THE SILENT GUARD

SOUTHERN STAR TRILOGY BOOK TWO

By K.J. Taylor

Published by Shooting Star Press

http://www.shootingstar.pub

1st edition 2018
2nd edition 2023

National Library of Australia Cataloguing-in-Publication entry:

Taylor, K.J. (Katie Jill) 1986–

Fantasy—Fiction
The Silent Guard/K.J. Taylor
Speculative fiction--Young adult fiction.
A823.4

Cover design by Sabrina RG Raven
Map by Allison Jones

ISBN-13- 978-1-925821-94-9

Shooting Star

*Dedicated to everyone who has stuck by the series
for all these years. I couldn't have done it without your support.*

Acknowledgments
Editor: Jessica Stewart
Typesetting: Saira Manns

Contents

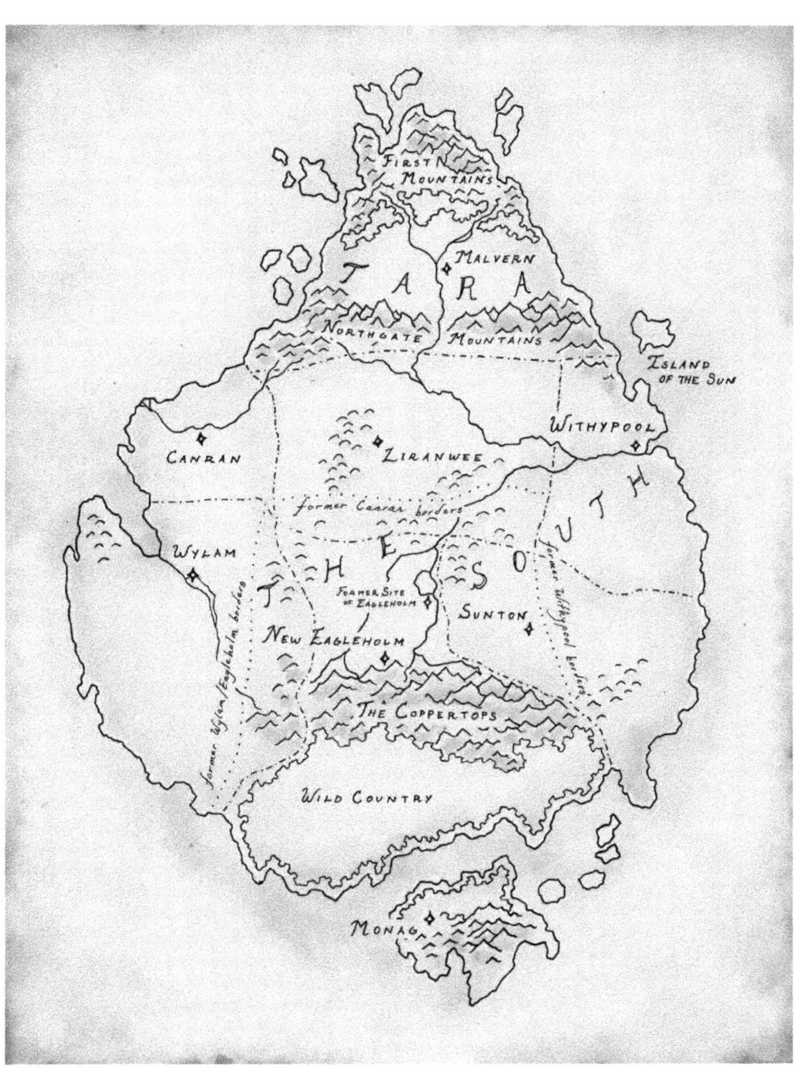

FIRST MOUNTAINS
MALVERN
T A R A
NORTHGATE
MOUNTAINS
ISLAND OF THE SUN
WITHYPOOL
CANRAN
LIRANWEE
former Canran borders
THE SOUTH
WYLAM
FORMER SITE OF EAGLEHOLM
SUNTON
former Withypool borders
former Wylam/Eagleholm borders
NEW EAGLEHOLM
THE COPPERTOPS
WILD COUNTRY
MONAG

Chapter One

The Pain of the Past

Senneck was dying.

Not that she would admit it to him; but Kullervo could see it. He knew if she could have, the proud old griffin would have flown away into the wild as griffins usually did, to die alone where her body would never be found. But her wings had gone stiff with age and she seemed to no longer have the willpower to say no when he offered her a warm barn to rest in.

She curled up there instead, in the straw, and Kullervo kept watch over her. The people in the village of Gwernyfed, where the two of them had settled down, quickly sensed what was going on. They had the sense to keep away from Senneck, but they visited Kullervo and quietly offered food and medicines for the only true griffin most of them had ever seen. He accepted their gifts politely and told them Senneck would soon recfover, but he knew she wouldn't. Medicines wouldn't do anything for her now. Maybe they would have helped if she had been dying from disease, but she wasn't. Old age had simply caught up with her.

Senneck said nothing about it one way or the other. She stayed in her barn, sleeping most of the day and eating very little. Kullervo stayed close by in case she needed him.

His niece, Flell, stayed too. But she was devoted to her adopted father and would have stayed close to him no matter what was happening. Kullervo hadn't been sure whether she would understand but like most children, the eight year old was more perceptive than she seemed.

'Senneck's going to die, isn't she?' she asked one day.

Kullervo looked down into his niece's small, solemn face. She had inherited a paler version of her Amorani father's brown skin and her fearsome grandfather's straight eyebrows, but the bright blue eyes had come from her mother.

'Yes, she is,' Kullervo answered at last. It was the first time he had admitted it out loud, and it made a lump form in his throat.

Flell clutched his hand more tightly. 'Are you sure?'

Kullervo closed his eyes for a moment. 'Yes.'

'Why?'

'She's very old,' said Kullervo. 'She was alive when your grandfather was young. She's older than I am.'

'You're old too, aren't you?' Flell looked him in the face as she spoke, and an edge of desperation showed in her voice.

Kullervo chuckled. 'I'm only thirty, petal.'

'Is that old?'

'Three times older than you, but not very old at all,' said Kullervo.

'How old will you be when you're old?' asked Flell.

'I have no idea,' said Kullervo. 'Humans can live to be seventy, but I don't know about myself.'

'Yeah, because you're not human,' said Flell. 'You're a man-griffin.'

She sounded so much like her mother that Kullervo shivered. 'Something like that. But don't worry; I'm not going to die soon.' The wings on his back twitched.

Flell didn't look very comforted. So far in her short life she'd never seen anyone die, and had never lost anybody. Or at least that was what she thought. Senneck was the closest thing to a mother she had ever known, and Kullervo knew that as far as she was concerned, he was her father. It didn't seem to matter if it was by blood or not.

Kullervo crouched down, awkward with his overly tall, lanky frame, and gave his adopted daughter a hug. 'It's all right, Flell. Don't cry.'

But Flell had already started to shudder lightly in his grasp. 'I don't want Senneck to die!'

'Neither do I,' said Kullervo, 'but everybody's time comes eventually. Nobody can live forever.'

'But it's not fair!' said Flell.

'Life isn't fair,' said Kullervo. 'It never has been. We just have to do what we can to make it fair.' He let go of her. 'Flell. Let me tell you something I've never told anybody.'

'Okay.' She sniffled a little, but listened.

'I don't talk much about my father,' said Kullervo. 'His name was Arenadd Taranisäii, but people called him other things as well. The Dark Lord Arenadd. The Shadow That Walked. The griffins called him Kraeai kran ae.'

'You mean he was…?' Flell began.

'Yes. Once he was an ordinary man, but he died. Then a griffin called Skandar brought him back, but dead people aren't supposed to come back. So he came back as something else, something that wasn't human. He was immortal – he couldn't age and he couldn't die. He was young forever.'

'I wish I could live forever,' said Flell.

'So do lots of people,' said Kullervo. 'Because they're scared of dying. But my father had already died, and he couldn't die again. He was trapped here in the mortal world, and couldn't leave it.'

'He did horrible things,' said Flell.

'Yes, he did. And he did them because he was forced to. The Night God was his master, and she told him to kill people. Including his own child.'

'You?' said Flell. 'He was meant to kill you?'

'No,' said Kullervo. 'It was your mother.'

Flell pressed herself against him. 'He killed my mum?'

'No.' Kullervo smiled sadly. 'He couldn't bring himself to do it. Otherwise, you wouldn't be here. But he was a miserable man. Do you understand that, Flell? He couldn't die, but he couldn't live either. He lost everyone. All his friends. The woman he loved – my mother. He had to stay here and watch everybody die. He was all alone. He wanted to die, but he couldn't.'

'That's so sad,' said Flell.

'Yes it is,' said Kullervo. 'And do you see what it means?'

'It's bad to live forever,' said Flell.

'You can't live without dying,' said Kullervo. 'To live properly, we have to get old and we have to die. You can't really make the best of something unless you know you won't have it forever. People weren't meant to be immortal, and when it does happen, it ends badly for everyone. Now do you understand?'

Flell nodded solemnly. 'I still don't want to die. And I don't want you to die either.'

'Well, don't worry,' Kullervo smiled. 'It won't happen for a long time.'

Flell looked a little happier. 'Can we go and see Senneck now?'

'All right.' Kullervo stood up, and they went into the barn together.

When he had first come to Gwernyfed to live quietly and bring up his sister's child, Kullervo had been unnaturally huge – taller than any other man, and powerfully muscled. It had been a side effect of an attempt to fix the malformed magic gland in his throat and help him control his ability to twist his shape from human to griffin and back again. By now, though, that side effect had more or less worn off and he had reverted to his old gangly, awkward shape. He was still unusually tall – so much so that he had to duck to get in through the barn door – but the muscular bulk had gone. He still had a pair of feathered wings on his back, and a tail poking through the seat of his pants, but while he was in human form they were useless.

Inside the barn, Senneck lay in her nest of straw. She had thrown off the blanket Kullervo had put over her, and her head rested on her taloned forepaws while she slept lightly. When Kullervo had met her she had already been ageing, but her long, leggy body had been strong and sinewy and her feathers glossy with health. Now both fur and feathers had faded, and the feathers had gone grey around her eyes and beak. Her joints had become stiff and swollen, and her eyes, once bright blue, had dimmed. When Kullervo and Flell came in, she stirred but didn't look up.

'Hullo, Senneck,' said Kullervo, raising his voice.

Senneck's eyes opened partway. 'Has day come?' she asked in a husky voice.

'Yes,' said Kullervo. 'It's noon.'

'I will miss the sun,' Senneck rasped to herself, and closed her eyes again.

Flell went over to the old griffin, and gently petted her head. 'Are you feeling better, Senneck?' she asked in slightly clumsy griffish.

'I am tired,' said Senneck.

Kullervo sat down on an upturned bucket. 'Maybe if you're feeling up to it, you could tell her a bit about her great-uncle,' he suggested. 'You're the only one left who knew him.'

Senneck raised her head a little, and peered at Flell. Then she looked at Kullervo. 'Perhaps you should tell her,' she said sharply. 'I think it is time.'

Kullervo looked away uncomfortably. 'I never knew him,' he said. 'You know that.'

Senneck snorted and laid her head down again.

'Tell me about great-uncle Erian,' Flell urged. 'I want to know!

Please?'

Senneck took in a slow, wheezing breath. 'Once I had a human,' she said. 'I chose him to be my partner. His name was Erian Rannagonson and he was born in a place called Carrick. He was the son of a peasant female and a griffiner called Lord Rannagon, from a city called Eagleholm.'

'What was he like?' Flell asked eagerly.

'He was brave and a great fighter,' Senneck said in a flat, careless kind of way. 'He was also a fool. But we fought together, he and I. We fought the dark griffin and his human. Tried to stop them in their conquest.' She shuddered in another breath. 'When Malvern fell… on that day… on that day my human, my Erian… died.'

'How did he die?' asked Flell.

'*Kraeai kran ae* killed him,' said Senneck, and closed her eyes again.

'What?' Flell looked at Kullervo.

Kullervo nodded sadly. 'My father Arenadd killed him. But that's not what I meant, Senneck. Tell her something real about him. About what he was like.'

Senneck gave an irritable groan. 'His eyes were blue, and his fur was yellow, and he had large front paws.'

Kullervo nodded again. 'I saw the carving on his tomb.' He smiled gently at Flell, who was listening with fascination, and added, 'I think you inherited those lovely eyes of yours from him as well as your mother.'

Senneck had already started to drift away again. 'He was a fool,' she rasped again in a distant, confused kind of way. 'He did not think before he acted. But he was my human.'

'Shhh.' Kullervo shushed her and gently stroked her neck. 'It's all right now, Senneck. You can rest now.'

Senneck stirred. 'Do not patronise me,' she said, and went to sleep.

Flell giggled. 'She's so bossy.'

'Always was.' Kullervo smiled to himself. 'We should stay here and keep an eye on her for a while.'

'All right.' Flell pulled herself up onto a beam and perched there in her favourite spot. 'I want to know more,' she said. 'Tell me more about the war!'

'Not now, Flell,' said Kullervo.

She pouted. 'Why not?'

'Because I said so.'

'Then tell me more about Uncle Erian,' said Flell. 'And mum as well, and my dad, and…'

'All right, all right!' Kullervo laughed. 'What else did you want to know?'

'Everything!' Flell said eagerly.

Kullervo frowned and absent-mindedly plucked a stray feather off his arm. He'd never kept anything secret from the child; she knew the names of her parents and the rest of her family as well, and he'd answered all the questions she'd asked over the years. But so far she hadn't asked one question in particular, and it was the one question he didn't want to answer – and would answer if she asked it, and truthfully as well, no matter how painful it might be. He had made a vow, years ago, that he would never tell another lie as long as he lived, and especially not to the only family he had left. But sometimes the truth hurt.

She hadn't asked, though, so he told her what she already knew.

'Your mother's name was Laela Taranisäii,' he said. 'She was the Queen of the North for about two years, after our father Arenadd went away.'

'And my father was from Amoran,' Flell supplied.

'That's right,' said Kullervo. 'Prince Akhane from Amoran. Senneck and I went all the way to Maijan to find him, because your mother needed his help. And when we brought him back to Malvern, she decided to make him her co-ruler, and she had a child with him. You, of course. Laela named you after her mother, Flell.'

'Flell was Erian's sister,' the younger Flell added.

'That's right,' said Kullervo. 'My father Arenadd was in love with her before he became the Shadow That Walked. But he didn't know her child was his own.'

'Why not?' asked Flell.

'Because when you die and come back, you forget who you were,' said Kullervo. 'I think that's how it works.'

Flell looked thoughtful. 'If my mother was Queen, does that mean I'm a Princess?'

'Yes,' said Kullervo.

'And your father was a King, so you're a Prince!' Flell added.

'I suppose so,' said Kullervo.

'Don't princes and princesses live in Eyries?' asked Flell. 'With crowns and treasures and things?'

'Sometimes they do,' said Kullervo. 'But Eyries aren't as nice as they sound, and crowns and treasures aren't any use to anyone in the end.'

Flell didn't look convinced, but Kullervo expected that. Some things you had to learn for yourself before you could believe them, and Flell was only a child after all.

They sat in silence for a while, watching Senneck sleep, and Kullervo thought about the past. It had been more than ten years since he had met Senneck. More than ten years since the day he had discovered his power to shape-shift, and had flown North in search of the family he had always dreamt of. He had found his half-sister, and a home of a kind, but nothing had been the way he had hoped or expected.

He looked around at the rough, simple wooden barn in the rough and simple village he called home now. Once he had lived in an Eyrie, and he had ruled his own Kingdom for a day. Now he was the elder of Gwernyfed, helping people with their troubles and doing what he could to treat illnesses and injuries. Some might have called it a sad outcome for someone who was more or less royalty, but Kullervo knew what suited him and made him happy, and it wasn't the life of a ruler or an ambassador. Gwernyfed was better.

But now Flell was getting older and asking harder questions, and he wondered how much longer she would be contented to stay where she was. Another child might have been happy to accept her lot in life, but Flell was a Taranisäii, and Taranisäiis had never had simple lives, or accepted anything easily.

*

Two days later, Senneck died. Her talk about Erian was the last real conversation she ever held; after that she slept even longer and said even less, and on the evening of the second day she quietly passed away in her sleep while Kullervo sat by her side.

He stayed there with her all night, not sleeping, but not really grieving either. Once the old griffin had meant the whole world to him. Now she was gone. Another piece of the past, fading away into history.

Early the next morning, Flell came looking for him. 'Uncle 'Lurvo?'

Kullervo looked up and smiled wanly. 'Good morning, petal. Did you sleep well?'

'No,' Flell looked a little pale. 'Senneck's dead, isn't she?'

'Yes, she is.' Kullervo gave his niece a one-armed hug as she came to his side to look down at the dead griffin. 'She died last evening.'

Flell looked at Senneck, dry-eyed and still. 'My mother's dead too, isn't she?'

Kullervo hesitated. 'Yes.'

'And my father?'

'They're both dead, Flell,' said Kullervo. 'That's why you're here with me.'

Flell didn't cry. Her expression was very steady, almost steely. 'How did they die?'

The question hit Kullervo like a blow. He started to speak, and stopped.

'Tell me,' said Flell. 'I want to know. Tell me!'

Kullervo stared at the floor. 'It was my fault,' he said, very softly.

Flell pulled away from him. 'Why? How?'

So Kullervo told her the end of the story. He did it quietly, eyes downcast, big, clumsy hands clasped together in his lap.

'After our father went away and Laela took the throne, our cousin Saeddryn rebelled. She wanted her son Caedmon to rule. When I came to Malvern, looking for my parents, I found out that Laela was the only family I had left. So I stayed with her, and promised to do whatever she told me. I helped her to look for Saeddryn and Caedmon as well, and when they threatened war unless Laela gave up the throne, I carried a message to them. I wanted to make peace. But they wouldn't listen. Saeddryn had me imprisoned and beaten to make me tell her what I knew about Laela's plans. That's why my teeth are like this.' He opened his mouth, showing the broken remains. 'Laela sent the unpartnered griffins to attack Warwick, where Saeddryn was hiding out. Senneck came with them, and she killed Saeddryn and helped me escape from prison. We thought that was the end of it, with Saeddryn dead. But she came back. Saeddryn returned, the same way my father had. She became the new Shadow That Walked, and set out to kill me and Laela, and Senneck as well. She still wanted to put Caedmon on the throne.

'So the war started. Every Northerner wanted to join Saeddryn, and we needed a way to stop her. To kill her for good – but nobody knew how to kill an immortal. So Senneck and I went to Maijan and brought back your father. He was a scholar, you see. He knew about magic and we hoped he could help us find an answer. But your mother had other ideas as well. She sent me south. We hoped to make peace with the Southerners and get them to help us. I gathered followers and came back north with new friends. Southerner friends. I thought I could change the world. Make peace between the races at last when my father had done so much to make the Southerners hate us,' Kullervo closed his eyes for a long moment. 'I was wrong. I couldn't undo centuries of hate and warfare. But I tried. By now your mother was pregnant with you, and she… she ordered me to help her capture Saeddryn. So I did, with the help of my new friends. We took her prisoner and I thought we would kill her, but we didn't,' Kullervo's face darkened. 'Your mother had her tortured, and I was forced to watch. They tore her to pieces. She went insane in the end, but I fooled her into betraying her own son after your mother ordered me to.

'And then we killed her. We tore out her heart, and that stopped her from ever coming back. We thought we'd finished it then, again, but we were still wrong. We had killed the Shadow That Walked, and to the Northerners that was a crime against them, and against the Night God as well. All of them rose up against us, and Caedmon led them.'

Kullervo had said all this in a monotone, but now his voice started to break. 'We had turned him vicious. What we did filled him with hate. Against us, and the Southerners who had helped us as well. He came to Malvern with an army and the Unpartnered joined him. All our griffins. He told us that if we didn't surrender, he would come in and kill everybody in the city. After your mother and I killed our father's cousin Saeddryn, the whole of the North went mad. Everyone rallied behind her son, Caedmon, and he led them straight to Malvern. We were outnumbered, and everyone knew it.

'I told your mother we should give in, but she wouldn't listen. We met with Caedmon – your mother, your father, and me. And when your mother said no to Caedmon, he killed your father. Your mother and I escaped back to the city, but she still wouldn't listen to me. And so… I betrayed her. It was the only way to save the city, and the country.' Kullervo looked up, red-eyed. 'I betrayed your mother, who was the only family I had in the world. She gave me a home when no-one else wanted me, and I turned on her. I killed her partner, Oeka, and had your mother locked up. Then I had myself crowned King of the North. But I didn't want to rule. I betrayed the Southerners as well. As soon as I was in charge, I ordered the city to surrender and handed the throne to Caedmon. I drove the Southerners out.' Kullervo took a deep breath, bracing himself for the end. 'I handed the crown to Caedmon.'

Flell stared at him. 'What…?' 'Your mother gave birth to you while she was imprisoned, and she warned me that when Caedmon came he would kill her and you as well,' said Kullervo. 'So I saved you. I switched you with another baby who had died, and ran away with you.'

'And my mother?' said Flell.

'She stayed behind in Malvern,' Kullervo said quietly. 'She was already badly hurt from giving birth, and if that didn't kill her, Caedmon did.'

Flell said nothing. She had gone even paler.

'So you see, we can't go back there,' said Kullervo. 'Caedmon is King now, and if he ever finds either of us, he'll kill us. I brought you here to protect you, but I promised I would never lie to you about who you are, or what I did.' He looked away. 'I didn't kill either of your parents, but if it weren't for me… if I'd only… if I weren't such a coward, then maybe I could have saved them.'

Flell stood up. 'Why didn't you stay?'

'You know why,' said Kullervo. 'I had to save you.'

'But you could've stopped him!' said Flell. 'He killed my mother and father.'

'We had killed his mother,' said Kullervo. 'He wanted revenge. And he wanted the North as well.'

'But you could've saved my mother!' said Flell. 'Why didn't you take her away with you?'

'I couldn't—,' Kullervo began.

'Yes you could!' Flell started to cry. 'You could've saved her!'

'Yes,' Kullervo said quietly. 'Yes, I could have saved her. But what's done is done. You can't change the past. You can only try and make the future better.'

'Shut up!' Flell shouted. 'You're stupid and you're a coward! It's your fault they're dead!'

The old guilt burned at Kullervo. 'It wasn't just—,'

But Flell wasn't listening any more. She turned and ran out of the barn.

Kullervo stood up. 'Flell—!'

But it was too late. He stopped himself from going after her – she needed to be alone for a while, and what could he say to her? That his naivety and his fear had stopped him from facing the truth and realising that his sister was going to destroy herself? And even if he had realised it sooner, would he have been able to stop her? He would never know, and that was what had made the knowledge so painful even after so many years.

The guilt rose higher, and the fear, and before he knew what was happening it was already too late. The emotion caught in his throat, and something deep inside him awoke. For the first time in years, his magic broke lose.

Kullervo fell over with a groan of pain, and started to writhe in the straw as the power twisted his body. Bones broke and re-formed, muscles shifted. Feathers spiked out through his skin, fur sprouted. His teeth pushed out of his mouth and fused together into a beak. Talons sprouted from his fingers, and his ears sank into his head.

Midway through the transformation, as always, the pain overwhelmed him and he fainted.

*

Kullervo stayed unconscious for the rest of that day – the change always drained his energy. He woke up as a small, ugly grey griffin with a chipped beak.

He stood up and stretched gingerly, feeling his reshaped limbs click and crack back into place. Then memory returned and he turned sharply to look around. There was no-one in the barn with him except for Senneck's body.

He lowered his head and gently rubbed his cheek against hers. 'Goodbye, Senneck. I love you, and I'll miss you.'

He limped slowly out of the barn, and went to look for Flell. Hopefully she would have calmed down by now.

But she wasn't in the house, and he couldn't find her or her scent anywhere. Some of the villagers were still up and about, and fortunately they all recognised his griffin shape – he'd transformed plenty of times during his life here, though then it had been on purpose.

'Kullervo!' one man hurried over.

Kullervo looked anxiously at him, and put his head on one side in an enquiring manner.

'There you are,' said the man – one of the Southerners who secretly lived in Gwernyfed, where the two races mingled peacefully. 'You haven't seen Flell, have you?'

Kullervo shook his head.

The man swore. 'She's run away, Kullervo. We've all been looking for her, but no-one knows where she went. She took some food and a knife from your house and left sometime last night.'

Kullervo hissed in shock.

'I know,' said the man. 'We're frantic. Everyone went out searching all day. Nothing.'

Kullervo nodded sharply, and loped away. As soon as he had a clear space he took off with a blow of his wings, and flew away from Gwernyfed as fast as he could.

*

Kullervo didn't return to Gwernyfed that day, or the day after that. He flew out from the village, circling the lands around it, and searched for Flell. He called for her, too, in his griffin's voice, which he knew she would recognise. Even in his griffin's shape, which dulled emotions, he could feel his heart aching with fear and despair. Senneck and Flell, the two people he cared most about, both gone in a day. And if he didn't find Flell soon, anything could happen to her. A half-breed with obvious signs of Southern blood in her wouldn't last a day among ordinary Northerners, who had become even more suspicious and hateful towards their neighbours since Kullervo's failed peace treaty.

The guilt pained him too, as it had every time he had thought of it since. And now it was his fault that Flell had run away, and if she died that would be his fault too.

Desperate now, panicking, he flew further and called louder. But he didn't find anything that day, or the next. His search eventually led him to a coastal town called Penarth, where he saw something that made his heart lurch.

Cautious now, but knowing he had to find out more, he flew

closer and saw everything.

Ships. Dozens of ships in the harbour, all flying the triple-spiral banner of King Caedmon Taranisäii. Ships with Northern troops on board, and griffins flying overhead. Some of them were setting sail as he watched, moving south along the coast. Kullervo knew only too well what that meant.

War had come to Cymria. At last, Caedmon had decided to follow his mother's dream and invade the South as his predecessors, Arenadd and Laela, had refused to.

It was enough to make Kullervo sick to his stomach. But what could he do? He had vowed not to take any part in the North's affairs, or the South's. His interference had only caused more harm last time.

But now that he saw this, his certainty wavered. He thought of all the people who would suffer and die. But what could he possibly do? Fly to the South with a warning? Nobody would listen, and he still had to find Flell.

But… he thought of the South, and the people he had met there. The scheming Lady Isleen, who had tried to seize Malvern for herself. Lord Resling, who had followed him faithfully until his death. Old Roland, who had died in the ruins of Eagleholm. And Red, the orphan boy from Liranwee who had travelled with him, and looked up to him as a second father. And so many others. Ordinary people, living their lives – lives that would be destroyed when those ships arrived.

It was the thought of them that made Kullervo fly closer, and that thought which doomed him. The Unpartnered there saw him and were soon on him, and he was too small and weak to stand a chance. They soon forced him to land, and pinned him to the ground.

'Where is your human?' one demanded. 'You are not one of us.'

'I don't have a human,' Kullervo gasped.

'Then you are a wild griffin.'

'No—,' Kullervo began, but it was already too late. Wild griffins had no rights, none at all.

But they didn't kill him. Humans came – Northerners all, black eyed and black haired. They put chains on him and forced him onto a ship, where they put him in a cage below deck and shipped him off with them.

From there, Kullervo slowly learned what was going on. He stayed on that ship as it sailed south, and met with other ships. Ships from Amoran, all loaded with dark-skinned Amorani troops. The Amoranis took Kullervo then — chaining him in another, much larger cage, which was just one of many. The largest cage was meant for griffins, but the others weren't.

Kullervo stayed there, and watched what happened next. He heard the faint sounds of battle as the Amoranis went ashore, and over the next day or so the prisoners began to arrive. Other griffins were herded onto the ship and chained in rows next to Kullervo, and after them the humans came. Southerners, captured in the sack of some city or other. They were bundled into the other cages. Hundreds of them.

Kullervo knew why, of course. He watched them through his yellow griffin eyes, and remembered the way things had been when he was very small.

Once, centuries ago, the Southerners had ruled the North. They had made the Northerners into second-class citizens in their own land, and sold others into slavery.

Now it was the Southerners' turn. The Amoranis would take these prisoners back to their own country and sell them in the slave markets there. It would be the ultimate revenge, and the ultimate humiliation.

But why did they want griffins? Kullervo didn't know.

And then, to his horror, Kullervo saw him among the others. A huge griffin, fighting against his chains and screaming in outrage. A griffin whose feathers were black and whose fur was silvery brown. And his eyes were as blue as the sky.

'I cannot be chained!' he screamed. 'I am the dark griffin!'

Kullervo's eyes widened. But before he could say that griffin's name, someone else said it for him.

'Kraego!' A man stood up in the cage directly in front of the one where Kullervo lay. He reached out for the massive beast.

Kraego subsided, and looked back at him. 'Red,' he said. 'So you are alive.'

The man, whose hair was indeed red, wore the uniform of a city guard and had a strong, square jawed face with a thick moustache. He looked as if he had been fighting recently; there were cuts and bruises on his brawny arms and his nose had been broken at some point in the past. In fact., he looked exhausted and miserable as well.

'Yeah,' he said. 'They got the both of us. But why'd they put you in here?'

'I do not know,' said Kraego. 'But the moment I am free, they will suffer. I will not endure this humiliation!' He wrenched at his chain, and snarled like a mad dog.

But Red shook his head. 'Forget it, Kraego. It's over. There's no gettin' out of this one.' He sat down and put his head in his hands. 'What do I do now?' he asked aloud. 'It's hopeless.'

Then Kullervo spoke. 'It's never hopeless, Red,' he said in a low voice.

Red froze. 'What? Who said that?'

'Down here,' said Kullervo.

Red turned, searching for the speaker. 'Where are you?'

'Red, I'm here,' said Kullervo. 'I'd be so glad to see you again, if only it weren't here.'

Red looked down and his eyes widened. 'Kullervo!' he said. 'It's you!'

Kullervo rubbed his head against the big Southerner's hands. 'Yes,' he said. 'It's me.'

Chapter Two

The South Will Rise Again

Red listened while Kullervo told his story. The small, grey griffin with the sad eyes spoke slowly and softly, telling him not just about how he had come to be on the ship, but about his sister's death and Caedmon's rise to the throne as well. He told it in a matter-of-fact tone and without bitterness, but there was sadness there, and gentle regret.

'So here I am,' he finished. 'And you and I have finally met again. You've grown up so much!'

'Yeah, I have, haven't I?' said Red. 'Toldya I'd be a big man one day.' He tried to smile, and failed.

'I remember!' said Kullervo. 'And you too, Kraego.'

The giant black griffin glared at them both. 'I have grown larger than even my father.'

'I think you may have,' said Kullervo. 'Your mother would have been proud.'

'Any female would take pride in such a powerful chick as I was,' Kraego said bluntly.

Red rolled his eyes. 'Kullervo, what're we gonna do?' he asked. 'How're we gonna get out of here? They're gonna sell me as a slave, but what about you? Why'd they want griffins?'

'I don't know,' said Kullervo. 'Amoranis believe griffins are sacred, so it makes no sense. They can't sell us as slaves. But what else could they want us for?'

'No idea,' said Red. He picked some dried blood out of his moustache. 'But maybe we oughta tell you our story.'

'Tell me,' Kullervo agreed. 'I can see you became a guard just as you said you were going to.'

'So I did,' Red nodded. 'An' what happened was this…'

He told his story, and Kraego's as well, describing his life as a city guard in Liranwee, and how Caedmon's invasion had ruined everything.

Kullervo listened. 'You sound bitter.'

'Well I am bitter.' Red thumped the bars of the cage. 'What'd you expect? We did everything we could, nearly died a dozen times, an' for what? I thought I'd win back my family's honour, an' my own too, an' here I am, about to spend the rest of my life wearin' an iron collar in Amoran.'

'Family honour?' Kullervo repeated. 'What do you mean by that?'

'Huh.' Red sat down again. 'I never told you my real name when we knew each other, or said where I really came from, did I?'

Kullervo's eyes narrowed. 'Why not?'

'Lots of reasons, but mostly just shame,' said Red.

'For what?'

Red sighed. 'I'll make it short. Your father Arenadd came from a city called Eagleholm, right? Well, so did my family.'

'I know,' said Kullervo. 'You told me. Your father Danthirk killed my father.'

'Yeah, he did,' said Red. 'He killed Arren Cardockson, an' if he hadn't done that he never would've come back as the Dark Lord Arenadd. Right? But that's not the whole story.'

'Yes?' said Kullervo. 'What's the rest of it, then?'

'It ain't much, really,' said Red. 'But you know yer father had a friend, right? His best friend, Branton Redguard. Guard Captain. Well, it's said the reason why Arren Cardockson got out of jail, the reason why my dad was chasing him that night, is because his mate Bran let him out. They said it was Bran's fault the city fell. Bran the Betrayer, they called him. His whole family inherited the shame of what Bran did.'

'Yes?' Kullervo said again.

'That was my family,' said Red. 'My dad married Bran's sister. My mother, Finna Redguard. My real name ain't Red. It's Kearney Redguard. The last Redguard. I took my mum's name. I wanted to make it a proud one again.'

'And you succeeded,' said Kullervo.

'No I didn't,' said Red. 'I failed.'

'But you tried,' said Kullervo. 'You're a hero, Kearney Redguard, and a good man. You can't be anything more than that.'

Red smiled ruefully. 'But I'd like to be.'

'Well then, keep trying,' said Kullervo. 'It doesn't matter if you succeed. It matters if you try, and if you learn from that trying.'

Red shook his head. 'Great Gryphus, Kullervo. Nothin' ever gets you down, does it?'

Kullervo scratched his beak with his talons. 'I like to think I take after my father there. Dying didn't stop him.'

'It just pissed him off,' said Red. He chuckled. 'I s'pose you're right. We ain't even dead, an' we'll think of something.'

'I will kill the first human that touches me,' Kraego promised.

'That's the spirit,' said Red.

Chapter Three

The Vision

The statue stood in the main square of the city of Malvern, not too far from the great Moon Temple where the Night God was worshipped. It was made from black marble imported all the way from Erebus, and depicted a man and a griffin side by side. The griffin was larger than life-size, but it was said that, in life, he hadn't been much smaller. He stood proudly with one front paw raised, beak open to screech a challenge. The man beside him was a Northerner, of course, with a stern, angular face and a pointed chin-beard. His curly hair flowed over his shoulders, and he wore a long robe that had once been the outfit of a slave, but was now considered the robe of a King. Queen Laela had adopted the style, and so had her successor King Caedmon.

The man carried a sickle, and pointed it ahead, his face locked in an expression of fierce challenge. Both figures faced the South, eternally defending the land that had been their territory against the enemy they had defeated to take it.

On the stone block beneath them, a simple message had been carved.

KING ARENADD TARANISÄII AND THE MIGHTY SKANDAR. MAY THEIR SPIRITS GUARD US.

Teressa had always loved the statue, and she had been in the habit of visiting it whenever she wanted some time to herself. She would climb the base and sit down between the Mighty Skandar's massive forelegs and rest there where no-one would easily spot her from the ground. It was a good place to go, away from the stress and hard work of life in the Temple.

She went there now; to rest and contemplate as her mentor had taught her. Teressa was only a novice in the Temple and she wasn't sure if she wanted to go further than that. Part of it was simple self-interest – if she were promoted, she would have less time to herself. But it was also fear. Greater prominence meant greater scrutiny, and more chance of being discovered.

Not that what she was doing was *illegal*, as such, but she knew the priesthood wouldn't approve of it, and if she was found out then maybe they would make it a heresy. She would rather not have to find out. Best keep it a semi-secret and not talk about it, just in case. Besides, in a way the secrecy only made it more exciting. Everybody understood the wicked thrill of doing something furtive and forbidden.

Leaning back against the Mighty Skandar's leg, Teressa reached into her silver robe and brought out her talisman. It was a piece of polished stone, carved with a triple spiral. The King had adopted that symbol as his personal emblem, but it was older than that — maybe as old as Cymria itself.

Every phase of the moon had its symbol, and the triple spiral was the most powerful. It represented the full moon — the Wolf Moon, some called it. The Night God's eye was the moon, and when it was full, that eye was fully open and at its most aware.

On the other side of the stone, opposite the triple spiral, was another symbol. A rounded triangular shape — the universal symbol for the human heart. That was the true symbol of Teressa's secret cult, but some of the other stones like this one showed the triple spiral inside the heart. That didn't matter. It stood for the same thing.

Teressa made a quick check to make sure nobody was watching her — unlikely as the statue put her well above the street and she was almost invisible under Skandar's talons. She put the stone down and took a small knife from her belt. There was already a healing cut on her thumb — she reopened it now, and gingerly squeezed some blood out onto the carved heart where it joined the stains of dozens of other offerings.

Teressa began to recite the ritual words — words she herself had invented, and passed onto others who believed in the new religion she had created and inspired.

'With this offering of true Northern blood, I call to ye,' she murmured. 'To ye who came to us from nothing, sent by the Night God's grace, I offer ye my loyalty and my soul. Blessed one, heartless one, mighty Shadow That Walks, ye are the master I choose. Watch over me, give me courage, help me to stand up when the whole world tries to push me down, let me serve my people beyond life, beyond pain and beyond hope, as ye did.' Those were the words she always said, but once she had finished, she moved on and began her real prayer. 'Arenadd,' she said softly. 'Ye were the first Shadow That

Walked and ye were the one who showed me my path in life. Ye saved me, and ye saved all of us. I know ye can hear me now, wherever ye are. I believe it with all my heart and I know that ye'll guide me when I need ye to. But I want to help, too. If I can do anything at all, I will. I know our King and our armies will conquer the South with the Amoranis' help. I know they'll try, at least, but… I just feel helpless now, as if I'm cut off from everything else. I wish there was something I could do. I know that, sometimes, one person can make all the difference. Help me to make a difference. It's all I ask.'

She had said all she wanted to say, and fell silent as she picked up the stone and held it between her hands. She sat back with it cradled against her chest and meditated as the priestesses had taught her. When the mind was still and the body at rest, peace and insight would come. She hoped it would come now.

After a while, as she relaxed further, she felt her mind start to drift away into a dream.

*

She dreamt of a day long ago, when she was a child. Confusion and fear gripped her as she sat in the back of a wagon with a group of other children. Like her, they wore black robes cut down to fit them, and some of the older ones wore the iron collars of slaves. She herself was too young for a collar – only five years old. But she had spent her entire life for as long as she could remember, working and doing whatever she was told. She had been born into a life of slavery, to parents who had died when she was small – killed in an accident in the mine where they worked. But when Arenadd Taranisäii and his followers had begun their uprising against the Southerners, slaves throughout the South had started to rebel along with them. Many had died for their pains, but others had escaped, or even risen up and killed their masters.

And then she had come. A woman – not even a Northerner. Her hair was silvery grey and her eyes were yellow and fierce, and her voice was harsh and commanding.

They said her name was Skade. Lady Skade. She was strange and savage, said to be a lover of Arenadd himself, and pregnant by him.

Skade was the one who showed the slaves the way home. She and her Northern companions, and the griffin that travelled with them, gathered up the runaways and the rebels and formed them into an army. They bought or stole others.

Teressa and the other children were some of the first to join them. Slave children weren't much use anyway, and the slavers were becoming nervous and starting to sell off their wares quickly and cheaply.

Teressa didn't want to go. She was afraid of Skade, and afraid of going to the North. It was said to be her people's homeland, but she had never seen it and the story of this man who was trying to conquer it frightened her. But she had no choice – she had never had any choice with anything that happened in her life. All her decisions had been made for her, from the moment she was born.

So she went North with the others. She saw the followers of the heartless man, Arenadd. She never saw any fighting, but she saw the aftermath of it. Saw the dead and the dying, the wounded, and the burning cities. She saw the Southerners die or be driven out, and the Northerners triumph. She saw the beginnings of the Kingdom of Tara.

After the war was over, she heard that Skade was dead – killed in the fighting. Arenadd was said to be dead as well, but he reappeared and went among his followers, pale faced and red eyed but steady, wearing the silver circlet that would one day be passed on to his cousin, Caedmon.

That was when Teressa met him. Some of the other children had been reunited with their parents, but she and plenty of others had no parents, and nowhere to go. Some of the newly freed slaves were already settling down, into houses taken from dead Southerners. A few of those chose to adopt orphans, but nobody took Teressa. She stayed, waiting silently for her future to be decided for her just as it always had been.

That was when Arenadd came. She saw him walking by, and her carers stepped forward to bow to him. She heard them talking – telling him about what they had been doing. Then they pointed to her, and in a moment he was there, coming towards her. He was so tall, so huge to her, and so dark – shrouded in a black robe as if he too were a slave. His eyes were as deep and black as the night sky.

Teressa wanted to run away from him, but she didn't. It wasn't allowed. But she felt the fear chill her.

Arenadd stood over her for a moment, and then knelt to look at her. Suddenly, when his face was level with hers, he didn't seem so big or scary. But he didn't smile.

He reached out to her, and touched her on the forehead. His hand was cold. He spoke, and Teressa remembered the words he said for the rest of her life.

'Teressa, you're an orphan without a place in the world. But sometimes we all feel that way. You're going to have to choose what you want to be, but I'm going to help you now.' And he blessed her, speaking loudly so everyone there could hear. He blessed her in the name of the Night God.

And from that moment on, she was indeed blessed. Arenadd had never blessed anyone before, and he never did again, though plenty of people asked him to. It made Teressa special, and by the next day the new High Priestess, Saeddryn, had taken her into the Temple. But Teressa had always believed that her life belonged not to the Night God, but to him. To Arenadd, who had given her a life. If a man could be a god, then he was the god she chose, and when she was older she found others who felt the same way. Others chose to worship only the idea of Shadow That Walked, and some were more devoted to Saeddryn, who had become like Arenadd many years later. But Teressa's faith belonged to Arenadd, and always would.

She dreamt all of that in moments, and her passionate belief swelled in her. She kept returning to that moment though, as the dream repeated itself. That moment when he had stopped to talk to her, and laid his hand on her head. And, as that moment returned again and again, it began to change. Arenadd spoke, but his blessing started to fade, and other words came through.

Teressa, his voice whispered. *Teressa.*

Teressa, still trapped in her child's body, nodded silently. She couldn't speak.

There's something you have to do, Arenadd whispered. His voice seemed to be coming from far, far away.

She felt the dream starting to unravel around her. Shape and sound faded, and blackness began to take its place. The voice grew louder.

I hear you. Louder all the time. Now I have the strength to answer.

His face filled her whole world.

Find them. She's coming. Searching. Find the child with the Southern eyes. Find the dark griffin.

Where is he? Teressa's voice was silent, but she thought she could hear it anyway.

You need help, said Arenadd. *Go to the Hatchery. Find help. Find the child. Go…*

Go where? Teressa wondered.

Arenadd began to fade into the void…*East, his voice called back. Find the dark griffin in the East. Find my…son…*

'I will!' Teressa shouted aloud, but the darkness closed in, and swallowed the sound of her voice.

*

Teressa drifted back into the waking world, only moments after she had fallen asleep. Her back ached, and the stone had fallen out of her hands. Maybe the noise of it had woken her up.

She picked it up and stowed it away in its pocket. While she stretched and rubbed her back, the memory of the dream suddenly snapped back into her mind. She froze and stared into space, not so much thinking about what had happened as just letting it wash over her. Arenadd, she had dreamt of Arenadd! She had prayed to him, and he had come.

When she realised that, she instantly decided that the dream had been a message. Arenadd wanted her to do something for him, so she would do it – it was as simple as that. But what did he want? She had to find something, that was it. Go east and look for a dark griffin, and…Arenadd's son? But he didn't have a son. He'd never had any children; there had only ever been liars and imposters. Teressa was certain of that.

But maybe he did have a real son – one no-one knew about. And if that was true, then she would find him in the East. Maybe that was the child he had said was coming.

But first…first he had said to go to the Hatchery. That was the closest place, so she would go there before she decided what to do next. Maybe she would find another sign there.

Filled with excitement, she quickly climbed down from the statue and set off towards the Eyrie.

The royal Eyrie of Malvern consisted of five towers, linked by covered walkways. The tallest and the largest of them was the Council Tower and it stood at the centre. It held the great Council Chamber, where the King met with the senior griffiners, and the

King's own quarters were right at the top. With griffiners, as with griffins, the highest roost went to the most powerful.

But Teressa's destination was one of the other towers – the widest one. Some of its lower levels were used for storage, but everything above that was given over to one big open space where the unpartnered griffins lived. Normally, the Hatchery Tower would be festooned with griffins flying or perching wherever they chose. Now, though, the building was quiet. The Unpartnered had left with the King and his army, to fight together and help with the conquest of the South.

Teressa thought of that on the way to the Eyrie, and wondered what she would find if she managed to get into the Hatchery. She would have to come up with some story for the guards on the gate if she wanted to find out.

On the ground, the Eyrie was surrounded by walls. There were gates in them, of course, and the largest was at the front – opening out onto a public square where market stalls clustered together. There was also a platform right at the centre, used for executions. It wasn't in use today, though, and the square was packed with people buying and selling.

Teressa wove her way through them to the main Eyrie gates. One of them was closed, but the other was open, and a few tradespeople were going in and out. Four guards stood by, but they looked relaxed enough. Things were quiet in Malvern at the moment.

Teressa made for the open gate, wondering if she would be able to get through without being noticed. And, at first, it looked as if she would. But when she was a few paces away one of the guards held up a hand.

'Stop. Who are ye?'

Teressa stopped and nodded politely. 'I'm Teressa, from the Temple.'

'What do ye want in the Eyrie?' the guard asked. He asked it in a businesslike way, without any overt threat.

'I'm bringing a message from the High Priestess to the Master of Taxation,' said Teressa, hoping the lie would be enough.

The guard glanced at his colleagues. They didn't look overly interested, and he turned back to her and nodded. 'All right, then. In ye go.'

Hiding a sigh of relief, Teressa went in.

The Hatchery Tower was locked on the ground floor, but the Council Tower wasn't, so she went in there and climbed a few levels until she found a walkway that went in the right direction. She had only been in the Eyrie once before, and she took her time now to admire her surroundings. Like every building intended for griffins, it had been built on an exaggerated scale – all the doorways and passageways were huge, and there were openings in the walls here and there with curtains over them, but no glass or shutters. Teressa knew they were for the griffins as well – to let them fly in and out as it suited them.

There were also no stairs anywhere, at least in the main passageway that spiralled up the tower. Griffins couldn't use them very well, so the floor was a ramp instead, with rough carpeting to help them grip. It was hard going for a human, but Teressa managed it, pausing occasionally to inspect a tapestry or decorated shield that hung on the wall.

Fortunately, she didn't run into any griffins. They were notoriously suspicious of anyone wandering around their territory, and she might have been asked questions she would have found difficult to answer. Of course, any question was difficult to answer when you had a griffin glowering at you.

Finally, Teressa found the walkway she was after which led over to the Hatchery tower. She followed it cautiously, on the lookout for more guards. There weren't any, but the passageway ended in a space dominated by a huge set of double doors. They were reinforced with steel, and decorated with carvings of griffins.

Teressa gave one a careful push, and to her surprise it swung open without much effort at all. She peered through the gap.

The Hatchery was enormous – even bigger than she had expected. The ceiling was so high she could barely see it, and the entire space above a certain level was criss-crossed with huge wooden beams for perching. On the floor, thick wooden walls had been constructed to make nesting stalls for any griffin who preferred the ground, and the walls were full of uncovered holes to serve as entrances.

Normally the place would have been teeming with griffins, but now it was almost completely deserted. Only a few of the Unpartnered would have stayed behind. Teressa had heard that in some places, when unpartnered females laid eggs, the chicks would be handed over to human carers who would raise them until they were old enough to go in with the adults. If any mother tried to raise her young while surrounded by other adults, they would probably be killed by jealous females or males wanting to possess the mother.

Here in Malvern, though, the pregnant females were in the habit of flying off into the wild to raise their young, so there were no chicks here. Instead, as Teressa nervously entered the Hatchery proper, she saw other kinds of griffin who had stayed behind. There were a few youngsters, and an adult perching above who was nursing a crippled leg. On the floor, she noticed a few elderly griffins dozing in the afternoon sun. Only the very young, the very old, and the sick would have stayed behind. Any griffin with its youth and full strength would be far too proud to say no to a fight.

Teressa stood uncertainly near the door while she took all this in, and wondered what she should do next. If she was supposed to find help here, then she couldn't see it.

But she did have one advantage. One of the priestesses who had raised her had hoped to become a griffiner, and had learned griffish – and Teressa had gone to learn with her. Once it had been forbidden for a Northerner to learn it, but King Arenadd had been very firm about that – he wanted as many of his people as possible to learn griffish if they could.

Teressa spoke up now, hesitantly. 'Uh…I mean…' she cleared her throat and broke into her best griffish. 'My name is Teressa, and I'm here to find help.'

Nothing happened. One of the youngsters on the floor looked up briefly from the bone it was busily tearing at, before going back to its meal as though nothing had happened.

Teressa tried again, louder this time. 'I had a dream today, where King Arenadd told me I should come here. He said I had to find a child, and a dark griffin, and his son. He said I'd find help here.'

It sounded utterly ludicrous, and she cringed as she said it. But if she didn't say it, she would always wonder what would have happened.

More silence followed, and then the griffin with the crippled leg dropped out of the rafters. It landed awkwardly and with a hiss of irritation, but quickly recovered and started to limp towards her.

Teressa, thinking she was about to be chased away, took a step back towards the door.

The griffin came on. Its front leg looked deformed – it bent sideways at an unnatural angle, and the talons were thin and twisted. The eyes were an unusual pale violet colour, and the feathers were slate grey.

'What is this you have said, human?' it rasped at her.

Teressa cringed. 'Er…I, uh…I said I had a dream, that's all. I'll go now.'

The griffin huffed. 'A dream of what?'

Teressa explained.

The griffin listened with its head on one side. 'And it said that you would find help here?'

'Yes,' said Teressa, who was already regretting having come to the Hatchery at all.

The griffin pecked idly at its crippled leg. 'I too have had a dream today.'

Teressa's heart fluttered. 'Ye did?'

'Yes. I dreamt of a griffin whose feathers were black. He told me that even though I am weak, I may become great, and that a silver human would show me the way. He said that I must find a dark griffin in the East.'

Teressa gaped. 'Then it was real! Ye saw it too!'

'I saw something,' the griffin said unhelpfully. 'I do not believe in dreams.'

'But if this one told ye about meeting me, then it can't just be chance,' said Teressa.

The griffin eyed her silver robe. 'Perhaps. What is your name?'

'Teressa. I'm a priestess.'

The griffin lowered its head so that she could see the feathery ear tufts that meant it was a male. 'I am Orak.'

'So what are we going to do?' Teressa asked after an awkward silence. 'It seems as if we're supposed to do something, and together, but what? And how?'

'I do not know,' said Orak. 'But I am willing to go with you.'

Teressa started. 'Really?'

'Yes.' Orak raised his lame leg. 'I am a cripple, and a weakling. My life has been nothing but a struggle to survive, and before the Unpartnered left, I slept in the open, in the rain and the snow. They would not let me live here, and when they return I will not live much longer. They will kill me, or drive me out until I am dead of starvation and cold. My only chance to live is to leave here, and I cannot do that without a human, but until now I have not had the chance to choose. Now you have come, and I will take that chance.'

'Ye mean, choose me?' said Teressa.

'Yes. I will make you my human and we will leave here together. And perhaps we will find this dark griffin. I am willing to take any opportunity if it will save my life.'

Teressa took a deep breath, and rubbed her face. 'All right. Yes. Great gods. Let's go, then!'

'I will need a harness so that I can carry you,' Orak said matter-of-factly. 'You must make one or find it. And if we leave this city, we must take food.'

'All right.' Teressa thought fast. 'We should go back to the Temple. I'll pick up my things, get some money. Maybe we can buy a harness.'

'Come then,' said Orak, and limped over to the doors.

Teressa opened them and together the two of them left the Hatchery behind.

Even on the walk back to the Temple, Teressa was amazed by how different everything had suddenly become. On the way back down through the Eyrie they bumped into a pair of griffiners, both of whom nodded and said polite hellos before going on their way. The guards let them past with low bows and mutterings of 'My lady'.

The two of them were allowed out of the Eyrie with no questions asked, though the guard on the main gates who had first let Teressa in stared at the pair of them with complete astonishment. Teressa had to suppress a giggle.

Out in the city, people stood aside to let them pass. Those closest to them bowed just as the guards had done. It was strange, exciting and wonderful all at once, but it also made Teressa a little nervous.

'Ye should wait out here,' she said when they had reached the Temple. 'If the priestesses see us together they'll ask questions.'

Orak flicked his tail. 'I will stay here, but do not be gone for long. We must leave before night comes.'

'I understand. I won't be long.' Teressa hurried into the building.

Luckily it was quiet – all worshipping and ceremonies took place at night, and the Temple was generally deserted during the day. The only person there now was another apprentice priestess like herself, who was busy sweeping the floor.

Teressa hurried past her and made for the back of the Temple interior where hidden doors led into the living quarters and store rooms.

Once upon a time, the Night God had been worshipped in the open air and the only temples built to her were stone circles. The Southerners had destroyed most of those when they had conquered the North, and Teressa only knew of one that was still standing – the great circle of thirteen stones up in the mountains, called Taranis' Throne. She had always wanted to see it for herself.

Malvern's Moon Temple had been the first ever formal building dedicated to the Night God, and its interior had been designed to bring back something of the past. There were no chairs or benches, or any furniture at all for that matter. The pillars that lined it had been placed at irregular intervals – not in rows or any straight lines at all, but spaced out randomly in the manner of trees. They had been made to look like trees, too, each one covered in tiny tiles in varying shades of brown and grey that looked just like bark. The branches were stylised, curling things, made out of silver. Blue glass lanterns hung from them. The floor was covered in tiles, too – around the base of each pillar they depicted roots and fallen leaves, and further out they made pools and streams, grass and other plants.

Right at the centre of the space, where the pillar trees thinned out, and a circle of stones stood around the moon-shaped altar. They were much smaller than the ones that had been used to make Taranis' Throne , but they had been polished and carved with spirals to look the same. Or so the High Priestess had once told her. Inside, standing over the altar, was a white stone statue of the Night God herself, looking down on the altar with her mismatched eyes – one a black gemstone and the other a silver disc.

Teressa skirted around the edge of the stone circle and went through the door into the apprentice quarters. These were much plainer than the Temple itself, of course, but her own small room had some stars on the ceiling – she'd put them there herself with some leftover paint that had been used to touch up the ceiling mural in the Temple.

Teressa's room didn't have much in it; just a bed and a small cupboard where she kept her belongings. She opened the cupboard now, and brought out a leather satchel. It was the only bag she owned, but she remembered hearing that griffiners didn't carry much in the air anyway – they couldn't risk making themselves too heavy.

A griffiner! She thrilled at the thought. *I'm a griffiner now!*

Grinning with excitement, she packed the bag with a few items – money, some dried food she'd been saving, a tinderbox, the old ceremonial knife she'd rescued after the priestesses had replaced it with a new one, a water bottle, and – wrapped carefully in cloth first – her prayer stone. She also found some ointment and other medicines she kept for emergencies, and packed those in.

She didn't own any clothes other than a spare silver robe, but she did have a fur-lined cloak, given to her as a birthday present by the priestess who mentored her. She put that on, made a last check for anything else she might need, and left.

As the door closed behind her, it occurred to her that she might never return. But she pulled herself together – of course she would. In the meantime, she should get back to Orak – she shouldn't keep her new friend waiting.

The grey griffin was sitting just where she had left him, and he stood up the moment he saw her coming. 'You are ready?'

'I think so,' said Teressa. 'What're we going to do about a harness, though?'

'You must find one,' Orak said unhelpfully.

'I suppose we could go to the markets,' said Teressa. 'It's worth a try.'

Orak turned and started to limp back towards the Eyrie and the market square without comment.

Teressa followed him. 'We should decide where we're going to go,' she added. 'What do ye think?'

'The dream said that the dark griffin was in the East,' said Orak.

'Aye, but where in the East?' said Teressa, unconsciously using the old word she had picked up from her mentor. 'Is it actually in the East, or just *to* the east?' She strained to remember the exact words.

'First we can look in the east side of this land,' Orak decided. 'There is not much beyond here but the sea, but we can go to the shore and follow it. A dark griffin should not be hard to see, and if we do not see him we may meet others who have.'

'And if we don't,' Teressa said slowly, 'Then we'll have to assume the dream meant in the East. And that means leaving Cymria.'

'I do not understand,' said Orak.

'Oh,' said Teressa. 'Well, "in the East" means Amoran and Maijan. Countries over the sea to the East. And past them there's Erebus.'

'I have not heard of them,' said Orak. 'But if we must go to those places, we will.'

Teressa grinned again. 'I hope we do!'

Chapter Four

Bought and Sold

Red's journey to Amoran took months, and afterwards he dearly wanted to forget it. He and the other prisoners stayed below decks, crammed into the cages for days on end. Every so often they would be taken up on deck in small groups, and allowed to take some fresh air while the floor of the cage would be given a quick scrubbing. They were fed every day – bad food, and not too much of it, and a hole in an internal ledge that jutted out over the water served as a toilet. It was enough to keep them alive.

But overcrowding, the heat, the stench, the constant lurching of the ship, and pure despair, was enough to wear down even the strongest of them. A month or so out to sea, Red saw the first prisoner die. He passed away in his sleep after days of illness, and Red and the others watched the guards drag the body away. Others followed. They died of sickness, or starvation, and one of the smaller women tried to escape by climbing out through the lavatory hole. They heard her scream and a faint splash as she landed in the ocean, and none of them ever saw her again.

The griffins fared just as badly. They were too large and powerful to go up on deck, so they stayed chained down, forced to lie on their bellies and relieve themselves where they were. At first, being griffins, they tried to fight back. But even Kraego eventually saw that struggling and threats couldn't save him, and even he grew too weak to want to try. All of the creatures quickly lost condition, but the Amoranis seemed very concerned about keeping them alive. They started bringing in more food for the weaker ones, and letting them stand up and groom every so often.

Red would have expected Kullervo to be one of the fastest to weaken, but the shapeshifter proved to be surprisingly resilient. He lost weight and his feathers grew bedraggled, but he stayed alert enough, and he and Red would talk to pass the time.

Red, of course, asked one question very early on.

'Why don't you turn human again?' He asked it in plain Cymrian, not wanting to draw attention to himself by using griffish.

'I can't,' said Kullervo.

Red frowned. 'Why not? I saw you do it before. You can switch back an' forth whenever you like.'

'Not always,' said Kullervo. 'I can't now. They've made sure of it.'

'How?' asked Red. 'What d'you mean?'

'Look around,' said Kullervo. 'Don't you think it's odd that none of the griffins here have tried using their magic to escape?'

Red eyed the sulking, stinking creatures, lying in their rows. 'I dunno…'

'We can't,' said Kullervo. 'They've drugged us. There's a plant they call griffinsbane. It paralyses the magic gland, stops the griffin using its power. They've been mixing it in with our food. None of us can do anything now.'

'Damn!' Red swore.

'Yes,' Kullervo said in his slow, sad voice. 'But there's something I want to know as well.'

Red sat down on his bench. 'What's that?'

'How do you know griffish?' asked Kullervo. 'You can understand me.'

'Oh,' Red grunted. 'My dad was a griffiner, wasn't he? He had to learn griffish, so I learned too, when I was just a lad. I was meant t'be a griffiner too, when I got older.'

'You never told me,' said Kullervo. 'Why not?'

Red shrugged. 'My dad was dead an' I wasn't gonna be a griffiner anymore. Common guardsmen ain't supposed to know griffish. Could've gotten me into trouble. So I kept my trap shut. I figure it doesn't matter now. I couldn't be in any more trouble than I am now.'

'And besides, you are a griffiner now,' said Kullervo. 'I always thought you and Kraego went well together.'

Red glared at the sleeping Kraego. 'We ain't partners. I thought we might be, but Kraego doesn't. He's a wild griffin an' proud of it, an' once this was over he was gonna fly back to the mountains an' I was gonna go back to being a guard. If anyone still wanted me, anyway.'

Kullervo shook his head. 'I have a feeling it won't end the way anyone expects. Especially for you.'

'No,' said Red. He looked at his fellow prisoners, and could almost smell their despair. 'I'm never gonna see the South again. None of us are.'

And, as the voyage dragged on, that came true for many of the prisoners.

Two of the griffins died as well, and their fellows on either side ate most of the remains before they could be hauled away. The air grew steadily hotter as the ship moved closer to Maijan – the island nation that was part of the Amorani Empire. The heat only made conditions worse in the cages. Food rotted, excrement stank, and flies crawled and buzzed. More people died. Red could see himself losing weight and muscle, but he didn't care so much anymore. The days started to slip away from him as he slept and woke, ate and slept again, and dreamt of a rope that strangled him and a pair of icy hands that reached out to drag him into eternal darkness. He felt as if he were slowly resigning himself for what was coming, but he had no idea what to expect. What would Amoran be like, and what sort of life would he have there? He asked Kullervo, but Kullervo didn't know.

'You'll have to be strong, Red,' the small griffin said one day. 'And you are strong. Your father was strong, your uncle was strong, and so are you.'

Red couldn't find anything to say to that. He had tried to be strong for so long, had held onto hope for longer, but now…now he felt lost.

And then, at last, Maijan came. Red felt, and heard, the ship dock. He waited in silence, with the other prisoners, and after a while their jailers came down and started to empty the cages. The prisoners were taken above decks, cage by cage, and didn't return.

Red was in the last cage, and his turn came last. A group of Amoranis came and made them stand up, and one by one the prisoners were shackled onto a long chain and made to shuffle out in single file.

Red didn't resist when his turn came. He was too tired and besides, what was the point?

'Goodbye,' he called back to Kullervo. 'An' good luck!'

'And to you as well, Kearney Redguard,' Kullervo called back. 'Be strong!'

Kraego raised his head to watch his friend go. 'Red! One day we will see each other again! One day we will fly together again, and our enemies will fall.'

'They will!' Red yelled back defiantly, before one of the guards smacked him in the head and the column moved out.

They walked up a wooden ramp and onto the ship's deck. The sunlight hit Red's eyes in a painful flash, and he grimaced and turned his head away. Around him the other prisoners were blinking and groaning.

The Amoranis urged them on, across the decks and down another ramp onto the docks. It was the first time in months that Red had set foot on a surface that didn't lurch or sway, and it made his stomach give a queasy jolt. He winced and straightened up, doing his best to keep steady.

The sun here was blazing hot — at least as hot as the strongest summer back in Cymria. As Red and the other prisoners went on shore, it heated up the chains holding them together and made Red wince. He hoped they wouldn't have to stay out of the shade for too long.

The locals had gathered to watch, and Red looked back curiously at them — he had never seen a Maijani before. He'd expected them to look like the Amoranis, but they weren't. Their skin was even paler, and most of them had flat or beakish noses. Their eyes were dark, and they had black hair. They stared at the prisoners with open curiosity, and talked among themselves in their own language. Red wondered if they'd ever seen Southerners before. Some of them had definitely noticed him — he saw them staring at his red hair with fascination.

He had expected to be put onto another ship — after all, they were supposed to be going to Amoran. But instead the column marched on and up into the harbour-side town — it was too small to be called a city. The buildings were unlike any Red had ever seen; flat roofed, and painted in bright colours. But he saw the market stalls and the people going about their business and his heart swelled painfully. Some things may have been different, but the sight of it made him desperate for home. He thought of Liranwee, remembered its grubby streets and the houses, the Eyrie tower looming above everything else. He remembered the markets, colder and dirtier than this, but full of the same buying and selling. He remembered patrolling with his partner, Ranulf, chasing thieves through the marketplace.

A terrible sadness filled him, and he looked away to stare at the ground. This market might have reminded him of the ones at home, but he wasn't home, and in this market, one of the things for sale would be him.

And that was exactly what happened. He and the others were taken to an open square, surrounded by stalls, and placed in holding pens not that different from the ones on the ship. The prisoners from the other cages were already there, along with more brought from the other ships that had come from Cymria. Some Maijani and a handful of Amorani prisoners were there, too.

They even sell themselves, Red thought. He wondered if they were prisoners of war like himself, or criminals being sold as punishment. He knew his own people had once sold their Northerner vassals into slavery for similar reasons.

He stood patiently in his pen, crowded in with the others, and waited to see what would happen next. The Amoranis who had brought them were talking to some of their friends, who had been waiting in the square, but of course they were using their own language, and Red had no idea what they might be saying.

To occupy himself, he stretched his legs as well as he could and looked around to see if he recognised any of the others.

His eyes widened. 'Lady Isleen!'

The woman who had once been Eyrie Mistress of Liranwee didn't look like a city ruler any more, or a griffiner. She wore a stained and torn wool dress, and her wrists were shackled just like his own. She had lost weight, and her bland, square face was downcast and pathetic.

She looked up at the sound of her name, and showed a brief moment of surprise. 'Captain Redguard. You're alive.'

'Yeah,' said Red. 'Didn't think I'd see you again.'

'I didn't think to see you again, either,' said Isleen. She turned away and pressed her forehead into the bars. 'Did you succeed?' she asked. 'Did you warn the other Eyries?'

'I did,' said Red. 'Kraego an' me did our best.'

Isleen smiled weakly. 'I'm sure you did.'

'But it wasn't enough,' Red added, half to himself.

'No,' Isleen mumbled. 'Nothing could have saved us except Gryphus himself.'

Red nodded grimly.

'Alaric could have saved us,' Isleen muttered to herself.

She obviously hadn't intended for Red to hear that part, but he did, and pulled a puzzled expression. 'What, Alaric the Dashing? From them storybooks?'

Isleen reddened. 'Never you mind!'

'Did you say Alaric?' said a small, sad-looking man from beside her.

'That's none of your business,' Isleen snapped, obviously embarrassed.

The man blushed. 'B…but you did say it.'

Isleen ignored him.

'I'm sorry,' the man added. 'I just thought you were talking to me.'

'What?' said Isleen.

The man's blush deepened. 'I… I'm Alaric. From Withypool.'

Red rolled his eyes. 'She didn't mean you. She meant Alaric the Dashing. Y'know, the one what rides a golden griffin called Sunfire an' saves the world from evil an' gets the prettiest women.'

Alaric cringed. He was indeed a small man, and might have been pudgy once as well. His curly hair was a dull brown, and he had a bad squint that suggested he was short-sighted. 'Oh. But I…I mean, I…'

'What is it?' Isleen said irritably.

'I wrote those books,' Alaric said meekly.

Isleen stared at him. 'You did?'

'Yes,' said Alaric. 'I put myself in them. I never wanted to be a hero, though, I just wanted to tell stories.'

'About you bein' a hero,' said Red.

'I just liked to pretend,' said Alaric, looking as if he wanted to sink into the ground and never be seen again.

Red looked away, faintly amused, but behind him, he could hear Isleen and Alaric talking. The world had gone mad. Alaric the Dashing was a real person…more or less. Isleen had found her hero. And now she and him and everyone else were about to become somebody else's property.

A short time later, the buyers began to arrive. A small group of Amoranis, and two Maijanis, all richly dressed and accompanied by personal slaves. The slaves were easy to spot. They wore iron collars around their necks, and identical clothing – plain pieces of white cloth wrapped around the hips, with another piece for the breasts if the slave was a woman. All of them, even the women, had shaved heads.

The buyers stood by in a loose group, while the prisoners were brought out for their inspection. The buyers picked out the ones they apparently liked the look of, and Red saw money changing hands. The sight of it made him feel sick to his stomach. How could anyone be treated like this? How could this even *happen*? Was this really what his parents' generation had done to other human beings?

Once again Red thought of Caedmon and his followers, and the hatred and malice in their faces. And he saw, now, what they had seen when they looked at him. They had seen, not a human being, but a slaver. A piece of scum no different to the people here, busy prodding and poking at the prisoners as if they were oxen for sale.

Red's head drooped, and a terrible shame and humiliation came over him. And, just for a moment, he found himself wondering if he deserved this. Not for what he had done, but for what his people had done.

Maybe, in the end, they had brought this on themselves.

His own turn came, and he stepped out of the pen in line with the others and stood with them while the buyers came forward to look at them. Just as the Amorani lord back in Cymria had done, they inspected Red closely – felt his muscles, made him flex his arms and legs, roughly patted him down to check for injuries. They even checked his eyes and ears to see he had all his senses. When they saw the guard tattoo on his shoulder they paid close attention to that, and before long one of the Maijani buyers had pointed at him and given a nod.

Red stood still, gripped by a sense of numb unreality while they inspected him. One man, a native Maijani with a lined and arrogant face made note of his guard tattoo and nodded at once. Red's guards unshackled him from the line and pushed him over to stand with the others who had been chosen. Isleen and Alaric were with them, and several other former guardsmen.

They weren't chained up again, but none of them tried to run away. Running now would mean death, and on an island, there was nowhere to go. The Maijani's personal guards herded them away, and Red went with them, still feeling numb.

Their new master took them to a rich-looking building made of mud bricks painted white and blue. Inside, the prisoners were put into a plain wooden room and made to wait, while a pair of guards came in every so often and took them away one by one. Red stood in silence, head spinning. He felt close to vomiting.

He didn't have to wait long. Soon enough, two Maijani guards gestured at him to come with them. He went quietly, and they escorted him into a room where a group of three male slaves waited. There was a large bucket of steaming water on the floor between them, and a fire burned in an open brazier.

The guards stood aside and waited, keeping a close eye on Red.

One of the slaves nodded briefly at him. 'Take off,' he said, and tugged on Red's tunic.

Reluctantly, Red took off his tunic. But that didn't satisfy the slave, and he realised that he was expected to strip. He did, and stood there embarrassed while one of the other slaves there gathered up his clothes and his boots and unceremoniously threw them onto the fire.

'Hey!' Red yelled. Nobody listened. He watched as the tattered remains of his guard uniform went up in smoke.

The slave who had made him strip gestured at the bucket of water. 'Wash.'

Red was happier to do that. He splashed the water over himself – it was hot and soapy, and two of the slaves gave him a scrubbing brush to help him get the dirt off himself, and fresh water to rinse off. He washed himself all over, and once he was finished one of the slaves picked up a razor.

Red froze. 'No—,'

They didn't listen. Two of the slaves held him still, and despite his protests the third one took the razor and silently shaved him. They took everything – his hair, the beard he'd grown on the voyage, even the thatch of hair on his chest and back. Red could only be grateful that they left his groin alone, but before long the rest of him was as smooth and hairless as the day he was born.

After that they gave him a white cloth to tie around his hips, and some leather sandals for his feet. And the collar. It was big and heavy, made of solid iron with some kind of writing etched into it. Red tried to pull away, but they held him still again and the collar snapped shut around his neck. He tugged at it once they let go of his arms, but it wouldn't budge. It rested on his collarbone, heavy as shame.

Then they let him go on into the next room. He shuffled off, awkward in his new sandals, feeling the air on his bald scalp. He felt naked and defiled, helpless as a baby.

But there was something worse to come.

In the next room, two more slaves and two more guards waited by a brazier. An iron rod poked out from among the glowing coals. Red knew exactly what that meant when he saw it, and he turned and tried to run back out of the room. But the two guards had been prepared for this. They took him by the shoulders and twisted one arm behind his back, just as he would have done in an arrest back home. They pulled the other arm out in front of him, and pressed his right hand down on a tabletop while one of the slaves took the rod out of the brazier.

On the end was a strange symbol, glowing red hot.

'No!' Red yelled. 'Stop!'

But the brand pressed into the back of his hand, and his throat went raw with the sound of his scream. The smell of burning flesh hit him as the brand lifted, and when he returned to his senses he found himself shaking between his captors.

The other slave, the one who hadn't branded him, slapped some gritty ointment over the burn and turned dismissively away.

The guards took Red out of the room, and he went meekly, feeling his hand tremble. Among all his fear and pain and humiliation, he found himself remembering the cold hatred he had seen in the face of King Caedmon. He remembered the sneering mockery of the Northerners.

Once we did this to them, he thought.

He had always known that, but he had never thought of what it might have been like. He had never imagined the humiliation.

Shivering, he let himself be shown to his new quarters. It was a simple long room full of bunks, but at last he had a place to lie down. He chose the nearest bunk and flopped down on his back. Immediately the collar pressed into the back of his neck, and he winced and tried to adjust it. It fitted so tightly that he could scarcely move it, and when he pulled, it crushed his windpipe. For an instant – one horrible, sickening instant – he thought he could feel the chafing of the Hangman's rope around his neck. Panic-stricken, he yanked at the collar, desperately trying to make it come off, but the more he pulled the more it throttled him and the worse his terror became.

'Stop!' A pair of hands tugged his away from the collar. 'Stop, now.'

Red lurched upright, banging his head on the bunk above him, and tried to pull away from the stranger.

The hands let go of him. 'Breathe deep,' said their owner. 'Breathe!'

Red made himself breathe deeply and slowly, and his panic subsided. 'I thought it was gonna strangle me. I thought...'

The stranger was another slave – an older slave, a Maijani. He smiled, showing brilliantly white teeth. 'Collars are not made to strangle. Dead slaves are no good,' he said, in thickly accented Cymrian.

Red made himself relax. 'I'm never gonna sleep in this thing.'

'Then you never going to sleep,' said the Maijani.

'I'd rather die,' said Red. He clenched his good fist. 'I'd rather die than live like this.'

'So many men say, but they live on,' said the Maijani. 'You come from Grephe, yes?'

'Red,' Red muttered.

'You come from Grephe, Yes?'

'What's that?' asked Red.

'The land of griffins.'

'Cymria,' said Red.

'Yes, that is Grephe,'

Red sighed. 'Doesn't matter; I'm never gonna see it again. What're they gonna do with me now?'

'You will not stay here,' said the Maijani. 'You and the new slaves will go to Amoran tomorrow. To the markets in Instabahn. My master is a seller, not a keeper.'

'Who'd want to buy me?' Red wondered.

'You have no fear!' the man grinned and slapped Red's tattooed shoulder. 'You have this. Strong arms and the mark of a Grephe guard. My master is pleased. In Amoran, a man like you is worth much.'

Red looked at him curiously. 'Why? Ain't slaves just meant for mining an' building an' whatnot?'

'Some. But in Amoran they have many uses for many kinds.

Soldiers, guards, teachers and speakers to make one language another.'

'Oh,' said Red. In Cymria, slaves had never been used for anything but unskilled labour. No wonder the Amoranis who'd brought him here had asked him if he could read or write.

'Yes,' said the Maijani. 'You will be a guard or used for fighting. If you have other things you do, tell them so. More value to them means a better home for you.'

'Thanks,' said Red. 'I'll remember.'

'You remember!' the Maijani said cheerfully. 'And see what life brings to you next. Always there is surprises.'

'You can say that again,' Red muttered.

Chapter Five

The Slave Whore

The Maijani slave had been telling the truth, and the very next day, Red and the other new slaves were taken back down to the docks and loaded onto another ship – this one a smaller ship of Maijani design, made from rich, spicy smelling wood. This time they weren't locked up below decks. They were given a place to sleep down there, but were allowed to come and go from it as they pleased and given jobs to do. Isleen and Alaric, being educated but not strong, were put to work in the galley. Red and the other stronger slaves worked for the crew, tying ropes, cleaning up, fetching and carrying. It was hard work, especially in the blazing Eastern sun, but it kept them busy, and they were fed reasonably well.

After a few weeks, Red had started to put weight back on and regained some of the muscle tone he had lost on the voyage from Cymria. But he was expected to keep his head and face shaved, and before long the sun had tanned him all over. His scalp peeled and his nose turned red, and his hands became splintered and callused. The brand slowly healed, and thanks to regular applications of ointment, it stayed clean. But it was extremely painful for many days before the scar finally began to form.

Isleen and Alaric were both bald and collared, and so were the others who had been bought that day; all guardsmen like Red, whose tattoos were clearly visible now they had to go shirtless. Red didn't know any of them, but the slaves were allowed to talk amongst themselves while they worked, so he soon got to know them. Most of them were from Withypool, but two were from Sunton, having come along with their territory's army.

But, in the end, he found he didn't have much to say to any of them. Most of them were sullen and angry, and all they could do was curse the ones who had put them in this situation and try and make plans for escape and revenge. Red didn't join in with that. He had more sense than to think there was any chance of going home now. And even if they did get home, what would they be coming back to?

A country that had been overrun by Northerners, where their friends were dead and their cities overthrown? Going back there would mean nothing but death or a return to slavery.

Red felt paralysed by the knowledge. And, when once he would have talked to the others and tried to keep their spirits up, now he kept to himself, working in silence and feeling the shame and humiliation of what had been done to him burn through his mind. It was numbing.

He went about his work in silence, the way a man without hope works: slowly and methodically, not caring about speed, doing it just because there was nothing else to do and no other choice. His new masters weren't cruel – more indifferent. They gave him his orders without calling him by name or looking him in the eye, as if they knew he would obey without argument.

And, hating himself for it, he did. So did the others – even the angriest and most resentful stopped trying to argue or resist very quickly. Not because they wanted to obey the hated foreigners who owned them, but because they had no other choice. Disobedience got you nothing but a blow from a whip or a stick, and stronger resistance got you flogged in front of everyone. That, and back-breaking labour, was enough to stop the grumblers and the schemers after a while.

Red watched it all happen with resignation.

The journey to Amoran was shorter than the one that had brought them to Maijan. The slaves and the normal sailors worked efficiently together, and after a few weeks the continent that was home to the great Amorani Empire came in sight on the horizon. Red saw it, and felt his mind finally start to lift out of its stupor. In spite of everything, he couldn't help but be a little excited by the prospect of seeing a new land. And who knew what Amoran would be like?

He found out some days later, when the ship finally reached the shores of Amoran. Red had expected it to dock there, but instead it sailed on inland along a huge, wide river, and followed it for another day and a night.

Red watched the landscape beyond the river, and took everything in. Amoran was a desert country, sandy and dry. But close to the river, crops had been planted, and he saw the farmers wading through the shallows at the water's edge, collecting rich river mud in baskets to fertilise their fields.

Smaller boats sailed up and down the river, bobbing in the wake left by the slave ship, and Red watched the Amoranis on board casting nets or throwing spears to catch larger fish and ducks. Most of them were men, but he saw his first Amorani women, too: small, delicate and dark eyed. Further along, outside the first of the villages they passed, he saw huge crocodiles slide off the river banks and into the water where they floated just at the surface, golden eyes staring coldly at the foreigners sailing into their land.

Strange trees grew near the river as well, unlike anything Red had ever seen before, with thin, branchless trunks and fronds sprouting from the top like spiky ferns. Birds perched in them, of course, but so did another winged creature – unlike anything he had ever seen or heard of. They were about the size of chickens, but much slimmer, with scaly serpentine bodies mounted on two clawed legs. But they had wings. Wings with big, flattened scales instead of feathers which they used to flit about among the ship's masts, hooting to each other like a flock of parrots. Red saw their pointed reptilian heads, and the tiny fangs and horns.

'Dragons,' one man murmured to another.

Dragons! Red stared in wonder, and when he had the time he watched them closely to see if they would breathe fire. Fortunately, they didn't. Maybe that part was just a myth.

Meanwhile, under the merciless glare of the sun, the ship moved on. On the morning of the second day, Red went up on deck and saw their final destination.

A great city lined the river on both sides, built right up against the water. The buildings were different to anything he had seen at home, but not so different from the ones in Maijan. Smooth, light brown walls, some of them painted in bright colours, with flat roofs and open, glassless windows. Shade -cloths protected doorways and rooftops where the locals had set up tables. Red saw a family eating at one, while they looked down idly at the ship docking below.

At a place where the river was a little wider, dozens of piers jutted out into the water. Other ships the size of the one Red stood on had already docked there, but his own was the largest new arrival. Urged on by a shout from one of the free Amorani sailors, he obediently grabbed a rope and helped them to furl the sails, while others threw a rope to a man waiting on one of the largest piers. In no time at all, the ship had been docked and the slave master and his guards brought the entire human cargo together on deck. There they were chained together, wrist to wrist, and herded down a ramp and onto the pier.

Red shuffled along obediently between Lady Isleen and another former guardsman, wondering where they were going next. The slave markets, presumably. And once he got there, he would just have to hope that whoever bought him would be…

…would be what? Kind? Unlikely.

He would just have to hope that, whatever happened, he would have the strength to survive.

*

They didn't go to the market that day, however. Instead, the slaves were forced to walk with their master and guards to a house that he must have owned. It was bigger than the place in Maijan, built close to the river, which had been tapped to provide a private pool. The rest of the building encircled it in a horseshoe shape, and the presence of the water helped keep the interior blessedly cool.

Red and the other slaves were locked up in the slave quarters, along with some others who must already live there as household servants. It was surprisingly comfortable, with enough narrow wooden beds for everyone, and even another, smaller pool set into the floor to serve as a bath. The slaves were left to their own devices, provided with a fire and food, and the slaves already living there – mostly Amoranis, Red noticed – silently and efficiently made a meal for everyone.

Freed from the running chain, Red took advantage of the pool to wash himself, and ate as much as he was allowed. It made him feel much better, and even a little optimistic. If this was going to be his life from now on, at least he knew that slaves weren't treated as badly here as he had imagined.

'What will happen to us?' Lady Isleen said suddenly, breaking into his thoughts. It was the first thing she had said in days.

Red looked up from his bed where he had lain down to rest. 'What d'you reckon?' he said shortly. 'Tomorrow we'll be off to the markets an' we'll be sold.'

Isleen looked utterly miserable.

'Cheer up,' Red snorted. 'You're a noble, remember? You're

gonna get a job teachin' some Amorani lord's kids or whatever. It'll be a cushy life for you.'

'The life of a slave,' Isleen muttered.

'At least it's life,' said Red, not troubling to show her respect as he would have if she was still an Eyrie Mistress and he was still a guard in her city. Now they were equals, more or less. 'Would it be better if they just stove yer head in?'

'Yes.'

Alaric shuffled closer to her. 'It's all right,' he said timidly. 'We'll be all right. We'll find a way to get out of this.'

'D'you really think that?' Red said sourly.

'You escaped,' said Alaric, with a boldness that took him by surprise. 'You were on the gallows and you escaped. Isleen told me.'

'Yeah,' Red admitted. 'Got away from the Northerners, got away from Isleen. Done a lot of escapin' lately. But I reckon my luck's just about run out. I might've gotten away with a lot, but that doesn't mean I made a difference. I mean, look where it got me. Look where it got the South.' The bitterness in his voice surprised even himself.

'Captain Redguard,' Isleen stood up. 'You can't blame yourself for what happened to us. You did your best. One man can't fight an army. What happened to our country was something none of us could stop. Even if I had listened to you when you tried to warn me, it would have been too late. You know who is to blame.'

'Yeah,' Red muttered. 'Yeah. I do.'

'Then blame him,' said Isleen. 'And forgive yourself.'

Red softened. 'All right, milady. All the same, don't go thinkin' you're gonna get out of this, because you ain't. None of us are.'

'We might,' said one of the other former guards.

'Like how?' said Red. 'Even if we got out of here, how'd we get home? Steal a ship? You know how to sail one all by yourself?'

'There's always hope,' said Alaric, with a kind of forced bravery, as if he were trying to sound like his imaginary counterpart, Alaric the Dashing.

Hope. Red sighed. He had spent so much time holding onto it, in the face of everything, but now he felt as if it had finally slipped away from him.

He didn't bother to argue with the puny former storyteller, but he shot him a pitying look and slumped onto his bed to get some rest.

Isleen, though, moved closer to Alaric and silently pressed herself against him. Alaric put an arm around her and gave her a tentative hug. He looked as if he couldn't believe his luck.

The sight of them made Red's heart ache. So strange that anyone would be able to find love here, of all places. For the first time, he found himself wishing that he had given less time to his career in the guard and allowed himself the time to find someone he could love. His whole life he'd been determined to win back the Redguard family honour, but without a wife, that family would end with him. And now it was too late. Any children he fathered now would be born into a life of slavery like his own.

The night was hot outside, but the pool in his new quarters helped to keep it pleasantly cool, and Red was too exhausted to be kept awake by much anymore. He drifted off to sleep, bitter about the past, and feeling no hopefulness for the future.

*

Morning came, and at dawn the slaves were taken out in a column — the new arrivals who had come with Red on the ship, and others who had already been there when they arrived. Chained together by the wrists as before, they walked slowly through the sandy streets of Instabahn and then to the great slave market that brought so much wealth to the city. Long rows of sturdy wooden posts fitted with chains lined a wide walkway, which at the moment was taken up by other groups of slaves with their masters.

Red's group was driven along to a particular cluster of posts, where they were taken off the running chain one by one and each attached to a post by another chain which latched onto a ring that protruded from their collars.

Red soon found himself chained to a post of his own, unable to sit down, tethered in place like a donkey. He scowled down at his big callused hands, and waited in silence.

By the time the sun had finished rising the slave markets were already bustling. Every post had been occupied, and the first customers had begun arriving. Red's owner walked back and forth among his wares, ready to pounce on anyone who came by. Every now and then, he bellowed something in Amorani. Red wondered what he was saying. Crying his wares, like a stallholder in the marketplace back home, maybe?

"Finest human beings, fresh off the boat, get them while they're alive!"

Red watched the customers. They were mainly Amoranis, richly clad, many of them accompanied by griffins. Most of them came accompanied by a slave or two to shade them. Even the griffins had their own attendants. Red looked at those griffins with particular curiosity.

Amorani griffins were a different kind to the ones back in Cymria. Desert griffins: smaller and slimmer, most of them with coats of sandy or dark brown. Some of them sported colourful head-crests, and many of them had splashes of bright colours on their wings or necks. A lot of them were dressed up, too, wearing elaborate headdresses strung with beads, or jewelled gold sheaths on their beaks. Red even saw one whose talons had been coated in gold leaf.

It was hard to imagine that people who pampered their partners this much would chain up griffins like Kraego, especially when, as Kullervo had told him, the Amoranis held griffins to be sacred. It made no sense.

He glanced at the slave next to him – an Amorani man with a scar on his chest.

'Hey you,' he hissed. 'D'you speak Cymrian?'

The man glanced at him, but said nothing.

'Why'd they want griffins in Amoran?' Red asked.

The man looked puzzled, and shook his head.

'I don't mean for partners, I mean as like slaves,' said Red. 'They brought some over with us in chains. What for, d'you know?'

'I hear the Emperor asked for griffins to be sent,' the Amorani slave said unexpectedly. He spoke Cymrian very well. 'What for, I do not know. But say nothing.' He immediately fell silent as their master passed close by.

Red nodded back and didn't try to talk again. He'd already found out that his master didn't like it when slaves talked in his hearing. In Amoran, slaves were expected to speak only when spoken to.

The day grew brighter, and the heat increased unbearably. Thank gods; their rank of posts had a shade cloth over it. Red saw other slaves on the other side of the road who weren't so lucky. Left out in the blazing sun, they cringed and picked at their collars, which had already blistered the skin around the necks. Their master, pacing back and forth to keep an eye on them, smacked them with the fly swat in his hand to make them stop. Red winced at the sight.

Meanwhile, his own master had already begun making his first sales. Alaric and Isleen and another former griffiner were among the first to go, sold to a wiry old Amorani who seemed very pleased to have found three such high-class slaves.

'Come,' Red overheard him say in griffish as they were unchained from their posts and pushed towards him. 'Come, you will be a gift to my grandson. You will be teachers for his sons.'

Red waved to Isleen. ''Bye, milady.'

She smiled back weakly, and allowed herself to be led away to begin her new life. Alaric stayed protectively close to her, looking pale and drawn, as if he couldn't quite believe what was happening to him.

Red shook his head and settled down to wait until his own turn came.

Sometime close to midday, the Amorani slave beside him stirred and pointed. 'Look,' he said softly. 'See the lady there?'

Red followed his pointing finger, and quickly saw who he was talking about. An Amorani lady came walking their way. She was attended by two slaves of a race Red had never seen before; their skin a little darker than those of the Amoranis.

The woman herself looked Amorani to him. She was tall and full-figured, and there was something loose and seductive about the way she walked. She wore green; a small piece of clothing Red had no name for covered her breasts, sparkling with green gemstones, and a long sash of dark green fabric hung from her hip and swept over one leg as she walked. Her hair was long, coloured a rich brown so dark it was almost black. Red saw her face, with its full sensual lips and high cheekbones, the eyes dark and watchful.

'Whoa,' he mumbled to himself.

'They call her the slave-whore,' his new friend whispered. 'She comes to the markets here every week, and buys only the strongest men. It is said she keeps them to pleasure her, for no lady needs so many guards as she has.'

Red grinned to himself. 'Sounds like the kinda master I wouldn't mind having.'

As if she had heard him, the green-clad woman came closer. She looked at him, then at the other slaves around him, and smiled briefly.

Red shifted nervously, making his chain clink. The sound must have attracted her notice, because she came straight to him, and as other buyers had done, she gestured at him to come closer.

Obediently, Red stepped towards her and held his arms out from his sides as the others had done so she could inspect him. She did, running her delicate hands down his arms and legs to feel the muscle, testing the flexibility of his joints and moving a finger in front of his eyes to see if he had his full sight.

Red's master appeared at once, speaking to her in Amorani. A brief conversation took place, while the woman checked Red's fellow Southerners, and then inspected Red again. She seemed pleased, and soon gestured at him and every other man there who had a guard tattoo as he did. Red's master replied, and after some more discussion she handed over a bag of money.

In a moment, Red and every other former guard there had been unshackled from his post and attached to another running chain like the one that had brought them to the market. Then their new owner and her two attendants led them away with a nod and a curt command.

But that wasn't all. Red and his fellows followed their new master through the markets, and several more times she stopped and purchased other slaves – all Southerners, and the occasional Maijani, but not one single Amorani. Maybe this lady objected to buying members of her own race, Red thought.

Either way, by the time she finally left the market she had a train of at least fifty slaves following her, mostly men, and all strong and fit. Clearly, she had no interest in educated slaves like Isleen and Alaric.

That afternoon, her buying over, the woman in green led her new possessions to the river, where a small ship was moored. It was crewed by more slaves, and they immediately lowered a gangplank and helped the newcomers aboard. Red and the others were quickly directed below deck to a long room lined with hammocks, where one of the lady's attendants took them off the chain and gestured at them to make themselves comfortable.

Red was more than happy to take a hammock and relax in it. After an entire day spent standing up, a hammock was very welcome.

A short while later, he felt the ship lurch as it set off along the river, and he dozed on and off, in between wondering where he was going now and who this lady really was. Somehow, he doubted that she was really going to use himself and the others as the Amorani slave had suggested. He couldn't help thinking that he wouldn't complain if she did, though. He grinned wickedly to himself at the idea.

*

The journey to his new owner's home took longer than he expected. Several days passed while the ship journeyed up the river, sometimes driven by the wind and other times by the oars that Red and his fellow slaves had to handle. But it was a pleasant journey; the work wasn't too hard, there was plenty of food, and their new master treated them much more gently than the last one.

Red soon learned a few things about her from some of the other slaves there who had been with her for a while. Her name was Lady Ahamay, and she owned a large riverside estate North of Xanthium, which was the capital city of Amoran. She was unmarried, and very wealthy, with a reputation for hosting the most luxurious parties. Even members of the Imperial family would come to them, sailing upriver in their pleasure barges to watch the swimming races she would organise, and to compete in fishing games and other contests which sometimes went on for days. Even the Emperor himself was one of her circle of friends.

'With such a large home, and so many important guests, the lady likes to have many guards,' Red's informant told him. He was one of the two attendants Ahamay had had with her in the marketplace, whose race Red hadn't been able to guess.

'So that's why she bought us?' Red asked.

'Yes, that is why.'

Red had too much common sense to ask if the stories about her taste in slaves were true, but his disappointment must have shown, because his new friend grinned and added, 'She does not use us for her pleasure, though new men like you sometimes wish she did!'

'Where'd the stories come from, then?' asked Red.

'They began most likely because the Lady Ahamay sometimes dines in private with new slaves and treats them as equals.'

'Why?' Red wondered.

'It is said that she asks them questions,' said the man. 'And asks them to tell her of their lives. Perhaps because she is curious, or perhaps she likes to hear stories.'

Red frowned his puzzlement.

'She will like to dine with you or one of the others who have come from Grephe, I think,' the other slave added. 'We have never had men like you before.'

'She didn't buy any other Amoranis back there,' Red recalled. 'Can't see any here either. Unless you're one?'

The man shook his head. 'I am from Erebus, which is east of Amoran. My name is Tototl. Lady Ahamay does not buy Amoranis; only those from Maijan, or Erebus, or Grephe. Why, I do not know.'

'What's Erebus like?' asked Red. He'd only ever heard it mentioned, and knew nothing else about it.

'Ah,' Tototl looked wistful. 'Erebus is a land as big as the whole of the Empire, and it is covered in great jungles. It is ruled by the all-knowing priesthood in the name of the Great Serpent, Itzcóatl.'

'It's not part of the Empire?' asked Red, who knew at least that the Amorani Empire had conquered a good part of the Eastern world.

'The Empire would like it to be,' said Tototl. 'But over all these centuries my people have refused to bow to their armies. Amoran and Erebus have been bitter enemies through all of living memory.'

'Like us and the Northerners back home,' said Red, half to himself.

Tototl grinned. 'Not so much! You white-skinned ones fight your own countrymen. You are all men of Grephe.'

'Tell that to the bastards who took my home an' sold me over here like some cow goin' to market,' Red growled.

Tototl lost his grin, and shook his head. 'Conquerors are all the same, yes?'

'Yeah,' said Red. 'Did you come from Erebus? Were you born there, like?'

'Yes,' said Tototl. 'But I was brought to Amoran when I was very small. My village was destroyed by the Emperor's sons.'

'Mine too,' said Red. 'The Emperor's sons helped, anyhow. It was one of them what came over an' crushed us at Withypool.'

Tototl hissed to himself like a snake. 'You in the West have been lucky that the Empire does not consider your country worth fighting for, or it would have done to you what they have done to Maijan and so many others.'

Red shook his head silently. He didn't want to think of his home any more. It was too painful.

'Still, now,' Tototl added. 'If you must live this way, then Lady Ahamay is a fine master to own you. She does not flog or starve; you will be fed well and treated kindly.'

That was a comfort, at least, but as the journey continued, Red noticed his new master starting to pay him some attention. Sometimes he noticed her looking at him in an appraising kind of way, though she never spoke to him directly. He wondered if she was curious about the faint stubble of red hair that had started to reappear on his head and chin; as far as he knew, there was no such thing as a red-haired Amorani.

Eventually, after about a day of sailing on past Xanthium, they reached their new home.

It was as magnificent as Red had expected. A great, domed building loomed over a complex of other, smaller domes spread out along a good stretch of river bank. The bank itself had been modified; dug away to create a semicircular bay edged by a stone wall, with piers at either end. The water's edge was lined with those strange Amorani trees Red had seen before – palm trees, he'd been told they were called – mixed with others that he'd never seen; which had dark, rich bark. The water of the bay was lush with reeds, where unfamiliar water birds flocked.

Lady Ahamay's ship docked at the first pier, and there the slaves disembarked and were led inside to their new quarters. They shared a home, as they had done back in Instabahn, and it was just as comfortable, with individual beds and a pool.

They were indeed fed well, and left to sleep. Red couldn't help but feel lucky that he'd been sold to a place like this. If it must be slavery, as Tototl had said, at least he had a master who was apparently going to treat him well. It was better than nothing.

*

Next morning, each of the new slaves was taken out into an open courtyard not far from their sleeping quarters. Unlike the lush, plant-filled courtyards Red had seen in Instabahn, this one was plain, boasting nothing but an open stretch of sandy ground dotted with the odd palm tree. But it offered something else instead: a row of archery butts along one wall and racks of weapons by another.

Red realised quickly what it was, because he'd seen something like it plenty of times before in his old life. A training ground.

Sure enough, once the newcomers had been made to stand in a neat rank, another, older, tough-looking Maijani slave appeared and spoke to them in rough Cymrian.

'You are here to be guards to my Lady,' he said. 'Today you will use weapons, and show me how well you fight. If you fight well, you will have better weapons and armour.' He gestured at the racks of weapons. 'Now take spears, one each, and make pairs. Quickly!'

Red obeyed, helping himself to a long, light wooden spear with a fine steel tip. The design was a little different to what he had used back in Liranwee, but not too different. A spear was a spear.

Once everyone was armed they split into pairs and sparred as if they were on a parade ground back home, while their instructor went from pair to pair, watching without comment. After a while he called a halt and ordered everyone to put their spears back and take a sword instead. After that, they had to demonstrate their archery skills, and finally, hand to hand.

It was all the sort of thing Red had done a hundred times before in training, and he handled it without any difficulty now, though he was best with the short sword, and hand to hand. He'd taken his job very seriously back home and had spent plenty of his spare time practising. It was why he'd been promoted to Sergeant as early as he had.

The instructor seemed pleased by what he saw. Once everyone had gone through their exercises and put their weapons back, he nodded and smiled and said, 'It is said that men of Grephe make fine guards, and it is true. But you…' he pointed at Red.

Red stood a little straighter. 'Sir?' he said, guard-like.

'It has been said that you can read and that you know the griffin's tongue,' said the instructor.

Red nodded. 'Yes sir,' he said.

The instructor nodded. 'Then my Lady will want to speak with you. Go to your sleeping place and wash yourself, and you will be sent for.'

'Yes, sir,' said Red.

Chapter Six

A Tale for a Tale

Red returned to his quarters and cleaned himself up as instructed, full of curiosity. He felt a little proud, too. Out of all the newcomers, he was the one Lady Ahamay had chosen to meet. He'd get the opportunity to find out what his new master was really like, and maybe there would be some other opportunity in it, too. He'd have to keep his eyes open and find out.

A short while later, one of her attendants – Tototl himself – appeared. He smiled at Red in a friendly way and said, 'So it is you the Lady has chosen this time! Come with me, Grephian.'

Red followed him. 'Is she gonna ask me questions, then?'

'She will ask for your story,' said Tototl. 'Answer with the truth and you will please her.'

'Right,' Red nodded and hurried after his new friend, impatient to see what would happen next.

Tototl led him away from the slave quarters, which were in the western wing of the estate, along with the kitchens and other lower class parts of the building. Ahamay's own living area was in the centre of her estate, under the biggest of the domes Red had spotted from the boat. Tototl showed him to a particular room close to the front of the building, with a large window that looked out over the waters of the river. Thin, gauzy curtains stirred in the hot breeze, and carried the scent of unfamiliar spices to Red as he entered.

He stopped in the doorway, and quickly took in the room itself. A low table stood in its centre. There were no chairs around it – in Amoran, it seemed, people preferred to sit on cushions on the floor. There was a couch though, a little further back from the table. Lady Ahamay lounged on it, as scantily clad as she had been when Red first saw her in the marketplace. She smiled lazily at him, and called to Tototl in Amorani.

Tototl pushed Red gently on the back. 'Go. Do not keep her waiting.'

Red entered. Lady Ahamay didn't get up, so he went up to her couch. He bowed awkwardly. 'Milady.'

She smiled. Her eyes were heavy-lidded, dusted with some kind of makeup that made them sparkle pale green. There was a hint of green in her eyes as well.

'You are from the land of griffins,' she said, using griffish. 'You know the language of griffins, yes?'

'I do,' said Red, using griffish as well.

'But your language is this,' said Ahamay, switching to heavily accented Cymrian.

'Yes, milady,' said Red, surprised.

She smiled again. 'You did not think to hear your language from me, Grephian. But I have learned many tongues. What is your name?'

'Kearney Redguard.'

Ahamay put her head on one side as she listened. 'Your hair is red. I see those tiny hairs on your head there.'

'Yeah,' said Red. 'A bit of it's grown back.'

'Then I will call you Desher,' said Ahamay.

'What does that mean?' Red ventured.

She smiled. 'In my tongue, it means… Red.'

Red smiled back.

'Sit, Desher,' said Ahamay. 'Eat.' She gestured at the table.

Red glanced at it. It was laden with dishes of foods he had never seen before. 'Is it all for me?'

'Eat,' Ahamay said again.

Red was more than happy to obey. He sat himself on a cushion at the table and helped himself. There were spiced meats and strange sharp cheeses, and some kind of cooked grain he had never seen before. Weird, exotic fruit filled a bowl in the middle of the table, and there was flat, oiled bread to go with it all. He tried some of everything. Some of the spices made his tongue hurt, but he ate it anyway.

Lady Ahamay ate nothing, and only watched him, mysterious and silent.

While Red ate, Tototl and his fellow attendant slave appeared and provided him with a jug full of what turned out to be wine. It was strong and sweet, and very good. He drank it very gladly, casting grateful looks at Ahamay. It was true, he thought – she really was good to her slaves.

She waited patiently until he had finished eating before she spoke again. 'Now that I have given you a gift, you must give me something in return, Desher,' she said.

Red put his cup down. 'What d'you want me to give you?' he asked cautiously.

She smiled that mysterious smile. 'Give me a story.'

'What about?' asked Red.

'Your story,' said Ahamay. 'Whether it is good or bad, tell it truly. Tell it all to me.'

Red hesitated. 'All of it?'

'From the beginning,' she said.

Red took another drink, mulled things over for a moment, and then obeyed.

He told her everything: his whole story, beginning with his parents. He told her about his mother, a toymaker, and his father, a sergeant in the guard. He told her how his father had killed a young Northerner called Arren Cardockson, and how that Northerner had returned from beyond the grave to destroy Eagleholm in revenge. He told her about his travels with Kullervo, about his time as a guard in Liranwee. He told her about how the war with the North had begun, his travels with Kraego as he tried to rally the Eyries and save the South, and the battles he had fought in. He told her about how he had fought King Caedmon, leader of the Northerners, and almost killed him. He told her how he and Kraego had been captured and taken away in chains to Amoran. He told it all, in detail.

It took a long time, but Ahamay didn't interrupt. She listened seriously, as if she were truly interested, and she must have heard the bitterness and anger in Red's voice as he talked about how his quest to save his country had failed, with a life of slavery his only reward.

When at last he was finished, she sat in silence for a moment longer, apparently digesting everything he had said.

'Desher is a brave man,' she said at last. 'Noble and good.'

Red looked at her with surprise, but said nothing. His throat hurt from so much talking.

Lady Ahamay finally sat up. 'It is a good story you have told,' she said. 'It pleased me. Now, in return, I will tell a story to you.'

Red nodded silently, curious. Would she tell him her own life story in return?

She didn't. What she was to say instead was something far stranger than any life story could have been.

'What I will tell you is deep knowledge,' she said. 'Magical knowledge. The greatest scholars have studied it. Listen now, Desher, and remember it always.'

Red listened, utterly silent and almost unmoving.

'This world has many races,' said Ahamay, 'Grephians, Amoranis, Erebians, Maijani, Eireans, Taians… Many, many races live in this world. For every race there is a language, for every race a god. And for every race, a guardian.' She smiled to herself in that mysterious way she had. 'It is said that every race had its guardian. Sent by the gods, many worshipped as gods themselves – they were sent to lead and protect. And they were powerful, very.'

Red resisted the temptation to ask questions, but he looked enquiringly at her. She must have guessed what he was wondering, because she answered anyway.

'In Amoran, it is said that there was once a great master. A creature who was neither man nor griffin. A griffin with the heart of a human, or a human with the heart of a griffin. There was once a golden egg that sat in a temple high in the mountains of this country; an egg that would hatch into this being. But that egg was stolen many hundreds of years ago by one of your race. It is said that he took this egg west to Grephe, and so the guardian of Amoran became the guardian of your race.'

Red had never heard anything about this.

'Now my people have no guardian, and there are some who believe that this is why they have become as they are,' Ahamay went on. 'Eternally hungry, never satisfied, always seeking what they do not have. Never to be content until they have rulership over the entire world. There are others who say that this is not true; that this golden egg, this man-griffin who was our guardian, never existed but in myth. But the Emperor himself changed his mind when the guardian of a different race came here to Amoran some years ago.'

Red found himself thinking of Kullervo. Kullervo was neither man nor griffin but both – could he have something to do with this story?

'Your enemies,' said Ahamay. 'The enemies who put that collar on you. They too have a guardian.'

The Northerners, Red thought. Was she talking about the Night God?

'That guardian came here,' said Ahamay. 'His name was King

Arenadd Taranisäii—,' she pronounced the Northern name awkwardly, 'and he was a man only on the outside. The guardian of the Tarans is the dead who walks. A shadow made flesh, partnered to a black griffin. Sent to lead his people, and to kill all those who would threaten them.'

The Shadow That Walks. Red shuddered.

'Yes,' Ahamay nodded. 'The one that your father killed became the shadow. The guardian.'

'But he's gone,' Red blurted. 'King Arenadd's dead now – I mean, properly dead.'

Ahamay shook her head. 'Then the Tarans, too, have lost their guardian now. But for the gods, all is never lost. A guardian can return. That is what the Amoranis hope – and fear.'

Red didn't try and interrupt again. He sensed that she was reaching the end of her story now.

'You know that the bitterest enemy of the Empire is the country of Erebus,' said Ahamay. 'You have been told that they are enemies because Erebus will not allow itself to be made a part of the Empire, but it is not true. Not entirely. For you see, Erebus too once had a guardian. The great serpent, Itzcóatl. Not an ethereal being, but a creature of flesh. A serpent longer than a ship and thicker than a tree, whose scales shone with the colours of the rainbow. Once he lived among his people, and it is said that he could speak to them as a man would. But when my people invaded Erebus the first time, it is said that they slew Itzcóatl. Then they burned his body and scattered his bones to the far corners of the world, so that he could not rise again. For this, the Erebians never forgave us. They have said that they will fight the Empire until every man, woman and child of their people is dead. They say that what the Empire has done is something that can never be forgiven.' She fixed Red with an unexpected, penetrating stare. 'But I think you, too, have no love for the Empire, Desher.'

Red hesitated.

'Speak,' Ahamay said in a low voice. 'You have my permission to say whatever is in your heart. Do you think that it is right for my people to fight outside their own country? The Empire claims that it brings civilisation and culture to those countries it conquers.'

'I don't care about that,' Red growled. 'We never did nothin' to them, an' they should've left us alone.'

'You resent what has been done to you,' said Ahamay. It wasn't a question, but it wasn't quite a statement either.

Red tugged at the collar around his neck. 'My country's been overrun, an' my people are under the thumb of the Northerners, or they're here like me. If the Empire hadn't helped, we could've had a chance to win. An' you say they're doin' all those things to other places as well. But why'd you want me to say it? You're an Amorani.'

'I am,' said Ahamay. 'And I have entertained the Imperial family here many times. But that does not mean I agree with all they have done. I cannot speak this way to my countrymen, and so I speak of it to those like you, whose lives have been taken by the Empire.'

'Well then, I hate them,' Red said boldly. 'If you wanna hear the truth. It was just the Northerners we were fightin' before — now it's the Empire as well. If the South is ever gonna be free again, it won't be until the Empire's driven out. Maybe we could handle the Northerners, but if the Empire's gonna help them, we don't have a chance.'

Ahamay nodded thoughtfully. 'You are more clever than you seem, Desher. Thank you. I have enjoyed your story. Now you and I must rest, but… I would like to speak with you again.'

'Really?' said Red.

'Yes.' She smiled. 'I will eat with you again soon. Tomorrow you will begin your work protecting my home, and I will hear of how well you do this work. Be loyal and steadfast, and you will be rewarded.'

Red stood up from the table, and saluted like the guard he had once been. 'You can depend on me, milady. I might be a slave now, but I'm a Redguard too. Loyalty's our code.'

'Even loyalty to one who owns you as if you were a horse in her stable?' said Ahamay. She asked the question without any trace of mockery.

'If I have to,' said Red. 'I'm a guard, an' I'll do that job the way it was meant to be done, no matter who I'm guarding or where.'

'Then that is good,' Ahamay nodded. 'Go now, and I will see you again soon.'

Red nodded back respectfully and left with Tototl.

The other slave kept close to him. 'So!' he said once they were out of earshot. 'You have become one of her favourites.'

'She does that with other people?' asked Red.

'Yes, with the slaves she likes the very best,' said Tototl. 'She will eat with them and speak with them for a time, until she grows bored with them and finds a new favourite. Some last longer than others.'

'Why'd she like me?' Red wondered aloud.

'She likes a man who speaks his mind,' said Tototl. 'Not those who tell her only what she wishes to hear.'

'I never was much good at bein' a yes-man anyhow,' said Red, and privately determined that if being outspoken meant better food and special treatment, he'd be more than happy to oblige.

And he couldn't help but be attracted to Ahamay as well, he admitted to himself. There was something so self-assured but restrained about her, as if she could be open but still keep enough back to make her interesting. And there was something about the way she had spoken to him that made him feel special, as if she were taking him into her confidence as she would only do with someone she admired. He liked that, and he knew he was already looking forward to their next meeting.

*

It came sooner than he expected. After a day spent standing guard outside her private chambers with another slave, Red was summoned to have dinner with Ahamay again. This time she ate too, sitting opposite him and offering him the best dishes as if he were her honoured guest. She talked about Amorani politics, and asked for his opinions, and asked him to tell her more about Cymria as well and how its own government worked. When he asked she told him about other countries she knew of as well, and something of the Imperial family.

'The Emperor has four sons,' she said. 'The eldest is in Erebus, leading their father's armies there. The second eldest is here in Amoran, with his father. Two govern colonies away from Amoran. The youngest, Prince Akhane, went to Grephe to wed the Queen of the Tarans, but was killed there when she was overthrown. I met him here once. He was a great scholar, fascinated with magic. It was he who told me the tale of the golden egg which he had heard from the priests of the temple where it was once said to be.'

She had other stories like that to tell, but seemed more interested in what he had to say, asking him for his opinions on everything she told him. She asked him about fighting, too; about his training and experience.

And that was how it went on for many nights after that. The other slaves quickly became envious and stopped talking to him, but he didn't care. All he wanted was to stay with her, to keep her favour. Not just because she was beautiful, but because she treated him like a human being, and that was something he didn't want to let go of. He kept reminding himself of what Tototl had said; that she always got bored with her favourites, but he tried to convince himself that she wouldn't get bored with him.

Nor did she seem about to lose interest. She soon promoted him to her personal bodyguard, along with another of the burlier slaves – a scarred Maijani named Tamaku, who said he had been beside her for the last five years.

Now Red had to be with her all day every day, and he even guarded her bedchamber at night while she was asleep. He shared his duty with others, so he would have time to sleep, but he didn't want to be away from her for any longer than he had to. He had begun to live for the glances she sent his way, for the smiles she favoured him with.

He knew he was becoming obsessed, but he didn't care. Here, in this place, she was all he had.

She seemed to know it, too, but it didn't seem to bother her. If anything, she seemed amused by it.

Weeks passed, and she was there every day, in her beads and silks, smiling those smiles that were just for him, giving him those favours that lifted him above everyone else. He was her favourite, he was the one she talked to and ate with. He was hers, and not just because he was her slave. He wanted to be hers; hers completely and utterly. She sensed that, too.

At last, one hot night when his obsession had grown to agony pitch, she quietly summoned him into her room and closed the door behind them both.

'Lay down your spear,' she told him.

He leaned it against the wall. 'What d'you want me to do?' he asked, already more than ready to do it.

She smiled that smile, and backed away towards the couch she slept on. 'Come,' she said softly. 'Come and do as you wish to do, Desher.'

Red smiled back. He felt wild and stupid and hot all over. He stripped off his armour and dropped it carelessly on the floor, and reached out towards her.

She moved back slowly, not to discourage him, but to tempt him forward. He followed her.

'Come,' she said again. 'I want you now.'

Half mad with desire, Red tore the cloth away from her breasts and took her in his arms, caressing her as gently as he could with his big rough hands. She touched him back, and she was hot and strong; stronger than he had expected. 'Yes,' she whispered, kissing him. 'Yes, now.'

Locked together, pulling at each other's clothes, the pair of them stumbled back towards the couch.

Red's last lover had been a barmaid back in Liranwee, and it had been a long time since he had felt a woman's touch. But Ahamay was unlike any woman he had ever known. She was lithe and sinuous, refusing to let him take control, but not taking it herself. She encouraged him just enough, and held back just enough to inflame him, just as she had done with their conversations. But she was passionate and alive, more than any woman he had loved in the past, as if he were the finest lover she had ever had.

That night was more than just physical sensation for Red; it was a kind of ecstasy. It was everything he had wanted and more.

It wasn't the only time, either.

After that, Ahamay took him into her room several more times, quietly and confidently, without explanation or indeed many words at all. It turned Red's new life into something more than slavery, or imprisonment. To him, for a time at least, his new home became paradise.

Then, after another night of love, while they lay in each other's arms, Ahamay finally spoke.

'Desher,' she said softly. 'Would you like to be free?'

The question caught him by surprise. 'Free?' he murmured. He'd almost forgotten the idea by now.

'Yes.' She reached up to touch the collar. 'You were not always a slave. What would you do to remove this collar and become a true man again?'

'To be free…' Red said slowly.

'To be free, and to go back to the land where you belong,' said Ahamay. 'Yes?'

'I'd do anything,' said Red.

'Truly, anything?' said Ahamay.

'Yeah, I would.'

'And you are loyal to me?' said Ahamay.

'I am,' said Red.

She sighed deeply. 'Then it is time.'

'Time for what?' asked Red.

'I have a task for you,' said Ahamay. 'You must do it, with the others who will follow you. I have searched for many years for the man who can do what must be done. If you succeed, then you and your friends will be set free. I promise it.'

Red tensed. 'What d'you want me to do?'

'First you must be certain,' said Ahamay. 'If it meant your freedom, would you be willing to fight?'

'Yeah, I would,' said Red.

'And to kill?'

'I would,' said Red.

'And to do exactly as I say and ask no questions?'

'I would,' said Red.

'Then it is good,' said Ahamay. 'Rest now. Soon, I will tell you what must be done.'

'All right,' said Red, and obediently let himself rest without asking any other questions. But for the first time since he had been taken away from his homeland, he let himself feel that faint, wavering thing that made him feel closer to the man he had once been: hope.

Chapter Seven

The Child

Teressa flew out of Malvern on Orak's back – the first time she had ever flown. She had seen partnered griffins in the air before, but had never realised how difficult flying really was. It had looked effortless, and she'd assumed it was without even thinking about it. After all, how hard could it be? You just sat there, surely, while the griffin did all the work.

But it wasn't like that, she soon discovered – though not before she'd almost fallen off her new partner's back and badly unbalanced him in the air for a few terrifying moments. You couldn't just sit there; you had to move as your partner did, leaning to one side when he turned, and so forth. Flying was a delicate business and the slightest shift in weight could send a partnered griffin into a deadly barre roll, or worse. As it was, Teressa only survived because of the harness she had bought.

A griffin harness was a little like a horse's bridle, but whereas a horse would hold a bit in the mouth that allowed the rider to direct her mount, no griffin would ever stoop so low as to let a human control them that way. A griffin harness was strapped around the head and neck, and allowed a rider to hold on – nothing more. And if that rider got any ideas about trying to pull the griffin's head this way or that, they were liable to be bitten. Teressa had no intention of trying that herself; but when she did accidentally pull Orak's head to the side he wrenched back so hard that he nearly sprained her arm. After that she was very careful not to bother him while they were in the air.

But the harness did help her to hold on; without it, she was certain, she would have wound up dead or maimed.

She soon started to get the hang of flying, and she and Orak started to learn how to work together. Though Orak did most of the work in the sky, he expected her to help him navigate. She did her best; though she didn't have a map, part of her training in the Temple involved studying the stars and she knew how to recognise constellations and find the four directions. So, when they stopped for the night, she would check their direction and help Orak decide what to do in the morning.

They went east first, to the coast, and then began to systematically search the land between Malvern and the sea, gradually working their way towards the North. They spent nights wherever they could; sometimes sheltering in barns or staying in small outposts built for travelling griffiners, or, when they had to, in crude shelters Teressa built out of sticks and bark. Both of them kept their eyes open for a child, or a black griffin, or someone who might be Arenadd's son. Unfortunately, they had no idea what the child or the son might look like – or even if they might be the same person. The black griffin would be easier to spot, but they saw very few griffins at all and none of them were black. Teressa questioned everyone they met, but none of them had seen a black griffin, and none of them seemed to know what she was talking about when she asked about a child.

The travelling was hard, and quickly started to look pointless, but the sense of adventure Teressa felt, and her conviction that she was doing Arenadd's will, kept her going long after someone else might have started thinking about giving up. Orak, meanwhile, just seemed happy to be away from the Eyrie.

But by the time their journey was reaching the end of its third week, the lame griffin started to grow impatient.

'It has been many days, and we have found nothing and heard nothing,' he said one evening. 'If there were a black griffin in this place, we would have found some sign by now. But we have not.'

Teressa nodded. 'Ye may be right. What should we do?'

'That is simple,' said Orak. 'If the griffin we are searching for is not here, then he must not be in the East of this country, but in the East that is over the sea, which you told me about.'

'That's most likely true,' said Teressa. 'The part I remember most about the dream was "in the East." That's what people say when they're talking about Amoran – if they don't say "it's in Amoran", they say "it's in the East." We don't know enough about this "child" or the son, but a black griffin should be the easiest thing to find. And if we do find him, then maybe he can tell us where the rest of them are. Maybe they're together somewhere.'

'Then we have agreed,' said Orak. 'We must go over the sea to Amoran. Do you know how we may do this?'

'More or less,' said Teressa. She paused to think it over. 'We'd have to take a ship, but we have no money.'

Orak snorted. 'I am a partnered griffin, and you are a griffiner. We should not have to give money to common humans. They will take us to this place because we shall command it. Otherwise, you shall tell them that if they do not, I will tear them to pieces.'

Teressa didn't know what to say. For a long moment she sat there stupidly and stared at her new partner. 'Er,' she said at last. 'Er, I suppose we could try that.

'Or… or maybe we could just lie? I know some of our griffiners are in Amoran now, staying with the Emperor as ambassadors. Maybe we could say we're going to join them. I could say I'm an ambassador too…' she hesitated. 'I don't look like one, though. I don't have any fancy clothes. Maybe I could just say we're carrying a message to them. Something like that.'

Orak put his head on one side while he listened. 'Trickery,' he said. 'Yes… humans are cunning creatures. Perhaps you could use this power to fool them.'

'I'll do my best,' Teressa said, trying hard to sound bold.

'Do this, then,' said Orak. 'And if you do not succeed, I shall force them to take us to Amoran.'

'All right,' said Teressa, privately hoping it wouldn't come to that. 'That man we talked to yesterday said there was a port town not far from here – Abertawe, remember? We can go there and look for a ship docked there that could carry us. It's a bit further North, so we should be able to make it there some time tomorrow.'

Orak flicked his tail. 'We will go, and search along the way. It would not be good to make this journey to Amoran if we do not need to.'

'Agreed,' said Teressa.

And so the next day, they did exactly that. Orak headed north and east, zig-zagging along the way to cover more ground, though by now, with the decision made to go to Amoran, it had begun to feel rather pointless. Never mind; he did it anyway, and towards midday, it finally made a difference.

Teressa, balancing carefully on her partner's back, suddenly felt uneasy. A coldness started to needle at her, somewhere deep inside. She frowned and shook her head slowly, unable to shed the feeling that something was different. Somewhere under the whistling of the wind in her ears, she thought she heard something. Some other sound, hidden in the meaningless rush of noise that she had grown used to by now.

She frowned to herself and began to concentrate, trying to identify the sound, which grew louder and clearer as the cold inside her grew. But before she had made any progress at all, Orak lurched underneath her and a jolt of panic snapped her out of it. She gripped his harness more tightly and leaned forward against his neck when, without any warning, the lame griffin swooped. He had never done it before, or at least not as fast or steeply as this, and Teressa was completely unprepared for it. Instinctively, she leaned backwards hard, flat along Orak's back, and yelled in terror.

It felt as if they weren't flying at all now, but falling – rushing straight downward. The wind bit into her eyes, forcing tears out from under the lids which dried instantly on her face. She closed them, but darkness only made the falling worse and she forced them open again, barely able to see anything anyway. Panic-stricken, she wrenched at the harness, trying to pull Orak out of his dive. He didn't respond at all.

Teressa could barely see out of her streaming eyes. The sheer force of the wind had pulled her head back, so all she did see was the sky, all blue and blurry.

She didn't even have the strength to scream again. This was it. She was going to die…

She caught a brief glimpse of something else: a quick flash of green and grey as they passed through the treetops, and then –

Orak's wings opened, and he levelled out with a violent jolt before hitting the ground with a thump that threw Teressa off his back. She fell backwards onto the griffin's haunches, and then rolled off onto the ground with a painful thud.

She sat up, stunned and aching in a dozen places, and stared dazedly at nothing in particular.

Orak hadn't taken the landing easily either. He must have landed too hard on his crippled leg, because Teressa saw him half fallen to that side, hissing and struggling to get up.

'Curse this leg!' he snarled.

Teressa managed to stand. Her back hurt the moment she straightened up, and she winced and rubbed it. 'Argh. Ow. Dear Night God, what…?'

Orak had recovered himself now, and he limped over to her. 'You are not hurt?'

'I think my whole body's turned into one big bruise,' said Teressa. 'Orak, what was that?'

'I tried to land too quickly,' said Orak. 'I have hurt my weak leg. Your weight on my back made the fall faster than I am used to.'

'But ye did that on purpose?' Teressa exclaimed. 'I thought… I don't know what I thought, but I didn't think… what was that for?'

Orak shook his head dazedly. 'I do not… I am not certain.'

Teressa stared blankly at him. 'Uh, why not?'

'I was flying,' Orak said slowly. 'And then an urge came to me that I must fly down at once, as quickly as I could. I had an instinct that there was something here on the ground.'

Teressa pulled herself together as well as she could. 'Wait,' she said. 'I had a funny feeling too, just before ye started diving like that. It felt like… I don't know, I thought I could hear something.'

'What did you hear?' asked Orak.

'I don't know,' said Teressa. 'I couldn't work it out. But now we're down here, maybe we should look around. We could have a rest at least.'

'Yes,' said Orak. 'That would be a good idea. I shall scent the wind.'

He put his head up and sniffed, the air whistling through his nostrils. Teressa, thinking she should stretch her aching legs, started to limp around the clearing where they had landed. It wasn't much of a place, she thought. It was far away from any civilisation; just an open space in a forest of white-trunked spice trees. No sign of anyone anywhere. She was about to say so, when Orak's harsh voice broke the silence.

'Teressa! There is a scent!'

Teressa froze. 'What is it? What scent?'

'Human,' said Orak. 'I can smell a human. There.' He pointed his beak towards a wattle thicket at the edge of the clearing.

'Is it an old smell?' asked Teressa, remembering what he had said about a scent lingering long after whatever created it was gone.

'No,' said Orak. 'It is fresh. There is a human there. Come.'

He limped towards the thicket.

Cautiously, Teressa reached for the old sacrificial dagger she had taken to carrying in her belt. 'Is it just one person?'

'Yes,' said Orak.

But before they could go and investigate, the stranger chose to come to them. Teressa saw a small figure push its way out of the wattle, and she relaxed at once – it was only a child.

The child stood cautiously at the edge of the bushes that had sheltered her, and peered up at Orak. Then she looked at Teressa. 'Are you a griffiner?' she asked.

Teressa eyed her curiously before she answered. The child looked about eight years old, maybe a little older, and she was filthy. The plain woollen dress she wore was torn and grubby, and there were leaves and bits of twigs in her hair. But she looked surprisingly bold considering that she was all by herself. She was also, very clearly, not a Northerner. Her skin was light brown, her hair very dark – almost black but not quite. Her eyes though were bright blue, startling in her dusky face.

'Are you?' she asked again.

'Yes,' Teressa said slowly. 'I'm a griffiner. My name's Teressa, and this is my partner Orak. Who are ye?'

The child eyed her warily. 'I'm Flell. What are you doing here?' She had an odd accent. Not quite Southern, but there was definitely a touch of something Southern in it. Teressa felt sure of that.

'I'm looking for a black griffin,' she said honestly. 'What are ye doing here?'

'There's no black griffin here,' said Flell. 'The black griffin's dead.'

Teressa took a step closer to her. 'Are ye lost?'

Flell scowled. 'No. I'm travelling.'

'Where to?' asked Teressa. 'Are ye all by yerself?'

'Yeah,' said Flell. 'I'm goin' to Malvern.'

'Why?' asked Teressa. 'What about yer parents?'

'Don't have any,' said Flell. 'They're dead.'

'Then what about yer home?' asked Teressa. 'Where did ye come from?'

'Doesn't matter,' said Flell. 'I need to go to Malvern.'

'Why?'

Flell pulled a knife out of her pocket. It was small and cheap looking, with a wooden handle – probably stolen from a kitchen somewhere. 'I'm gonna kill the King,' she said. 'He's in Malvern.'

Teressa stared at her, and then glanced at Orak.

'What is this human pup doing here?' the griffin asked.

Flell scowled at him. 'I told you. I'm goin' to Malvern. I'm gonna kill the King with my knife.'

Teressa frowned. 'Ye can't do that,' she said. 'We should take ye home. Wait.' She stopped as realisation dawned on her. 'Wait a moment. How did ye know what Orak said just now?'

''Cause I know griffish,' said Flell. She looked at Orak with interest. 'Can you take me to Malvern an' help me? What's your name?'

'I am Orak,' said Orak. 'Do you truly understand me?'

'I do,' said Flell. 'Look, I can do it.' She broke into griffish. 'My name is Flell and I know griffish.' She used the language a little clumsily, but with confidence, like someone who had grown up speaking it.

Teressa couldn't believe her ears. 'Holy Night God. Where did ye learn griffish? Where did ye come from?'

'From Gwernyfed,' said Flell.

'That's a Northern place name,' said Teressa. 'But how can ye be in the North? Yer not a Northerner. Ye must have some Amorani in ye, or some Maijani maybe, and those eyes…'

'There's lots of half-breeds in Gwernyfed,' Flell said carelessly. 'Will you take me to Malvern now? Please?'

Teressa wasn't listening. She looked at the scowling child, and another part of the dream rose up in her mind. …the child with the Southern eyes. That was what Arenadd had whispered to her.

She looked straight at Flell, at those bright blue eyes, and felt as if she were falling.

'My gods,' she breathed. 'Orak, look at her. Look at her eyes.'

'I am looking,' said Orak.

'It's her eyes,' said Teressa. 'Remember the dream? "Find the child with the Southern eyes."'

'My mum was half Southern,' said Flell, sounding a little uncertain. 'Uncle 'Lurvo says I got my eyes from her.'

'We've done it, Orak,' said Teressa. 'We've found her. This is the child, it has to be. The child with the Southern eyes.'

Orak looked at Flell again, more closely. 'Her eyes are blue. Do Southerners have eyes like them?'

'They do,' said Teressa.

'What are you talking about?' Flell finally demanded.

'Orak and I both had a dream,' Teressa said grandly. 'A dream where the great King Arenadd himself told us to find a black griffin, his son, and a child with Southern eyes.'

'I know about Arenadd!' said Flell. She looked excited. 'Am I the child he said you should find?'

'We think so,' said Teressa. 'Have, uh...' she hesitated, embarrassed. 'Have ye had a dream about him too?'

'No,' said Flell. 'But I bet he wanted you to find me. He's my grandfather.'

Teressa frowned. 'He's what?'

'My grandfather,' said Flell. She took a deep breath. 'My grandfather was Arenadd Taranisäii, and my grandmother was Flell from Eagleholm, who I'm named after. My mother was Queen Laela Taranisäii and my dad was Prince Akhane from Amoran. That's why I'm going to go kill the King. It's because he killed my mum and dad, and I should be Queen because my mum was Queen.'

Teressa and Orak exchanged glances.

'This pup thinks she is the offspring of Laela Half-Breed?' said Orak. 'Insanity. That child was born dead.'

'But Queen Laela had blue eyes,' Teressa said slowly, hardly believing as she said it that it could be true. 'And she married an Amorani. And this child...'

'I didn't die,' Flell went on blithely, apparently completely oblivious to the fact that she was giving away information that would make her a target for every griffiner in Malvern. 'Uncle 'Lurvo switched me with another baby who died so the King wouldn't know I was really alive. And then him and Senneck took me away to Gwernyfed.'

'Who's this Uncle Lurvo?' asked Teressa.

Flell looked unhappy. 'He was my mother's brother. He's a man-griffin, with wings and a tail. When I was little I thought he was my dad, but he's not. He can't have children. He loved Senneck, but she died and then I ran away so I could go kill the King.'

'Ye mean Kullervo?' said Teressa. 'Kullervo the shape shifter? That's yer uncle?'

'Yeah,' said Flell. 'I dunno where he is now. He's Arenadd's son. His mother was Skade, so he's only my mother's half-brother anyhow.'

Teressa frowned. 'Arenadd's son... but he was just an imposter, wasn't he? Is he in Gwernyfed, then?'

'I s'pose,' said Flell. 'But I'm not going there. Please can you take me to Malvern?'

'No we can't,' said Teressa. 'We have other things we have to do. And anyway, the King's not in Malvern. He's in the South, fighting our enemies. Can ye tell us where Gwernyfed is?'

Flell scowled. 'No. It's a secret. I want to go to Malvern.'

Teressa hesitated, not knowing what to do. She couldn't just take this child to Malvern – it would be the death of her. Going to the South was out of the question as well. But she couldn't very well leave her here by herself.

While she stood there in indecision, Orak suddenly spoke up. 'Teressa,' he said. 'We must keep this child.'

Teressa gave him a blank look. 'What?'

'I have decided,' said Orak. 'We shall continue with our plan to go to the East. We shall take this child with us.'

'What for?' asked Teressa.

'If she is truly the half-breed Queen's heir, then she could be of use to us,' the crippled griffin said patiently. 'If she is what she claims to be, then she is also a member of the Emperor of Amoran's family. If we were to give her to him, he may reward us for finding his grandchild.'

Teressa thought quickly. 'One thing's certain: she's not safe in the North. Maybe the Emperor could give her protection. But what about Kullervo?'

'Forget him,' said Orak. 'The dark griffin is more important. If this dark griffin is like the Mighty Skandar, then he may have his power. Have you considered that?'

Teressa's heart beat faster. 'The power to make the Shadow That Walks…'

'Yes,' said Orak. 'If this griffin is in the East and we have been sent to find him, then it may be that he needs our help. If we can help him, we may gain his allegiance. The one with the power of the dark griffin on his side is unimaginably powerful. And if we can win the gratitude of the master of Amoran, she may help us to find him.'

'"She"?' Teressa repeated. 'The Emperor's a man.'

'The ruler of Amoran is the great Zaerih,' Orak said impatiently. 'Most powerful of griffins in the East. Her human is the Emperor. Do you agree with what I have said?'

'I'm not going to Amoran!' Flell snapped.

Teressa ignored her while she mulled over what Orak had said. She had never spent any time among other griffiners, and so had no familiarity with the intrigues and backstabbing of typical griffiner politics – she had never learned to think with this kind of deviousness. Now, hearing this, she couldn't help but be excited by what Orak had suggested. It was the kind of plan she would never have imagined on her own.

'Let's do it!' she said.

'You think it is a good plan?' asked Orak.

To her surprise, she realised that he sounded slightly anxious. 'I do,' she said. 'It's clever.'

'I am as cunning as a human,' Orak said smugly.

Teressa turned her attention back to the child. 'Flell,' she said. 'I think Arenadd wants ye to come with us.' By now she was so accustomed to the idea that she was doing her idol's work that she said this without embarrassment.

Flell looked doubtful. 'What for?'

'He sent us to find ye,' said Teressa. 'And we still have to find a dark griffin. I think ye are supposed to help us. Anyway… don't ye want to meet the Emperor? If ye really are Laela Half-Breed's daughter, then he's yer grandfather.'

'But I want to kill the King,' Flell insisted.

'Ye can't,' said Teressa. 'So forget about it right now.'

'Why?'

'Because it's impossible and because I won't let ye,' said Teressa. 'And ye'll never get to him anyway. Now, are ye coming with us or not?'

Flell looked as if she were considering it for a moment, and then she nodded. 'All right. I want to go see my grandfather.'

Chapter Eight

Going to Maijan

So Teressa and Orak took the child with them as they journeyed on towards the port town of Abertawe, where hopefully they would be able to find a ship to take them to Maijan, or even all the way to Amoran. Either way, she wasn't expecting it to be easy. She had no money to pay for passage, and nor did she know how she was going to go about pretending to be an ambassador. And besides, would anyone believe her?

But when the three of them arrived at Abertawe, a very unexpected sight awaited them. The small port town was swarming with griffins. On their approach Teressa saw at least a dozen of them circling over the buildings. None of them showed much interest in the newcomers, but Orak sensibly chose to land well away from the port where they seemed to be concentrated. Approaching another griffin's territory on foot was the most polite way of doing so, since a griffin on the ground was at a disadvantage if it came to a fight, and therefore seen as unthreatening. The crippled Orak certainly wasn't the kind of griffin who would ever look for a fight if he could possibly avoid it.

Teressa watched the circling griffins while she dismounted and helped Flell down. 'What do ye suppose they're doing here?'

'Maybe they're goin' to Amoran too,' Flell piped up.

'The human pup may be right,' said Orak. 'Why else would they have come here?'

Teressa shrugged. 'We'd better go and find out.' She hoped they wouldn't ask too many inconvenient questions.

Orak started to limp down the town's main street towards the shore, and Teressa and Flell kept pace with him on either side.

'Now,' Teressa told the child. 'When we talk to people, just keep quiet. From those eyes they're going to guess ye've got Southern blood in ye, and that won't win ye any friends.'

'I'm not scared,' Flell lifted her chin.

Teressa gave her a look. 'Is that so? Well, then, let me ask ye something. Have ye ever wondered why people in Gwernyfed live secretly?'

''Cause Southerners aren't allowed in the North,' said Flell. 'Everyone knows that.'

'And do ye know why half-breeds like ye are so rare?' asked Teressa.

This time Flell didn't seem to have an answer. 'I dunno,' she said lamely.

Teressa kept her gaze steady and her voice cool, so that what she said next would have as much impact as possible. 'Because out here in the real world, half-breeds die. Sometimes their own mothers kill them in the womb, or they're killed by their own relatives, or left for the wolves. There's no laws that say half-breeds have to be killed, but there might as well be. So unless ye want to die young, say nothing and leave the talking to me.'

Flell went pale. 'They'd kill me?'

'If they knew who yer mother was, they certainly would,' said Teressa. 'Or they'd give ye to the King, who'd kill ye. I'm probably risking my own neck by not doing that myself.'

Flell had gone very quiet. 'Then why are you helping me?'

'Why?' said Teressa. 'Because…' she hesitated. Up until now she hadn't really considered the fact that sheltering this potential rival to the throne might count as treason. 'Because ye are Arenadd's granddaughter,' she said. 'And to me, he's the only true King I've ever had. He saved my life once, and he'd want me to protect ye.'

'Uncle 'Lurvo says he died to save my mum,' said Flell.

'Well then, that settles it, doesn't it?' Teressa gave her a reassuring smile. 'Don't worry, Flell. If I have to, I'll give my own life to keep ye safe. Now let's go and see what these griffins are up to, shall we?'

Flell nodded and kept quiet after that, apparently determined to do as she'd been told. Teressa's attempt to scare her had obviously succeeded, but she looked comforted as well – Teressa noticed that she moved a little closer to her as they moved on.

She watched the child for a moment. Flell frowned ferociously to herself as she walked, looking ahead as if to check for the dangers Teressa had warned her about. She didn't look very strong; in fact, she was short for her age and somewhat on the scrawny side, but in her own way she was impressive. Teressa could sense that there was steel inside her, despite her young age. She was intelligent, too. If only she had a little less stubbornness and a lot more common sense.

Teressa smiled to herself, and made a silent promise that she would do as she had said she would, and protect Flell at all costs. Even if she wasn't who she said she was, she still needed help. But in her heart, Teressa believed that she was Arenadd's grandchild. She looked like him, didn't she? Teressa thought she did. She had seen the child's mother, Laela, once or twice, and thought that Flell looked like her, too.

'Stop there,' a voice interrupted her thoughts. 'Who are ye?'

Teressa stopped, and eyed the man who'd put himself in the way. He was another Northerner, and from his fine clothes he was obviously a griffiner.

She cleared her throat hastily. 'My name is T— ahem, Lady Teressa, and this is Orak. We're going to Amoran.'

'Ye look like a priestess,' said the man.

'That's because I am one,' said Teressa.

'Going to Amoran, are ye?' said the man. 'Are ye— wait,' he frowned, and then smiled. 'Of course! Ye must be the priestess we've been waiting for. Yer going to the celebration in Xanthium, yes?'

'Aye, that's me,' Teressa said immediately. 'Were ye all waiting for me, then?'

The man nodded. 'Yer the last one to arrive. Just as well ye got here now. We were getting impatient.' He glanced at Orak. 'They didn't say ye were a griffiner though; we thought ye were coming by cart and that's why ye were taking so long.'

'Only just got chosen,' Teressa smiled. 'Sorry we kept ye waiting.'

'Fair enough,' said the man. 'Who's the child?' he appeared to notice Flell for the first time, and frowned at the sight of her.

'Oh,' said Teressa. 'Er, this is Urbi,' she said. 'She was visiting Malvern from Amoran, and I've been asked to take her home.' She stopped there and looked hopefully at her questioner. "Urbi" was the only Amorani name she knew.

The man looked suspicious. 'Why is she by herself?'

'She's an orphan,' Teressa said truthfully. 'She came to Malvern with her mother, but she died from a chill. Now I have to take her home to her father.' She had prepared this story during the flight.

The man looked at Flell. 'Where'd she get those blue eyes from?'

'I don't know,' Teressa lied. 'Anyway… she doesn't speak Northern. She's so upset since her mother died that she won't speak griffish either. I think its best that she be left alone during the voyage.' She knew that if Flell spoke her accent would immediately reveal that she wasn't from Amoran. Besides, she'd already shown that she wasn't much of a liar.

'Understood,' the man cast a rather unpleasant look at Flell. 'Anyway, ye'd better come with me. It's time we got going!'

Teressa nodded politely, hoping like mad that her relief wouldn't show. She couldn't believe her luck.

'You have done well,' Orak said softly as they followed their guide to the ship that would take them to Amoran.

'I reckon I have,' Teressa murmured back.

Flell, thankfully, said nothing.

*

There were several ships moored in the harbour, all Amorani in design; long and narrow, built for speed, but very tall. They had been made specifically to carry griffins, and had plenty of deck space for them to nest on, as well as specially built stalls below deck where they could escape from the sun. There were plenty of cabins for their human partners as well, and fortunately the one given to Teressa had two beds.

Orak, though, refused to nest with the other griffins on the grounds that they would bully and attack him. He found himself a secret spot down in the hold, among the cargo, instead and avoided coming up on deck when the other griffins were about. Teressa and Flell spent plenty of time with him during the voyage, partly so that Teressa could see to his needs, but also to avoid their fellow passengers who might ask inconvenient questions. Unfortunately, without much else to do during the long, tedious months it would take to reach Maijan, most of them had plenty of time for that sort of thing.

But their luck held out, and the other griffiners they encountered seemed to accept Teressa's claims without much trouble. Once they learned that Flell supposedly didn't speak their language, they lost interest in her quickly enough. Some of them asked about her Southern eye colour, but Teressa only said that she didn't know where she'd got them from and assumed that one or other of her parents must have had Southern blood in them. That didn't make anyone particularly happy, but since Flell was a child, a supposed foreigner, and leaving the country for good, no-one made too much of a fuss about it.

Teressa, of course, had plenty of questions of her own to ask, but she found the answers easily enough. It seemed that there was a great celebration due to happen in Xanthium, the capital city of the Amorani Empire. As an ally of the Empire, the King had sent a good number of griffiners to take part in the festivities, and now Teressa was one of them.

It was just as well, she reflected more than once, that she really was a priestess and hadn't lied about that as well. If she had lied on that front, she would have quickly gotten into trouble, because some of the more devout griffiners there soon started seeking her out and asking for her to say prayers for them, or invoke the Night God to send them strong winds and powerful currents to help them on their way. She was able to do that without much trouble, and even enjoyed it. Prayer had always made her feel good, even if her faith only partly belonged to the Night God.

She prayed in private as well, to Arenadd, asking him to give his protection to her, to Orak, and to Flell – and to give her his guidance so she could do what he had asked. She hoped that she would dream about him again, but no more dreams came. She could only hope that she was doing the right thing.

Once, Flell came across her in the midst of her prayers.

'What are you doing?' she asked loudly, interrupting her travelling companion's fervent murmurings.

Teressa blinked and shook her head as her concentration broke. 'I'm praying,' she said sharply. 'To the Night God.'

'But I heard you say Granddad Arenadd's name,' Flell said obnoxiously.

Teressa sighed and put her prayer stone back into its wrappings. 'He was a holy man.'

'No he wasn't,' said Flell. 'He was bad. He killed my grandmother. She was called Flell too.'

Teressa shook her head irritably and stuffed the stone into her bag. 'Maybe he did, but he sent me to protect ye, so speak more respectfully, girl.'

'He was a murderer,' said Flell. 'Everyone says so.'

'He was a great man!' Teressa snapped. 'He saved the North and its people. He set us free in the Night God's holy name. And when I was even younger than ye, he saved my life. So don't ye dare insult him.'

'Huh!' Flell gave her a sulky look, but desisted.

Teressa went quiet as well. She was actually surprised by how angry she'd gotten, but she'd never heard anyone insult her idol before, and she felt personally offended as well as offended on his behalf. But she admitted to herself that Flell had every reason to dislike him, considering what he had done to her family.

Still.

'I suppose he wasn't perfect,' she admitted. 'But nobody ever won a war by being kind or gentle. But listen,' she looked seriously at Flell, 'I know yer doing the sensible thing and not talking on this voyage, but if ye ever do speak to another Northerner, don't tell them about what I'm doing.'

'What d'you mean?' asked Flell.

'I mean, don't tell them about this stone, or that I prayed to Arenadd,' said Teressa.

'Why?' asked Flell. 'Aren't you allowed to?'

'No,' said Teressa. 'There are lots of us who pray to him, or Saeddryn, or just the Shadow That Walks. But we do it secretly. The priestesses in Malvern wouldn't be pleased if they found out and they'd probably make it a heresy.'

'What's a heresy?' Flell looked puzzled.

Teressa gave her a serious look. 'Let me put it this way: back when the Southerners ruled the North, they made it a heresy to worship the Night God. If ye were caught doing it, they burned ye alive.'

Flell yelped in fright. 'No way! They'd burn you?'

'We don't burn heretics in the North,' said Teressa. 'But I might still be put to death. So keep quiet about it, all right?'

'I will,' Flell said immediately.

'I know I can trust ye,' Teressa smiled. 'Ye and I both have secrets and we should keep them for each other, yes?'

'Yes,' said Flell. She looked thoughtful. 'I never prayed before. Do you get special powers if you do it?'

'No,' said Teressa. 'But it's good for ye. It's good for the soul. It's a way to find guidance. I came and found ye because I prayed, and asked for a chance to make a difference. My prayer was answered. And ye know what I think?' she added playfully.

'What?' asked Flell.

'Arenadd was yer grandfather,' said Teressa. 'I bet if ye prayed to him, he'd be even more likely to listen. I know he loved yer mother very much. He took good care of her. If he were here, he'd want to care for ye as well.'

'How can he care for me if he's dead?' asked Flell.

'He might speak to ye, or keep ye safe from danger,' said Teressa. 'Ye'd have to try it to find out!'

'I wanna try it,' Flell said immediately. 'How do I do it?'

'I could teach ye,' Teressa offered.

'Yeah, teach me!' said Flell.

So Teressa did. Unable to talk to anyone else during the voyage, Flell talked to her and Orak and spent most of her time with them, and Teressa taught her what she knew, passing on the knowledge she had gained from her time in the Temple. She taught the girl about prayer, about meditation, about the rituals and the sacrifices. Being a child, Flell particularly wanted to know about the sacrifices – especially the human ones.

'Oh, they're very rare,' Teressa told her. 'They only sacrifice people on the night of the Blood Moon. Yer grandfather didn't used to come to the Temple much but when the Blood Moon came he'd perform the sacrifice himself.'

Flell looked disappointed. 'Who'd they sacrifice, then?'

'Condemned criminals,' said Teressa. 'But sometimes people would actually volunteer for it. The most devout of all, who wanted to go straight to the silver fields to be with the Night God.'

'That's stupid,' said Flell.

Teressa chuckled, but didn't argue. She'd certainly never felt the urge to offer herself up for sacrifice. A little blood from her thumb was more than enough.

She taught Flell about her own secret worship as well, showing her the prayer stone and teaching her the chants and prayers she had written herself and distributed in secret to those who wanted to follow in her footsteps. The child listened seriously, and seemed to actually take in what was being said. Apparently she was more interested in learning than Teressa had expected.

'Can you do magic too?' she asked one day. 'Are them ritual things magic?'

'Teressa thought it over. 'Aye, they are,' she said. 'But not like a griffin's magic. Ye can't light a fire with it or anything like that.'

Flell scowled. 'Why not?'

'We're human,' said Teressa.

'Humans do not have magic,' Orak put in. 'These prayers are only words, and words do not have power.'

'They do,' said Teressa. 'Just not in the same way. But,' she added, seeing the disappointment on Flell's face, 'I can teach ye one other thing. The divining ritual – that's the only one that I think does something special.'

'What's that do, then?' Flell asked suspiciously.

Teressa smiled conspiratorially. 'It's the ritual to see the future. Fortune tellers use it in the marketplace, and some people come to the Temple to do it themselves, but they need a priestess to teach them the words.'

'Ooh!' Flell got excited again. 'Can I see my future?'

'Maybe,' Teressa shrugged. 'It's said every Northerner can use the divining ritual to see their future just once. Once in their whole life. When I was young I tried it, but nothing happened. Maybe I didn't do it right. But if ye want to try it, I can teach ye how.'

Naturally Flell said she did, so Teressa taught her that as well – reciting the incantation and making her repeat it back until she knew it by heart.

Plentyn yn tyfu'n ddyn,
Gorffennol ddaw'n bresennol,
Rhaid i amser fynd rhagddo
Arglwydd tywyll y nos, gweddïaf
Cwyd len y nos, rho i mi ond trem
Yn y nen, tair lleuad lawn ar ddeg,
Pob un yn fywyd blwyddyn,
Llygad y nos, agor led y pen,
Dangos fy nhynged i mi.

Flell knew some Northern, but she seemed puzzled by the words of the chant. 'What's it mean?' she asked.

'It's old Northern,' said Teressa. 'In Cymrian the chant goes something like this:

From child to man,
Past to now,

Time must run ahead
Dark god of night, I pray

Lift aside the veil, give me but a glimpse
Thirteen full moons in the sky, each one a year of life
Eye of night, open wide,
Let me see my fate.

Flell listened. 'How does it work?'

'Wait until the moon is full,' said Teressa. 'Then find a pool of water, or fill a bowl with it. Make sure the moonlight is shining on the water. Then put yer finger in the water and move it in a circle. Do it thirteen times – once for each full moon of the year – and chant the words. Then stare into the water, and maybe, just maybe, ye'll see a vision.'

'Wow!' Flell grinned. 'When's the moon gonna be full again?'

'In seven days,' Teressa said promptly – knowing the phases of the moon and being able to predict them had been one of the most important parts of her training.

'I'm gonna try it then,' said Flell.

'If ye want,' said Teressa, privately thinking that it was unlikely the ritual would work for someone who was definitely more Amorani than Northern, and one who didn't worship the Night God either. But Flell needed to keep herself busy, so it couldn't hurt to let her play around with it. Most likely, the child would forget about it well before the moon was full anyway.

But Teressa was wrong. Flell asked every day if it would be a full moon that night, until finally Teressa said yes. Flell grinned with excitement before disappearing around some grain sacks and producing a bowl. She must have scouted around for it all week; Teressa watched as the young girl carefully filled it with water. Once the full moon had risen on that night she took her bowl and went up on deck with it, wearing a determined scowl.

Teressa let her go, despite the temptation to go with her and see what happened.

Flell didn't return for a long time, but she eventually reappeared with water down the front of her dress and tears on her face.

'It didn't work!' she wailed. 'I tried an' tried an' tried an' it didn't work!'

Teressa gave her a hug. 'There, there, it's all right.'

'Why didn't it work?' Flell demanded.

'Maybe ye just aren't meant to see yer future,' said Teressa.

'But I wanna see it!' said Flell.

'Then maybe ye can try again next time,' said Teressa, more to calm her down than anything else.

Flell sniffled. 'Yeah,' she said. 'I'll try again. When's the next full moon?'

'Not for thirty days,' said Teressa. 'But don't worry. There'll be at least two more before we get to Maijan.'

As promised, that was how Flell occupied herself for the rest of the journey, while overhead the sun steadily grew hotter and hotter. Before long everyone on board wanted to spend their time below deck, and someone asked Teressa to pray for some soothing rain, which she obligingly did. But the Night God seemed disinclined to help this time, and every Northerner on board suffered. Their pale skins weren't meant for such a hot climate, and all of them got horribly burned if they spent any length of time in the sun.

Flell, thanks to her dusky skin, seemed better able to cope with it though she complained along with everyone else. But she kept up her determination to try the ritual again until it worked; Teressa heard her repeating the words to herself as she went about. She didn't bother to make sure no-one was in earshot when she did it, but Teressa covered that by explaining that she had been teaching the child Northern. Luckily, nobody seemed that interested in her anyway. Some of the women on board might have tried to tend to her since she was an orphan, but Flell showed no interest in being mothered. She was a surprisingly independent child.

Eventually, the full moon came again, and as promised Flell went up on deck with her bowl of water. This time she didn't come back at all, and Teressa finally caved in and went looking for her. She found her seated near her bowl, which was sitting in a puddle of water. At first it looked as if Flell was still staring into the bowl, but when Teressa went closer she realised that the child was asleep. She didn't do much more than mumble sleepily when Teressa picked her up and carried her below decks to her bed.

Next morning, though, Flell didn't wait to be asked about her latest efforts.

'I saw it!' she said excitedly, before Teressa had even gotten out of bed. 'I saw the vision like you said!'

Teressa mumbled and rolled over.

'I saw it!' Flell said again. 'I saw the future! Wake up, Teressa!'

'Mnph?' Teressa looked up blearily.

Flell scowled at her. 'Get up, lazybones! I wanna tell you what I saw.'

Teressa sat up, rubbing her face. 'What'd ye see?' she asked.

'I saw the future,' said Flell. 'I saw the sunwheel, and a big snake, and griffins, and—'

Teressa was only half-listening, but as she woke up properly and reached for the water jug she began to feel relieved. As Flell went on, describing all sorts of fantastical visions, it quickly became obvious that she had actually fallen asleep without meaning to and had some dreams. But since she believed those were the vision she'd been promised, they should satisfy her.

'Well,' Teressa said when Flell's excited descriptions finally petered out. 'Sounds like yer going to have quite an exciting life. With snakes and griffins and – what was it? A giant chair?'

'Yeah,' said Flell. 'I was sitting on it.'

'Fancy that,' said Teressa. 'I hope ye were happy with what ye saw, because it won't work again. Once in a lifetime, that's it.'

'That's okay,' Flell nodded. 'I don't wanna sit up all night again.'

'Don't become a priestess, then,' Teressa sighed. 'We have to do that a lot. All our rituals are held at night.'

'I don't wanna be a priestess like you,' said Flell. 'But thanks for teaching me that.'

'Yer welcome,' said Teressa. 'And now we should really spend some time thinking about what we're going to do when we get to Amoran.'

'Find the black griffin, you said,' said Flell.

'Aye,' said Teressa. 'We'll have to hope yer grandfather can help us with that.'

'He will,' said Flell. 'I'll tell him to help you, 'cause you helped me.'

Teressa gave her a quick hug. 'Thanks, Flell. And don't worry. With Arenadd's help, we'll do it.'

Flell rolled her eyes. 'You're so stupid sometimes. But I like you.'

Chapter Nine

Doing Good Works

Eventually, after months of sailing, the ship arrived at the Islands of Maijan — a long chain of islands that made up a single country, ruled by the Empire, which had installed governors on two of the larger islands. The largest of the islands, called Aotea in the local language, had a small city on it, and a port where ships like this one could dock. The flotilla on its way to Amoran stopped there to resupply, and the passengers were allowed to go ashore. Teressa, Orak and Flell were very glad to be among them.

'We'll be here two days,' Teressa told Flell. 'So we have time to explore.'

Flell bounced with excitement over the idea, and Orak too was curious. So was Teressa, come to that. None of them had ever left Cymria before.

Maijan didn't disappoint them either. It was very far from Cymria; in a different climate and the culture, and the people were far away from anything any of them had experienced.

They toured the marketplace — though of course none of them had any money to spend — and were allowed to see the governor's palace, where some of the local Amorani dignitaries were pleased to receive their visitors from the West. The governor himself turned out to be an old Amorani man — short and slight, his dark hair gone to grey. But his thin moustache was as neat as his clothes. He had his wife beside him, and to Teressa's surprise she was a Northerner. Apparently, Amoranis weren't so against the idea of interracial marriage as people back in Cymria.

She smiled politely, and introduced herself when the opportunity arose.

The governor smiled. 'Greetings to you, priestess. I am Lord Vander, and this is my wife Inva. And who is this child?' he frowned politely as he saw Flell.

'This is Urbi,' said Teressa. 'From Amoran. I'm taking her home.'

Vander's frown deepened, but he only said, 'We do not have

much here to entertain a child, but my own son is nearby. Shall I bring him to meet you, Urbi, if you would like another child to play with?'

Flell nodded – keeping silent as Teressa had instructed.

As promised, Vander's son soon appeared. He was a year or so younger than Flell, and looked more or less like an Amorani, though his skin was about the same tone as hers thanks to his Northern mother.

'My name is Yafeu,' he said shyly to Flell.

'This is Urbi,' said Teressa. 'She can't talk, so please be kind to her.'

'Treat her gently,' Vander advised.

'I will, Father,' Yafeu said formally, and beckoned to Flell to follow him.

Teressa let her go, a little cautiously. By now she trusted Flell to be sensible. She was glad to get some time to herself, too, as Vander soon invited her and Orak to help themselves to the food provided.

The evening passed by very pleasantly, and when night came the guests were informed that they had been provided with quarters in the palace. Flell and Teressa shared theirs with Orak.

'So how did ye enjoy playing with that little boy?' Teressa asked.

'It was nice,' said Flell. 'He kept talking in Amoran language, though. I had to pretend like I understood.'

Teressa shifted uneasily. 'Yes, well. That's good. I hope ye didn't say anything.'

'No,' said Flell. 'I wish I could…'

'It's a nuisance,' said Teressa. 'But don't worry. Once we get ye into yer grandfather's protection, ye can talk. None of the others will dare touch ye once we've done that.'

'All right,' Flell sighed.

Teressa said nothing more, but internally she was hoping that nothing bad would come out of this. She hadn't missed Vander's frowning look, and she hoped it didn't mean that they had attracted unwanted attention. But if they had, they would be leaving him soon enough, so what harm could it do?

On the last day of their time in Maijan, though, she overheard Vander speaking to Curig – the man who had welcomed them onto the ship back at Abertawe.

'Yer cabin is prepared, my Lord,' Curig was saying when Teressa came into earshot.

'Excellent,' said Vander. 'Ymazu and I shall be there well before you are ready to set sail.'

Once Curig had left, Teressa couldn't resist asking Vander what was going on. 'Are ye coming with us?'

'I am,' Vander smiled. 'Before I was made Governor of Maijan, I was the Emperor's chief diplomat. And he is an old friend. My partner Ymazu and I have been invited to come to the celebrations. Inva will stay here with our son, to govern Maijan in my absence.'

'Oh,' said Teressa.

Vander smiled again. 'I am glad to see you, Priestess Teressa,' he said. 'I have wanted to speak with you.'

'Ye have?' Teressa said nervously.

'Yes.' Vander lost his smile. 'There is a question that I want to ask. Come with me.'

Teressa glanced cautiously at Orak, who was with her. Flell had wandered off to explore the palace with Yafeu, who had become a fast friend.

Vander said nothing more, but led the two of them away and into a large airy room that must have been his own private chamber. There was an aged griffin in there – a smaller, Amorani female whose dark brown feathers had begun to grey around the beak. She was dozing, but looked up when the visitors arrived.

Orak bowed his head politely to her, and she yawned and looked away.

'This is Ymazu,' said Vander. 'She does not often come with me now. She deserves her rest; it has been well-earned. Now come. Sit.'

Teressa sat on the low cushion offered, while Orak settled beside her. 'What did ye want to ask?' she said. By now her nerves had increased horribly. Her stomach was twisting.

Vander sat opposite her, cross-legged on his own cushion.

He smiled mysteriously, and smoothed down his moustache with his finger. 'That child you have brought,' he said. 'I wanted to ask about her.'

Teressa's heart pounded sickeningly. 'What about her?'

'She is only a human pup,' Orak interrupted. 'There is nothing special about her.'

'Perhaps not,' said Vander. 'But I wanted to ask – what was the name of her mother, who died in Malvern?'

'I don't know,' said Teressa. 'I think they told me once, but I forgot it, and Urbi won't speak to me, so I couldn't ask her.'

'And can I ask why she was in Malvern?' asked Vander.

'She came to visit the city,' said Teressa. It was at least true that several Amoranis had come to see it for themselves – mostly nobles with money and time for travelling.

'And the child is most definitely from my country?' said Vander. 'I can see that she is not purely Amorani.'

'No, I think her father has some Southern blood in him,' said Teressa.

'But she was still raised in Amoran,' said Vander.

'Aye, she was,' said Teressa. She wondered how long she could keep this up, before Vander finally caught her out.

He didn't keep her waiting any longer to find out. 'And yet my son tells me that she speaks no Amorani,' he said.

Teressa's heart sank. 'She doesn't speak at all.'

'But she does not understand my language,' said Vander. 'My son is quite certain of this.'

Oh damn, thought Teressa. Beside her, Orak tensed.

Vander didn't need to probe any further; Teressa's expression must have told him everything he wanted to know. He leaned forward. 'Tell me where you found her,' he said. 'The truth.'

Teressa gave in. This man wasn't a Northerner, and he was loyal to the Emperor. Maybe she could trust him. But she wasn't about to betray Flell just like that. 'How do I know ye don't want to hurt her?' she asked cautiously.

Vander smiled. 'If you think I am the kind of man who would harm a child, then perhaps it is not surprising that you have lied to me. But you have been lying ever since you first found her, yes?'

'I…' Teressa trailed off lamely.

'You have done this to protect her,' said Vander. 'But do not be afraid. I will not tell your countrymen what you tell me, and I will not hurt the child. I promise it on my honour as a true man of Amoran. Now tell me the truth.'

'Ye are loyal to the Emperor, aren't ye?' said Teressa.

'I am,' said Vander. 'We have been friends since we were boys in training as griffiners.'

'Well then… I'm taking the child to him,' said Teressa. 'She wasn't safe in the North, and if any of the other Northerners here find out the truth, they might kill her. They might kill me too.'

'Then you found her in the North?' Vander asked quietly.

'I did,' said Teressa. 'And her real name—,'

'Flell,' said Vander, even more quietly. 'Flell Taranisäii, daughter of Queen Laela.'

'How did ye know?' Teressa asked softly.

Vander smiled again. 'Because I helped Kullervo to smuggle her out of the city. The dead child that we replaced her with in the cradle was my own daughter, who died at birth. Only I, and Inva, and our partners, know the truth. Then you are taking Flell to her grandfather the Emperor?'

'I am,' said Teressa. 'He can protect her. He will, won't he?' she added anxiously.

'He will,' said Vander. 'He was distraught at the news of the deaths of his son and grandchild. He would be most pleased to have that grandchild returned to him alive. And with my testimony, we will be able to prove that she is not an imposter. But where is Kullervo? He took the child to raise her himself.'

'I don't know,' said Teressa. 'Flell says she ran away to try and kill the King and avenge her parents. She was going to get herself killed.'

Vander frowned. 'Then Kullervo must be searching for her. I can only hope that he does not run into trouble. But why have you decided to help the child? You knew you were risking death by protecting her.'

'Because I'm loyal to King Arenadd,' said Teressa.

'As I am loyal to my Emperor,' said Vander. 'Very well. I will keep your secret, and protect you as well as I can, and when the time comes, I will help you to present the child to the Emperor. But it must be done in secret. If your countrymen were there to see you do this, you would be in danger. And I cannot be seen to be involved, or our alliance with your King would be damaged. He would not be pleased to know that the Empire was sheltering his rival for the throne.'

'What'll happen to Flell in Amoran?' asked Teressa. 'What will the Emperor do?'

Vander shrugged. 'She will be given a home and a husband will be found for her when she is old enough. The Emperor has four sons and six grandsons – you will see them all at the celebrations in

Xanthium. A woman may only claim the Imperial Throne if there are no male heirs left alive, so Flell will not rule the Empire. But one day, perhaps, her sons or grandsons will.'

Teressa nodded in relief. She wanted Flell to be protected, and in Amoran the King would never find her. But if she became Empress… well, maybe nothing would come of it, but it would be better if she didn't. She was hardly Empress material anyway.

'Thank ye, Vander,' she said. 'It's good to have someone else on my side here.'

'Yes,' Vander sighed. 'But I hope that this does not… ah, I have become sentimental in my old age. Go now, Teressa, and take good care of the child. You have done well so far.'

Teressa smiled her gratitude as she left with Orak. Silently, she thanked Arenadd and the Night God. Now she had Vander on her side, her quest would be easier. And once Flell was safely in her grandfather's protection she, Teressa, could go back to her search for Kullervo and the dark griffin. Arenadd's will would be done.

*

The ships set sail for Amoran the next day, with Vander and Ymazu now on board the same ship as Teressa and Orak. The longest part of the journey was now over; they would be in the Amorani capital in another month or so.

During this last leg of the journey, Vander quickly proved that he was serious in his promise that he was on Teressa's side. He took to spending time with Flell, quietly telling her things in Cymrian, which he spoke very well. Teressa politely kept her distance, but she heard enough to know that he was teaching her about the history of her family, telling her stories about her forebears. He also started teaching her Amorani. If she was going to live in Amoran, she would need to know it.

Flell seemed happy enough to go along with this, and actually appeared to have forgotten her original plan of trying to kill the King who had killed her parents. At least, she didn't argue with the plan for her to go and live with her grandfather. Which was just as well — aside from anything else, Teressa had no desire to listen to a child's whining, especially in this heat. To a Northerner like herself, being in this sweltering new climate was something of a nightmare.

At last the coast of Amoran came in sight, and after that the ships began to sail up the great River Erech, which would take them all the way to Xanthium. Now they were able to dock and go ashore every night, first at the smaller city of Instabahn – where Flell's parents had been married, according to Vander – and later at other, smaller settlements.

By now Teressa had adapted to the heat, and she watched the strange sandy land they were now in with wonder. It was unlike anything she had ever seen before. Flell seemed to like it too.

Teressa could only imagine what the capital city would be like, but after a long voyage up the River Erech she finally found out.

Xanthium was huge – easily the biggest city they had seen so far. It had been built on both sides of the river, which had been artificially widened to accommodate docks on either side, where ships, fishing boats, pleasure barges and other vessels Teressa didn't recognise bobbed gently in the current. Great palm trees grew along the banks, and behind them, buildings rose high into the sky as far as the eye could see, up and over the hills on either side. But straight in front of them, towering above everything else, was the Imperial Palace.

Built of the same sandy-yellow stone as everything else, it was absolutely enormous, with numerous towers built in a similar style to the ones in Cymria, with ledges and openings all the way up for griffins to fly in and out of as they chose. But their roofs were domed rather than flat, and decorated with golden sunwheels.

Unlike important buildings in Cymria, which were generally built on hilltops or at least high ground of one kind or another, the palace – the Hall of Suns, Vander said it was called – had been built close to the river. In fact it had been built over the river, with a great archway beneath it to let ships sail through it. On top of the archway was a statue of a griffin, standing proudly with one forepaw raised. Its smaller siblings stood on either side, lining the bridge – "small" was a relative term, since even the smallest of them was larger than a real griffin by a considerable amount. Teressa could actually see a few live griffins perched on them quite comfortably.

'Holy Night God,' she mumbled to herself.

Flell was almost dancing in excitement, obviously desperate to say something, but still sensible enough to keep quiet. But her eyes had gone wide and bright with excitement.

Even Orak looked astonished. 'What wonders humans can

make!' he exclaimed.

'I know!' said Teressa.

The crippled griffin gave her a serious look through his purple eyes. 'This is why we griffins choose to ally ourselves with your kind,' he said. 'Because of all the creatures of this world, only humans have the power to make such things as this. Sometimes I forget that, but when I see such a sight as this, I remember.'

'I don't think I knew what we could really make until now,' said Teressa. 'Though…' she thought wistfully of the great Temple back in Malvern.

The Hall of Suns had its own dock under the archway, and the ships stopped there. Once they were underneath Teressa could see that the archway's underside had entrances in it – smaller, open archways big enough for both humans and griffins to enter by. Once she had disembarked with Orak, Flell, Vander and the other guests, they were allowed to enter by those archways, which were guarded on either side by several Amorani and Maijani men, armed with spears.

Teressa looked curiously at the guards as she passed them. All of them were simply clad – a white kilt around the hips, helmets and bronze breastplates. Heavy iron collars had been clamped around their necks.

'Slave guards,' Vander explained, seeing her look. 'They are raised from birth to do nothing but fight, and to be absolutely loyal to their masters.'

Teressa shivered. Once some of these slaves might have been Northerners like herself, but there weren't many Northern slaves left in Amoran. The King had renewed the alliance with Amoran by promising that if they helped him in their invasion of the South, they could take as many of its citizens as they liked to sell in their slave markets. In return, they would send slaves of Northern blood home to be set free. Teressa had seen some of them herself, all bewildered and lost in the ancestral homeland they had never seen before. Most of them didn't even speak the Northern language. But that didn't matter. What mattered was to bring them home.

Inside, the palace was even more impressive. Teressa quickly saw why it was called the Hall of Suns. The interior had been coated in clay that hid the lines of the stonework and that clay had been covered with designs in brightly coloured paint. Not a single wall, pillar or ceiling had been considered unimportant enough to go undecorated. Teressa saw flowers, dancing women, griffins, dragons, birds and other animals, painted everywhere. But mixed in with all that, and visible on just about every surface, were the suns. They were painted in gold – sunwheels, just like the ones that decorated temples in the South. Teressa had seen that symbol before: a circle, with three waving lines that met in the middle to represent sunbeams. She wondered why it would be the same symbol as the one used in Cymria, and asked Vander as much.

Vander nodded as he listened to her question. 'The people in the South of your country may think that symbol is their own, but it has been in Amoran for thousands of years. It is said that the sun-worshippers of your own country were taught to worship that way by us, and that it was we who gave them this symbol. The truth of that, however, is lost: there is no record of our dealings with your country that go back that far, and all we have to learn from are myths.'

Teressa listened curiously, and couldn't help but wonder if her own people had learned about the Night God from somewhere else. But surely not. The Night God belonged to the North; nowhere else.

After that, she and Orak were shown to their new quarters – by slaves. These were Amorani slaves, clad just as simply as the guards outside, but without the armour. Since they went bare-headed, Teressa could see how their hair had been shaved off. Even the women were bald. She wondered why. Maybe it was to keep fleas away.

The slave assigned to take her to her quarters was a woman who silently led her, Orak and Flell to a modestly sized but beautifully furnished and decorated pair of rooms. One room was for Teressa – and a smaller bed had already been installed for Flell – and the second was for Orak, and came complete with a velvet pad on the floor for him to lie on, a carved stone water trough, and a golden dish set into the floor which had been stocked with meat. There was even a second slave waiting there to attend to the griffin's needs.

Teressa stared in wonder, but didn't remark on anything. Both she and Orak had received similar treatment in the places they'd stayed along the way, assigned personal slaves to wait on them, if only for one night.

Now her own slave bowed formally as the others had done,

saying, 'I am Halima, and I will care for you and obey your every command while you are here in Xanthium. Does my Lady wish for me to bathe her before the celebrations begin?'

Teressa nodded. 'Yes, thank ye. Urbi, ye should have a bath as well.'

Flell looked resigned, but said nothing.

Halima bowed to Orak. 'In the meantime your own attendant shall groom and annoint you, sacred griffin.'

Orak looked pleased, and swaggered off into his nest. All griffins loved to be pampered.

Teressa didn't mind it much herself. She waited happily while Halima filled a bath with the help of a second slave, who showed up as if from nowhere, and then she and Flell were allowed to share it while the two slaves – both very well trained – washed and massaged them and even combed their hair for them before decorating it with beads and anointing it with some kind of sweet-smelling oil that made it shine.

After that they were both offered new clothes made in the Amorani style. Teressa preferred to keep her silver robe, but Flell accepted hers eagerly, probably because it was heavily decorated with shining glass and gold beads. She wanted to wear makeup like an Amorani lady, too, and got what she demanded.

Teressa, watching, shook her head. Childhood didn't last all that long in the scheme of things, but for some reason most children wanted to be adults, or at least be allowed to dress like them. Or maybe Flell just liked being fussed over; that was certainly understandable.

Vander had informed her that the celebrations would begin that evening, when the Emperor officially announced them open. They would go on for several days after that, though, and from the descriptions Teressa had been a little shocked by just how extravagant this birthday party would be. But Vander had added that this wasn't just any birthday – the Emperor was turning sixty, and this year would mark the thirtieth year of his reign.

Teressa had never been to any celebration that extended beyond beer and cakes, and despite the importance of her quest, she was looking forward to this one. By the sound of it, the Amoranis knew how to enjoy themselves. She only hoped that Vander would succeed in winning her and Flell an audience with the Emperor before it started – the sooner that was done, the better.

The former diplomat did not disappoint them. Not long after Teressa and Flell had finished dressing, and Orak had emerged from his nest – now wearing a fine beaded headdress and a golden sheath on his beak – Halima answered a knock at the door and returned to announce that Vander and Ymazu had come to see them.

Teressa hurried to the door, and found Vander waiting. He was wearing a fine set of clothes, and Ymazu had been groomed and decorated like Orak.

'Vander,' Teressa smiled. 'How did it go?'

Vander nodded formally. 'The Emperor has asked to see you,' he said. 'We must go to him immediately.'

Teressa's heart beat faster. 'All right. Flell, Orak, come on.'

Neither of them needed to be prompted. They joined up with Teressa, their attendants quietly following in the rear, and Vander and Ymazu escorted them to where the Emperor of Amoran waited.

They found him in a pleasant courtyard, which had been planted with all kinds of lush plants and even featured an ornamental pond with fish in it. Several guards had been discreetly posted around the walls, but they only glanced briefly at the visitors before returning their gazes to the middle distance.

The Emperor sat cross-legged by the pond, with his dark brown partner lounging behind him.

He looked ordinary enough to Teressa – she was even a little disappointed. After so many descriptions and so much build-up, the all-powerful Emperor of Amoran had grown large in her mind, like a figure from a legend. Now that she saw him in person, she found herself looking at… well, just a man. A man who looked rather smaller than she had expected, and older as well.

He wore an elaborate headdress: striped blue and yellow cloth that framed his head and shoulders like a lion's mane, and which featured a golden griffin's head over the forehead. A wide, jewelled necklace covered his chest, which was otherwise bare, and below that he wore a simple cloth kilt made from the same blue and yellow cloth as his headdress. A griffin's tail, sewn together from real fur and feathers, hung from the back – Teressa could see it lying on the grass beside him.

His partner Zaerih was more impressive, as griffins generally were. Her brown coat was patterned with yellow, with a splash of green on the wings, and her eyes were the colour of sand. She did not stand up, or look even mildly bothered by the arrival of two other griffins. She barely flicked her tail. Somehow, that only served to give her a faint aura of menace – as if she were so powerful she didn't need to acknowledge her visitors at all.

The Emperor, though, stood to receive them. 'Vander,' he said, speaking griffish.

Vander bowed and smiled. 'Sacred Ruler, I have brought the woman and the child as commanded.'

'Yes…' the Emperor looked past him to Teressa.

Vander gestured at her to come forward. She did, holding Flell by the hand, and bowed low. 'Sacred Ruler,' she said, echoing Vander.

The Emperor inclined his head in return, but his eyes were on Flell. 'Speak,' he said.

'I— my name is Teressa,' said Teressa. 'And this is my partner Orak.'

'You have come as a guest to my celebration here, then?' said the Emperor.

'I have,' said Teressa.

'But that is not the only reason you have come,' said the Emperor. 'So Lord Vander here has told me.'

'No,' said Teressa. She hesitated, not sure how to proceed.

Flell, though, took the opportunity from her. She pulled her hand out of Teressa's and went forward to confront the Emperor, not showing the slightest sign of caring about who he was, or that there were guards there, or the looming shape of Zaerih.

'My name's Flell,' she said loudly, using griffish. 'Flell Taranisäii. My dad was your son Akhane, so I'm your granddaughter.'

The Emperor's dark eyes widened. 'You?'

'Yeah, I am,' Flell said boldly. 'Teressa and Orak brought me here to live with you because you're my granddad.'

The Emperor looked sharply at Vander. 'I was told that my son's child had died.'

'It was a lie,' said Vander, shaking his head. 'This child speaks the truth. I helped her uncle to rescue her from her cousin, who would have killed her. She was given to her uncle to raise, but now… now this priestess has found her and has brought her here to be reunited with you. I recognised her in Maijan, and decided that I would help her to do this. She would not have been safe in the West, not for long.'

'I ran away from Uncle 'Lurvo,' Flell said helpfully. 'Now I want to live here with you.'

The Emperor looked at Teressa. 'Where did you find her?'

Teressa explained.

'Then you have done a great service to the Empire by bringing this child to me,' said the Emperor. He inspected Flell. 'I do not doubt that you are telling me the truth. You have never lied to me Vander, and you, child—,'

'Yeah?' said Flell.

The Emperor smiled. 'I have met both your mother and your grandfather, and I can see them in you. I can also see my son. You are my grandchild, and a member of the Imperial Family. As Emperor, it is my duty to care for my country, but as a father it is my duty to care for my children and their children. Therefore, you will be given a home here in Amoran, and when you are older I shall find a husband worthy of you.'

'I'm never getting married!' Flell snapped.

The adults chuckled, and the Emperor's smile grew warmer. 'Every child says that at least once,' he said.

'Now.' He looked at Teressa. 'Teressa of Tara, you have done a great service to my family. If there is a reward that I can grant to you, name it.'

Teressa smiled, partly in gratitude and partly in relief. 'There is a reward I'd like, Sacred Ruler.'

'Then speak now,' said the Emperor.

Teressa took a deep breath – this was going to sound odd. 'I came here on a quest,' she said. 'A holy quest. I'm looking for a black griffin. Have ye seen one, Sacred Ruler? Is there one here in Amoran?'

The Emperor looked puzzled. 'A black griffin? Why would you be seeking one?'

'Because the great King Arenadd came to me in a dream and told me to,' Teressa said honestly. Seeing the bewildered looks on all their faces, she went on quickly. 'He told me to find a black griffin in the East. This is the East. He also told me to find a child with Southern eyes.' She pointed at Flell. 'I found her. He told me to find his son, as well. I think that might be Kullervo. But first, I must find this griffin. Is there one here in Amoran, Sacred Ruler? If ye can help me find him, that's all the reward I want.'

The Emperor frowned.

Behind him, Zaerih suddenly spoke up. 'There have been tales of black griffins,' she said in low, lazy tones – almost a purr. 'And I did once meet one. The Mighty Skandar, who was ruler of all griffins in your own country, Orak. But we have heard that the Mighty Skandar is dead, and there has been no other word of such a griffin.'

Teressa thought it over. Could it be that Skandar was still alive? But if he was, why would he be in the East?

'Well,' she said. 'I intend to stay here in Amoran until I've found him. If I have to I'll travel the whole country, or even go to Erebus.'

The Emperor smiled. 'If you are so determined to find this griffin, then so be it,' he said. 'I shall not force you to search yourself. As your reward, I shall send out word through the whole of my Empire, commanding every citizen that if a black griffin is ever seen, they must send news of it at once. You may stay here in the Hall of Suns until it arrives.'

Teressa bowed low. 'Thank ye, Sacred Ruler.'

'It is no great thing to ask after you have brought my grandchild to me,' said the Emperor. 'But for now, it is time to celebrate!'

'Aye!' Teressa said excitedly. 'Thank ye again, Sacred Ruler. And also…'

'Yes?' said the Emperor.

Teressa smiled. 'Happy Birthday.'

*

Teressa left Flell with her grandfather and returned to her quarters with Orak to rest. As she left the Emperor's presence, she felt as if a great weight had been lifted from her shoulders. She had succeeded – her and Orak both. They had found Arenadd's granddaughter and got her to safety, just as he would have wanted. The first part of their quest was done, and now, with the Emperor's help, the next part should be much easier.

'We have done well,' Orak agreed. 'Now we have the allegiance of the master of Amoran, and with the child out of our care, we are safe. The others from the North will not discover us, and we can trust Ymazu and her human to keep our secret.'

'I'm sure we can,' said Teressa, sitting down to rest. 'Arenadd and the Night God protected us.'

Orak snorted. 'Foolery. But now we must find the black griffin.'

'Aye.' Teressa sighed. 'I wonder how long it'll take before we do? I don't want to have to fly halfway across Amoran looking for him. I've a feeling Arenadd wants us to find him for a reason. Surely it must be to help our people. If the King succeeds in conquering all of Cymria, he might need the dark griffin's power to help keep it.'

So far, she hadn't really thought about what purpose finding this mysterious griffin might serve. But if he did indeed have the same power as Skandar, then surely it must mean…

Teressa smiled to herself, as the obvious answer came to her. 'I know what this is about,' she said.

Orak looked up from his grooming. 'What have you thought of, Teressa?'

Teressa nodded. 'Aye, I know what this is about. Don't ye see? It's obvious. We have to find this dark griffin for a reason. Arenadd's trying to tell us that it's time for a new Shadow That Walks to rise. His successor, and Saeddryn's. The Night God's servant, come to help our people the way Arenadd and Saeddryn did. The Night God wants us to help this griffin find the right Northerner and give him the dark power. And then…'

'And then you will want to serve this human,' said Orak.

'I will,' said Teressa. 'It would be what Arenadd wants. And what the Night God wants too.'

She frowned thoughtfully and drank some water, while the idea settled comfortably into her mind. It felt right, and as a priestess-in-training she had become used to trusting her feelings. The mind and the heart weren't the same thing, and when the mind was at rest, the heart could come to the fore and show the way. That was how the gods worked; through the heart. She did just that now; and what her heart told her was that she was right. She must help the dark griffin to be united with the one the Night God had chosen, and once that man or woman had been given the power of the Shadow That Walked, she must stand beside whomever it was and give them her undying loyalty. And the loyalty of her fellows as well – every Northerner who worshipped the Shadow That Walked, as she did, If she called on them, they would follow. They, too, would serve the new avatar of the Night God.

That was how it was; that was how it must be, and she swore to herself, then and there, that she would follow this destiny of hers to the death. She would do Arenadd's will, and together, she and Orak would help the Shadow That Walked to join the King and crush the South once and for all. Her people would rule all of Cymria in the name of the Night God. That was what the Night God wanted, so that was how it would be.

'That's what I'll do,' she murmured aloud. 'Come what may, I will find the dark griffin. I will find the Shadow That Walks. I will give my life for him. I swear it on my soul.'

*

Close by, Orak said nothing. But his own thoughts weren't so far away from his partner's. If he did indeed find this griffin, he too would be prepared to follow and obey. He was a cripple, and with his weakness, could never hope to dominate others. No, his own glory must come out of the glory of another: a griffin stronger than himself. If he could win the gratitude of the mighty black griffin that he had seen in his dream, then he too could become powerful. He would fight beside this griffin with all his strength, until at last the day came when nobody, man or griffin, would ever mock him again. He would not die, as other griffins – even his own mother – wanted and expected.

He cast a glance at Teressa, and felt glad that he had chosen her. She was cunning, as a human should be, and strong – at least as strong as a tiny human could be. At the very least, she was brave. She would serve him well.

All these thoughts put him in a good mood, and he stood up with a flick of his grey feathered tail. 'We have done well!' he said loudly. 'And we must be rewarded. Before our work continues, we shall celebrate!'

Teressa smiled. 'We will!' she said. 'We've earned it.' She looked out the window, where the light had turned red and orange. 'The sun's setting. It's time. Let's go and have some fun.'

'We shall!' Orak declared, and led the way out of the room and into the palace, where the celebrations were about to begin.

Chapter Ten

The Imperial Birthday

At the centre of the Hall of Suns there was indeed a hall — perhaps the same hall that gave the palace its name. It was huge — big enough for entire houses to be built inside it, Teressa thought. If it had been empty it would have looked even bigger, but as it was it was crowded and that made it look rather smaller than it might have.

Everyone was there — all the party guests gathered into the hall, standing among the massive stone pillars that held up its roof. Those pillars were decorated, like everything else in the Hall of Suns — carved and painted to look like lotus flowers. The ceiling had been painted with a massive mural, and at the very centre of that was a golden sunwheel — a sunwheel bigger than a griffin. There were actually griffins, flying in a circle, painted around its inside. At the very centre, a golden man stood with his arms outstretched and a faint smile on his face, staring down at the guests through a pair of rich blue almond-shaped eyes.

Beyond all of that was a profusion of painted flowers, fields, rivers, oceans — and after a few moments of staring at it in wonder, Teressa realised she was looking at a map of the world. The sunwheel was at the centre of what must be Amoran, and beyond that — painted much smaller than the great Eastern continent — were the other countries of the world. She saw what must be Cymria, painted with snow-covered trees much larger than life, and Maijan stuck in-between. She had never seen a map of the world before, but she assumed that was what it must be like — Amoran, the greatest of all, at the centre. Amoran, the land of the sun, to which all the other lands of the earth were subordinate. It was humbling.

Below that, the gathered guests chattered excitedly among themselves. They were standing quite close together, forced to stay around the edges of the hall, since the rest of it had been fenced off by a group of guards. A great throne, carved out of stone, sat on a plinth in the very centre, and upon it sat the Emperor with his family standing around him. Teressa counted them, and quickly saw that there were indeed four men there who must be his four surviving sons. Each of them had their own children with him, and at the very back stood a group of women who must have been the wives of the Emperor and his sons. In Amoran, she had been told, noble men were allowed to have as many wives as they pleased. Either way, it was a big group, and she guessed that the entire Imperial family must have been called back to Xanthium for the celebration.

If the Imperial family were all griffiners, their griffins mustn't have been with them – Teressa only saw the Emperor's own partner, Zaerih, standing behind his throne. She had reared onto her hind legs and rested her forepaws on the back of the throne, directly behind her partner's head. It only served to make her partner look more impressive to Teressa.

The Emperor himself was still wearing the headdress he had had on earlier, but now he had also donned a white tunic – very light and loose-fitting, but plain. His sandals, though, were gold, and his face had been painted to make his eyes look bigger.

Teressa scanned the faces of the Imperial family, but couldn't see Flell anywhere. Just as well. It would be best that the Northern guests there didn't see her.

As for the guests themselves, they stood between the pillars – the griffiners with their partners just behind them, rearing protectively over them. Orak had stationed himself just behind Teressa like the others – she could sense his great grey head looming over her own, without having to look, and his chest feathers brushed against her back. It was comforting to have him there.

There must have been at least two hundred other guests – mostly Amoranis, but all the Northerners she had arrived with were there too, along with some Maijanis, and some from races she had never seen before, all wearing what must have been their ceremonial outfits. Her fellow griffiners from Cymria wore theirs – gowns or tunics decorated with griffin feathers, with the long flight feathers hanging down the back. Teressa wished she had one of her own, but she would have had to pay a tailor a lot of money for it. An outfit like that probably cost hundreds of oblong.

There were guards everywhere too – she saw them stationed, two at every entrance. Slave guards, of course.

She had just finished taking all this in when Zaerih screeched. The sound cut across the chattering of the guests, and silence quickly fell. Everyone there looked expectantly at Zaerih and the Emperor.

The Emperor stood up, and raised a gracious hand. 'Welcome!' he said loudly, speaking griffish. 'Welcome to the Hall of Suns, and welcome to Xanthium if you are a visitor here. Many of you have come a very far away to be here today, and I thank you for your courtesy.' He smiled. 'Today is the sixtieth year of my life, and the thirtieth year of my reign as Emperor of Amoran. Thirty years, I have ruled this great Empire. It has been the task of my life, and one I have always taken pride in. Therefore you who have come here today are hereby invited to celebrate with myself and my family. Eat, drink, and enjoy yourselves!'

The guests cheered.

'But first,' the Emperor added with a smile, 'It is time for the giving of the gifts.'

At this signal, several guests came forward one after another, to present the Emperor with gifts – some from wealthy families, and others from rulers of nations. One of Teressa's fellow Northerners was among the first to go forward, and he presented the Emperor with a white Cymrian parrot in a cage. The parrot raised its yellow crest, and squawked "Hello!" in Northern, much to the amusement of the onlookers.

'They can be taught to repeat words, Sacred Ruler,' the Northerner holding the cage explained.

'A fine gift,' the Emperor smiled.

After that there were other Amoranis, who presented him with all kinds of different things – jewellery, books, carved wooden furniture decorated with gemstones… more beautiful things than Teressa had ever imagined. The Maijani dignitaries, led by Vander, presented him with a fine set of clothes, and an elaborate bone carving. Two finely-dressed guests from a race Teressa didn't know came forward after that, accompanied by four massive dog-like creatures she had never seen before, and presented a chest full of intricately wrought gold ornaments. The dog creatures stood by, grunting deep in their chests.

After a while, though, Teressa, started to lose interest. She only perked up again when one of the Amorani guests – a lady dressed in green – came forward with the last gift, and that was only because the gift was so large. It had to be carried in by a team of slaves, all strong young men. They placed it down, and their master came forward and dramatically lifted away the cloth that covered it.

Underneath was a huge model building, carved out of dark wood. It looked like a palace of some kind, and it was astonishing. The windows were carved gemstones, and the roofs were ivory. It must have taken months to create.

'A magnificent gift, Lady Ahamay!' the Emperor said with a smile.

The lady bowed and smiled in return. Her slaves, having deposited the gift, silently returned to stand guard on either side of her. Teressa, watching, was shocked to notice that these slaves were different from the others. They were heavier than the Amorani slaves she had seen; wider in the shoulders, and paler in the skin. Their eyes were paler, as well.

Southerners, she thought. Southerners, all the way from Cymria. Had they been sold over here as prisoners of war, or had they been here already?

She hadn't seen a Southerner in years – not since she was a small child – and she inspected these with great curiosity.

The biggest of them was the one who stood the closest to his master. He was square-jawed and big-handed, and she shuddered to think of how strong he must be. Most interesting of all, she could see faint stubble on his head, and it was red. She had never seen a red-haired man before.

As if he knew that she was looking at him, the red-haired slave turned his head towards her. His eyes narrowed, and she saw the expression in them.

It was full of hate.

She stiffened, and hot fear swelled in her stomach like molten metal. She wanted to look away, but she couldn't.

Then the Emperor spoke again, and the moment ended. 'Excellent!' he said loudly, causing a stir among the crowd. He nodded to his own slaves, who came forward to clear away the gifts. They left the carved palace, though – only moving it aside, so that some of the Emperor's grandchildren, who had been eyeing it with interest, could come forward to examine it while their grandfather spoke on.

'Now,' he said. 'It is time! On this most important of days, you here may all see a great treasure. It is only rarely brought out, but you may have the privilege of seeing it.'

The guests murmured excitedly, and settled down expectantly to wait. They didn't have to wait long. Moments later, obviously having been waiting close by for just this moment, a team of slaves appeared, carrying something enormous wrapped in cloth on their shoulders.

Whatever it was, it was massive – easily as big as a large griffin. The muscular Maijani slaves carried it with difficulty, and laid it down at the Emperor's feet with obvious relief.

The Emperor had stood up again, and now he waved a hand to the slaves, who came forward and silently removed the cloth.

Everyone there gasped.

Teressa leaned forward, dumbstruck, not quite able to believe what she was seeing.

It was a colossal skull – a skull made of some kind of black material that looked vaguely like stone. It wasn't plain black, though, but shiny and iridescent, like the scales of a fish.

The skull itself was elongated, the eye sockets so big that Teressa could have curled up inside one. She could see the teeth from here – thin, sharp teeth, each one longer than her arm. The fangs at the front were as long as her whole body.

'Holy Night God,' she breathed.

Behind her, Orak hissed. 'What creature could have such a skull?'

The Emperor spoke up. 'This is the skull of the great serpent of Erebus,' he said loudly. 'Which my family has guarded for many centuries. It is our greatest treasure.'

'That thing was alive?' Teressa exclaimed, but nobody heard her over the shouts of astonishment. Surely, she thought, nothing that big could ever have existed.

'Now you may—,' the Emperor began, and broke off suddenly. Teressa saw him frown in puzzlement.

The lady in green, Lady Ahamay, had come forward. Ignoring the Emperor, ignoring the slaves, she went towards the skull. Her red-haired bodyguard followed close at her heels, along with his burly Maijani partner.

Lady Ahamay walked along the length of the skull, gently running her fingers over its shining surface. She murmured something to herself. The Emperor glared. Clearly, Teressa thought, Ahamay was being very rude.

She reached the Emperor, and faced him with the skull between them. She smiled. He gave her a puzzled look in return. 'What is this, Ahamay?'

She spoke in some language Teressa didn't recognise, but as her voice grew louder it began to sound more and more like a chant – rhythmic and strong. Behind her, the two guards stayed impassive and blank faced as slaves in Amoran always did.

The Emperor said nothing. He looked puzzled. Around him, his family had also gone quiet, apparently not knowing quite what to make of this.

Lady Ahamay smiled widely, and then without any warning she shouted a word. 'Itzcóatl!'

With that she pulled a dagger out of her clothes, stepped forward, and stabbed the Emperor through the heart.

'Now!' the red-haired slave behind her roared in his own language, and before the Emperor could even fall he had rushed forward and brought his big fists down on the carved wooden palace. It broke instantly, splitting right down the middle, and as it fell apart, something came out.

Screams split the air. The Imperial family fell back in terror, but too late. There was no room to escape.

Snakes emerged from the broken carving – dozens and dozens of them. They whipped away into the crowd, hissing and rearing up to bite anyone who came too close. The Imperial family was right in their path. None of them, not even the raging Zaerih, stood a chance.

Teressa saw them fall, one after another, covered in snake bites. In front of them, completely calm, Lady Ahamay gestured to her slaves. They came forward and lifted the skull, carrying it with them away through the crowd, which was too panic-stricken to try and intervene.

Teressa had frozen to the spot without even realising it. Pure terror and shock had turned her spine to ice.

Orak had more presence of mind. His beak hooked her by the back of her silver robe, and he pulled her away from the panicking guests, dragging her towards the exit.

Teressa finally came back to her senses, and managed to find her feet. 'We've got to get out of here!' she said stupidly.

'Hurry!' Orak rasped. 'Run!'

He went ahead of her, shoving people out of the way to clear the path. Teressa kept close to him.

'Teressa!' a voice yelled off to her left. She turned her head, and saw Lord Vander hurrying towards her with Ymazu.

'Vander!' she yelled back.

'You must come with me!' the old Amorani called. 'Help me!'

Teressa nodded sharply and ran to him, elbowing the fleeing guests aside. Behind her Orak realised what she was doing and followed.

Vander had gone pale. 'The Emperor is dead. We must not let his murderer escape. Come with me!'

Without a thought, Teressa followed him. Ymazu helped to clear the way just as Orak had done earlier, and the two humans followed, with Orak somewhere behind. Teressa didn't stop to wonder if he approved of this plan, and there was no time.

The assassin and her slaves weren't hard to track. They had taken the same door that must have been used to bring the skull into the hall, because it was the only one big enough. A few people had gone in pursuit, and now Vander and Teressa joined them.

The door led down a ramp, and a steel gate had been lifted to clear the way. The fleeing slaves carried the skull down it, ignoring their pursuers.

'They are going to the river!' Vander shouted. 'They must have a boat waiting!'

They did, and more than that. Other slaves were waiting – dozens of them, all powerfully built Southerners and Maijanis. As their friends carrying the skull came down the ramp, they emerged from hiding and attacked their pursuers as they flooded out of the hall in confusion.

There were four griffins with Vander and Teressa, including Ymazu and Orak – but in the confined space, their size was a hindrance. The slaves attacked them and the humans there indiscriminately, and as Teressa lurched back in fright she saw several of the guests fall. Their killers disposed of them quickly and efficiently, with brutal stabs and slashes of their short swords or spears. When one of the griffins there shoved his way forward, a Maijani slave stood in his way and calmly thrust a spear through his throat before he could give himself the space to strike back. The griffin fell, killing several people in his death throes, and those behind him fell back, giving the assassins time to escape.

Teressa kept close to Orak and Ymazu. 'They're getting away!' she shouted.

Vander's dark eyes narrowed. 'They will not get far,' he said, and to her amazement he went on, shoving his hesitating fellows out of the way. Ymazu went with him, and pushed the dead griffin aside.

'Come!' Orak called, and limped after her.

Teressa followed against her better judgement,. 'Orak, we should go back!' she yelled.

Orak ignored her.

Down by the river, the slaves had already loaded the skull onto a boat where more of their comrades were busy covering it up. Meanwhile the bearers and the defenders took up position on the bank, ready to stop anyone who tried to interfere.

Some of the others had followed Vander and Teressa, and more were starting to appear – guests and guards who had managed to gather their wits and come after the fleeing assassin.

Vander, though, was first to reach them. 'Stop!' he roared. 'Murderer!'

Lady Ahamay was still in sight, standing on her boat. There was a strange smile on her face. 'In Itzcóatl's name, justice has been done,' she called out in griffish. She waved to her slaves. 'Kill them.'

The slaves on the bank charged.

'*No—*!' Teressa screamed, but too late. With people pressing up behind her and the slaves charging from the front, there was nowhere to run to.

She saw Vander fall, stabbed through by a sword. Ymazu, trying to defend her human, fell as well not long afterward, speared in the chest and throat.

Half mad with terror, not knowing what to do, Teressa did what may well have been the stupidest thing possible. She ran forward, straight at the slave guards charging towards her.

The first one aimed a blow at her with a dagger. She dodged sideways and ran on, ducking a second slave. Her feet suddenly sank into mud, and she realised that she had reached the boat. An idea suddenly came to her and, ignoring the chaos on the bank, she dived into the water. The boat was already pulling away, but she didn't care about that. All she wanted to do was escape.

She swam around behind the boat, keeping away from the oars thrusting at the bank, and made for the other side.

Behind her, Orak saw what she was doing. 'Teressa!' he screeched, and charged. Bowling his attackers over, he bounded to the bank and leapt at the boat. His outstretched forepaws cleared the side and hit the skull, cutting through the cloth to touch its shining surface.

The instant Orak's talons touched the skull, a great blast of force shot outward from it. Everyone there, human and griffin, toppled over like trees struck by a hurricane. Orak fell back with a scream, and landed in the water.

The force struck Teressa as well, thrusting her backward through the water. For a moment she went limp with shock, but fortunately that made her float to the surface.

Bewildered, she recovered herself and swam for the shore as quickly as she could.

As she reached the shallows, a hand grabbed her and hauled her out, dragging her free of the water. She had thought she was making for the opposite bank as she'd planned to, but the invisible blow from the skull had confused her, and she had swum back the way she had come, wanting nothing but to get out of the river before something else happened

Teressa clung to her rescuer. 'Thanks,' she spluttered.

The hand had not let her go, and as she tried to recover herself she felt its grip tighten and lift her up. She shook her head dazedly, not knowing what was going on, and found herself looking up into the face of the slave with the red hair.

His hate-filled brown eyes were on her, and as she began to struggle he raised a short sword with his free hand. 'Northerner scum,' he growled in his own language.

Teressa clutched at his thick, muscular arm. 'No!' she cried. 'Oh no! Help!'

The Southerner only snarled and pushed her away, giving himself room to stab her to death.

'No!' Teressa pleaded. 'No, please don't! Let me go!'

The man paused ever so briefly.

'Please don't kill me,' Teressa babbled. 'Please, I never hurt anyone, I—,'

The Southerner hesitated, sighed, and lowered the sword. 'Get out of here, you stupid bloody darkwoman,' he said, and shoved her away, sending her sprawling in the mud.

A moment later, someone grabbed him from behind. He turned and began to fight back, trying to defend himself as half a dozen Amorani guards closed in.

Teressa, keeping low, watched in silent horror as the full force of the Imperial guard finally arrived, and silently and brutally beat down the assassin's lackeys. Some died, others surrendered, or were fought into submission.

Teressa saw the one with the red hair go down, roaring defiance, his sword lost. But he was outnumbered, and his attackers finally knocked him down and took him prisoner with the other survivors.

'The bastard had it coming,' he snarled, as his wrists were shackled together behind his back.

A blow to the head silenced him, and he and the other prisoners were hauled away. The boat was long gone by now, with Lady Ahamay and her remaining slaves still on it. On the bank, the guests and others who had first gone after her began to recover themselves. Or some of them did, anyway. Others lay dead or dying where they had fallen.

Teressa looked around frantically for Orak, and saw him shivering on the bank nearby. She ran to him, and found him standing over the bodies of Vander and Ymazu.

Teressa sighed – a long, deep sigh of exhaustion and shock. 'Orak,' she rasped. 'Are ye all right?'

Orak said nothing. He seemed to be staring at the bodies that lay at his paws.

Teressa knelt, and lifted Vander's head. His face was flecked with blood and mud, and more blood had wet his tunic. She gently brushed the hair away from his forehead, and placed a hand on his chest. 'Lord Vander?' she said softly.

Vander did not reply, and she knew he was dead. Ymazu, beside him, was dead as well. Someone had put a spear clean through her throat.

'Who were they?' Teressa mumbled. 'Why…?'

'They came to steal the skull,' Orak said quietly. He didn't look up as he spoke.

'But why?' said Teressa. 'Why kill everyone, why…?'

'It is not just a skull,' said Orak. 'It is a powerful object. Very powerful.'

'Was that what knocked everyone over?' asked Teressa.

'Yes,' said Orak. 'When I touched it, its power…' He still hadn't looked up.

Teressa stared at him in confusion.

Silently, Orak raised his crippled foreleg.

It was healed.

Chapter Eleven

The Search for a Guardian

The Emperor was dead. Red knew that. Even if Ahamay's blow had missed the man's heart, she had poisoned the blade. She had told him so. She hadn't told him what was inside the carving, but now that he knew, he saw it all clearly at last.

She's an Erebian, he thought numbly as his captors dragged him away. *That's what all this was about. They killed Itzcóatl and took his skull, an' she didn't just want to take it back. She wanted revenge. Revenge on all of 'em.*

Now she had taken that revenge, and Red had been her lackey. The Emperor was dead, along with his entire family, and Ahamay had fled.

Red wondered briefly if she had always meant to abandon him like this, to leave him to take the fall for what she had done. But he found that he didn't even care any more. Because what he had helped her do wasn't just for the sake of her revenge – it was for his own as well. He had avenged the massacre at Withypool and the fall of the South, and with the Emperor and his family dead, his home country might finally have a chance.

Chaos would take hold of the Empire now. Amoran would be forced to withdraw its troops from Cymria, and with them gone...

Red knew that his time was up now. He knew it as his captors hurled him into a cell with the rest of Ahamay's surviving slaves. As a slave he had been almost worthless, but now he was worth less than nothing. They would kill him, most likely as painfully as possible. But that didn't matter, not any more. He had struck a blow for the South and its people, and would die knowing that no matter what happened, that blow could not be taken back.

He lay on his back on the floor of his cell, not even noticing the crazed smile that had spread over his face, not feeling the pain of the cuts on his arms and chest.

Nothing matters, he thought. *Nothing matters any more, not a damn thing.*

Fear would not come back to him until later, after things had calmed down and some Amorani official came and gave some orders to the guards that he couldn't understand. Not until after that, when he and the others were chained together and taken away.

He thought they were being taken to their deaths at last, and his heart beat fast, expecting that at any moment he would emerge into the daylight and find a scaffold waiting for him, or a chopping block.

But none of those things came. Instead he and the others were taken downward – down into the bowels of the palace, where the only light came from stone lamps, and several heavy wooden doors had to be unlocked to let them through.

The prisoners started to mutter uneasily among themselves.

Then, when the last door opened, the smell hit Red's nostrils: the heavy, sickly stench of rotting flesh.

He retched and stumbled briefly, and the first real stirrings of fear came back to him then. He realised where he must be going now. Not to a public execution, but to a torture chamber.

'Shit,' he muttered to himself. 'Oh shit.'

He started to struggle against his chains, along with several others who had caught the stench and probably realised where they were going. But they didn't stand a chance. Their guards quickly beat them back into line, and they were dragged on down the passageway and into another room – a long, low stone room with a cage along one wall, already filled with prisoners.

One by one, the new additions were unchained and thrown into the cage.

Red stumbled in and nearly fell, his nose now filled with that sickly rotting stench. The cage was crowded and dirty. The prisoners in it barely looked up at his arrival. They stood or sat, all hunched and gaunt, staring at nothing, many of them caked in filth.

Red managed to find a spot in a corner and pressed himself into it while his fellow prisoners came in after him, some of them still fighting back before they were shoved through and the door slammed and locked behind them.

There was already a small group of guards there to watch over the cage, and the ones who had brought them down walked out, leaving them to continue their duty.

Red stared dully at the men who stayed behind. He wondered if any of them felt any pity for their prisoners, but then… had he ever felt pity? He had never been a prison guard, but he had arrested people in the past and taken them to be locked up. Some of them would have been executed. Maybe even tortured.

Had he ever felt any guilt for that, he wondered? Any sympathy?

He didn't know. He couldn't remember. He didn't know if he even deserved sympathy any more.

He turned to look at the prisoner next to him – a miserable looking Maijani who shivered constantly where he stood.

'Why are we here?' Red asked gently. 'What're they gonna do with us?'

The Maijani said nothing. He didn't look as if he'd even heard what Red had said.

Red looked around the cage. 'What's going to happen to us?' he asked again, not sure who he was asking, or if he wanted to know the answer.

One of the Amorani prisoners stirred. 'When they take you, you will know,' he said in a dull, flat voice. 'Pray that you die first.'

Red said nothing, but that was when the true fear came.

Later on, while some of the other prisoners slept, he fixed his gaze on the lamp flame nearby and offered up a final prayer – but not to his own god.

'Night God,' he muttered. 'You ain't my god, I know. But you're the god of death. So I'm prayin' to you now.' He closed his eyes. 'Kill me. Kill me now, so it can be over. Kill me…'

*

Kraego and Kullervo had been in the cages underneath the Hall of Suns for a long time.

When they and the other griffins captured in Cymria had come to Amoran, they had been brought straight to Xanthium, and then to the prison they had occupied ever since. None of them had seen the sun in that time, and by now none of them expected to survive, let alone escape.

They occupied a huge cage that filled half of the chamber they were in, all of them chained to the floor by collars around their necks, to stop them from turning on each other. Not that any of them had the strength by now. Their water was drugged to stop them from using their magic, and the drug also served to keep them sleepy and weak.

At first, none of them could guess why they were there – but it didn't take long for them to find out. All they had to do was wait until they were fed, and then the truth began to dawn on them all.

They knew that there were other chambers down in this place. Every other day, a griffin would be taken out of the cage and dragged away. None of them ever returned. There were humans being kept down here as well – unseen at first, but sometimes the griffins would hear their screams.

When food came, all of them soon realised why.

Griffins would be taken away, and returned dead or dying, with pieces of their bodies hacked off or organs removed. They were thrown into the cages to serve as food for their fellow captives who, with nothing else to sustain them, tore the remains to pieces.

But there was worse.

The human prisoners were dying as well, and their bodies were also thrown into the cages as fodder. And they weren't just dead, but mutilated, sometimes grotesquely so.

It was Kullervo who first guessed at the truth. The other griffins were too crazed by hunger and captivity to care much; they snatched the corpses thrown to them and tore them apart in a frenzy without bothering to inspect them.

Kullervo refused to touch any of it, and when the first human corpse came within his reach he gently pulled it towards himself and turned it over.

Even in griffin form, he felt the horror freeze in his throat.

The man was an Amorani, and it was obvious what had killed him. Someone had cut him open and then sewn the hole shut again, as if he were a piece of clothing to be altered. The shock of that mutilation had obviously been too much for the man; the wound hadn't even begun to heal before it killed him.

Kullervo didn't have long to look. The griffin beside him snatched the body away and ripped it open, gulping down the organs inside.

Kullervo could only stare. 'What have they done?' he rasped. 'What are they doing?'

Kraego had been chained beside him. 'I do not know,' he said, sounding as if he didn't care either. 'They must be torturing these humans for some crime.'

'But why?' said Kullervo. 'What crime? And why us? Amoranis

worship griffins.'

Kraego snorted. 'It is food. Eat, or die. When I am unchained, I will teach them to fear me.'

Kullervo gagged at the very thought. 'No,' he said. 'No, I won't. I can't. Not people. Not other griffins.'

'Then you will die,' said Kraego.

'I would rather die,' said Kullervo.

'Then you are a fool,' said Kraego. 'There is nothing more important than to live.'

But Kullervo didn't believe him, and as the weeks dragged by, he refused to eat the corpses offered to him.

With nothing else to eat, the flesh slowly wasted away from him until his ribs showed. Much longer and he would die. But by the time he finally understood just what was happening here, he started wishing for it.

More human corpses arrived, day after day, all of them cut open and sewn back together. Then others came, and these – these had been altered on the outside. Kullervo saw the first of them for himself, and that was when the truth dawned.

Someone had hacked off a griffin's wings, and sewn them onto the man's back. The wounds had festered and the wings had rotted, and the man was barely alive.

Kullervo watched as the man was devoured by his fellow prisoners.

'It's me,' he said, barely audibly. 'They're trying to… they're trying to create me.'

Kraego lay beside him. His fur was bedraggled by now, and his feathers dull. He stared blankly at Kullervo. 'What is it?'

'They're trying to create the Winged Man,' said Kullervo. 'A man like me; both human and griffin. They want…'

He trailed off there, but he could see it all now – see it with horrible clarity. When he himself had gone to Maijan as his human self, with his griffinish wings in plain sight, the Amoranis who saw him wanted to worship him. They had believed he was the legendary Winged Man – a messenger from the sun god.

He wasn't, of course. He had turned his back on both gods long ago. But the Amoranis still believed, and now they were trying to recreate what they had lost. Out of desperation, perhaps, or insanity.

'They want their guardian back,' Kullervo said, mostly to himself.

And now he could see the depths they were willing to sink to. That was when he truly wanted to die.

But as time dragged by and he lay there, suffering in agonies of hunger and listening to the screams of butchered men, he knew what he had to do.

'I have to make the change,' he said aloud. 'I have to change back into a human. Then I could be… I could be their guardian. But…'

But his magic gland had been numbed by the drug, and if he changed now, in his weakened state, it would kill him.

He still refused to resort to cannibalism, but now he stopped taking the water as well. If he waited long enough, the drug might wear off. Maybe.

*

Kraego watched Kullervo as the next few days dragged by, and felt contempt for him. But mixed in with that very normal griffish emotion was some admiration as well.

At first, when the shapeshifter refused to eat the dead humans and griffins offered to him, Kraego thought it was simple stupidity. No true griffin would ever choose to die rather than live, no matter what the cost. If he must eat humans or fellow griffins, so be it.

But over time, he began to feel disgusted with himself. He ate the corpses offered to him because he had to, but he didn't take any pride in it. He was a griffin, a predator, and should be hunting for himself – not lying here in chains, eating this foul food thrown to him by human captors. When he thought that, he found himself admiring Kullervo just a little, who had been offered the chance to live in the same way Kraego had, but had the pride to refuse. Their captors wanted to force him into this, but he wouldn't bow to them.

When Kullervo stopped drinking the water, Kraego finally saw what had to be done and he too stopped taking his water. Maybe, he realised, he could wait until the drug wore off and use his power to escape. Unlike Kullervo, though; he didn't go thirsty – the blood of the bodies he ate was enough to stop him declining too quickly. In fact Kraego, as the largest griffin in the cages, was strong enough to seize plenty of food for himself and had kept himself in better condition than most, despite the lack of exercise.

'You are right,' he said softly to Kullervo one day. 'You and I must regain our magic. Then we shall escape.'

And then, he added to himself… and then, when he was free, he would make these humans pay. Until he had come to this place he had never known what captivity was truly like. He had never felt such humiliation as he did now, and that humiliation only fed his hatred.

I am the dark griffin, he thought obsessively, over and over again as the time dragged out unbearably. *I will not die here. I will not be kept prisoner. I will escape this place. I will break free. And then I will kill them all.*

Leaving the water untouched worked; he could feel it. Little by little, the numbness in the magic gland which sat in his throat began to fade. Little by little, the faint burn of magic returned. He could feel it. Soon, he thought. Soon it would be strong enough to use.

Beside him, Kullervo lay on his belly. Perhaps his own magic was starting to come back to him, but by now it was already too late. Starvation and thirst had all but killed him. He barely had the strength to raise his head any more.

'Do not be afraid,' Kraego told him one night. 'I will find a way to escape from here. I will kill the ones who have done this to you.'

Kullervo's voice was a low moan. 'No,' he said. 'No killing, no…'

Kraego didn't listen. *One more day, he thought. One more meal, and one more day without that drugged water. Then I will be ready. Then I will be strong enough.*

The next day came, and the next meal arrived in their part of the cage. It was a human body, and Kraego snatched it away from his fellows before they could touch it. He hissed to himself in satisfaction as he pulled it closer. It was a good, big one with plenty of meat on it. It would make a solid meal.

He pinned the corpse down with one huge forepaw, and opened his beak to bite into it. But then, as it turned over under his weight, he froze.

The man under his paw was a Cymrian, a Southerner. His red hair had been shaved off, but it had begun to regrow down here. That, and the scent of him, was enough to make Kraego hesitate.

'Red,' he said softly.

Beside him, Kullervo slowly opened his eyes. He peered at the body. 'Red?' he rasped.

Red lay at their paws, scarcely breathing. He was naked and vulnerable, like a baby. The collar was gone, and his throat was hideously swollen, the rough stitching along the front of it barely holding the wound closed. It oozed black, stinking pus.

'Red,' Kraego said again, blankly.

Kullervo managed to drag himself upright, and he leaned forward as far as he could, reaching his front paws out to touch Red's burning hot chest. 'Red,' he said in a low, dull voice. 'Red. No. Oh no…'

Neither griffin wanted to eat him. Even Kraego balked at the idea. They held onto him instead, protecting him from the other griffins who tried to snatch him. Kullervo managed to splash some water out of the trough and onto his face to try and cool him down. But there was nothing either of them could do for him.

They sat there together for a long time, watching in silence as Red's breathing grew more and more laboured. Ugly, swollen veins had spread out from the infected wound on his throat and put poison into his blood, and fever had consumed him.

Both griffins kept watch over him, neither one speaking at all, keeping up a vigil for what they both knew would happen. Eventually, as the night drew on, they heard Red give one last feeble gasp, and then stop breathing.

'Goodbye,' Kullervo said softly. 'You're away from this cruel world at last, Red.'

Kearney Redguard did not move, and little by little they both saw the colour drain out of his skin and leave it white and ghastly, while his limbs began to stiffen. He was dead, and his sufferings were over.

In that moment, a sound came from the void – a sound that no-one heard. Somewhere beyond the mortal world, the dark spirit that had once been Arenadd Taranisäii chuckled softly as he dragged Red's soul away into the void.

Chapter Twelve

The Unthinkable

After a while, as they looked down at Red's body, Kraego began to speak.

'I am not just the Mighty Skandar's son,' he said. 'I am his successor. I have inherited his power.'

Kullervo said nothing. He lay on his belly in despair, and listened while the black griffin spoke on.

'I have known that the dark power was mine for many years,' said Kraego. 'I can use the shadows just as my father could. I have never used it, but if I unleashed the magic in my throat I am certain that it would kill everything it touched. When I was young, all I wanted to do was defeat my father and have his territory for myself. But that chance was taken from me, and I swore that one day I would return and kill Shar, who took that chance away. But before that time came, I had a dream.'

Kullervo stared at him, still saying nothing, though he had a feeling he knew what was coming.

'I am a griffin, and do not believe in human gods,' said Kraego. 'But a god came to me. The Night God, which humans from the North worship. She told me that I had the same power which she gave to my father and which he had passed on to me. She had a command to give me. She told me that there was a human I must find – a Northern human called Morgan Taranisäii. She told me that I must kill him, and when he was dead I must give him the power. I must create the next Shadow That Walks, and together we would crush the sun-worshippers and give her people power over all of Cymria.' He stood up. 'Her offers were tempting. Offers of power. But I did not do as she commanded. I am a griffin. I am the dark griffin, I am the mightiest of all my kind, and I am no-one's lackey. My will is my own, and I shall not serve this creature who calls herself a god.'

'Good,' Kullervo whispered. 'Don't listen to her, Kraego. She's a liar who only wants power.'

'I serve no-one,' Kraego repeated. His voice had steadily grown stronger, but flatter as well, before it rose higher and became a scream. 'I serve no-one! I am a griffin, and I shall be free! And for this outrage, I shall have revenge!'

As he screamed, he arched his neck and began to retch, as if he were about to vomit. But he didn't. His throat pulsated, faster and faster, harder and harder, and then… then he went rigid.

Kullervo stumbled upright. 'No!' he cried. 'Kraego, no! No!'

But Kraego would not be stopped. He stood there for a moment, absolutely still, beak pointing downward… and then he screamed.

The scream came not from his throat, but somewhere deep inside his huge body, and it was not a griffin's voice. It wasn't loud, but it was powerful – so powerful that every griffin there faltered and pulled away from him, straining against their chains in sudden desperation to escape from a sound and a sight that put terror into their hearts.

Because with the scream came the light.

Black light. A blackness that went beyond mere darkness, and became a hole that went through the world, a freezing, life-sucking void. The light came from Kraego's beak, pouring out of him and into Red's dead body, more and more of it until even the massive Kraego began to shake.

Then, without warning, the black griffin collapsed.

'No,' Kullervo said again, but it was already too late. All his emotions welled up inside him – human emotions, and unable to control himself any longer, he fell too and began to thrash and scream as his own magic took hold of his body and twisted it. Bones cracked, muscle stretched, and fur and feathers fell away in handfuls. He was changing.

Everyone there could hear that, and they had heard the scream of Kraego's magic. But no-one heard the other scream.

But Red heard it. From some place where there was nothing but absolute blackness and freezing cold, he heard it. He heard the voice of a woman, screaming a single word.

NO!

It was a word that contained more absolute rage than he could ever have imagined. But, hidden somewhere behind it, he heard a man – a man laughing in horrible triumph.

For just a moment he thought he saw him. Saw a face that he had seen once before and remembered all too well. A thin, Northern face with a pointed chin beard, the eyes black and glittering.

'Go back, Kearney Redguard,' the face said, and laughed again. 'Go back!'

Then he vanished, and Red fell into the void.

*

Red woke up in pain. He felt himself twitch all over – his whole body jerked sharply and then went limp, and he lay very still for a moment, before his mouth opened of its own accord and he started to breathe.

He sat up with sudden strength, frantically gasping. His mind seemed to have gone blank. He coughed – his throat felt wrong. Not painful really, but uncomfortable. He groaned to himself, and rubbed his face.

'Red,' a voice said from nearby.

Red turned vaguely, and saw Kraego. He was chained to the floor by his neck, and he looked thin and unhealthy. But he was alive; he was there, and Red smiled at the sight of him.

'Kraego,' he said, and stopped. His voice… there was something wrong with his voice. It didn't sound right.

Kraego's blue eyes were fixed on his face. 'Are you strong?' he asked.

Red shook his head dazedly, and flexed his arms. 'I reckon so,' he said. Once again, his voice didn't sound right. It came out all rough-sounding. But it was clear enough, at least. He could still talk.

'Good,' Kraego tugged at his chain. 'It is time, Red.'

'Time for what?' asked Red, still confused.

'Time for us to be free,' said Kraego. 'Quickly, take off this chain. Open the cage. We must leave this vile place.'

'All right.' Red stood up and patted himself down. Everything still seemed to be there. He was fine.

He went over to Kraego and removed the pin that held his collar shut. It fell away, and Kraego shook himself vigorously. 'At last!'

Red scratched him under the beak. 'Kraego, what happened?' he said.

'You are dead,' Kraego said bluntly.

In that moment, everything came back. All of it.

Red froze, and then staggered backward as the memory of everything that had happened slammed through his brain.

'Oh shit,' he said. 'Oh shit. Shit, dammit, oh gods, what…?' he pawed at his throat, and felt the blood drain out of his face. 'Oh gods, they cut me open, they… and then there was all this pain, and… oh gods. No!'

He was dead. He knew he was dead. He remembered dying.

'Oh gods,' he said again. 'Oh gods. I remember… I saw him. I saw that face. He tried to take me away when the Hangman got me. He pulled me away, and it was so cold, and I heard… oh gods. Oh gods, I'm dead!' Frantically, he put a hand to his throat and felt for a pulse.

There was nothing. His heart wasn't beating.

'Red.' Kraego came forward and touched him with his beak. 'Red, listen.'

Red stood still, and listened.

'You died,' Kraego told him. 'You died, and your body was given to me to eat. But I did not eat you. I have brought you back.' He hissed. 'The Night God wanted me to give my power to a Northerner, but I have not. I chose you, Kearney Redguard. Now, you are the Shadow That Walks. You are my partner. And together, you and I shall have revenge on the scum who have done this to us.'

Red didn't hear him. He stood there paralysed, as hideous visions filled his mind.

He remembered the cage where he had sat for days, half-starved and gradually succumbing to fear and despair, while those around him were dragged away, day by day, never to be seen again. He remembered the day when he had been chosen.

The bloodstained stone table where they had tied him down, a young griffin trussed beside him, ready for whatever happened next. They had drugged him, but it hadn't been enough to make him sleep. He had been aware enough to feel it as they slit his throat open from his chin to his collarbone. He had seen through a haze of agony and terror as they tore something out of the griffin's own throat, and hastily thrust it into his own before stitching the wound closed over it.

Pain and blood loss had all but killed him – but not quite. He only vaguely remembered those last days while he lay in a stupour, feeling the burning and the itch as the wound grew infected.

They'd tried to keep him alive – he remembered that. They'd given him water and tried to feed him, and given him medicines.

Others had lain beside him, suffering too, and their captors tried to care for them. But they died, sometimes as soon as they arrived, and when Red's fever finally rose high enough he sank into unconsciousness – and never woke up.

He had felt, and seen, the icy void that waited beyond life. The void of death. He had heard his heartbeat grow steadily fainter and weaker, until it stopped altogether. He remembered the face. That awful, cold face, reaching out to drag him away into nothingness forever.

I'm dead, he thought. He didn't need Kraego to tell him that – he hadn't even really needed to feel for a pulse. He knew he was dead. He remembered dying so clearly.

'You died in agony,' Kraego interrupted sharply, as if reading his thoughts. 'You have suffered here, and now you have been killed. I have brought you back.'

Red couldn't think. 'I'm the Shadow That Walks,' he mumbled. 'You made me… like him.'

'Yes,' said Kraego.

'But that's not…' Red coughed. It felt as if there was something stuck in his throat. 'I can't be… I ain't a Northerner, an' the Night God…'

'You were not chosen by the Night God,' said Kraego. 'The choice was mine and I have made it. I chose you.' He hissed horribly. 'The world has never known a thing such as this. The power of the dark griffin has gone to a Southerner. It has been given to you, and you may do with it as you please. Now come, Red. There is no more time. We must escape this cage.'

Fear and confusion had frozen Red's mind so badly by this point, that it was almost a relief to be told what to do. 'Right,' he mumbled. 'Yeah.'

He could see the door directly in front of Kraego, and now he reached an arm through the bars and started to fumble with the latch. It was awkward, but he managed it, and the door swung open.

Kraego surged forward, shoving Red aside. Standing in the open, he stretched his wings wide and gave them a vigorous shake. 'At last!' He started to snarl. 'Come, Red. Come!'

But Red hadn't moved. He stopped and looked back at the cage and the bedraggled griffins inside it. 'No,' he said. 'Wait. We gotta help them too.'

Kraego growled at him. 'Be quick.' Red had already gone back into the cage. The griffin who had been standing beside Kraego hissed warningly at him, but he barely paid attention. What did it matter if he got bitten? He was already dead, wasn't he?

'It's all right,' he said, speaking griffish in his new, growling voice. 'I'm gonna set you free.'

The griffin only snarled and tried to lash out at him.

Red ignored the danger. He ducked in under the beast's chest, and before it could get him with its beak he snatched it by the collar and pulled out the pin that held it shut.

Freed, the griffin made a break for the way out, shoving him onto his back in the process. Red curled up to protect himself, but luckily the griffin's claws missed him.

The griffin ignored Kraego as well. Bent on making its escape as fast as possible, it pushed past him and ran away out of the room.

'Be quick,' Kraego urged again. 'Our enemies will see that one and come to see what is happening.'

Red nodded briefly, and he would have gone to free the rest of them – but then he saw Kullervo.

The shapeshifter lay on the bottom of the cage not far away, the collar he had worn still sitting loosely around his neck. He was human again, naked and wasted almost to nothing, with his wings lying uselessly over his back.

Red ran to him. 'Kullervo!'

Kullervo stirred when Red turned him over, and clutched weakly at the Southerner's arm. 'Red,' he whispered.

Red held onto him. 'Kullervo. What happened…?'

Kullervo coughed. 'Kept here with the others. Changed back now. For the last time. Red, the others. Help them, Red. Quickly, before…'

'I will,' Red promised, but first he gently pulled Kullervo out of the cage and laid him down close to Kraego. 'Keep him warm,' he told the giant griffin. 'I gotta get the others out.'

He went back into the cage, and did just that. The griffins quickly realised what he was doing, and they didn't try to attack him. Each one stood still and waited eagerly while he unfastened their collars, and the moment they were free, they fled from the cage. Red heard some thumping and a brief scream from outside, and guessed that some of the guards had tried to stop them and died for their trouble.

Finally, when the last of them had gone, he went back to Kraego's side. The giant griffin had stayed by Kullervo, keeping him safe.

Red crouched again, and lifted his old friend's head in his hands. 'Kullervo?'

Kullervo barely moved. His skin had gone cold.

Red held him. 'Kraego, what're we gonna do?' he asked. 'We can't just leave him.'

Kraego lay down to see the pair of them more easily. 'There is nothing either of us can do for him,' he said, with surprising gentleness. 'And we cannot stay here.'

But it was already too late. Man and griffin looked up sharply as the sound of crashings and breakings came from somewhere outside the prison, mingled with the tearing of talons.

Kraego stood up. 'They have broken the doors down. Red, come. Now, before…'

Red shook his head. 'I can't leave him, Kraego.'

Kraego looked about to grab him, but in that moment the sound of running feet came from outside, and a group of people burst in. Most of them were guards, and they advanced on Kraego, who started to hiss and raise his beak ready to attack.

'No,' Kullervo rasped from the floor. 'No, don't.'

The guards saw him, and froze. One of them shouted something in Amorani.

'I am the Winged Man,' Kullervo said, speaking griffish. 'Let them go. There's no need to fight.'

Seeing the guards starting to lower their weapons, Kraego relaxed slightly.

For a moment, nobody moved – but then someone called out from among the group of intruders.

'The black griffin!'

Red looked up, and saw a woman push her way through to the front. A woman he recognised. It was the Northerner he had almost killed in the fight by the river. She wore a silver robe with a light cloak over the top, and her face was full of wonder as she stepped closer to Kraego. She spoke again, her voice awestruck.

'I found ye,' she said, using griffish. 'Ye are the black griffin!'

'I am,' said Kraego. 'Who are you, Northerner?'

The woman bowed reverently to him. 'My name's Teressa. I'm

from Malvern. I was sent to find ye.' Her black eyes shone. 'Ye are far more magnificent than I ever imagined.'

'Who sent you to find me?' Kraego demanded.

'The great King Arenadd,' said Teressa, with complete sincerity. 'He sent me to find ye, and a child, and his son.'

Red frowned at her; what in the gods' names was the woman blathering about?

But, cradled in his arms, Kullervo spoke up. 'Teressa…?'

The woman came forward, utterly ignoring everyone else. 'Ye have wings,' she said in wonder. 'Then ye must be…'

'I am Arenadd's son,' Kullervo whispered.

Teressa crouched close by, and reached down to touch Kullervo's face. 'I found ye,' she said. 'At last.'

'My father sent you?' said Kullervo.

'He did,' said Teressa. 'He came to me in a dream. I found Flell, too. She told me what ye looked like.'

'Why'd Arenadd want you to find him?' Red asked cynically.

'I think I can guess,' Kullervo whispered.

'Why?' Teressa leaned in close. 'Tell me why. Please! All I want to do is serve him.'

'What happened to Flell?' Kullervo asked.

'She's safe,' said Teressa. 'I brought her here with me. The Imperial family's all dead now, except for one of the Emperor's grandsons. He got bitten though, he won't live long. Flell's going to rule the Empire.'

There were tears on Kullervo's face. 'Wish I could help her. But… but…' he twitched and gasped in pain.

'What is it?' Teressa reached out, helping Red support him. 'Kullervo, please. Yer father sent me to find ye for a reason. What is it? Just tell me.'

'Come here,' said Kullervo.

Teressa leaned in close, and as Red watched, the man-griffin whispered something in her ear.

'That's it?' she asked afterwards.

Kullervo nodded weakly.

Now the Amoranis had begun to approach as well. The guards dropped their weapons, and all of them came towards Kullervo, pale with amazement, moving with absolute reverence. Kraego hissed at them, but they didn't seem to notice him. All their attention was on

Kullervo.

Kullervo saw them, and raised his head. 'I am the Winged Man,' he said. 'I am what you wanted. You did this because you were desperate. You wanted to be guided. Well then, listen. I don't know much, but I do know this.' He coughed. 'The gods give us hate, not love. Don't believe their lies. Set the slaves free. All of them. Nobody should live in a cage. That's all I know.'

He went silent and fell back, exhausted by the effort.

Red held him close. 'Kullervo,' he rasped. 'Please, don't…'

Kullervo looked up at him through eyes that had begun to go dim. 'Hate isn't the answer, Red,' he said, so quietly he was almost inaudible. 'I know it. Look at me. Look me in the eyes.'

Red did. 'Kullervo…'

Kullervo smiled at him. 'I'm looking into the eyes of my father,' he murmured, and went still. His own eyes closed.

Red looked up at the Amoranis. 'Do somethin'!' he said sharply, using griffish so they would understand. 'Help him!'

They came, guards and the nobles who had run in with them. They took Kullervo from him and began to carry him out of the room as well as they could – but it was too late for them or anyone else to do anything. Even as his hold on the shapeshifter fell away, Red felt something change in him. Some sense that he had never felt before which told him all he needed to know.

Kullervo was dead.

*

Kullervo heard Red's last call to him as they were pulled apart, but the Southerner's voice sounded muffled and far away. A much louder sound filled his ears. He could hear his own heart, pattering frantically for a moment before it slowed. For a long instant it went silent, and vision faded away from his eyes. He could feel his body growing cold.

His heart beat again.

Once.

A long pause.

It beat again, weaker this time.

Then it went silent, and did not beat again.

Kullervo felt himself gasp in one last breath, and then sigh it out again. The coldness in him grew, and his senses shut down.

He could still feel the hands, though – the hands carrying him, lifting him, taking him away. And they didn't fade away. They stayed… they changed.

He could feel them – hands holding him by the shoulders, hands that were as strong as steel and cold as ice. Hands that could not be escaped. Hands that pulled him away from the world, and into the cold blackness of the void.

Kullervo didn't try and fight back. He surrendered himself to those hands, and in that moment, he died.

The void took him into itself, and it was cold and dark and empty, and pitiless.

The hands let him go, and he found himself standing in absolute nothingness, all alone.

Fear filled him – but only for a moment.

'No,' he said, and was surprised to find that he could hear himself. 'No, I can't be…'

'…can't be dead?' a voice asked from behind him.

'No.' Kullervo turned around slowly. 'I can't be alone. Because this is where you live… Father.'

Arenadd Taranisäii heaved a sigh. 'This isn't living, son. Even being the Shadow That Walks was closer to living than this.'

Kullervo stared at him for a long moment. The spirit of his father didn't look ghostly, not here – here he looked like any other man. A Northerner, of course, tall and gaunt. He wore a long black robe, not much different to the one his successor Caedmon wore, and had a pointed chin-beard of the same style. But his long hair was curly, and where Caedmon had the blue, spiralling tattoos of manhood on his face, Arenadd had a scar under his left eye that looked like a tear-track.

'Father,' Kullervo said softly. '…Dad?'

Arenadd did not smile. 'I don't think I could manage "dad". "Father" will have to do. Welcome to the void, Kullervo.'

Kullervo looked around. 'Where's the Night God? She's here too, isn't she?'

'She is, but you won't see her,' said Arenadd. 'You rejected her, remember? You spat on her altar and said you'd rather die than worship her.'

'I did, and I don't regret it,' said Kullervo. 'I rejected Gryphus too.'

'So you did,' said Arenadd. He grinned wolfishly. 'There aren't many people with the balls to be godless.'

'That's why I'm not in the afterlife,' said Kullervo. 'I can't go there.'

'No, you can't.' Arenadd shook his head. 'I'm sorry, but there's nothing I can do for you. I did my best to help you before, but I'm a prisoner here now.'

'It's all right,' said Kullervo. 'I'm just so happy to see you.'

'You'd be the first,' said Arenadd. 'I was the last thing a lot of people saw before they came here. Now I'm the first thing they see afterwards. None of them are very happy about it. Some of them try to kill me on sight. Waste of time, of course.'

Kullervo smiled. 'Well, I'm happy to see you. I wanted to see you one last time before I went.'

Arenadd smiled back. Then, astonishingly, he lowered his head and bowed elegantly. 'Well done, Kullervo. I'm proud of you. You suffered so much in your life, but you proved you were the better man than most of the so-called real humans you met.'

Kullervo looked at him in astonishment. 'Do you really mean that?'

'I do,' Arenadd straightened up. 'You tried to change the world and make it a better place once. I know. I watched.'

'I did,' said Kullervo. 'But I couldn't. It was too much for me.'

'Maybe,' said Arenadd. 'But you changed people, and that's what will make the difference.' He smiled a secret little smile. 'You couldn't change the world, but he can. If he remembers what you taught him. And she'll help him.'

'You know what I told her?' asked Kullervo.

'Yes. And thank you. You were right, and she won't forget.'

'Well then…' Kullervo shivered. He could feel the last remnant of himself starting to fade away. A nothingness began to spread through the memory of his body. 'I can't stay… promise me, Father. Promise you'll watch over him, and her, and all of them.'

'I will,' said Arenadd. 'I already have been.'

'And afterwards?' said Kullervo. 'If she does help you, after that…'

'I'll do what has to be done,' said Arenadd. 'Just as I always have, and no matter what the cost.'

Kullervo's voice had begun to fade as well. 'And promise me one other thing,' he whispered.

Arenadd took a step closer to him. 'Anything.'

Kullervo reached out and took his father in his arms. 'Don't give up on yourself,' he said. 'You can be whatever you want to be. Promise me, Father, promise…'

Arenadd held him in return, and his embrace was icy cold. 'I do, Kullervo. I will. I'll try, I—,'

But Kullervo had already vanished into the blackness.

Gone forever.

*

Red looked at the Northerner, Teressa, who had stayed beside him in apparent shock.

'What did Kullervo tell yer?' he asked softly.

She looked absently at him. 'I don't really know. Who are ye?'

'I…' Red hesitated, and bowed his head. 'Nobody.'

Teressa looked back at him through narrowed eyes. She recognised him, of course – more or less, anyway. But now he had changed. His red hair had started to grow back, and he'd grown the beginnings of a beard as well. His collar had been taken off, and she could see a great, deep scar underneath. There was an odd little bulge there, too –just above his collarbone. But more importantly…

His tanned Southern skin had gone deathly pale and sickly looking, and his eyes looked wrong, though it took her a moment to work out why.

They had turned black. Not black like her own, but black like… black like a deep abyss. A black without any brightness to it. They weren't the eyes of a Northerner, but the eyes of a dead man.

'Who are ye?' she asked again, softly.

'Red,' he muttered. His voice sounded rough and damaged.

But Teressa had already guessed who he must be – and what as well. She looked at him, then at the black griffin that towered over them both.

'Ye are the Shadow That Walks,' she breathed. 'Ye are Arenadd reborn.'

He glared at her, but she didn't care. She threw herself down at his feet.

'Master,' she said.

Red stood up. 'I'm nobody's master,' he said. 'Sod off,

Northerner.'

'Wait!' Teressa called. She took off her cloak and offered it to him. 'Take this, Master.'

Red took it and put it on, covering his nakedness. 'Thanks,' he said shortly, and walked off.

Kraego glanced back at her. 'You are a fool,' he said, and went after his human.

Teressa stared after them both, unable to move. But only for a moment. She pulled herself to her feet, and ran after them.

Chapter Thirteen

The Follower and the Followed

Red left the chamber without looking back, though he knew Kraego was following him. He heard the Northerner call after him, but he ignored her. He didn't care about her. He didn't care about anything, not now. He didn't care that he was mostly naked, or that he might be recaptured. He was dead. Why should anything matter to him any more?

He went out into the corridor and followed it, passing the entrance to the room where the butchery of man and griffin happened, and went on back to the prison where the surviving captives were still hunched in their cage. The guards who had kept watch over them were gone – he saw their bodies lying in the corridor outside.

The prisoners looked up at him with puzzled expressions. Red ignored them, and went straight to the cage door. It was locked, but he grabbed it and gave it a brutal wrench.

The lock and the hinges broke with a loud crack of metal, and the entire door came away in his hands. He threw it down, and gestured brusquely at the prisoners.

'Go on,' he said. 'You're free.'

With that, he turned and left without waiting to see what they would do.

Kraego was waiting, and the giant griffin fell in beside him as he walked up and away through the broken doors to the palace above.

'Red,' he said. 'Where are you going?'

'Dunno,' Red rasped. 'But I ain't staying here.'

'Yes. We must leave this place as quickly as we can,' said Kraego. 'We must go—,'

'There's only one place I want to go now,' Red interrupted. He shivered, clutching at the cloak, and fought down the terrible sadness that had begun to rise inside him. 'I want to go home, Kraego. I never want to see this bloody place ever again.'

'Home,' Kraego repeated softly. 'Yes. It is time.'

The idea did something to bring Red out of his horrified stupor, and he looked down at himself. 'But first I'm gonna go find some pants,' he added.

He strode off through the palace, paying no attention at all to the guards and other people who got in his way. They backed off when they saw Kraego, and none of them dared to say anything.

Red searched through a few rooms until he found one that looked like a bedroom. He rummaged through the clothes someone had left folded on a low cupboard, until he found some light Amorani leggings. They were too small, but he pulled them on anyway, along with a tunic.

Outside, as he left, he spotted a slave guard and made straight for him.

'Gimme yer sword,' he said harshly.

The man shook his head – maybe to say no, or maybe just to say he didn't understand.

Red knocked him down with a punch to the jaw, and snatched the curved sword out of his belt. He took the man's spear as well, and went on his way.

At this point, his pursuer finally caught up with him. He heard her coming, and turned to see the Northern woman in the silver robe come running up.

Kraego hissed warningly at her, but she didn't seem to notice. There was a look of complete obsession on her face, and she called out to Red in her softly accented voice.

'Master!' she said again. 'Shadow That Walks. Let me come with ye. I am yer servant.'

'I ain't the Shadow That Walks,' Red said stubbornly. 'Bug off.'

'Ye are,' said the woman. She bowed. 'Master, I came all this way for ye. Now I know why I was sent. It was to find ye, and serve ye.'

'I'm a Southerner,' said Red.

'But ye are the Shadow That Walks,' said the woman. 'Ye are chosen by the Night God.'

'No I ain't,' said Red. 'I was chosen by Kraego.'

'Well then, whatever ye do is the Night God's will,' said the woman. 'Please, let me go with ye. I'll do whatever ye say, I swear.'

Red scowled and shook his head, and kept walking.

The woman followed silently, perhaps hoping he'd given some kind of consent.

'Do yer even know what I'm gonna do?' Red asked eventually.

'It doesn't matter,' said the woman. 'Whatever ye do, I must help ye do it.'

'I'm gonna go home,' said Red. 'I'm gonna go back to Cymria. Back to the South. An' then, I'm gonna find King Caedmon an' I'm gonna kill him. An' I'll kill anyone who tries t'get in my way.' Saying it out loud gave him an unexpected, savage pleasure. 'I'm gonna drive the likes of you out of my country,' he added. 'Kraego gave me the power, an' I'm gonna use it to do what I want, not what any god says. Now what do you say, blackrobe?' He glanced at the woman. 'Or maybe I oughta call you *silver*robe.'

The woman looked shocked. 'But ye are the Shadow That Walks.'

'Yeah, that's right,' said Red. 'An' that's what I'm gonna do.'

'Well then…' the woman looked even paler than before, but determined. 'Well then, if that's what ye are going to do, then I have to follow ye.'

Red looked her with slight shock. 'You'd help me do that?'

'Aye, I will,' said the woman.

'They're yer own people,' said Red.

'Doesn't matter,' said the woman. 'I don't know if that's what the Night God wants, but it's what Arenadd wants, and that's enough for me. He sent me to ye.'

Red frowned in puzzlement. 'What's your name again? Tressa?'

'Teressa,' she corrected. 'I worship Arenadd, and he told me…'

'I heard,' said Red.

'Can I come with ye, then?' asked Teressa.

Red shrugged. 'Fine, whatever.'

'I do not see why—,' Kraego began, but then he stopped and tensed. 'Stay away from me!' he warned, turning to confront something that had appeared to his left.

It was a griffin – male and of a decent size, though nowhere near as big as Kraego. His feathers were bluish grey, and his eyes were pale purple.

He didn't rise to meet Kraego's challenge, but instead bowed his head to the other griffin. 'You are the black griffin.'

'I am,' said Kraego.

The grey griffin looked past him to Teressa. 'We have found him,' he said.

'We have,' said Teressa. 'And the new Shadow That Walks as

well.'

'Then we both know what we must do,' said the griffin. He looked back at Kraego, and bent his forelegs in a kind of bow. 'Mighty black griffin, I have come to this land with my human to find you. Now I offer you my service.'

Kraego looked blank. 'You wish to follow me?'

'I do,' said the griffin. 'My name is Orak, and I am from Malvern. My human and I will follow you from this day, and do as you command.'

Red looked at Teressa. 'You're a griffiner?'

'I am,' said Teressa. She looked a little nervous, and then she knelt and bowed her head to him. 'I'm yer servant, Shadow That Walks. In the Night God's name, I swear to follow ye until I'm dead.'

'Get up,' Red said awkwardly. 'C'mon, stop that. This is no time for this kinda nonsense – we gotta get out of here.'

'It's all right,' said Teressa. 'Ye heard what I said to Kullervo. I brought Flell here, and soon she'll be Empress. She hasn't been crowned, but she's acting Empress at the moment. And she's my friend. She won't touch ye if I ask her.'

'Rise, Orak,' said Kraego. 'I accept your offer to serve me. Does your human have a plan?'

'I do,' said Teressa. She stood up as well. 'We don't have to run away. Let's go to Flell instead and ask for her help. She can give us a way home. Don't worry about being arrested again – they can't touch ye now.'

'Why not?' asked Red. 'I might be dead now but I helped kill the Emperor.'

'I've been here a while,' said Teressa. 'I know the Amorani law. Kraego's chosen ye now. Slaves and prisoners have to be set free at once if a griffin chooses them. Vander told me.'

'All right, then,' said Red. 'But I swear to gods, if this goes wrong, I ain't gonna be locked up again. I'll kill anyone who tries.'

'Don't worry,' Teressa soothed. 'I'll die before I let anyone touch ye, Master.'

'Don't call me Master,' said Red. 'My name's Red.'

Teressa raised an eyebrow. 'Just that?'

Red followed her off through the palace. 'Why, don't y'reckon the Shadow That Walks should have a name like that?'

'I was hoping for something a bit grander,' Teressa admitted.

'Well then, call me Captain Redguard,' said Red.

'Captain…?' Teressa repeated.

'Yeah. I was a guard captain, once upon a time,' said Red. 'Now where's this Flell?'

'This way,' said Teressa. 'Not far.'

Red followed her, with the two griffins close behind. He coughed. 'Ugh, it feels like there's somethin'… stuck in my throat. I don't reckon my voice is gonna sound the same again.'

'At least ye can still talk,' said Teressa. 'With that scar on yer throat, I thought… what'd they do to ye?'

'I don't want to talk about it,' said Red.

'All right,' she murmured. 'I can understand.'

Red went quiet after that and concentrated instead on keeping up with her. She seemed to know where she was going at least, and after a short journey through the different levels of the palace she took the four of them to a large and airy stone room. A magnificent chair stood in the middle of it, on a plinth. It had been made from black wood and decorated with semiprecious stones.

Guards stood on either side of it, and they, along with the size of the chair, served to make the chair's occupant look very small indeed. Then again, she was only a child. She was small and thin, with light brown skin. Her hair was black, and her eyes were blue.

She looked down imperiously at her visitors. 'Hello, Teressa and Orak,' she said.

Teressa bowed. 'Hello, Flell.'

'Empress Flell,' the child corrected. 'What d'you want?'

Teressa hesitated. 'I've got some news for ye, Flell, but ye… it's not good.'

'What is it?' asked the child. She frowned at Red.

'We found yer uncle Kullervo,' said Teressa.

Flell sat up straight. 'You did? Where is he?'

'He's here in Amoran,' said Teressa. 'They were keeping him under the palace.'

'Why?' asked Flell.

'I don't really know,' said Teressa. 'I'm so sorry. I didn't know, and by the time I got to him…'

'Can I see him?' asked Flell. 'I mean… bring him to me. I want him.'

'He died,' said Teressa.

Flell stared at her for a moment, before her small face darkened with anger. 'No he didn't! Bring him here right now!'

'He's dead,' Red interrupted. 'I was there.'

'But… but…' Flell started to cry. 'But I don't want him to be dead.' Teressa tried to go forward to comfort the child, but she only cried harder and waved her away. 'Go away! I don't want you here.'

Red watched gloomily as the child sobbed. This was the person who was in charge of the entire Amorani Empire now?

He stepped in now and spoke up, voice loud and harsh. 'He's dead,' he said. 'An' he died because of the people you're in charge of now. Amoranis killed him.'

Flell stopped crying and stared at him.

'They killed a lot of people down there,' said Red. 'Griffins too. Now if you want to make things right again, like he would've wanted, then you're gonna set us free. Me, an' the others from the South. You're gonna give us a boat so we can go home. And you're gonna order the Empire's armies to leave Cymria. You'll bring them back here, and you'll give orders that they're not allowed to go back there, ever. Understand?'

Flell's face was wet with tears, but she snapped back at him. 'You don't tell me what to do!'

'Yeah I do,' said Red. 'I've just told you, an' you're gonna do it or you'll feel the back of my hand. You're gonna break the alliance with King Caedmon. Got that?'

Flell froze. 'Caedmon?'

'Yeah,' said Red. 'The King of the Northerners. You ain't gonna let the Empire help him no more.'

Flell scowled. 'I know who he is. He killed my parents.'

'Then stop helping him,' said Teressa. 'You don't want to be on his side, do ye?'

'No.' Flell stood up. 'You go home, then,' she said to Red. 'I'll send you home with your friends, and then I'll tell the Amoran people not to help Caedmon any more. Promise.'

Red smiled. 'That's what Kullervo would've wanted,' he said. 'He was my friend, you know.'

Flell eyed him. 'Who are you, anyhow?'

'My name's Kearney Redguard,' said Red. 'They call me Red.'

'I know about you,' said Flell. 'Kullervo said.'

Red's silent heart ached. 'What'd he say?'

'He said you were a Southerner an' you were like a son to him,' said Flell. 'He said he wished you an' me could've met.'

'An' now we have,' said Red. 'Teressa said you could help me.'

'I did,' said Flell. 'I'm gonna.' She lifted her chin. 'I'm gonna be Empress,' she added. 'I'm gonna be a great ruler like my mum an' Granddad Arenadd was.'

'I'm sure ye will,' Teressa smiled indulgently.

'Now go on,' said Flell. 'I'm gonna go tell people about what we're gonna do.'

Red resisted the urge to wearily shake his head. 'All right,' he said. 'Thanks.'

As they left together, he muttered to Teressa, 'That kid's not gonna last a day.'

'She will,' said Teressa. 'She's Arenadd's granddaughter and the Night God is watching over her.'

Red stopped and turned to her. 'Teressa, I'm in charge of you now, right?'

'Ye are,' said Teressa.

'Good, then here's an order for you: stop talking about the Night God right now, an' don't mention her ever again.'

'Yes, sir,' Teressa said meekly.

*

The four of them stayed in the Hall of Suns for a few days after Red's transformation, and, as Teressa had promised, nobody bothered them. Nobody in the palace would speak to him, but under Flell's orders, he and Kraego were given food and a place to sleep. Teressa stayed close by, constantly ready to follow his orders, and Orak stayed servile to Kraego as he had agreed.

The Amoranis who had arrived in time to witness Kullervo's passing must have listened seriously to his last words, because the others who had been kept prisoner with Red were allowed to go free, and there were no attempts to hunt them down or any of the griffins who had escaped. Red saw no signs of anyone being about to free the slaves, though. He wasn't surprised. Letting the prisoners go free was one thing, but freeing every slave in Amoran was another.

They had kept Kullervo's body, and Teressa informed him that they had decided to build a temple out in the city where it would be entombed.

'Damned fools,' Red muttered on hearing the news. 'Kullervo wasn't holy. He was godless. He'd be furious if he knew people were gonna wind up praying over his bones.'

But at least he would have a proper resting place; there was that to be said about it.

Meanwhile, on Flell's orders, a boat was prepared to take Red and the others home. Dozens of slaves were brought to go with him. Other Southerners, as promised. Their collars had already been removed, and by the time Red, Teressa, Kraego and Orak boarded the ship, they were on board waiting for them.

Red saw them standing in a nervous cluster by the mast, and went up to them. Two of them came forward to meet him, staring in awe and fear.

'Captain Redguard,' said one of them. 'It's you. But…'

Red stared back at her, and couldn't help but smile. 'Hullo, Lady Isleen.'

The former Eyrie Mistress of Liranwee looked very different to his memory of her. Once she had been, if not fat, then at least somewhat on the pudgy side. Now, though, she was thin. Scars had appeared on her arms, and there were more on her neck where the collar had been removed. She'd been given some proper clothes to wear instead of the traditional Amorani slave's outfit of simple cloth wrapped around the hips and breasts, but above it her square, bland face was gaunt and browned by the sun, and the shaved remains of her hair had gone to grey.

She looked back at him uncertainly. 'Captain… what happened to you? And why are we here?'

'The new Empress has set you free,' said Red. 'I told her to.'

Beside Isleen, a small, once-fat man with a squint spoke up. 'Empress? You mean the stories are true?'

'They are, Alaric,' said Red, raising his roughened voice so all of them could hear him. 'The Emperor's dead. The only member of his family left is some little brat of a girl. She's havin' us sent home. All of us.'

'Why, though?' asked Alaric.

''Cause I said I'd give her a clip around the ear otherwise,' said Red.

The freed slaves laughed among themselves, somewhat nervously.

Red grinned. 'All right, that ain't true. Teressa here got her to do it.' He gestured at the Northerner, who was keeping a cautious distance.

One of the other freed slaves, a former guardsman, glared at her. 'That's a Northerner.'

'Yeah,' said Red. 'But you ain't gonna touch her, understand? She's with me, an' it's thanks to her we got this boat, an' thanks to her yer all free. Now, let's get goin'. We got a long way t'go, an' we can swap stories on the way.'

The ship had come with a crew, of course — Amoranis, and a handful of Maijanis, one of whom was the Captain. At a nod from Red he started shouting commands to his crew and in no time at all the ship had set out down the river.

Red stood up on the stern of the ship, and watched Xanthium gradually pass away behind them. 'An' that's that,' he muttered to no-one in particular.

Kraego and Orak weren't on board, though there were specially built spaces below for them. They flew overhead instead, lazily circling the ship, with Orak riding on his superior's slipstream as an inferior griffin often did.

Red felt glad to know that Kraego was there. During their separation, he'd come to realise just how much he had grown used to having him there beside him, and now that they were partners at last, it was a great comfort. The full horror of what had happened to him had only just started to sink in over the last few days, and he took solace in knowing Kraego was close by.

He supposed, as well, that he should consider how lucky he was. He could have stayed dead, down in that place under the Hall of Suns. The caged griffins could have eaten him, or his body would have been burned and the ashes thrown away. But Kraego had chosen him. Kraego had saved him.

He knew that he would never be the same again, of course. His heart would never beat again, his soul had been replaced by evil magic and would not return. The Redguard family would now definitely end with him; the Shadow That Walked could not have children.

But all that didn't matter as much as it might have. If Kraego had done nothing, then the Redguards would have been gone anyway. And now the last of them had been given another chance. A chance to make things right again. To use the Night God's gifts against her, and maybe…

Red smiled grimly to himself, as a new possibility occurred to him.

He knew whose fault it was that his family had been disgraced and all but destroyed. His uncle Bran had blamed himself, and Red's father Danthirk had blamed himself as well, but neither of them had been at fault.

No. There was a guilty party in their story, and it wasn't a Redguard at all. It was Arren Cardockson. Arenadd Taranisäii. He was the one who'd destroyed Eagleholm, even if Bran had ended up being the one punished for it.

But if Arren had just died, that would have been the end of it right there. Eagleholm wouldn't have been destroyed, and the Redguards would have been safe..

No, it was the Night God who had done it, wasn't it? She was the one who'd sent Kraego's father Skandar to him. She'd given him his orders. True, Arenadd had given her his loyalty voluntarily, so far as Red knew, but if it weren't for the Night God…

'An' now the power's come to me,' Red said aloud.

He had to save his friends and his country, of course – he knew that. But now, with the power of the Shadow That Walked, maybe he could do more than that.

What if he didn't just use it to kill ordinary people? What if he used it against the Night God herself? Could that be in his power now? Could he, Kearney Redguard, bring down a god?

'Maybe I could,' he said. 'Yeah, maybe I could. Aim high, Red, aim high.'

He decided not to tell anyone about it. But he'd think about it. He'd find out what he could, and maybe he'd find an answer.

He glanced back over his shoulder at the decks of the ship. Some of the freed slaves had gone below to be out of the sun, but others had stayed, maybe because they too, wanted to watch Xanthium disappear like a bad dream. He saw Teressa there with them, cautiously keeping her distance.

His black eyes narrowed. *Yeah,* he thought. *Her. What does she know?*

She was a priestess, after all. She'd told him so. Maybe she knew something about the Night God that he didn't. He'd have to find out.

While he looked at her, he accidentally caught someone else's eye. Isleen saw him and looked back. She gestured at herself and raised a questioning eyebrow.

Red paused, shrugged, and went down to her. 'Want somethin', Isleen?'

'I do,' she said. 'Will you tell us what happened now? Are we going home?'

Other freed slaves there, hearing her, came over. Alaric was among them, of course – Red had noticed that he rarely left Isleen's side.

'We're going back to Cymria, aren't we?' the puny storyteller asked.

Red nodded. 'An' along the way we're gonna be picking up the others. There'll be some in Instabahn, an' more in Maijan.'

'How did you really get this kid to agree to it?' asked one of the others.

Red pointed at him. 'What's yer name?'

'It's me, Neth,' said the man. 'Y'know, from Withypool? We met there once.'

'Oh yeah,' Red smiled. 'Another guard. I remember. You'd better ask her about what happened.' He gestured at Teressa. 'Like I said, it was her who got us all this.'

Everyone looked at the Northerner.

'Is that so?' said Isleen.

Teressa looked uncomfortable. 'Aye, it is. I came all this way to help ye.'

'Why?' asked Alaric.

'Well, really, I came to help him,' Teressa admitted, looking at Red. 'Don't pretend ye didn't do anything, sir. I only asked the Empress to do this because ye told me to.'

'But it was your idea,' said Red.

'It was,' said Teressa. 'Anyway…'

'Tell them, then,' said Red.

'We're listening,' Isleen added, eyeing the other woman with slight suspicion.

So Teressa told them, although Red was glad that she left out the part to do with Arenadd. She did say that she had been guided by a dream, though, and explained about Flell and Kullervo.

'Kullervo?' Isleen repeated. 'You saw him? He's alive?'

Teressa shook her head. 'I got to him too late.'

Isleen looked grim. 'The Winged Man is dead… this is a grim day for us all.'

'But,' Teressa went on, 'it's not over. There's still hope.'

'Oh yes?' said Isleen. 'And what hope would that be, Northerner?'

Teressa pointed at Red. 'Him,' she said. 'He's yer hope now. And yes I'm a Northerner, but I follow him, so ye can trust me.'

'Why, though?' asked Alaric. 'Why would you follow one of us?'

'Because…,' Teressa hesitated.

Red winced. 'Never mind. She just does.'

But Teressa shook her head. 'No, ye can't pretend about this, sir. The truth is the only way. The longer ye lie about it, the harder it'll get.'

Red sighed. 'Fine. But I'm gonna tell them, not you.'

'Yes, sir,' said Teressa.

'An' don't call me sir,' Red added.

'What's this all about, Captain?' asked Isleen.

Red hesitated just as Teressa had done, and probably for the same reason. But he supposed the direct approach would be the best, and plunged ahead with it.

'I died an' Kraego up there brought me back,' he said bluntly. 'I'm the new Shadow That Walks.'

His listeners froze.

'But,' Red added hastily, 'But I ain't the Night God's servant like the others. I can use my powers however I like, an' I'm on your side.'

'It's true!' Teressa put in. 'I came here because I knew another Shadow That Walks would rise. I found him, and I swore to obey him.'

Finally Isleen spoke. Her voice had gone shaky. 'This isn't funny,' she said.

'An' I ain't laughing,' said Red. He pointed at his throat. 'How'd you think I survived this? Easy. I didn't. My heart ain't beating — I can feel it… or not feel it. Ask Kraego if you still ain't convinced.'

Everyone there, even hardened former guardsmen like Neth, took a step backward.

Red sighed. 'This is why I didn't want to tell yer,' he said. 'I knew you'd be scared of me. But I swear—,' he put his hand on his chest, over where his heart had been, 'I'm still one of you. I'm a Southerner, right? You should be glad you got me, an' Kraego too.'

Alaric pointed at him. 'Y-you're the Shadow That Walks!' he stammered. 'You're the Night God's creature!'

'I ain't,' Red snapped. 'We all owe Kraego a big favour. Know why? 'Cause he wasn't meant t'do this. He told me the Night God came to him, an' she told him to give the power to someone else. A Northerner. An' then he was meant to help that Northerner destroy the lot of us. But he chose me instead. Now the power's on our side. An' I already know what I'm gonna do with it.'

'Which is?' said Isleen.

'I'm gonna take you all home,' Red said loudly. 'I'm gonna go back to the South, an' I'm gonna fight back against the Northerners. I'm gonna kill their King, an' I'm gonna drive the rest of them back where they came from. An' if no-one else wants to help me, then I'll do it by myself.'

For a long moment, nobody said anything.

Then Alaric stepped forward. 'I,' he said nervously. 'I, uh… I'll help you, Captain. If I can.' When Red looked at him, he winced and stared at his feet.

'Uh, I mean… I trust you,' he added. 'I know what you did for us before all this happened. You're a hero, like the people in my stories. And if – if I can do anything to help you save the South, I will.'

There was another silence.

Then Neth stepped forward. 'If a wimpy little sod like that's got the balls to sign up, I sure do,' he said. 'Count me in.'

'And me as well,' said Isleen. 'I don't have Arak any more, but… perhaps I could do something for you, Kearney. At the very least, I will follow you.'

Alaric smiled at her, making her blush.

'I'll come too,' said another former slave – one of Neth's friends.

'An' me,' said another.

'An' me too.'

'Yeah!' said a fourth. 'Let me at them Northern scum. We'll teach 'em a lesson.'

'We'll show 'em what true Southerners can do!' said a fourth.

'We will!' said another, and another, until every man and woman there had spoken up and offered their support. The rest had come up on deck to hear what was happening, and they too were quick to join with their friends.

'If what you say is true,' Isleen said formally, once the shouts had died down, 'Then we should indeed be grateful to have you, Captain. We all know what the Shadow That Walks did to our people not so long ago. Now, it would seem that power is working for us. With you, we may just stand a chance at beating this blackrobe scum.'

'Uh. Ahem,' Red coughed. 'Thanks, milady. But please—,' he glanced at Teressa. 'I'd prefer it if you didn't use that word again. Remember, it ain't just Southerners here. We owe Teressa a lot.'

'We do,' said Isleen. She took a step towards Teressa, and awkwardly held out her hand. 'I, uh… I apologise. I should not… that is, you've helped us, Priestess Teressa, and I would like to offer you my sincere thanks.'

Teressa smiled and linked fingers with Isleen before giving a quick tug and letting go – the traditional gesture of one griffiner to another. 'Thank ye, Lady Isleen.' She looked past her to the others.

'This won't be easy for me,' she added, 'I know what I've done and what I have to do. I've betrayed my King by helping ye, and so has my partner Orak. And if I stay with ye and help ye in this fight that's coming, I…' she shivered. '…I'll never be able to go home. Most likely, the King will put out a warrant for my arrest as soon as he knows what I've done. But I've made my choice,' she went on more strongly. 'I believe that following the Captain here is what the great King Arenadd wants. I've vowed to stay beside him and do what I can to help him until I'm dead.'

Several of the listeners looked surprised at this, or even admiring.

'I know ye don't like me,' said Teressa. 'After what my people did to ye, I'm not surprised. But for what it's worth—,' she touched her neck, 'I was a slave once, too. I was born a slave. King Arenadd set me free. Now the Captain and I have done the same for ye.'

'It's all right,' Alaric said timidly. 'I don't mind your being here. I'm grateful for what you've done.'

'An' so am I,' said Red. He put a big, rough hand on Teressa's narrow shoulder, and smiled. 'Don't worry, Teressa. You're welcome here. You're one of us now.'

Teressa smiled back. 'Thank ye, Captain Redguard. Thank ye with all my heart.'

*

The ship sailed on down the river Erech, and its passengers retired for the night. Some of them slept below, with the crew, but Red stayed up on deck with Kraego and slept on the bare boards, not seeming to notice how uncomfortable they must be.

Teressa didn't sleep at all, not at first. She sat by herself at the back of the ship, with Orak close by, and contemplated. She prayed with her stone, and afterwards looked up at the moon, which had risen high over the roofs of the outskirts of Xanthium.

Orak stood close to her, warm and protective.

'We have done well,' he rumbled. 'The dark griffin is with us now, and we have found our path. When this war is done, we shall be honoured for our courage.'

'Aye,' Teressa sighed. 'But it won't be easy.' She looked up at him. 'Have we done the right thing? I knew what we had to do, but I didn't know I would have to go this far. Betraying my King to Southerners…'

'We did what we had to do,' said Orak. 'Everything we dreamt of has led us to this. We know why we had to find the child, and the black griffin. But…' his violet eyes narrowed. '…but what about this other one? The man-griffin? We were asked to find him as well. I did not see him, but you did. Can you tell what part he had to play in all this?'

Teressa fidgeted. 'Well…'

'Did he speak to you before he died?' asked Orak. 'Did he tell you something?'

'He did,' Teressa admitted. 'I haven't told anyone what he said. It was just for me to hear. He whispered it to me.'

'What did he say?' Orak pressed. 'I am your partner, Teressa — you must tell me.'

'Aye,' said Teressa. 'But I think we should keep it a secret, even from Red and Kraego. I don't think Red would like it, at least. I know his friends wouldn't.'

'You have sworn to follow and obey this red-furred human,' said Orak. 'Have you been asked to do something he would not want you to do?'

'I don't know,' said Teressa. 'I didn't really understand what Kullervo said. But maybe…'

'Then tell me,' said Orak.

'He said "Her heart is in a hollow tree West of Gwernyfed, and his bones are in a cave above Taranis' Throne. Ye must bring the two together".'

Orak huffed to himself. 'A heart? Bones? What could that mean?'

'I don't know,' said Teressa. 'But I think I can guess part of it.' She looked up at the moon again. 'Nobody ever found King Arenadd's body, but I think Kullervo told me where it is.'

'What use would dead bones be?' said Orak.

'I don't know,' said Teressa. 'But I think we should go and look in those places and at least see what we find. And we should do it soon, before anyone knows what we did and we can still go into the North without being chased.'

'That is true,' said Orak. 'But you have sworn yourself to Kraego's human. They would not be pleased if we left without permission, or if we refused to say why we were going.'

Teressa thought it over for a moment. 'Aye, that's true,' she said. 'Besides, if Arenadd wants us to follow them, then maybe it would be what they want too, or be good for them.' She paused. 'I'll tell ye what I'll do then, Orak.'

'Yes?' said the griffin.

'I'll think it over on the voyage,' said Teressa. 'Pray some more. Maybe I'll have another vision. Either way, when I've got a better idea of what we should do, I'll talk to Red. I'll try and get his permission to do whatever it was Kullervo suggested. He trusts us now, after all. He might say yes. If not… then we'll think of something else.'

'Agreed,' said Orak. He lifted his wing, sheltering her under it. 'We have done well, Teressa. Very well.' He flexed his once-crippled leg, and the newly strengthened talons left gouges in the planks beneath them. 'I can fight now,' he said. 'I am whole. At last, I am a true griffin. Kraego does not need to worry himself over where my loyalty lies. The griffins of Malvern wanted me dead for my weakness, but when I return… it will be they who shall die.'

Chapter Fourteen

The King and the Prince

After the victory at the Battle of Withypool, King Caedmon and his followers had work to do.

Prince Caradoc stayed close to his father, and watched what happened. Father had been hurt in the fighting outside Withypool when a big Southerner with red hair had hit him with a sword. Afterwards, he had to keep his arm in a sling, and Caradoc didn't want to go too far away from him again.

The eight-year-old prince stood in Withypool's Eyrie council chamber with his yellow feathered partner Ereska standing protectively behind him. In the middle of the great rounded room, the King stood on the platform that had once been reserved for the Eyrie Master, Penrin. His partner Shar stood beside him. She was a big, red griffin, with scars on her hindquarters. One of her front paws was missing a toe. It was said that it had been bitten off by the Mighty Skandar himself, when she had fought him years ago before Caradoc was born. She had won the fight, and killed Skandar, and Caradoc's father had said that it was thanks to her that he had become King. When Shar killed Skandar, all the griffins who didn't have partners wanted to follow her instead, and they were stronger than any human army.

The Unpartnered were here in the city now, perching on rooftops or flying in big circles above the Eyrie. They weren't going to stay, though. When the King left, they would come too.

First, though, there was some work to do. Caradoc didn't like it when his father talked to his councillors – it was boring. But he had to go, because he was his father's apprentice and one day he would have to do all this himself, when he was King.

Today, though, it was more exciting.

King Caedmon and Shar looked down from the platform. Their highest officials stood in a group beside them – Caradoc and Ereska were among them. In front of them, a small group of people stood with guards around them. Their hands had been chained together.

Caradoc didn't think they looked very impressive, which was

funny because once they had been Eyrie rulers – like Kings and Queens, but they didn't call themselves that. They were Southerners, and there weren't any kings or queens in the South.

Caradoc looked at each one of them, and tried to remember their names. There was Lady Nelia, who had ruled Canran. Ekra, who'd ruled Wylam. Brannon and Larkin, the twins who had ruled Sunton, and Penrin who had ruled Withypool. They had all been griffiners once, like Caradoc was, but their partners were gone now. Locked up somewhere else, Ereska said.

Now King Caedmon stood over all of them, with Shar, and talked to them.

'You've been defeated,' he said brusquely. 'Your armies have been crushed, your griffins have died or betrayed you. Your cities have been destroyed or overrun. You've seen your people sold into slavery.' He smiled thinly. 'A scholar of history once wrote that history goes in a circle. So many things repeat themselves. Now you've seen the truth of that for yourselves.' He brushed some dust off the finely tailored black robe he wore. 'But we're not here to reminisce about the good old days, are we? No, we're here to talk about the future. So now, as your King, I'm going to tell you what the future will hold for all of you.'

'Don't toy with us, Northerner,' Lord Penrin spat. 'Just tell us what you're going to do with us. But I assume that you'll have us executed like the coward you are.'

Several of the Northern griffiners there hissed.

'That's up to you,' Caedmon said evenly. 'But now – your futures. And seeing as how I'm speaking to Southerners, I'll make it short and simple, shall I? Your country belongs to us now. In a few days, a ceremony will be held in which I will be officially crowned King of Cymria. From now on, I am your ruler, and any attempts to fight me or my people will be classed as high treason and dealt with accordingly. But I intend to be merciful as well as stern. You were Eyrie Masters once not so long ago, and if you're willing to co-operate you could be so again. My terms are simple. You can return to ruling your territories, but you'll do so under the supervision of griffiners appointed by me, and they and you will answer to me. Any decisions which you make must be approved by your appointed supervisors, and disobedience will be dealt with quickly and ruthlessly. I'm offering you a second chance – you will squander that chance at your own risk.'

The captured Eyrie Masters muttered and swore among themselves.

'This is outrageous!' Lord Ekra shouted. 'How dare you stand there and speak to us like that? You think we'd allow ourselves to become your puppets?'

Caedmon raised an eyebrow. 'Coming from you that's particularly amusing, Southerner. Do you honestly believe that you deserve anything better than that? Perhaps once you've been returned to your cell you can consider the possibilities, and honestly ask yourself what you would have done if it had been you who conquered us. But wait – I forgot. You already did that, didn't you? Call me cruel if you want, but remember: we learned it from you.' he coughed. 'I should add that if you don't take our offer, the alternative is that you will be immediately taken out of here and publicly executed. Now, speak and let us know what you decide.'

Silence fell.

Caradoc had listened to everything, and now his heart beat faster. He couldn't help but feel sorry for the Southerners. It must be horrible to be chained like that and then be told off in front of everyone. Father was scary when his eyes went narrow and his voice went all hard like that.

But it would be all right, of course. They would do what he said, because he was the King and everyone did what he told them to. Then they could go home, and everything would be fine.

Penrin pushed his way forward. He was an old man but he looked strong, and though scratchy, his voice was loud and angry.

'You arrogant scum,' he said. 'You really think you can make me accept your so-called deal?'

Caradoc gasped in horror, and looked at his father, waiting for him to get angry.

But Caedmon sounded perfectly calm. 'As I said, it's your choice,' he said.

'Well then, you can forget it,' said Penrin. 'I would rather die than be your vassal, blackrobe.' And then he actually spat, straight at Father's boots.

King Caedmon shrugged with his good shoulder. 'As you wish.' He nodded to the guards. 'Take him away.'

Two of them came forward and pulled Penrin out of the room.

He didn't fight them, but walked with his head held high, as if he didn't even care what was going to happen to him.

Silence followed. The remaining prisoners glanced at each other, as if to ask who would speak up next.

'So much for him,' Caedmon interrupted. 'What do the rest of you have to say? We await your answer with great interest.'

Lady Nelia coughed. 'Uh… I mean to say… if you're offering me the chance to go home to Canran, I'll take it. I don't know if I would be much use to you as an Eyrie ruler, though.'

'Your loyalty is all I ask for,' Caedmon said graciously.

'Thank you… sire.' Nelia smiled weakly.

Lord Ekra of Wylam shot her a disgusted look. 'You can't pull that trick with me, Northerner,' he said. 'You haven't captured Wylam. No army has ever conquered my city.'

'But we don't have to do that, do we?' said Caedmon. 'Your army has been killed or sent to Amoran. Who's left to defend Wylam now?'

Ekra sneered at him. 'You do realise, don't you, that if I go back to Wylam and begin ruling it in your name, I'll be dead in a day? My own Council would probably do it.'

'You're not afraid are you, my Lord?' Caedmon asked sweetly.

'I'm not stupid,' Ekra snapped.

'There's no need to be afraid,' said Caedmon. 'You'll be well protected by your new supervisors. I take care of my officials. Now, do you want to go home?'

'What choice do I have?' said Ekra. 'Penrin might be an old man, but I'm not, and I don't intend to let myself die just yet.'

'Then can I count on your loyalty?'

Ekra muttered something that might have been a yes.

'Excellent.' Caedmon looked at the others and raised his eyebrows. 'And the rest of you?'

Brannon and Larkin scowled and nodded. They looked like they were too angry to say anything.

'Excellent,' Caedmon said again. He nodded to the guards. 'Remove their chains.'

The Eyrie Masters rubbed their wrists once the chains came off. Caradoc wondered if they hurt.

'Now you can go,' his father commanded. 'You'll be given fresh clothes and something to eat, and be reunited with your partners.

Tomorrow morning, you can fly back to your homes with your new supervisors. This evening, each one of you will be presented with documents to sign, which provide the details of our new alliance, and the terms of your survival. If any part of what is written in those documents is violated, you will be found guilty of treason. I hope you all understand.'

'Perfectly,' said Ekra, through gritted teeth.

Caedmon smiled. 'Good. Let's part ways now, shall we, and I will see you later.'

He waited while they walked out with their guards still following. Once they were gone, he yawned and stretched. 'That's that dealt with, thank the Night God.'

One of his officials grinned. 'The looks on their faces! But… you don't think we can rely on them, do you Sire?'

Caedmon shrugged, keeping his wounded shoulder carefully still. 'Most likely not, but in the beginning at least, this will make things easier. Even their reluctant allegiance will help make the transition look more legitimate to the rest of their people. If any of them decide to rebel, we can say they betrayed their own people and have them executed. Now, if you'll excuse me, I need to get some rest.'

He stepped down off the platform, closely followed by Shar, who had stayed still and glared silently at the prisoners the whole time.

Caradoc followed them, and once they were out of the Council Chamber, his father turned to him.

'Did you pay attention to all of that?' he asked.

'I did,' said Caradoc. 'I didn't understand all the long words, but…'

'That's fine.' Father smiled at him. 'As long as you understood enough to know what was going on. Can you tell me what happened?'

Caradoc hesitated. This was another test. 'You told them they should go back and rule their Eyries, but they have to do what you say.'

'That's right,' his father nodded. 'And do you know why I did it like that? I could have executed all of them and replaced them with our own people, couldn't I? Can you guess why I didn't do that?'

'Um…' Caradoc scratched the back of his neck.

'Go on,' said Father. 'Try and guess.'

'I don't know,' Caradoc said apologetically.

'I didn't kill them because I want the Southerners to obey me,' said Father. 'Yes, we fought and killed their armies here, but they attacked us. Now that we've won, we have to show that we're here to rule, not destroy. If I took those people prisoner and then killed them when they were helpless, the Southerners would hate us. We need to show that we're here to do more than kill them. So we showed mercy to the Eyrie Masters who agreed to co-operate with us, and in that, they showed mercy to their own people as well – they knew that if they had chosen to fight back, the only result would be more dead Southerners and more burned cities.'

Caradoc nodded. 'But what about the old one who said he wanted to die instead?'

'He chose pride instead of common sense,' said Father. 'A mistake plenty of people make. But don't think he was a coward, Caradoc. It takes a lot of courage to die rather than betray what you believe in.'

'Are they really going to kill him then?' asked Caradoc.

'Yes.' Father hesitated. 'And… to be honest, if I were in his place I would probably have chosen death as well. But enough about that. It's getting late, and I think my bandages need to be changed.' He moved his wounded shoulder and winced.

Caradoc followed him as they went off up the ramp to the Eyrie Master's old rooms. They belonged to Father now.

'What are we going to do next?' he asked. 'Are we going back to Malvern?'

'No,' his father replied shortly.

'Is there more fighting?' asked Caradoc.

'Some, but not fighting that we need to be involved with. The war is more or less over now. What we need to do now is concentrate on building our new government.'

More talking, then. Caradoc pouted. He didn't want to see any more fighting; he just wanted to go home to Malvern. He'd thought it was over now.

'Where're we going to go, then?' he pressed.

'If we're going to govern all of Cymria, Malvern wouldn't be the right place to do it,' Father explained.

'No,' Shar added. 'The master of a territory must build his nest at its centre.'

'Exactly,' said Father. 'The Kingdom of Cymria will need a capital, and as it happens there's a city almost directly in the centre of the country that would be perfectly placed for it. That's where we're going, Caradoc. I'm going to move my government there, and appoint someone to be Eyrie Master at Malvern.'

Caradoc started. 'What? You mean we're not going to...?'

'No, Caradoc, we're not going back to Malvern, not for a while. The new capital city will be our home. But when you're older, you'll be made Eyrie Master of Malvern. It will be the last stage of your apprenticeship. By the time I die, you'll be ready to rule.'

Caradoc couldn't believe his ears. He couldn't think of anything else to say, either, so he mumbled, 'I don't want you to die.'

Father smiled and ruffled his hair with his good hand. 'It's all right, son. I'm not going anywhere. My cousin, the half-breed, did everything in her power to get rid of me, and never succeeded. I won't die until I'm an old, old man — after I've seen you become King and raise children of your own.'

Caradoc didn't like it when his father talked like this. He nodded unhappily. 'Where's the new capital?'

'You've already seen it,' said Father. 'It was the first place we conquered. Apparently, the Southerners call it Liranwee.'

*

They went to Liranwee two days later, once the Eyrie Masters had left with the people who were really in charge. Liranwee didn't have an Eyrie Master any more; there had been one called Lady Isleen, but Shar had killed her partner when the King's army had taken the city. Then Isleen had been sent to Amoran to be a slave. That didn't matter, though, because from now on Caradoc's father would be Liranwee's Eyrie Master.

Caradoc did remember Liranwee, of course. It was the first place they had captured when the war started. They had come through the Northgate Mountains together, and Liranwee was the first place in their path. But they'd planned it all before, of course. Caradoc's adopted brother Morgan, had gone to Liranwee by himself and spied on the Southerners there, and he had come back to meet them later with information that would help them win.

He had brought a prisoner, too — a guard with red hair and a big bushy moustache. He was the first Southerner Caradoc had ever seen. But he'd escaped, and it was Caradoc's fault. He'd gone to see him in his cage, and the Southerner had taken him hostage and escaped. Sometimes Caradoc still had nightmares about it.

Liranwee wasn't looking so good when he saw it again. The Unpartnered had dropped firebombs on it and big parts of it had been blown up or burned down. Even the Eyrie was damaged. Father had left some griffiners behind to keep an eye on everything, but not much had changed since the city's fall. He heard that a lot of the Southerners had run away. Most of them had stayed, though.

When the King arrived, everyone came to meet him. Caradoc kept out of the way with Ereska and tried to pay attention to what they were saying, but it was boring and he stopped listening.

After that, they were allowed to go and rest.

Father looked pleased as they went into the Eyrie Master's quarters. 'Everything's going very well,' he said.

'This city is not so good,' Ereska remarked. 'Many of its nests have been destroyed.'

'What has been destroyed can be rebuilt,' Shar said sharply. 'That is the power of humans.'

'Exactly,' Father smiled. 'The Southerners here need something to do with themselves, so we'll set them to work on the repairs. The city guards, for instance – we can't rely on them to stay loyal to us, but we can't let them sit idle either. We'll give them new jobs as builders.' He frowned. 'Yes… everything's going smoothly. There's only one thing that still bothers me.'

'What's that?' asked Caradoc.

'Your brother,' said Father. 'He's been gone far too long, and we haven't heard back from him or Lady Arwydd either. I'm worried about him.'

Caradoc sat down on a chair by the fire. 'Will you send someone to look for them?'

'I should,' said Father. He sat down too. 'But maybe we should give them a little longer first.'

'They went after that giant griffin, didn't they?' said Caradoc. 'The one that got away from the fighting.'

Father nodded. 'Whoever he was, he escaped from here with his partner. We were afraid they might warn the other Eyries. The other spies from Canran came back to Withypool and apparently Morgan helped them in their mission as planned. But then he went after the griffin again, and Arwydd went with him, and that's the last we heard from either of them.'

'I hope Morgan's all right,' said Caradoc. 'And Echo too. And Arwydd's nice.'

'Do not be afraid for them,' Ereska rumbled. 'Echo is a most cunning griffin – almost as cunning as a human, and powerful. He can protect your brother.'

Shar snorted. 'He wishes to mate with me. Perhaps his desire to impress me so that I will submit to him is what has kept him away. You must hope that this desire does not lead him to place his human in danger.'

Ereska purred softly and dipped her beak towards the superior griffin. 'If he comes back to you with his tail raised, I think that he shall go away disappointed. He is not worthy of you. But I shall be there to raise my own tail to him. He is worthy of me.'

Caradoc knew griffins well enough to guess what that meant, and he giggled behind his hand.

Father smiled to himself. 'Echo is a good griffin, and Morgan is a good man. I once promised his brother Henwas I would protect him, and it's time I acted to make certain that promise isn't broken. I'll send some griffiners out to look for him in the morning, though hopefully that won't be necessary.'

Caradoc listened. 'What did you promise his brother?'

'Ah, Henwas…' said Father, sounding sad now. 'He was one of the greatest friends I ever had. But he died. On his deathbed, he told me he had a younger brother called Morgan. He asked me to take care of him. So once I became King, I did what I could. Their mother had died, so I took Morgan in. Henwas was worthy to be a Taranisäii, and Morgan proved he was just as worthy. Cunning and honour; that's what a true Taranisäii must have.'

Caradoc frowned and twisted his hands together. He didn't say it, because that would be weak, but inside he wished he could be a true Taranisäii as well. But he didn't feel cunning or honourable, or brave either. He'd never even been into battle like a proper King should.

But I will, he thought to comfort himself.

But… how could that happen now? The war was over, wasn't it?

*

The next morning came, but before the search party could be sent out, someone arrived from Withypool.

It was Lady Arwydd. She came with her partner Essh, straight to the roof of the Liranwee Eyrie. Both of them looked exhausted and dishevelled, but they insisted on seeing the King and his partner immediately. Caradoc and Ereska came to watch.

Arwydd was said to be one of the most beautiful women in the King's court, but now she was a mess. Her clothes were torn and dirty, and her black hair was tangled. She bowed low while her partner lowered her head to Shar.

'Sire!' Arwydd burst out before anyone else could speak. 'Sire, it's…'

Father gestured at her to stand up. 'It's all right,' he said. 'Calm down and tell me what's happened.'

Arwydd looked close to tears. 'It's Morgan,' she said. 'The Southerners have him.'

Father froze. 'What? How did this happen? Tell me everything.'

'Is Morgan all right?' Caradoc interrupted.

Arwydd smiled weakly at him, but didn't answer his question. 'We went after the griffin, as commanded,' she said. 'We lost him, but after Canran we found him again in the city, with his partner. We chased both of them further southward, past where Eagleholm used to be. We caught up with them while they were camped for the night, and Morgan decided that we should ambush them while they were asleep. He went in with Echo and Essh – I stayed away, because I'm not a fighter. I only went with Morgan at all because… well, never mind.' She blushed a little and went on. 'I didn't see what happened, but Essh came back to find me afterward and said that they got Morgan. They caught him and took him away – he didn't know where.'

'What about Echo?' asked Father.

'I don't know,' said Arwydd. 'I saw him briefly, but he didn't come back with us. He went to find Morgan and get him back. Essh and I decided we had to come back to you with the news.'

'You don't know where they took Morgan, then?'

'No,' said Arwydd. She shuddered. 'It… it's worse than that, Sire. Much, much worse.'

'Why?' Father asked. 'What else happened?'

'It's the griffin,' said Arwydd. 'He's… Essh, maybe you should tell them. You understand it better than I do.'

Essh shook out her feathers. 'My human is right. Shar, this griffin that we went after is no ordinary griffin. We already knew that he was a giant, but I have seen him closely now, and I have seen his power. He is a black griffin. He is like the Mighty Skandar. I know this not just because of his coat, but because when Echo's human was captured, the black griffin seized him and dragged him away into the shadows. This griffin has the power to make the Shadow That Walks, but he flies with Southerners and has chosen one as his human.'

Shar hissed. 'You are certain?'

'I am,' said Essh. 'I have seen it with my own eyes, and so has Echo. This griffin is only young, but he is already almost as large as the Mighty Skandar, who is his father. He will be at least as dangerous.'

The King swore. 'What about the human? This griffin's partner – who is he?'

'We know who he is,' said Arwydd. 'His name is Kearney Redguard. A former guard captain from Liranwee – Morgan says he was our prisoner for a while but he escaped.'

Caradoc felt as if a big, cold hand had grabbed his heart. 'That's the one who took me and ran away! The Southerner with the red hair.'

'I think that I have seen this griffin,' Shar interrupted. 'What does he look like?'

'His feathers are black,' said Essh. 'But his hindquarters are silvery grey. He has blue eyes.'

'Yes… I know that griffin,' said Shar. 'His name is Kraego. He was at Withypool, and he challenged me. I defeated him. If he is not dead now, then the Amoranis have taken him.'

'Are you sure?' Father asked.

'Certain,' said Shar. 'Do not be afraid of this one, Caedmon. Whether he has his father's power or not, the black griffin is gone. His human is most likely dead as well, or collared.'

Father sighed. 'That's good to know. But if we'd known about this beforehand we could have put out an order to capture one or other of them so we could find out what they've done with Morgan. As it is, we'll have to look for him. Arwydd, you can help with that. You and Essh will have to lead the search party to where you last saw Morgan.'

'Yes, sire,' said Arwydd.

They talked some more after that, making plans for how she would help them find Morgan, but Caradoc's attention wandered away from them. He found himself thinking about the red-haired guard who had taken him hostage instead. Red, that was what he'd said his name was. Red from Liranwee – from here.

Caradoc had talked to him while he was locked up; he'd wanted to see a real Southerner, and ask him things. He wanted to know what they were like. Everyone knew they were the biggest enemies of the Northerners; once they had ruled the North and sold its people as slaves.

But Caradoc wanted to know what they were like.

It had been a horrible mistake. He had gotten too close to the cage, and the Southerner had suddenly lunged forward and grabbed him through the bars. He'd been so strong; he'd held him still with one hand, and after he'd gotten out of the cage he'd slung him over his shoulder and carried him like he weighed nothing at all.

Caradoc had been more scared that day than he'd ever been, but Red hadn't hurt him. He let him go once they were far enough away. And now, maybe he was dead. Caradoc was surprised when he realised that he felt a bit sad about it. It was strange to think of someone you had met being dead; it was hard to feel like they were really gone forever. And now his foster brother Morgan might be dead too.

Those thoughts left him feeling sad, and that night, once he was on his own and the moon had risen, he decided to pray.

He snuck out onto the balcony that the griffins used for flying off from, and looked up at the moon.

He kept his eyes on it and waited for a while, as he had been taught to by his father. When the inner stillness that prayer needed had come, he folded his hands and murmured a prayer to the Night God.

'Night God,' he said. 'Please don't take Morgan away. He's my brother. And don't take Father either, or Ereska, or Shar. I want them to be alive because they're my family.' He stopped there for a while, not sure if he should say anything else. Then, on an impulse, he added; 'And don't take that Southerner with the red hair either. I know he's one of the enemies because he's a Southerner, but Father says he's brave, and I think so too. So keep him safe too, Night God, and don't take his soul either.'

Silence followed his prayer. But he liked to think that the god of death had listened.

Chapter Fifteen

A Northerner in Eagleholm

Morgan was lost. But he didn't know it at first.

Everything had been going so well.

Morgan was a spy. He'd always been good at pretending, and his older brother Henwas had taught him how to use that gift to his advantage – the gift of mimicry, of altering the sound of your voice, of changing the way you moved and looked. To become someone else. Whoever you wanted to be.

Henwas had used that gift for his own purposes. He'd lived the life of a particular kind of thief; one who got what he wanted not by breaking into houses or waylaying people in the street, but by fooling people into giving him what he wanted. It was the subtlest way of stealing, and maybe Morgan would have followed his elder brother into the same kind of life one day.

But when he had been taken into Malvern's Eyrie as the King's own adopted son, Morgan had eventually begun to use his gifts for a far nobler purpose: not to serve himself, but to serve his King and his people. He had been the first of King Caedmon's followers to go through the Northgate Mountains and into the South, and once he had done that he had infiltrated the Southern city of Liranwee along with his partner, Echo.

That was where he had met Captain Redguard. And when Red had escaped the destruction of Liranwee and gone to warn the other Eyries with his new partner Kraego, Morgan had gone after him Echo. He had chased Red through the South of Cymria, never coming close enough to catch up to him.

Until Eagleholm, that is. Until Red and Kraego had flown on past Dead Mountain which had once been the city of Eagleholm. Morgan had followed them, with Echo, and Arwydd and her partner Essh. They had hoped to ambush the two of them while they were asleep, and kill them quickly.

But Morgan had made a mistake. The master spy had been caught out. Red had woken up at just the wrong moment, and he was much stronger than Morgan.

He and Kraego had captured the spy, and for a few horrible moments he had thought his time was up. After all, Red had plenty of reasons to kill him.

But Red hadn't killed him. He and Kraego had captured Morgan and dragged him away through the shadows, leaving his partner Echo behind.

They had taken him to a city he had never seen before, a city nobody in the North knew existed.

New Eagleholm.

It was tiny, only half built, and occupied by only a few hundred people. Northerners were absolutely forbidden to enter the city, but Morgan had been allowed in as a prisoner.

That was when he had realised Red's true motivation. He had expected the big Southerner to kill him by way of revenge, but this was far better. Morgan wouldn't be killed. No, instead he would be delivered into the hands of his enemies. Handed over, as Red had been. Imprisoned as he had been. Tortured to try and force him to betray his people, just as Red had once been.

Morgan had seen it all as he sat in the cell underneath New Eagleholm's half-finished Eyrie. He had seen the poetic justice of it all. And he had seen, too, that he deserved it.

But that didn't mean he would let it happen to him, and he hadn't. And, at first, everything had been going his way.

The guards watching over him were badly trained, inexperienced, and no match for a master spy. Morgan had escaped with ease, and killed three men in the process. He had slipped out, into the city, his mind already focused on a plan. Sneak out through the city, get out through a side gate, and find Echo. Then he would return to his King and give his report, and hopefully be allowed to stay by his side from then on.

Morgan was used to planning like that, and in the past it had always worked out. Like his brother before him, he led a charmed life.

He reminded himself of that now as he moved quickly and quietly through the night-time streets of New Eagleholm. It helped to reassure him.

Everything's going to be fine, he told himself several times. You were born lucky, right? Born lucky.

All was still, more or less. As in most cities, the lamps had been lit out in the streets, and there were a few people still out and about. Morgan avoided them with his usual skill. If only he had something with him, he could have made himself a quick disguise, but he had nothing with him but a dagger and a lock pick, and a short sword he'd stolen from one of the dead guards.

He could cover his eyes and play at being a blind man again, but he didn't have a razor to shave off his hair as he'd done last time, and by now more than enough of it had grown back to give him away. Nobody but a Northerner had black hair.

He could bluff well enough that people wouldn't notice the tall, narrow-shouldered build and long fingers, but hair colour wasn't something you could draw attention away from so easily. This time, he'd have to rely on stealth.

But that was all right – he could be stealthy when he needed to. He had crept out of Liranwee by the secret tunnel several times to liaise with Echo, and never been caught.

But while he had known his way around Liranwee, he didn't know his way around New Eagleholm. And in Liranwee he could rely on his disguise.

He slunk along a darkened street, keeping to the shadows. The best he could manage was to head towards the city walls, which were the most complete part of the partially built city. If he could make it to them, he could follow their length until he found a way through – and he would just have to hope that the guards posted on it wouldn't spot him.

As he hurried on, he saw someone coming towards him up the street. He quickly moved closer to the wall of the building to his left and kept going, hoping they wouldn't notice him.

The stranger came on and drew level with him. Morgan resisted the urge to pull away, which would make the man suspicious, but he couldn't stop himself from watching him as they passed close by each other. The stranger looked back with the kind of incurious stare of one man passing another he didn't know. Morgan was in the shadows, and he hoped they would hide his face. His heart beat faster.

The stranger looked away and kept going, and Morgan had to bite back a sigh of relief.

Thank you, Night God, he prayed silently.

Above, as if hearing his prayer, the clouds shifted away from the moon and the shadows retreated. Morgan quickly turned away to hide his face.

'Hey,' a voice said from behind him. 'Hey, you!'

Morgan put his head down and hurried on.

'Hey!' the voice called. The stranger was coming after him. 'Hey, wait a moment…'

Before Morgan could slip away, the man came up behind him and touched him on the shoulder. 'Hey—,' he said again, but Morgan didn't wait to find out what he was going to say. He pulled the dagger out of his belt, turned and stabbed the Southerner in one smooth movement.

The man jerked and gasped. The dagger had been expertly aimed, and he collapsed without a sound.

Morgan put the dagger back in his belt, and ran.

A shout suddenly split the air, from somewhere up ahead of him. 'Murder! Holy gods, murder! Guards!'

Morgan saw the witness appear from a doorway further along the street, and started towards him, reaching for his dagger. But it was already too late. The man's shout brought others running. Morgan swore and ran back up the way he had come, searching for an alleyway he could duck into.

Too late.

Two more people were coming down the street towards him, and there were no convenient alleyways in sight.

He kept going, intending to just shove the newcomers out of the way, but they had already noticed the commotion.

'Stop him!' one of the people behind him shouted. 'He just killed that man!'

The two in front hesitated and stared at Morgan.

'He tried to rob me,' Morgan lied with practised ease, putting a Southern accent into his voice. 'It was self-defence.'

'That's no—,' one of the two men in his way began, and then stopped. His eyes narrowed. 'Wait.'

His friend stared too, and then gasped. 'Holy Gryphus, he's a Northerner! That's a Northerner!'

Morgan could have done a dozen things to get out of this. He could have kept on lying, could have made a run for it, could have ducked into the nearest hiding place and lain low until things died down. But tiredness, hunger, and sheer terror stopped him, and the moment those words hit his ears he panicked.

He drew the dead guard's sword, and stabbed the speaker to death. The man's friend cried out and lurched towards him, and Morgan caught him by the hair and slit his throat. His pursuers were already on him, and as he tried to run again someone caught him by the arm.

Shouts rose from half a dozen voices, and more people were already emerging from houses to see what was going on.

'He's a Northerner!'

'It's a blackrobe!'

'Murderer!'

Morgan fought back. Cornered now and desperate, he drew his dagger with his free hand and lashed out, trying to make them back off. It worked for a moment, but then someone hit him from behind and he went sprawling onto the dirt. Someone stamped on his hand to make him drop the dagger. His sword was already gone.

Hands grabbed at him.

Morgan struggled. 'Get your paws off me, you filthy sun-worshippers!' he roared.

But the hands only took him by the arms and twisted them behind his back, and they pulled him up until he was kneeling.

Someone else pulled out a clump of his still-short hair. 'I don't believe it! He really is one of them.'

Others started jeering.

'All right, lads, we've got ourselves a blackrobe,' one man said loudly. 'What're we gonna do with him?'

'Let's hand him over to the guards!' a woman suggested.

'What, and let them have all the fun?' another interrupted. 'No way – he's ours!'

'Hang him!' said a man. 'Let's take him to the square an' hang him.'

The others gave shouts of approval.

'Go on, go an' tell your friends!' the first man said, taking charge. 'They'll all want to see this. It's been a long time since we've had a hanging.'

Several people ran off, some of them shouting as they ran. 'A hanging! We're gonna have a hanging!'

Morgan started to throw himself forward with all his strength, trying to make them let go of his arms. His shoulders screamed agony, but he didn't stop.

'No!' he yelled. 'Are you mad? Give me to the guards! You're breaking the law!'

One of his captors smacked him in the head. 'Ain't you heard the law in New Eagleholm? You see a blackrobe, you kill him on sight. Now shut up, scum, an' come quietly. We're gonna send you straight back to the Night God.'

They dragged him to his feet and made him walk. He tried to go along with them, but they didn't make it easy. Someone kicked him in the back of the legs, and he nearly fell over.

His captors jeered and wrenched on his arms to make him cry out. Morgan held back as well as he could, but a gasp of pain escaped him, and the Southerners laughed at the sound of it. Their voices were loud and crude, and full of hate.

Morgan made another effort to free his arms, and failed. Struggling only made them hit him again.

They took him away down the street and along another, many of them calling for others to join them. A mob had begun to gather, and as it grew the procession ground to a halt while the newcomers started to shove at each other, all trying to get at him.

Some of his original captors gathered themselves around the two holding Morgan and pushed through the crowd. 'Get out of the way!' shouted the man who had put himself in charge. 'We're taking him to the square!'

The mob only shoved harder. Some of them even started to fight each other. Morgan could hear them shouting.

'C'mon, let me at him! Get out of the way!'

The mob surged, and the people holding Morgan fell forward under the pressure. Morgan fell out of their hands, and an instant later he was on the ground. He curled in on himself, trying to protect his vulnerable parts, and gritted his teeth as the blows started to rain down on him.

Pain slammed through his back and shoulders. Something smashed over his right knee. Hands pulled at him, trying to make him expose his stomach. A boot caught him in the groin, and he screamed.

He vaguely saw someone pull out a knife, and feebly rolled over to try and get away. But before the mob could finish him off, someone grabbed him by the shoulder and pulled him away.

'Stop it!' a voice yelled. 'We're gonna hang him – come on!'

The mob jeered again, but backed off and let the man take Morgan. This time they didn't try and make him stand up, but took him by the arms and the back of his tunic and dragged him along the ground. His attackers followed along in the rear, some of them throwing things or yelling threats.

A broken bottle hit him in the face, but he was only vaguely aware of the pain. His mind seemed to have frozen. He felt the blood, though, trickling hotly down his chin to his neck.

The mob moved on, taking him with it, until the streets around them opened up into a square. There was a stone plinth there, and a statue stood on it. A woman with her arm extended.

Half a dozen people climbed over the statue and started throwing ropes over the arm, all wanting to be the first. One of them finally succeeded, and the others retreated. Morgan looked up through fuzzy eyes and saw the noose. The woman who had tied it brought it down while several others grabbed at the other end.

'C'mon, bring him over!' she yelled.

Two people started to pull Morgan to his feet, and he made one last wild effort to escape. The people nearby shoved him back and he fell again, and several more brutal blows smashed into him before his original captor managed to pull him away.

The noose went around his neck, and tightened.

'No,' Morgan choked. 'No…!'

But the Southerners only jeered louder, and started to pull the loose end of the rope over the statue's arm.

Morgan went up, and up; up until his feet left the ground and he dangled, kicking and clutching at the noose around his neck. He couldn't speak any more. He managed one last feeble gasp of air before the noose crushed his windpipe.

His tongue bulged and his eyes pushed out. His whole head and face started to throb. He could feel his heart, thudding, racing, drowned out by the screams and shoutings of the crowd that hurled stones and rotten fruit at his dangling body, and pulled on his legs to make him die faster.

The screams rose higher. Were they his? Could some part of him reach out past the noose and scream out his pain and terror? Or could he still hear the mob, somehow frightened by its own violence?

The sound grew louder, and stronger. Through the darkness that had started to close over him, Morgan thought it was strange that people – even people like this – could make a sound so loud, so powerful. It even seemed to frighten the ones pulling at him; their hands fell away.

'Run!' a voice shouted from somewhere far away.

Morgan's legs continued to kick feebly, as if they wanted to obey.

The rope suddenly went slack, and he thumped down onto the ground. He thought he was too far gone to even think, but it was as if his hands had a life of their own. They went to his throat and pulled at the noose. It loosened, and his mouth opened wider and sucked in air. It felt like knives in his throat.

It was all he could manage. His body had gone numb, and he lay there pathetically on his back and just breathed. Spots flashed in front of his eyes.

Something hit the ground close by, so hard the ground shook. Only half conscious, Morgan tried to turn his head and look, but he was too slow. Something hit him in the middle, something heavy, and a crushing grip closed around him and lifted him. A great gust of air blasted over his face, and he went up again, carried away by something with sharp points that stuck into his back. He realised that he was flying.

Morgan looked up, and saw a wall of feathers above him. He could see the great scaled foreleg that held him.

Echo.

He let his eyes close, and slid away into unconsciousness.

Chapter Sixteen

Homecoming

Red had been at sea for months now. Amoran was behind him, and Maijan as well. Cymria lay ahead.

It wasn't just one ship though. By now there were three, each one crewed by Amoranis but carrying dozens of Southerners. Freed slaves, all of them, going home on Empress-elect Flell's orders. Red doubted that all of the men and women sold by the Northerners were there, but a good number of them were and that would have to do for now. Putting a stop to Caedmon's invasion would come first; they could worry about Amoran later.

The original group from Xanthium had stayed with Red on his own ship, with Orak and Teressa among them. Isleen, Alaric, and the former guardsmen stayed close to Red and Kraego; Teressa stayed even closer. She remained as fanatically loyal to both of them as she had been on their first proper meeting, but Red suspected that she partly stayed so close out of fear.

Nobody else on the ship wanted to talk to her, and some of them – former guards in particular – were outright hostile.

Not that any of them would be likely to actually attack her; even if she hadn't had a griffin beside her, Red had made it clear that she was under his protection. But he overheard some of them muttering insults and racial slurs in her presence, and though Alaric and Isleen both treated her with cautious respect, neither of them was willing to speak to her or spend much time around her.

If Teressa minded she didn't show it, but Red minded. He himself hadn't spoken to anyone much on the voyage, and nobody seemed to want to speak to him much either. He could have made more of an effort, but he didn't. A terrible feeling of isolation had come over him, as if there were a wall between himself and his fellow travellers – a wall he felt unable to pass through, and which they were unwilling to venture too close to.

Only Kraego seemed not to notice it but all the giant griffin could talk about was war, and anger, and revenge. And power, that too. But almost all griffins cared about power more than anything else.

Red felt glad he was there anyway, but he couldn't really confide in him.

He didn't feel the need to sleep much anymore. During the day, he kept out of the sun as much as possible; once it hadn't bothered him so much, but now it felt so hot it smothered him. His skin had stayed sickly pale, and refused to tan under the sun – now it just burned. He felt as if he'd turned into a kind of Northerner. Not just because of that, or because his eyes had gone black, but because he felt like an intruder. An outsider.

At night, though, he felt better; especially when the moon was out. He spent his nights up on deck, not sleeping, but sometimes just staring at the stars. Kullervo had once told him that Northerners believed they were the souls of the dead, and he wondered if that could be true. If so, then his own soul must be up there somewhere.

He touched the side of his neck, just under the jaw, as he had done many times over the last few months. The big vein there was cool and still, and did not pulsate in time to his heartbeat. It, and his heart, had gone silent forever.

He sat there, feeling paralysed by the knowledge, and only slowly realised that he could hear a voice. He looked up, mildly curious. Kraego and Orak were both asleep, further back on the deck.

Ahead, at the very front of the ship above the figurehead, he saw Teressa.

The Northerner wore a silver robe like that she had had on at their first meeting. She refused to wear anything else.

Just now she was crouched on one knee, like a servant kneeling to her lord. But her eyes were fixed on the sky, and she was murmuring in a low, fervent voice.

Red watched her with interest. He had already guessed that she was praying, but he wondered what she was praying for – and who to. This strange personal religion she claimed to have invented seemed to involve worshipping Arenadd as well as the Night God, so she could be appealing to either of them.

Red had never been very religious himself, and it seemed particularly odd to worship an actual human being – even a dead one. Was that normal for Northerners, or anyone? He didn't think so. Then again, he knew what Arenadd had been to his followers. His enemies had considered him a monster, but the Northerners he had led to freedom saw him as their greatest hero – and a holy man as well, since the Night God had supposedly given him the power to do it. A saviour.

Lost in thought, Red didn't notice that Teressa's murmurings had stopped until she turned her head and saw him.

She started in surprise. 'Oh!'

Red took a step back. 'Sorry. Didn't mean to spy.'

Teressa stood up. 'It's all right. I just didn't hear ye.'

'Yeah,' Red smiled sadly. 'Seems I don't make a lot of noise when I walk nowadays.'

She smiled back. 'Aye, the Shadow That Walks moves in silence, like a shadow. That's where the name comes from; that and the ability to be unseen.'

Red grimaced. He hadn't tried to use any of his new powers. He didn't want to.

Teressa noticed the look. 'This must be hard for ye,' she said, coming closer. 'I can understand. Yer people have always hated and feared the Shadow That Walks. Ye must have been brought up hearing horror stories about him.'

'Yeah, it's true,' Red admitted. 'Us people in Liranwee all grew up afraid that one day the D— that King Arenadd would come through the mountains an' kill us all. Honestly, the first time I saw that Caedmon, I thought it was him. Even though I knew he was dead. When I saw him, I…' he shivered. 'He looked at me an' said "Southerner, d'you know who I am?" An' I looked back an' said "The Dark Lord Arenadd." I was so scared. He laughed at me. They all did. I've never been so afraid. I don't reckon I was that scared later on when I was on the gallows.'

Tentatively, Teressa put a hand on his arm. Her touch was light. Gentle, or maybe just cautious. 'It must have been awful.'

'Of course, he wasn't the Dark Lord at all,' Red added. 'I felt like a right idiot when I found out. Didn't help us, though. Caedmon's just as bad if y'ask—,' he broke off, embarrassed.

But Teressa smiled. 'It's all right; ye don't have to feel stupid. I saw Arenadd with my own eyes, and I've seen Caedmon too. It's said he's the very image of his cousin, and I know it's true. Arenadd didn't have tattoos on his face, though. And don't forget – Caedmon might look like Arenadd, but he doesn't have the same powers. He's not immortal.'

'Yeah, but he's laid waste to the South just like Arenadd

would've,' Red said bitterly.

'No,' Teressa shook her head. 'The South hasn't been destroyed. Ye can still save it. And if that's what ye want, I'll stand by ye to the death.'

Red shook his head. 'I still can't believe you'd turn on yer own King like that. Your own people. Just for me. A Southerner, of all things.'

'I serve the Shadow That Walks,' Teressa said, with that expression of utmost sincerity he had come to know so well. 'If the Night God chose ye or not, ye are the Shadow That Walks, and Arenadd's rightful successor.'

Red gestured at the ship's railings. 'Sit down. I should've talked to you like this a long time ago. Had a lot on my mind these last few days, that's all.'

Teressa sat. 'I understand. Honestly…'

'Yeah?' said Red.

'Honestly, I'm surprised by ye,' said Teressa. 'I mean, I honour the Shadow That Walks – always have. But if that happened to me… if it was me instead of ye, I don't know what I'd do. Cry, probably. Scream. Go mad. But ye… ye seem so calm about it.'

Red sat down. 'It's not gonna be easy,' he said. 'I know it. But right now, I just gotta be glad I've got a second chance. Anyway, this could've been a lot worse. If the power had gone to someone else, if it was a Northerner…' he trailed off awkwardly.

Teressa only smiled. 'It's not for me to know the Night God's will,' she said. 'If ye are the Shadow That Walks, then ye are doing what's right. Not just for yer own people, but for mine.'

'Teressa, I'm gonna kill the King,' said Red. 'I'm gonna stop his invasion.'

'Then maybe we weren't meant to rule Cymria,' Teressa said without hesitation. 'As I said, it's not for me to know the Night God's will. But I honour ye before even the Night God, so if ye do go against her, I'll still follow ye. I swear it on Arenadd's holy name.'

Red frowned. 'Some people'd say I shouldn't trust you. You're a Northerner, and honestly, I think you're too religious for yer own good. But you came all the way to Amoran just to find me, so I'm gonna trust you to stick by what you said.'

'I understand,' said Teressa. 'If I could, I'd fight for ye, but I'm not a fighter. But there is something I can do for ye. I've been meaning to ask about it.'

'Yeah?' said Red.

'I'm not the only one who worships the Shadow That Walks,' said Teressa. 'Others do too. I don't know how many. I started the faith, and converted plenty of people myself, but my converts converted others. There could be hundreds for all I know. But if I told them about ye, some of them might choose to follow ye as I do. Some of them are just commoners, but not all of them. Some of us are griffiners. I know Lady Arwydd is one of us, and she's an assistant to the Master of War. She could have valuable information.'

Red stared at her. 'You'd go and find these people?'

'Aye, I would,' said Teressa. 'But I'd have to do it quickly, before the King finds out about what I've done. With yer permission, when we get back, Orak and I will fly North and gather the others.'

Red hadn't shaved off the beard that had grown during his captivity yet. He rubbed his hairy cheek while he thought it over. 'You'd really do that? It'd be taking a huge risk.'

'I know,' said Teressa. 'But I'd do it for ye. If ye want me to.'

'I'll think about it,' said Red. 'Then I'll let you know. All right?'

Teressa smiled. 'All right.'

*

As promised, Red spent some time thinking over what Teressa had said, and he decided to talk it over with Kraego.

'I'm glad that Teressa's with us,' he told his new partner, when the haughty griffin had come to him demanding to have his talons cleaned.

Kraego lifted his forepaw a little higher. 'The talon on the smallest toe is broken; be certain to smooth the edges. Yes, it is good to have another griffin to follow us, and a partnered human as well. Orak speaks to me with the greatest respect.'

Red rolled his eyes and hoped his new partner wouldn't understand what the expression meant. 'It ain't just that, either,' he said. 'Teressa says there's others like her, an' she asked me if she could go get them when we're back in Cymria. Maybe some of 'em would want to follow us too. She said some of 'em are even griffiners.'

'That would be good,' said Kraego. 'Powerful ones like us deserve many followers, and we shall have them.'

'I don't reckon we can win this with just you an' me,' said Red. 'You're a damned strong griffin, but there's only one of you. They've got the Unpartnered, an' plenty of partnered griffins as well. You beat griffins with griffins. That's what they say.'

'Do not be afraid,' said Kraego. 'Once I have made myself known to them, many griffins will come. As they came to my father.'

'They didn't come before,' said Red. Once he might have been less blunt about it, but not now. It wasn't as if Kraego could kill him.

'That is because I was wild and unpartnered,' said Kraego. 'An unpartnered griffin does not have followers. Now I shall return, partnered to the most powerful human in the world.'

'You could've chosen me before,' Red pointed out. 'Before all this happened. I even asked if you would. We might've gotten followers back then an' then maybe we could've stopped any of this from happening. Then Withypool might not've fallen, an' I'd still be alive.'

Kraego huffed. 'Only the Shadow That Walks is worthy to be my human.'

Red stared at him in disbelief for a moment. Then he went back to cleaning the griffin's talons. 'You miserable son of a bitch,' he muttered in Cymrian.

Kraego's raised forepaw suddenly slammed down onto the deck. '*Red!*'

Red backed off, but not very far. He said nothing, but stared defiantly back at the black griffin.

Kraego hissed, 'Do not blame me for what happened to you.' 'I did not wish for you to die. My plan was always to stay by you until the war was done. But—,'

'But what?' asked Red.

Kraego calmed down. 'I never intended to obey the demands of the Night God, and you should be grateful for that in more ways than you know. She did not just wish for me to make Morgan the Shadow That Walks – she also told me that I must kill you. I could have crushed the life out of you with one paw. But I did not. Instead, I decided that I would stay with you, and that if you were killed, I would give my power to you. That was always my intention, Red – because you have always been a brother to me, and because after what we lived through together I decided that you were worthy.'

Red couldn't believe his ears. 'You did?'

'Yes,' said Kraego. 'Of all the humans I have known, you were the only one worthy to be my partner.'

'You said you were gonna leave me when the war was over,' said Red.

'I did, and I did not lie,' said Kraego. 'But after the Night God had spoken to me, I began to reconsider.'

'You could've asked me if I wanted this,' Red said without anger.

'It was my decision to make,' said Kraego. 'And I do not think you regret this.'

'Yeah…' Red said slowly. 'It's all right, Kraego. I'm sorry. An' I'm glad you're here, too.'

'Then that is good,' said Kraego. 'Now, you must finish cleaning my talons.'

'Righto.' Red chuckled. 'What's a partner for, after all?'

He went back to cleaning the griffin's talons, using one end of the tool to scrape out the inside of each one, and the rasp on the other to smooth off any broken edges he found.

'But what about Teressa and Orak?' he asked. 'Teressa's asked for my permission before she goes off to find her friends. Should we let her?'

'That is for you to decide,' said Kraego. 'You are the human, and it is your cunning that must help us choose what we will do.'

'I ain't that cunning,' Red muttered. 'Most of the time I feel like an idiot. I dunno. What if Teressa decides to just rat us out to the rest of her lot?'

'They would not believe her,' said Kraego. 'And besides, Orak has told me that they left Cymria to come looking for me without swearing loyalty to Shar.'

'So?' said Red.

'That is forbidden for a partnered griffin,' said Kraego. 'By law, once he has chosen a human, he must go to the master of his territory to swear loyalty. I know this because my mother told me.'

'So if they went back now they'd be locked up or somethin'?' said Red.

'Their loyalty would be in doubt,' said Kraego.

'I know I shouldn't be too worried about it,' Red admitted. 'I mean… she helped us get free. She turned her back on her own people just for me. But my Dad always said you gotta watch out for someone who helps you by betrayin' someone else, 'cause who's to say they won't do it again to you?'

'It is simple,' Kraego said rather impatiently. 'If they betray us, I will kill them both.'

Red paused. 'Uh… right, but maybe you shouldn't tell 'em that.'

'If I do, it will make them doubly loyal,' said Kraego. 'Go and tell them that they have our permission. It is worth the risk if we may win more followers.'

Red sat back and wiped the cleaning tool on his tunic. 'I thought you said I was meant to figure it out.'

'I did, but I was bored with waiting for you to decide,' said Kraego. 'Now I have decided for you. Go and do as I have said.'

Red shrugged. 'All right. I reckon you're right anyhow.'

'I am,' said Kraego. 'Go now, *Kraeai kran ae.*'

*

Below decks in the cargo hold, Teressa combed her hair and talked to her own partner.

'Do ye think he'll give us permission to go?' she asked.

Orak scratched his belly with a back paw. 'Kraego will need the followers that we can bring. Do not be afraid.'

'All right,' said Teressa. 'But ye know that if we go back North, we won't just be doing that. Don't ye?'

'Yes… you wish to seek out this heart, and these bones,' said Orak. 'But I still do not see what we have to gain from it.'

'But I do,' said Teressa. 'I've worked it out. And we have to do it. It's our sacred duty.'

'Yours, not mine,' said Orak, unmoved. 'Have you understood what the winged man meant?'

'I have,' said Teressa. 'We know the bones must be Arenadd's bones. And the heart – I've worked out whose it must be. It's Saeddryn's. Do ye know how she died?'

'The half-breed human had her killed,' said Orak.

'Aye, but do ye know how?' Teressa persisted. When the grey griffin didn't answer she went on. 'They did it by cutting out her heart. The half-breed did it, and Kullervo helped. I don't know why they didn't just destroy it, but maybe it's indestructible. And if that's true, then maybe Kullervo took it. Hid it somewhere.'

'And what does that matter?' asked Orak. 'What use are dead bones and a piece of human flesh?'

Teressa could feel her own heart beating faster. 'Don't ye get it?' she exclaimed. 'The heart is where the power of the Shadow That Walks lives! The heart that doesn't beat. If Saeddryn's heart is still out there, then her power must be inside it! And if we put her heart in Arenadd's body, he could rise again! Don't ye see, Orak? That's what we're meant to do! That's what Arenadd wanted us to do this whole time! We have to help him come back to us.'

Orak stilled. 'If Kraeai kran ae were to return with our help, he could be grateful. He may reward us.'

'Who cares?' said Teressa. 'It's our holy mission.'

Orak's eyes narrowed. 'If Kraeai kran ae rose again, you would wish to follow him instead of Kraego's human. Yes?'

Teressa stopped in mid-flight. 'I suppose… I hadn't thought about it.'

'But the Mighty Skandar is dead,' said Orak. 'Kraeai kran ae would be unpartnered. Kraego's human is stronger, and we must remain with him.'

'But we have to help Arenadd,' said Teressa. 'I have to. Once he returns, he can tell us what to do. Maybe he would want to help Red as well.'

'And if not?' said Orak.

'I don't know,' said Teressa. She twisted the comb in her hair. 'I don't know…'

'But I do,' said Orak. He extended his talons. 'I have sworn to follow Kraego, and I will not be moved from that path. Kraeai kran ae may help us in return for our help, so we will bring the heart to his bones. But afterwards, we shall go to gather followers for Kraego. We will not abandon him.'

'All right then,' Teressa said reluctantly. But she felt an odd certainty that whatever happened, it would be all right. Arenadd wouldn't have sent her to find Red if she weren't meant to follow him.

'Now, you must hope that your new master will grant you permission to go at all,' Orak added.

Teressa slowly went back to her combing. 'I don't like this. I want to be loyal to Red — I don't want to lie to him. But if I tell him about the bones and everything, he won't like it. He'll forbid us, I'm sure of it.'

'Then say nothing,' said Orak. 'It is none of his concern.'

'But if I lie to him and he finds out—,'

'He will not find out,' said Orak. 'Leave it, Teressa. Seek his permission to go North and find him followers, and say nothing about Kraeai kran ae.'

'I won't,' Teressa said reluctantly. She put the comb away. 'I should go and see him. Ask if he's made up his mind.'

'Do so,' Orak commanded.

Teressa left obediently, but she couldn't shake off her feelings of guilt. She had betrayed her King. Now Red was all she had left, and if Arenadd did not return there would be nobody else. She had to stay loyal, and lying was not loyalty.

But if she asked Red for his blessing to try and resurrect her idol, he would say no – and then she would have thrown away her chance to bring Arenadd back and go on the greatest quest of her life.

So that was what it came to, she thought as she went up on deck. Lie to Red, or betray Arenadd.

I owe it to him, she thought finally. I owe it to Arenadd. One last service to him, before I turn my back on the North forever.

That made her feel better. But not as better as she had expected or wanted.

Up on deck, she found Red walking around in the shade. When he saw her, his face lit up and he came towards her.

'There you are,' he said. 'I was lookin' for you.'

Teressa bowed. 'I came to ask ye if ye'd decided whether to let me go North.'

'Good, because I was lookin' for you so I could say yes,' said Red. 'You got my permission.'

Teressa smiled her relief. 'Thank ye, sir.'

Red smiled back. 'Call me Red. Now, when we get back, you an' Orak will go off together. Go to Malvern, or wherever you reckon the most of them will be. I ain't sure where I'm gonna be yet, but I'll tell you once I know an' you'll bring them there to meet me, right?'

'I understand,' said Teressa. 'And thank ye for trusting me.'

'You've offered to take a big risk for us,' said Red. 'I reckon you've earned some trust. Oh, an' one other thing…'

'Yes?' said Teressa.

'If you get into trouble, send me a message,' said Red. 'I'll come.'

Teressa stared at him. 'Ye will?'

'Yeah. You came for me, so if you need it, I'll do the same for you.'

She stared at her feet. 'All right… Red.'

Chapter Seventeen

A Cave of Bones

Lady Arwydd prayed again shortly after the beginning of her search for Morgan. She had already prayed to the Night God, but when she and her four companions stopped to rest on the second night she felt the need to pray to another power as well.

Her fellow travellers were both griffiners, of course. One was Leolin – a friend of Morgan's who was also an assistant to the Master of War like herself. He was a good fighter, along with his partner Rukeera, and should be useful. More than that, he had asked to go.

The other two were Lady Nelwyn and her partner Serraka. Nelwyn was a healer – young, but apprenticed to the Master of Healing and already a good healer in her own right. Her silver feathered partner was unusually large – probably one of the Mighty Skandar's many offspring – which would be an advantage.

Arwydd didn't want to admit it to herself, but she felt inadequate to be in charge of the other two. She had never commanded anyone in her life. But she wasn't going to let her uncertainty show. Morgan needed her now, and she would do whatever she could to help him.

She left her partner Essh to sleep, and slipped away into the darkness of the trees where they had made camp. Once she thought she was far enough away, she pulled out the prayer stone she kept hidden in her clothes. Nobody knew about it, not even Essh.

As always, she found a moonlit spot and settled down with the prayer stone between her hands. Once she felt comfortable, she took out her knife and tentatively sliced it across her thumb. The blade was sharp, and the skin split open under it.

Arwydd winced, but quickly put the wound close to the stone and squeezed some blood out onto the carved design of a heart with a triple spiral inside.

'With this offering of true Northern blood, I call to you,' she said softly. They were the same words used in the great Moon Temple in Malvern, where a knife lay on the altar ready for anyone who wanted to pray to the Night God. An offering of blood had always been the proper summons.

But Arwydd offered her prayer up not to the Night God, but to someone else – just as the apprentice priestess she had met had taught her.

She remembered the woman very well. She had been in her thirties, but young for her age, full of a passion and conviction that Arwydd had never encountered before. She had persuaded the initially sceptical griffiner to follow her new faith, and done it very well. Arwydd had been praying to the Shadow That Walked ever since.

And, like Teressa, Arwydd had chosen to pray to one in particular.

'Great Arenadd,' she murmured, putting her hands around the stone and closing her eyes, 'I ask you to give me strength. Help me to serve the Night God faithfully, and with courage. And help me to do what I have to do now. I…' she hesitated. 'Help Morgan. Keep him safe. Help me find him. I know he needs me now. Help me get to him before it's too late. There were so many things I wanted to tell him. Please…'

She continued to pray like that for some time, but she had said what she wanted to say, even if she still couldn't bring herself to put the wild feelings that had begun to live inside her into words. It was enough to ask for courage.

Praying made her feel better, and when she had finished she carefully wrapped the stone up and put it away again before she returned to Essh and her bed-roll by the fire.

She hated camping, but she was so tired by now that she had no trouble falling asleep. She lay on her back and looked up at the moon, one hand unconsciously resting on her tunic where the prayer stone lay concealed in an inside pocket. Before long, her eyes closed and she fell asleep with the white moonlight shining on her face.

Her sleep was deep – deeper than the normal sleep of someone lying on hard ground in a cold forest. She could feel that she was asleep, but in such a way that she felt convinced that no power on earth could wake her up.

As she lay there in the comforting blackness, the dream came.

She dreamt of Arenadd.

He stood there, robed and bearded, staring at her. He did not smile, but he inclined his head towards her, in a gesture that might have been respect.

Arwydd stood and stared back at him, wanting to reach out to him but unable to move. A thousand questions filled her head, but she couldn't speak. But she smiled. She could do that, at least.

Arenadd smiled back, knowingly. Then he changed. The eyes stayed, but the face and the body changed around them. Now she was looking at someone else, someone she vaguely recognised. She saw a Southerner, big and burly, with red hair. He wore the armour of a guard, and his face was strong and square-jawed.

A Southerner. But a Southerner with Arenadd's eyes staring out of his face.

The Southerner spoke, and his voice was Arenadd's voice.

Serve the Shadow That Walks.

The dream ended there, but it would stay in her mind, as Teressa's dream had stayed with her. She found herself thinking about it the next day, and the day after that, endlessly turning it over in her mind, unable to shake off the feeling that she had finally been given the guidance she needed – but guidance to do what, she wasn't sure.

*

Several more days passed, while Arwydd and her companions travelled southward. They had to travel carefully; the Southerners might have been subdued and their leaders captured, but the whole country hadn't been brought under control yet, and there could well be enemies about. Luckily, though, the three Northerners barely saw anyone – only a few farmers working in the lands they flew over.

They were getting close to the last place Arwydd had seen Morgan and Echo; she knew it for certain once they had passed Dead Mountain. The great plateau at its top that had once been home to Old Eagleholm still had plenty of ruined buildings in evidence, but it was obvious without even landing there that the last of its inhabitants were long gone. Arwydd had no desire to go any closer to it than they did; even in the North, Dead Mountain was said to be cursed.

Beyond it, they found themselves in lands that were surprisingly well-populated. Before Dead Mountain, former farmlands had become largely barren. Beyond it, though, new farms and villages had begun to be built. The travellers saw plenty of crops and cattle, and Southerner peasants hard at work. They decided not to risk bothering them, but Leolin wasn't above stealing some food out of a field when their supplies ran low, and the three griffins helped themselves to some livestock.

Nobody would be likely to try and stop griffins from taking what they wanted.

'What I want to know,' Nelwyn said one evening, 'is what Eyrie owns these lands now? Somebody must be taxing these farmers and organising these villages. But who?'

'No idea,' said Leolin. He took out the sickle he favoured as a weapon, and started to sharpen it. 'According to the maps these are Eagleholm's lands, but Eagleholm is gone.' He looked at Arwydd. 'Do you have some idea, Wydd?'

Arwydd paused to think it over. 'We've picked up some things from the Southerners we captured. Most of Eagleholm's lands were seized by the other Eyries, or just left to rot. Anyone could have claimed all this,' she said, adding, 'We could ask the locals, of course.'

The other two laughed. 'Maybe we'll find out later,' Arwydd smiled.

And, some days later, they did.

They flew on, and soon reached the last campsite that Arwydd and Morgan had shared. There was nobody about, so the three of them split up and began quartering the lands around and beyond it, meeting up each evening to compare notes. At first they found nothing, but they persisted, gradually working their way further south until the Coppertop Mountains were in sight.

And there, right at the base of those mountains, in the middle of what had once been farmland, they found it.

A city. A new city. A city none of them had heard of. Though only half built so far, out of the coppery coloured stone that gave the mountains their name, all of them could see the handful of griffins circling above it, and the guards posted on the walls.

All six of them stood and stared at it from a safe distance.

'I'll be damned,' Leolin said eventually. 'Did anyone know this was here?'

'None of us knew,' said his partner. 'I did not, and nor does Shar.'

'This must be the seat of the one whose territory we are in,' said Essh. 'Echo's human was captured in this territory, so perhaps this is where he has been taken.'

Arwydd's heart sank. 'But if he's in there, how do we get him out?'

'Simple – we can't,' said Leolin. 'What we'll have to do is try and make certain that he's in there, before we go and report back to the King. Either way, this place will have to be captured as well. Don't worry, Wydd,' he added. 'If Morgan is in there, we'll free him when we take the city. And if they've hurt him, you can take revenge for him. The King won't show mercy to anyone who lays a hand on his own son.'

Arwydd felt ill, but she knew she had to take charge. 'How are we going to find out if he's in there?'

'We can't infiltrate the place,' said Leolin. 'None of us have the skills for it. We could try kidnapping one of the Southerners.'

'Or we can search for Echo,' Essh put in. 'If he has not been captured, then he will be here somewhere, seeking for a way to take his human back. It may be that he is hiding somewhere – perhaps in those mountains.'

'That's a good thought,' said Arwydd. For some reason, the thought of Echo made her feel better. The spotted griffin could change his coat at will – maybe he would be able to sneak into the city. Maybe he'd done it already.

Nelwyn, Leolin, and all three griffins were looking at her, waiting for her to make a decision.

'All right,' she said, doing her best to sound strong. 'We'll go into the Coppertops. But we'll do it carefully – we can't fly over the city without being spotted, so we'll have to go around. We'll search around in the mountains and see if Echo is there, or some clue that he's been in the area. If we don't find anything, then we'll try your plan of capturing someone from the city and questioning them.' She dearly hoped that it wouldn't come to that.

'All right,' Nelwyn nodded. 'Let's go, then.'

'Echo is the key,' said Essh. 'Come, get onto my back.'

The three griffiners mounted up, and the three griffins flew – westward until the city was nearly out of sight, and then south once again, into the Coppertops.

The Coppertop mountains were one of the few wild places left in Southern Cymria, mostly because they were too rugged to build on, and too impassable for the land on the other side of them to be worth it. Thick, lush forest covered the lower-lying areas, populated by wild goats and striped Southern wolves. Wild griffins lived there, too – though not many of them.

The three partnered griffins flew in over the mountains, and chose to land on the top of one, where their humans dismounted and all six of them surveyed the landscape.

Arwydd took in the dense forest that lay below them in every direction. 'How are we going to find anything in this?' she wondered.

'There is a way,' said Serraka, Nelwyn's partner. 'If we send out a call, Echo will know our voices. He will come to us.'

'Wild griffins may hear as well,' Leolin's partner Rukeera put in.

'They may, but they will not dare to challenge us,' said Serraka. 'We are three, and larger than them. I will call now.'

And, without further ado, she did just that – raising her big rough-feathered head to the sky and letting out a deafening screech. The other two joined in, while the three humans cringed and covered their ears.

Every griffin could call, of course. It sounded like a mixture of a lion's roar and an eagle's cry; a screech with a snarl and a rumble behind it. But calls could be modulated to include the sound of the griffin's own name, and that was the territorial call, and the one used to summon their partner.

All three griffins did that now, screaming their names to the sky so that they echoed over the mountains, again and again. It would be audible from miles away to a human, and from even further away to another griffin.

After a while, the three griffins fell silent and everyone there listened intently.

'I hear him!' Essh said sharply. 'Quickly. Call again!'

They called again, and then listened again.

'I hear him too,' Serraka said. 'He is further to the North. Come.'

Arwydd hadn't heard anything at all, but she eagerly climbed onto Essh's back. The three griffins set out again, sometimes calling while they flew, and as they went further on, Arwydd started to hear Echo's replies. She had grown up among griffins and could recognise their individual calls, and as this one grew clearer, she recognised it as Echo's.

Eventually, as they got closer to the edge of the mountains and the new city, they could see him. The spotted griffin was circling over a mountaintop above a valley, calling them to him.

Essh, Serraka and Rukeera flew to him, and when they were close enough, Echo went down to land. They followed.

Echo had landed in an overhang partway down the mountain, which was easily large enough for the three griffins. He stood on a heap of tumbled rock, waiting for them.

Essh landed, and her paws had barely touched the ground before Arwydd leapt off her and ran to meet Echo.

'Echo, there you are!' she called. 'Thank gods. Where's Morgan?'

Echo had indeed reverted to his customary spotted hide, but he looked thin and bedraggled. 'Essh,' he said. 'You have come to find us. You – human – Arwydd? You must come with me immediately. Morgan needs your help.'

'Where is he?' Arwydd asked sharply. 'Take me to him.'

'He is here,' said Echo. He jumped down from the rock pile and led her around it to a deeper part of the overhang. It went deep into the mountainside, and as Arwydd entered she saw the strange pictures painted on its walls. Images of human hands, and stylised animals with their bones clearly visible inside them. At the centre was a painting of a griffin, spewing magic from its beak.

She had no time to wonder about any of that though, because of what lay on the floor.

Bones. Human bones. They lay scattered around the sandy floor, most of them blackened with mould. She saw a skull, so small it must have belonged to a child, which had a big hole smashed through it.

In the midst of all that, someone had cleared a space and piled it high with dry grass and leaves, and that was there Morgan was.

He lay on his back on the makeshift bed, one hand clutching a long rope with a noose on the end. His clothes were ragged and filthy, and she could see painful looking bruises on his exposed skin. His cheeks were hollow and sunken with hunger and exhaustion, and one of his legs was in a crude splint.

Arwydd ran to him. 'Morgan!'

Morgan coughed and opened his eyes. He made a sound that might have been speech.

Arwydd crouched by him, and reached down to touch his face. 'Morgan, it's me. It's Arwydd. And Leolin and Nelwyn are here. We came to find you.'

Morgan smiled. 'Glad,' he said in a strangled whisper.

Nelwyn and Leolin had already come running, and Arwydd

turned to them.

'Nelwyn!' she said, in a sharp voice that surprised her. 'Quickly. Morgan's hurt.'

The healer didn't need telling twice. She sprinted over, and Arwydd stood aside to let her examine him.

Nelwyn pulled Morgan's torn tunic open, and expertly ran her hands over his chest, throat, and limbs. She examined his face as well, and his leg.

'Is it bad?' Arwydd asked, unable to stop herself.

'Broken ribs – they've mostly healed by now,' said Nelwyn. 'And that leg was obviously broken… I don't think it's healed straight.'

Morgan nodded weakly. 'Southerners got me,' he whispered. 'Been stuck here for months… they were hunting for us.'

Leolin swore. 'Those sons of bitches. Don't worry, Morgan – we'll get them. That city's done for. I wouldn't be surprised if the King razes the whole thing to the ground once he finds out about this.'

Morgan coughed. 'Like to do it myself.'

'That's enough,' said Arwydd. 'We'll take you back to Liranwee, and you'll recover.'

Morgan smiled weakly and clutched at her hand. 'Thank you.'

Arwydd gave Morgan an encouraging smile. She couldn't quite believe that she had taken command like that, but she was glad. Maybe she could do more than she had thought, and that was just as well. She wasn't going to let Morgan die; not before she had told him how she felt. Not ever.

But, to her surprise, while she and the others got to work preparing some food for him, she found herself thinking of the dream, and murmuring those sacred words to herself.

'Serve the Shadow That Walks…'

Chapter Eighteen

Serve the Shadow that Walks

Many long months later, Red's ships reached Cymria. The Amorani captain of the lead ship had asked Red directly where they should dock, and Red, seeing sense, had ordered him to follow the coast southward. Docking at Withypool or any of the South's major port towns would only lead to instant capture.

'No, we gotta land somewhere safe,' he declared. 'Somewhere out of the way, where we can do it quietly. It'd be hard not to get noticed with there bein' so many of us.'

'Then where shall we dock?' the captain asked politely.

'Not sure,' said Red. 'Let's just follow the coast at a distance, an' keep an eye out until we spot somethin' what looks right.'

Isleen had been standing by and listening, along with Alaric and Teressa. Now she stepped forward.

'May I make a suggestion?'

'Yeah, sure,' said Red.

The former Eyrie Mistress coughed. 'There is one place we could go to hide for a time. I don't think the Northerners know about it. In fact, scarcely anyone knows about it.' She turned to the Captain. 'Do you have a map?'

The Amorani nodded and quietly fetched one from a cupboard in his cabin. He spread it out on the table so they could all look at it.

It was a map of Cymria – slightly out of date, but fairly accurate.

Red inspected it. His home country was shaped vaguely like a teardrop or an egg, with the North at the pointed end. Liranwee wasn't on the map, but he thought he could estimate where it should go.

Isleen pointed. 'There,' she said.

Red looked at the spot she had indicated. At the bottom of the map, just below the main continent, was an island. It was large, and separated from the rest of Cymria by what looked like a fairly narrow channel.

'Monag Island,' said Isleen. 'Hardly anyone ever goes there. It's on the far side of the Coppertops, as you can see, so the only sensible way to get there is by boat, or on griffin-back. But it's inhabited, and it has a port. I seriously doubt that the Northerners know about it, or would bother with it if they did. There's nothing of any value on it. But we could land there, and not be noticed.'

'You sure?' asked Red.

Isleen nodded. 'I don't think many people in the South know about it, for that matter. I only know about it because of some obscure book I found in the library.'

'Could be worth a try, then,' said Red. 'Let's head that way.'

'It will be done, my Lord,' the Captain said with a bow.

'Monag it is,' Red repeated to Teressa in private later. 'But not for you.'

'No, Orak and I should leave sooner,' she nodded. 'When we're in sight of the North.'

'Exactly,' said Red. 'An' maybe I should've stopped you from knowin' about where the rest of us are goin' in case you get caught, but now you'll know where to send a message if you wind up needing help.'

'I won't betray ye,' Teressa promised.

'Well... if anything gets tortured out of you, I wouldn't blame you,' Red sighed. 'That ain't betrayal. Trust me. I know how it works. Just try an' make sure it doesn't come to that.'

'Ye don't have to tell me that twice, Red.' Teressa smiled to hide her fears.

'Didn't think so. You ain't stupid,' Red grinned back. 'Anyway, we'll be right by the coast this time tomorrow. That'll be your time to get goin'. Oh yeah, an' before I forget...' He drew his sword, and gave it to her. 'In case you get into a tight corner.'

Teressa held it cautiously. 'I don't think I'd know how to use it.'

'There's nothin' to it,' said Red. 'Someone gives you trouble, you stab 'em one. But mostly you don't have to; just hold it like you mean business an' half the time they'll back off. I could give you a quick lesson, if you like. Mind you, you'll have Orak helpin' you out. But just – here, give it back a moment.'

Teressa handed it over.

Red took it, and showed her a fighting stance. 'See?' he said. 'Y'just hold it like that. No quaverin', no lettin' them see how scared you are. Try it.'

Teressa took the sword back, and tried to imitate the pose.

'See, when you get right down to it, most people don't want to hurt anyone,' Red explained. 'Or get hurt either. So if you make it look like you might just hurt 'em, like you really might be serious, that'll scare a lot of people off. If you look scared, that's when they know they can do the hurtin' because you ain't gonna fight back.'

Teressa put the sword into her belt. 'I'll remember.'

''Course, most people ain't gonna mess with a griffiner anyway,' Red added. 'Let's just hope Orak's all you wind up needin' on this little trip of yours.'

'Aye,' said Teressa. 'Aye, let's hope.'

Red grinned. 'That's a funny word, "aye".'

'It's a Northerner word,' said Teressa. 'I just use it sometimes out of habit.'

'Hey, I didn't say apologise,' said Red. 'Anyway… you'd better rest up. I should too, come to that.'

Teressa watched him go, and smiled to herself. 'Serve the Shadow That Walks,' she murmured, and touched the hilt of the sword.

*

The next day came, and the ship drew closer to the Northern coast of Cymria. Red ordered the captain to go as close as he could without being noticed – fortunately he had already chosen to approach a part of the coast that didn't have a port, and there weren't any other ships about.

When they were close enough, Teressa and Orak were ready to leave. Travelling by griffin-back meant travelling light, and Teressa took nothing but her spare robe, a small bag of supplies, and the sword.

Red gave her an encouraging pat on the shoulder before she got onto Orak's back. 'Good luck, you two,' he said.

'We won't let ye down,' Teressa promised.

'I shall protect her,' said Orak. 'And work faithfully for you, Kraego.'

Kraego snorted. 'You have done well so far, Orak. Go now, and come back to me soon.'

'I shall,' said Orak.

Teressa climbed onto his back, and Red and Kraego stepped

back to give him room. The grey griffin took off with a graceful leap, and flew up and over the ship and away towards the looming coast of Cymria.

Several people had come up on deck, and they watched the two of them go.

'Where're they off to?' Neth demanded.

'North,' said Red.

'What for?' asked another former guard. Everyone there looked suspicious.

'Teressa reckons she can gather followers for us,' said Red. 'Friends who feel the same way she does.'

Neth shook his head. 'That was a mistake, sir. You shouldn't've let her go. First chance she gets she'll stab you in the back. You know what Northerners are like.'

Red had expected something like this, and he only shook his head. 'That's enough, Neth.'

'But she knows where we're going!' Isleen objected. 'What if she—?'

'She won't,' Red said sharply. 'She came all the way to Amoran to help us. She's not gonna turn on us now.'

'For everyone's sake, I hope you're right,' said Isleen.

'I trust her,' said Alaric.

Neth curled his lip. 'Shut up, you little runt. Nobody gives a damn what you think.'

The storyteller cringed and obligingly shut up.

'Leave him alone, Neth,' said Red. 'Cowards pick on people weaker than they are, an' I'm not gonna have a coward following me.'

Neth started, glared, and walked off muttering.

'You didn't have to do that,' said Alaric.

'That's right. I did it 'cause I wanted to,' said Red. 'Now let's get out of this damned sun.'

He walked off, and Alaric followed – nervously, but with his head held just a little higher.

*

Meanwhile, Orak and Teressa flew. They made straight for the shore, and flew on past it until they reached a small griffiner outpost – a lone tower built for a griffin to rest. Most outposts like it came stocked with some dried food and other supplies, but this one obviously hadn't been visited in a long time and boasted nothing more than some water in the trough, which was fed by a pipe that gathered rainwater from the roof.

They stopped there, and Orak drank.

'Now,' said Teressa. 'We just have to find out where Gwernyfed is. Do ye remember the place where we found Flell?'

Orak lifted his dripping beak from the trough. 'I do. I believe that I could find it again.'

'Good, because she came from Gwernyfed, and she was on foot,' said Teressa. 'She can't have gone far from it. It was inland from Abertawe, wasn't it?'

'Yes,' said Orak. 'We shall go that way. I think it is further south from here.'

Teressa agreed, and once they had rested a short while, they did just that. Orak flew steadily, following the coast until the port town of Abertawe had come in sight. The grey griffin landed there to rest again, and then flew on inland, retracing their last journey.

Orak hadn't lied, and after some searching he located the clearing where they had found Flell wandering around.

'It's got to be somewhere in walking distance from here,' said Teressa.

'The human pup came from that direction,' said Orak, pointing with his beak. 'I will fly that way.'

Teressa got back onto his back, her heart pumping with excitement. Despite what she was truly in search of, the thought of finding the hidden village alone was enough to thrill her. Southerners, living in the heart of the North! That would be a sight to see.

Orak headed northwest for a short distance, and then started to quarter the land as he had done on their first journey together, flying lower whenever he spotted clearer land that might hold a village.

It took a long time, longer than Teressa had expected. Orak didn't hurry, and for a good part of that afternoon the grey griffin gradually searched the entire area around the clearing, as far as he thought a human child might be able to walk.

But when they finally did find the place, it was further than either of them had thought — and it was so tiny that they nearly missed it altogether.

But they found it. A tiny village; just a little cluster of houses with some farmland around them, hidden away from the world with forest all about. It was no wonder that nobody had found it before now; it was so small that most people wouldn't even notice it, let alone bother to go any closer.

There were some people around, but when they saw Orak coming into land, they screamed and ran for cover. When the grey griffin touched down in the patch of dirt that passed for a village square, all of them had vanished and the place looked utterly deserted.

Teressa jumped down. 'Hello?' she called. 'It's all right! I'm a friend!'

Nobody answered.

'It's all right!' Teressa yelled. 'Ye can come out!'

After a while, a man ventured into the open. She was disappointed to see he was just another Northerner. He looked like a peasant, but he carried a sickle. Not the kind of sickle used as a weapon, though; it was just a rusty farming tool.

'Who are ye, milady?' he asked cautiously, speaking Northern.

Teressa hadn't heard the language in a long time, and she stumbled over her reply. 'My name's Teressa. I'm a priestess. And this is Orak.'

The man bowed. 'My name's Merwin. What can we do to serve ye, milady?'

'Is this Gwernyfed?' Teressa asked.

'It is,' said Merwin. 'Do ye need food? Water? A place to stay?'

'No,' said Teressa. She hesitated. 'Look, it's all right. I know there are half-breeds living in Gwernyfed, and I don't care. I'm not going to tell the King about ye. So the others can stop hiding.'

Merwin froze. 'Half-breeds?'

'Aye,' said Teressa. 'There are Southerners living here, and half-breeds as well. But they don't have to be scared of me. Kullervo sent us.'

Merwin stared at her. 'Kullervo? Did ye say Kullervo?'

'That's right,' said Teressa. 'He told me to come here.'

'Do ye know where he is?' asked Merwin. 'An' Flell?'

'I do,' said Teressa. 'Go and get everyone together; they should all hear about it.'

'Yes, milady,' said Merwin. 'Right away.'

He dashed off.

A short time later, the people of Gwernyfed began to gather. There were more of them than Teressa had expected – but not that many; maybe thirty or thirty-five in all. Most of them were Southerners of varying ages, but many of the younger ones were half-breeds.

Teressa had never seen a half Northerner, half Southerner since she had seen Queen Laela some years ago. It was bizarre. She saw children with the burly build of Southerners, but black hair or eyes like a Northerner. She saw one girl who was tall and bony like a Northerner, but with long blonde hair. There was even a boy with one blue eye and one black.

All of them were looking at her with a mixture of suspicion and fear.

Teressa smiled to reassure them. 'Kullervo sent me,' she said again, using Cymrian this time. 'I'm Teressa, and this is Orak.'

'Where is Kullervo?' asked one of them – Merwin, standing beside a Southern woman and a pair of half-breed children who must have been his own.

'I'm sorry,' said Teressa. 'He died.'

The people of Gwernyfed murmured among themselves.

'How did he die?' Merwin's Southerner wife asked.

'Please,' said Teressa. 'Sit down. I have a long story to tell ye.'

She sat down, cross-legged, and her listeners did the same. Orak lay down on his belly behind her and groomed, apparently content to let her get on with it.

Teressa told them everything – or at least the parts to do with Kullervo and Flell – explaining what had happened to each of them. She had expected them to be surprised when she revealed Flell's identity, but none of them did.

'We knew she was Queen Laela's child,' said Merwin. 'Kullervo told us. So ye say she's going to be Empress of Amoran now?'

'Maybe,' said Teressa. 'I helped her as well as I could, and I wish I could have helped Kullervo too. But I was too late.'

'It's all right,' said Merwin's wife. 'You did what you could for him, and if you were a friend to him then you're a friend to us.'

Teressa smiled awkwardly. 'Kullervo didn't just send me here so I could tell ye what happened to him. I'm here to find something. But before I ask, I think Kullervo would want me to help ye.'

'What could you do for us?' asked one of the children.

'I don't think ye should stay here,' said Teressa. 'It's not safe in the North. Laela Half-Breed wouldn't have bothered ye if she'd found out ye were here, but Caedmon's not like her. If he ever knows about Gwernyfed, he'll have ye all killed.'

None of them looked bothered.

'Gwernyfed's our home,' Merwin said firmly.

'But I think ye should leave it,' said Teressa. 'Maybe just for now, but to keep yer children safe, ye should go. My master Red is a Southerner. I could send ye to him. He'd keep ye safe.'

'We're not going anywhere,' said Merwin. 'If this Red wants to protect us, he can come here himself.' He said it firmly, but not rudely.

Teressa shrugged. 'Well… that's yer choice. But if ye won't let me help ye, maybe ye can help me.'

'What do ye need?' asked Merwin. 'Ye've done us a favour by telling us about Kullervo, so if we can help ye in return…'

'I think there's something here,' said Teressa. 'Or near here. Something Kullervo hid. I think he wanted me to take it away.'

The listeners looked puzzled.

'What kind of thing?' asked a woman.

'Something he didn't want anyone to find,' said Teressa. 'Something he didn't want to end up in the wrong hands.'

'Well then, why did he want it to fall into your hands?' asked Merwin's wife.

'He trusted me,' said Teressa. 'And I think it's best if I take it away.'

'It'd help if you told us what it was,' said a Southerner.

'A heart,' Teressa said at last. 'A human heart.'

Nobody spoke. People glanced at each other with disturbed and puzzled expressions.

'All I know is that he hid it in a hollow tree somewhere outside Gwernyfed,' Teressa added. 'But if he didn't want anyone to know about it, then maybe he didn't tell anyone here about it.'

'He didn't,' said Merwin. 'Not to my knowledge. But…'

'Aye?' said Teressa.

'Well…' Merwin glanced at some of his friends, checking to see if any of them were going to object. 'I know the woods around here, an' so do my sisters. We could show ye all the hollow trees we know of around here.'

'I think,' Teressa added on an impulse, 'I think the tree might be dead.'

'Wait!' a Northerner woman who must have been one of Merwin's sisters stood up suddenly. 'Wait. I think I know the place.'

Everyone looked expectantly at her.

'I was out looking for firewood,' the woman explained. 'I walked a bit further than I should've, an' I found somethin' weird. There was a tree, see – a hollow tree, like ye said. It was dead. But the weird thing is… everything around it was dead too. The grass, the bushes – a whole ring of trees. All dead. It was a horrible place, really. Completely silent, like everything was dead, even the birds an' the insects. It gave me the creeps. I never went back. Never wanted to.'

Teressa stood too. 'Can ye show me? Can ye take me there?'

The woman grimaced. 'If what I felt there was right, whatever made it happen wasn't somethin' I ever want to go near again, an' I don't think it'd be good to have it near our village. I'd be glad if ye took it away.'

'Good!' said Teressa. 'Take us there.'

'Do it, Owena,' Merwin agreed. 'If she wants it so badly, help her take it away.'

The woman, Owena, had already started to walk away. 'Follow me, then, priestess.'

Teressa nodded to Merwin. 'Thank ye,' she said. 'And if ye ever change yer mind, then go to Monag Island. That's where Red will be. But I'll tell him where ye are anyway. Send him a message when ye need help, and he'll come.'

'We'll remember,' said Merwin. 'Good luck, Teressa, an' thank ye too.'

Teressa smiled and hurried off after Owena, already gripped by the thrill of adventure. Orak followed close behind, and the three of them went in among the trees – luckily the undergrowth wasn't too dense for him to get through.

Owena seemed to know where she was going, but before they left the outskirts of the village she stopped to take a lantern from a hook. 'It'll be dark by the time we get there, probably,' she said.

Teressa kept close beside her. 'Is it far?'

'Not too far, but it's dark under the trees,' said Owena. 'Are ye really a priestess?'

'Well, maybe I'm just an apprentice,' Teressa admitted.

'Never met a priestess before,' said Owena. 'Why are ye serving a Southerner, then?'

'I never went into that, did I?' said Teressa. 'I'll tell ye, then.'

So she did, giving the gist of her story in bits and pieces while they trekked through the leaf-litter, up a hill and down the other side. Owena listened with interest.

'Ye've betrayed yer own King,' she said baldly once Teressa had finished. 'Ain't ye scared?'

'I am,' Teressa admitted. 'But I have to follow my…'

She trailed off, as she found herself in a landscape that looked utterly alien.

Everything was dead, just as Owena had said. The grass was grey and crackled under her feet. The trees ahead of them had gone equally grey; their leaves and bark gone. It was as if they had been dead for years. Some of them had started to rot.

'Holy Night God,' Teressa breathed.

'See what I mean?' said Owena. 'Makes the hair on yer neck stand up, don't it?'

Teressa's skin was indeed prickling. 'I didn't think it'd be so… stark.'

'It's like a forest of bones, ain't it?' Owena agreed. 'Now… look there. That's what we came for.' She pointed.

Sure enough, right at the centre of the dead patch, there was a large tree with a hollow. The hole looked big enough, but it was too high for Teressa to reach.

'Lemme give ye a hand,' said Owena. 'It's lucky ye don't look too heavy.'

She gave Teressa a boost, and balancing awkwardly with one foot in her friend's hands and the other on her shoulder, Teressa groped her way up the tree trunk until she found the hollow.

She pulled herself higher with one hand on the edge and reached inside with the other. Her fingers brushed against dry, crumbling wood, spiderwebs…

She gritted her teeth and reached in further, and her heart leapt when she touched something rough. She managed to grip it between her forefinger and thumb and pulled. It stuck for a moment, but she pulled harder and it came free in a sudden jerk that sent her flying. She fell off Owena's shoulders and landed on her backside, clutching her precious burden in both hands.

It didn't look like much: just a small bag made of cracked, rotting leather. It was about the same size as her prayer stone, in fact.

The drawstring holding it shut was also leather, and had perished to the point that it broke when she pulled on it. She stuck her fingers through the opening instead and tugged. The bag came open, and unexpected fear lunged through her.

Inside was a heart. A human heart. Dried and withered, its outside covered in shrivelled black veins. Teressa touched it cautiously, and a hideous cold bit into her flesh.

'Augh!' she stuck her hands under her armpits, wincing.

Owena crouched to look. 'What happened? Is it sharp or somethin'?' She saw the heart. 'Holy gods…'

Teressa rubbed her hands together, shivering. 'Don't touch it. It's so damn cold…'

Owena pulled a face. 'Ugh, it's so… it's horrible. Wrap it up or somethin'.'

Teressa rummaged in her bag, and found a roll of bandages. 'This should do it.'

Orak had come closer as well. 'That is the heart?'

'Aye,' said Teressa. 'But we have to be careful with it.' She carefully tipped the heart out of the bag onto the loose end of the bandage, and wrapped it up without touching it for more than a brief moment at a time.

'I'm glad yer takin' it away,' said Owena. 'Get rid of it. Burn it or somethin'.'

'Don't worry. I'll get rid of it.' Teressa finished wrapping it up, and stuffed it into her bag.

'What do ye even want with it?' the peasant woman wanted to know.

'It's all right,' said Teressa. 'I'm going to use its powers for good.'

Chapter Nineteen

Teressa's Task

Teressa and Orak wasted no time once they had found the heart. Though the inhabitants of Gwernyfed offered to shelter them for the night, Teressa didn't want to stay – after seeing what the heart had done to the trees, she didn't like the idea of what it might do to people. She didn't like the idea of what it might do to her, for that matter, or Orak. The sooner they found the bones of King Arenadd, the better.

Fortunately, the stones of Taranis' Throne were easy enough to find. But it took them several days to get there, and neither of them enjoyed it.

Teressa felt the effects of the heart first. Within a day of finding it, she started to feel sick and listless. She slept badly, and had nightmares when she did.

Dreams of dying.

Dreams of murder.

A coldness started to prickle at her skin.

Before long, Orak started to show signs of feeling it as well. He grew restless and irritable, and looked more and more tired at the end of each day. He didn't say anything, but Teressa guessed that he was sleeping badly as well. She wouldn't have been surprised if he had been suffering from nightmares too.

She might have been afraid that her partner would want to stop but he dispelled that fear quickly enough, and when the First Mountains came in sight, all he said was, 'The sooner we are rid of this thing, the better for us. I shall fly quickly tomorrow.'

He pushed himself hard the next day, as promised, and after a time Teressa could see the stones.

When the Southerners had first conquered the North centuries ago, there had been many stone circles scattered through the country. They had been the Night God's first temples, and so the sun-worshipping Southerners had destroyed them, deliberately knocking the stones down and burying them, or even breaking them up for masonry. But the stones of Taranis' Throne had stayed.

Maybe the Southerners hadn't known about them, or maybe they were just too hard to get to. They had been built on a plateau high in the mountains, and had been a place for rebels to go ever since Caedmon's grandmother Arddyn had gone into hiding there with the last of her followers. That was where Arenadd had found her, and it was said he had sacrificed a man to the Night God at the stones, and that the god herself had come to him.

Teressa had always wanted to see them, and when she laid eyes on them for the first time she found herself thinking that of all the final resting places for the North's greatest leader, this was the most fitting.

Orak landed among them to rest and Teressa walked around to look at them, keeping her bag close, despite her newfound urge to get rid of it so she wouldn't have to feel its icy touch.

There were thirteen stones, as there were in every stone circle, each one carved with the phases of the moon and decorated with intricate spiralling patterns. They were taller than she had expected; grey, weather-worn, ancient. At the very centre, the altar stone stood.

It too had been carved with spirals, and there were old, brownish stains on its top. The blood of old sacrifices.

On an impulse, Teressa took the heart out of her bag and put it on the altar. It was still covered in bandages, but she could feel the icy sting of it on her fingers before she let it go. It looked strangely insignificant lying there, even though she knew how important it really was.

She stood there a moment and contemplated. She wondered if she should pray.

A faint sound came to her ears, and she stilled and listened.

Just for a moment, just barely, she thought she heard a scream. A man's scream, full of terror and agony.

She shuddered, and her eyes snapped open. The wind had begun to blow powerfully, whistling and howling among the stones. There was snow here on the ground, and it whipped up into the air in little flurries, chasing the wind.

Teressa quickly snatched up the heart and stuffed it into her bag.

'Let's go,' she said to Orak.

The grey griffin was looking away from her, at the mountains around and above them. 'I think I can see a cave,' he said. 'There.'

Teressa followed his gaze. Sure enough, she could see an opening in the side of one of the mountains overlooking the stones. She started to wonder aloud if that could be it, but the urge to leave was so powerful that she only nodded and got onto Orak's back. She took hold of the harness, and waited.

Orak took off with a lurch, and flew to the opening. It was indeed a cave, its entrance partly obscured by fallen rocks. The grey griffin landed awkwardly at an angle.

Teressa clambered off him, and nearly lost her balance on the loose rock. She sat down hastily.

'I cannot go in there,' said Orak. 'The hole is too small. Go in and see what you can find.'

Teressa nodded, and started to clamber up over the boulders piled at the entrance. They wobbled under her weight and threatened to fall on her, but she had come too far to give up now. She wedged her fingers into whatever gaps she could find, and if anything looked too precarious she simply shoved it and let it fall past her and out of the way.

She hadn't come properly dressed for rock climbing, and before long her silver robe was dirty and torn in several places, and her arms and legs had gathered plenty of grazes and bruises. But she reached the top of the heap with a mighty effort, and hauled herself up and over and through the hole into the cave.

She landed with a painful thump, and picked herself up. There was enough light from the entrance to see by, luckily.

The cave was long and low, but much bigger than she had expected. If the entrance weren't half buried, Orak would have been able to come in easily. After all, another griffin had already managed it.

Teressa stood there, her heart in her mouth.

The corpse of a griffin lay in front of her – a massive one. In life, the creature must have been at least as big as Kraego, if not bigger.

Its body lay in a mass of fallen feathers, some black, some silver, some white. Some of the fur still clung on – it was black. But she could see the bones showing through where the skin had rotted and pulled back from them.

The eye sockets were as big as her head, staring emptily at her, as if to accuse the trespasser.

'The Mighty Skandar,' Teressa whispered.

So this was where Kraego's father had come to die.

Slowly, reverently, Teressa edged around the griffin's body.

Beyond it, she found Arenadd.

The mortal remains of the first King of the North were much further gone than Skandar's. She could see the remains of his boots and trousers, but the corpse was bare-chested, and by now the skin was almost entirely gone, leaving only a few scraps clinging to the ribs. She could see the bones of his hands, entirely exposed. They were so clean by now that she could even see the ugly lumps of deformed bone on the left hand, where they had been broken and healed badly.

The face was a skull, its jaw open in a silent, mocking grin.

Fear and disgust caught in Teressa's throat, but she only hesitated a moment before she knelt and bowed her head.

'Great Arenadd,' she breathed. 'I found ye.'

The only reply was the howling of the wind from outside.

Teressa raised her head. She wanted to pray, but she knew there was no time to lose. She had come with a task, and now she had to fulfil it.

She opened her bag, and brought out the heart. Then, grimacing at the pain, she unwrapped it.

It was agony on her skin but she threw the bandage aside and gently put her hand inside Arenadd's ribcage. She found the spot where she thought the heart should go, and placed it there.

She pulled her hand out, and sat back.

'There,' she said. 'As ye commanded, great Arenadd.'

She wasn't sure what she had expected to happen. A great burst of light, maybe, or a ghostly visitation. A vision, maybe. Something miraculous.

But what actually happened was nothing.

She sat there for a long time, watching in silence. Nothing moved.

After a while, she started to wonder if there was something else she should do. Some sort of ritual, maybe? Or maybe she had just put the heart in the wrong place.

On an impulse, she took out the sacrificial knife she had saved, and cut her hand with it. She made it a big cut – not just a little nick on the thumb. It produced plenty of blood, and she sprinkled it over the corpse.

'With this offering of true Northern blood, I call to ye!' she said loudly.

Nothing happened.

Teressa started to feel embarrassed. She picked up the discarded bandage, and wrapped it around her injured hand.

'Teressa?' Orak's voice called faintly from the entrance. 'Have you found it?'

Teressa took one last look at Arenadd's body, and went back to the entrance.

'I found it,' she called back. 'It's done. But nothing happened.'

The grey griffin's head appeared, haloed by light, peering in at her. 'Come back to me, then,' he said. 'Unless another vision comes to you, there is not much more we can do here. I am only glad to be rid of the heart.'

'But we can't just leave it, can we?' said Teressa.

'What else shall we do?' Orak asked impatiently. 'Carry a bag of human bones about with us? You have done as you were asked.'

Teressa's stomach had started to rumble. 'All right,' she said. 'But maybe we should come back later. Stay here in the mountains for a little while, and check back in case something's changed. If Arenadd really does come back, he'll need our help.'

'Come out of the cave,' said Orak. 'We will rest for the night, and come back in the morning. If nothing has happened, we will leave.'

'All right.' Teressa adjusted the hang of her bag, and clambered out through the hole.

They made camp nearby, in the place called Taranis' Gorge, which still housed the remains of the old rebel settlement. Arenadd himself had stayed there once, and Saeddryn as well. Teressa thought of searching for the cave that Arddryn had lived in, but she was too tired to bother with it. She settled down in the remains of a lean-to instead, and lit a fire.

Her hand was still bleeding a little, so she wet her prayer stone with it and prayed before she went to bed. Maybe she would have another vision. Just one.

All she wanted now was a message, some sign to tell her that she had done the right thing.

That night, she did have another dream – or thought she did. She thought she saw Arenadd – not as a living man, but as the corpse from the cave. It sat up with a grinding of bones, and stared at her with its empty eye-sockets.

Thank you, it whispered.

*

Teressa woke up with a feeling of foreboding. Without waiting to eat anything, she woke Orak up.

'We have to go and check the cave,' she said.

Orak growled deep in his chest, but didn't argue. He took her back up to the cave, and she climbed inside, clumsy in her eagerness. She ran to see Arenadd's bones.

They were still bones. They hadn't moved, or changed.

Disappointment sank into her stomach like a brick.

'Damn it!' she swore aloud. 'Why isn't it working? What didn't I do?'

Naturally, nobody answered.

She decided that she must have put the heart in the wrong place. Reluctantly, she crouched and put her hand inside the ribcage. She found the heart, and pulled it downward.

It wouldn't move.

Teressa tugged a little harder, and felt a resistance. Something springy, like soft leather.

Bewildered, she leaned down and looked inside the ribcage. The heart was there, sure enough, but now it was anchored in place by several huge veins. Veins that had grown up over the bones of the neck and into the skull, and spread outward and downward to the rest of the body.

Teressa let go of the heart, and sat back. 'What…?'

She looked again. This time, she kept her gaze on one spot and waited to see if anything would happen.

The thickest vein, just above the heart, was moving. Ever so slowly, a bump formed on its surface. It grew, and split, and as she watched it made another vein, and another, branching out like a tiny tree.

She moved back further and looked at the outside of the body. Nothing much seemed to have changed. Had there been that much skin on the ribcage before? She wasn't sure. But it didn't matter. She had seen enough.

'It's working,' she mumbled. 'My gods, it's working!'

She ran to tell Orak.

'It's working!' she shouted. 'I can't believe it – it's bloody well working! The heart's growing. I mean, it's making veins! His body's rebuilding itself!'

'You are certain?' Orak exclaimed.

'Completely,' said Teressa. 'Orak, we've got to stay. We've got to stay in the Gorge for however long it takes. A few more days, maybe.'

'We must,' said Orak. 'If it is working, then we cannot leave until it is done.'

Teressa could hardly contain herself. A great and ferocious excitement had caught hold of her, more powerful than anything she had ever felt before. It was working! Arenadd was going to return. His body would heal, and then he would come with her. He would help her, maybe. Maybe… maybe he would even be a friend to her.

She hardly dared imagine that.

*

So Teressa and Orak stayed. They lived in Taranis Gorge for three days. Orak hunted to feed himself, and Teressa ate the supplies she had and the few things she could forage. Every day, the two of them went to the cave to see what was happening.

And, day by day, Teressa saw the changes.

She watched as organs grew inside the ribcage, bit by bit. She watched muscle grow over the top, and then skin. Pale, Northern skin, unmarked by scars or tattoos. Then, after that, fingernails and hair – long, curly black hair – and a ragged beard.

The eyes grew back, too, but they stayed closed.

On the third day, Teressa came to the cave and found him lying there. Whole and intact. His chest moved up and down slightly – he was breathing.

She just stood there for a moment, taking him in – all of him.

To her, he looked perfect. Tall and lean, with a pale, angular face. The fingers on his left hand were twisted, but other than that there were no signs of any of his old injuries. His body had been remade without any marks or blemishes.

Teressa dared to lean down and touch his face. 'Master,' she said.

Arenadd didn't stir. He lay there inert, scarcely breathing.

'Master,' Teressa said again. 'Master, it's me – Teressa. Ye've been remade. Ye've come back to us!'

Nothing happened.

Teressa shook him gently by the shoulder. 'Master?' she said. 'Arenadd? Wake up!'

But he didn't move, or show any sign at all that he had heard her.

Teressa kept trying. She shook him again harder, shouted his name, and finally, in desperation, slapped him across the face.

He still didn't wake up.

Teressa pulled his eyelids back. His eyes were unfocused, and didn't react when she waved a hand in front of them. When she took her hand away, they closed again.

Teressa wanted to swear. It wasn't supposed to be like this! She had brought him back, but he was comatose, and was that ever going to change?

She decided to give it one more day. Maybe his mind hadn't been rebuilt yet.

But the next day she returned to find him unchanged.

'Then we must leave him,' said Orak. 'He is no use to us.'

'But—,' Teressa began.

'See sense!' the griffin interrupted. 'Without a mind, he may as well not be alive. You and I have other things we must do.'

'All right,' said Teressa. 'But I don't want to just leave him in that cave.'

'He is immortal,' said Orak. 'He does not need you to take care of him. You have done enough. If he ever does wake, perhaps he will come to find us. For now, we must go to Malvern.'

Teressa was crestfallen, but she knew he was right. She had spent enough time on this; there were living people who needed her help.

'All right,' she said. 'But I'll leave some food with him.'

She put the last of her dried food in the cave beside Arenadd's silent body and murmured a prayer over him before she left, taking one of Skandar's feathers with her as a relic. Maybe, one day, she would return.

Behind her Arenadd lay still and silent, only moving to breathe.

An empty shell.

Waiting.

Chapter Twenty

Monag Island

Red and the others sailed on after Teressa and Orak's departure. As planned, they followed the coast at a safe distance, and attracted no attention. The Captain knew what he was doing. Now they could only hope that Monag Island would indeed have a port.

At first glance, the island looked uninhabited. It wasn't heavily forested; the island seemed to consist mostly of grassy plains. Its shores were high and rocky, and looked very uninviting. But when the ships ventured into the channel between it and the mainland, they found a port about halfway along, and that was when they saw the first signs that Monag was inhabited.

The port only had one pier – a heavy wooden affair, where a few small fishing boats were moored. There wouldn't be room for all three Amorani ships at once. In fact, there would barely be any room for one. Further back from the pier they could see a cluster of stone buildings, and there were a few people about, though no griffins so far.

The people on the pier had already seen the oncoming ships, and Red saw them start to run – some to the end of the pier to better see what was going on, and others back to the shore, probably to report to someone.

'Now we'll just have to hope they're friendly,' he murmured to Kraego.

Kraego said nothing, and only stared at the shore.

By the time the ship had come up alongside the pier – nearly capsizing some of the smaller boats there in the process – a small group of people had gathered. The Amorani sailors threw them a rope, and a man caught it and tied it to a post.

'We'd better go ashore, Kraego,' said Red.

'Agreed.' Kraego crouched low to help his partner climb onto his back, and once Red was in place, the giant griffin jumped down onto the pier with a powerful kick and a blow of his wings. People scattered out of his way.

Red slid off Kraego's back. His boots hit the wooden planking without a sound and he hurried over to the Monagians, who were backing off nervously.

'Hey,' he rasped. 'It's all right. We ain't here to make trouble.'

They calmed down, and a couple of them came forward.

'Who are ya?' one asked. He was a stringy blond-haired man, with an accent unlike any Red had ever heard. It sounded high and harsh.

Red nodded politely to him. 'Captain Kearney Redguard, from Liranwee. An' this is my partner Kraego. Are there any griffiners here?'

'A few,' said the man. 'Someone's already gone to tell 'em ya here.'

'Good,' said Red. 'We'll come ashore an' wait here.'

The man didn't argue. He stood by with his fellows while the Amorani sailors threw down a gangplank and the other passengers came ashore down it. The Captain came with them, and bowed politely to Red and Kraego.

'We have brought you home. Now I will take my ship from here, and the others will dock so that your friends can come ashore,' he said. 'Then we will leave. Our task is done and we will go back to Amoran.'

'Understood,' Red nodded. 'Thanks. An' you ain't gonna tell nobody where we are, right?'

'I shall say nothing, and return directly to Xanthium,' the Captain said immediately.

'Good.' Red nodded again and let him go.

The Amorani went back on board the ship, and Red watched patiently with the others while it pulled away from the pier and headed back out to sea, leaving room for the other two to begin unloading.

Alaric was already looking around with interest. 'Amazing,' he murmured. 'I never knew Monag was inhabited. I have to write about it. Alaric the Dashing should come here.'

Isleen moved closer to him. 'Are you going to write more books?'

'I think so,' said Alaric. 'I was thinking that in the next one…'

Red discreetly moved away. Once the pudgy storyteller got started on his books, it would take him a very long time to shut up again. He didn't seem to mind that nobody except Isleen wanted to hear about it, or that most of his fellow travellers would quietly disappear the moment the topic came up.

This time around, though, Red couldn't help but overhear one thing.

'I've been doing a lot of thinking,' Alaric was saying. 'While we were at sea. I think I know what's wrong with the series.' He paused to make sure Isleen was listening. She was. 'Alaric the Dashing doesn't suffer enough. His adventures are always too easy for him. I didn't realise it before, but now I've met Captain Redguard, and he's a hero, like Alaric is. And he's suffered. You can see it in his face. I think suffering teaches people how to be brave. It makes them better.'

No it doesn't, Red thought grimly. *It just makes them suffer.*

He moved further away and didn't hear any more of Alaric's excited chatter.

The second ship finished docking, and its passengers came ashore. While it was pulling out and the third began its approach, Kraego gave a warning huff and Red looked up to see a group of other griffins approaching from inland.

He glanced quickly at Kraego, and then hurried off further along the dock so they could wait for them in a spot where there was plenty of room for the newcomers to land.

There were three griffins, and they landed rather untidily on the shore not far from the end of the pier. Red and Kraego reached them shortly afterward, and Red stood back to let Kraego approach.

The leader of the little deputation crouched to let their partner dismount, and then came to meet the black griffin. She was female, and not very big – barely half Kraego's size which was probably why she approached him with far more caution and less aggression than a griffin would normally would have when faced with an intruder. Her fur and feathers were shaggy and unkempt, but the feathers on her tail had attractive banded patterns on them.

Kraego did not bow to her. 'I am Kraego,' he said. 'Do not be afraid – I have not come to take your territory from you.'

The female hissed. 'You are on my land, Kraego,' she said. 'Speak with more respect.'

Kraego gave a perfunctionary dip of the head. 'I lower my beak to you, who are master of this territory,' he said, speaking quickly and carelessly.

'I am Tarak,' said the female, slightly mollified. 'My human is Lady Merca, who is Eyrie Mistress of Monag.'

'Mine is Lord Kearney Redguard, who is *Kraeai kran ae*,' said Kraego, without the slightest hesitation. 'Let our humans speak now.'

Red winced, but came forward to meet Tarak's human.

Lady Merca turned out to be a small, chunky woman of indeterminate age, with a mop of curly hair decorated with wooden beads. Her clothes were plain and made of rough woollen fabric. She cocked her head towards Red, and said, 'Heya. Welcome to Monag.' She finished by clicking her tongue.

Red stared at her for a moment, but quickly remembered himself and bowed. 'Thank you, milady. I hope we ain't caused any problems by turning up like this.'

'No, no problems,' Merca answered. 'What did ya griffin say ya name was again? My hearing's not so fine.'

'Uh, Captain Kearney Redguard,' said Red.

'A captain with a griffin, hey?' Merca put her head at an odd angle and peered at him as if her eyesight were bad.

'I ain't sworn myself to anyone,' said Red. 'Ain't got an official position. I don't really wanna be a Lord anyhow.'

'And what brings ya here, then?' asked Merca. 'Fleeing from the Northerners too, are ya?'

'No,' said Red. 'Coming home. Have other people come here, then?'

'Many, many!' said Merca. 'A whole city-worth. Anyhow, are ya seeking to stay here in Monag awhile? I'll add ya can't stay long — there's no food here for so many.'

'If we can stay just a while, we'd be real grateful,' said Red. 'I don't think it'll be for long. Just long enough to rest up a bit an' make plans for what we're gonna do next.'

'Then that's good,' said Merca. 'Ya welcome, all of ya. Come and eat with me tonight, Captain, and tell me ya story. My other guests will want to hear it too, methinks.' She pronounced it "metinks".

'Thanks,' said Red. 'Is there room for everyone?' he added, doubting it.

'Nay, there's not,' said Merca. 'Too many here already from the mainland! But there's the tavern with a room or two, and barns, and we can put up tents and lean-tos and whatnot. It's only lucky the new ones brought food and so forth, or there'd be nothing to feed ya at all. But come now! All of ya, come!' She gestured expansively at him.

The others who had come with her had stayed silent through all this, but now they came forward a few paces, and the humans nodded. Both of them were elderly; the man on the right so ancient and doddering that Red wondered how he'd even made it down here.

'Come and share our Eyrie,' the old man wheezed. His partner, beside him, was also old – a scraggy female whose head had a slight, constant tremor.

Kraego looked at them all with contempt. 'We shall do so,' he said. 'Come, Red – we will go and tell the others.'

Isleen, Alaric and Neth had followed them part of the way, and Red found them waiting. 'We're stayin' here a while,' he told them brusquely. 'I'm gonna stay here with you an' help everyone get themselves up to the city. If there is one.'

'Excellent,' said Isleen. 'Leave it to me, Captain. I can organise everyone.'

'An' me,' Neth added sharply. 'I'm a guard. I know how to get people movin'.'

'Get goin', then,' said Red. 'All three of you. Neth – I'm puttin' you in charge of the other guards here, so get them together an' have them direct everyone.'

Neth saluted. 'Yes, sir!'

'An' you, Alaric,' Red added. 'You… uh… you stay with Isleen an' help her out, right?'

'Yes, sir,' said Alaric, sounding just a little crestfallen.

'I should probably go see the Eyrie,' said Red. 'But I'll come back.'

'It's all right, Captain,' said Isleen. 'Leave it to us and we'll see you there.'

Red nodded. 'Thanks. I'll see you later.'

Kraego had been waiting impatiently. 'Come,' he said.

Red climbed onto his back, and the black griffin took off.

They hadn't flown together in a while, and Red lurched a little at first. But he soon got the hang of it again, and once Kraego had settled into a steady glide he looked down from the griffin's back to get a better idea of what Monag was like.

He quickly saw that his first impressions had been right: most of the island was just open fields. He could see flocks of what were probably sheep, or maybe goats, roaming wherever they chose. There didn't even seem to be any fences to speak of.

Inland, not too far from the dock, a tiny city stood on a hill.

It was so small that it barely would have qualified as a town on the mainland, but oddly enough it featured not one Eyrie tower but two – one on either side of the hill. They weren't even close enough together to be linked by a bridge.

Kraego had left Tarak and the other two griffins behind, but now he hung back and circled over the city until they caught up. They made for the tower on the left, and he followed.

Like all Eyrie towers, this one had a flat top for griffins to land on, and Tarak touched down there, closely followed by the others. Once everyone was down, Merca turned to Red and said, 'There's plenty of empty rooms, so go below and choose whatever one ya want. Settle in, have a rest. At sunset, come to the dining hall and we'll eat.'

'Got it,' Red nodded. 'Thanks. I'll see you later.'

He and Kraego went inside, using the large opening in the roof which led to a ramp. Griffins couldn't use stairs very well, so every building meant for them had ramps instead. And very large doors and passageways.

The Monag Eyrie turned out to be not much different from that standard, but as they headed down through it, Red noticed how run-down this one looked. There were some tapestries hanging on the walls, but they were dusty and faded. Around them, the stonework looked equally aged; the mortar was crumbling, and dust and cobwebs had gathered in the corners.

'This place is a disgrace,' Kraego said haughtily.

Red glanced sideways at him. Since they'd become partnered, Kraego had become even more vain and demanding than before. He must have decided that being a partnered griffin made him better, or at least more deserving of special treatment. Red hoped the attitude wouldn't last.

'It ain't fancy,' he admitted. 'But they're helpin' us out for free. You oughta be more polite to 'em, Kraego.'

Kraego only snorted and poked his head into an entrance. 'This one is empty,' he said.

Red peered inside. The room beyond was grubby and disused, but it was indeed empty. 'Let's take this one, then,' he said. He was in no mood for wandering through the Eyrie any further.

The room wasn't in very good shape – it was furnished, but the furniture had been left out to gather dust, and the bedding had been just about destroyed by moths. The adjoining griffin's nest wasn't in much better shape.

Red took it all in, and sighed. 'I'll do some cleanin' up, then.'

'No!' Kraego said harshly. 'You shall not!'

Red stared at him. 'What? Why not?'

'You are a griffiner now, and it is beneath you to do this,' said Kraego. 'Find a servant and they shall clean this place for us both.'

Red rubbed his head. 'I s'pose we'll be needing fresh bedding anyhow. I'll go see if I can find someone.'

Someone else must have already done it, though, because he had barely gone anywhere when a pair of elderly servants arrived.

'Ya Lord Redguard?' one of them wheezed.

Red took a moment to decipher what the man was saying. 'Yeah, that's me, I guess. Were you lookin' for me?'

Both of them were carrying armloads of linen. 'So we were!' said the second of them, a woman. 'Lady Merca asked us to come clean ya room out an' whatnot an' so forth.'

'Good,' said Red. 'Come with me, then.'

He led them back to his new quarters, where the pair of them set to work dusting and replacing the bedding. Red had to resist the urge to help them – Kraego was still watching.

The two servants worked with surprising speed and efficiency, and once they'd finished with Red's room they left and returned a while later carrying baskets of straw. They swept the rotten remains of the old nesting material from Kraego's nest out and off the balcony outside, and replaced it, though it took several trips for them to bring in enough straw. Finally, they brought water to refill the termite-ridden wooden trough, and a sheep carcass.

Kraego settled down to eat it very gladly, leaving Red to thank the servants before they went on their way.

Once they were gone, Red lay down on the bed and stayed there for a while, staring at the ceiling.

He'd made it. He was home.

Or, at least, he was back in Cymria. From here, he could return to the mainland, and find out what the situation was. Merca clearly wouldn't be able to tell him much.

But she'd said Red and his friends weren't the only refugees here, hadn't she?

*

That evening, at sunset, Red and Kraego went to find the dining hall. It wasn't hard to find – there was only one in the tower, and the corridor outside it was crowded with servants bringing food.

Inside, a large table stood in the middle of an even larger room, which must have taken up most of that level of the Eyrie. It left plenty of room for the griffins. Food had already been laid out for them on stone ledges set into the walls, but there was only a handful of griffins actually there, which made the room look much bigger.

Kraego loped off to assert himself over his fellows, and Red made for the table where a good number of people were already sitting down. There were more humans in the hall than griffins, in fact. He recognised Lady Merca and her two friends – they'd now been joined by a third; a woman who looked just as doddery as her fellows. The others looked like minor griffiners, but only one or two of them looked younger than fifty.

They looked happy enough though, sitting together in little groups and sharing some wine.

Red stood there for a moment just watching them talk among themselves and all of a sudden a terrible loneliness opened up inside him like a chasm. He had meant to go and join them but in that moment, as he stood there outside their company, he felt utterly unable to.

The wall he had sensed between himself and others on the voyage rose again, but now it felt even bigger and more impassable than before.

He stood there, frozen in sudden indecision, but then one of the diners noticed him. She stood up and took a few steps towards him, but as she came closer she slowed. Astonishment showed on her face.

'Red?' she said. 'Kearney Redguard, is that really you?'

Red gaped. 'Liantha! Great Gryphus! What're you doing here?'

Liantha came to meet him, her face lit up by a smile. 'I don't believe it. You're alive!'

Before he could answer, she put her arms around him and hugged him tightly.

Red hugged her back. 'Liantha, it's so good to see you.'

The Eyrie Mistress of New Eagleholm let go and backed off slightly. Her smile had disappeared. 'You're so cold. Red, you look awful. What happened to you?' She looked at him more closely, and her concern became bewilderment. 'What happened to your eyes?'

Red shook his head. 'I'm fine, Liantha. Don't worry about it. But what about you? How'd you get here?'

Liantha sighed. 'It's a long story, so come and sit with me and I'll tell you.'

Several of her fellow griffiners from New Eagleholm were there with her. There were only a handful of them, but New Eagleholm hadn't had many griffiners in the first place. Liantha went back to her seat, and gestured at the empty one beside it.

Red had already guessed what she was going to tell him. 'New Eagleholm's been taken, hasn't it?' he said.

Liantha and her friends all looked pained.

'Yes, it has,' said Liantha.

Red set his jaw. 'Destroyed, or taken over?'

'Only taken over, thank Gryphus,' said Liantha. She was still looking at him with shock. 'What happened to your throat? You sound so different now. I barely recognised you.'

Red rubbed the scar. 'Just an injury. What about Eagleholm? How'd they know you were there?'

'It was that spy you handed over to us,' Liantha said grimly. 'Morgan. We had him in the cells, but he picked the lock and escaped. Killed several guards in the process.'

Red's heart sank. 'He got out of the city, then?'

'Not alone,' said Liantha. 'He was spotted in the streets and attacked. A mob tried to hang him. But it seems he had a partner. A griffin rescued him.'

Red swore. 'Echo. Did Morgan get hurt?'

'It sounds like it,' said Liantha. She shook her head. 'I know he was an enemy, but it was a horrible incident. My guards didn't have a chance of breaking it up, but from what I heard he was severely beaten. We thought he would have died anyway, but it seems he didn't. He came back months later, and this time he brought an army. We were outnumbered.'

Red said nothing. Visions flashed into his mind; memories of city streets where griffins rampaged and Northerners ran beside them, black eyes full of hate.

Above, smoke billowed into the sky as houses burned, and screams filled his ears.

He shuddered.

'It was like a nightmare,' said Liantha. She had gone a little pale. 'But we escaped. Thanks to you. Because of what you told us, we knew we could expect an invasion – sooner or later the Northerners would find out where we were. We had made plans – we knew we wouldn't stand much of a chance if they came, so we planned an evacuation of the whole city. Some of our unpartnered griffins started flying out Northward every day or so, to scout out the land and see if anyone was coming. So we had plenty of warning.'

'Did you try an' fight at all?' asked Red.

'No… it would have been suicide. We fled, and the Northerners overran the city. Most of us escaped, but not all. No, not all.' Liantha shook her head.

'Don't blame yourself,' said Red, as gently as his damaged voice would allow. 'It wasn't your fault what happened.'

Liantha still looked bitter. 'I built a city, and lost it. Some Eyrie Mistress I turned out to be.'

Red touched her on the shoulder. 'It ain't the city what matters, Liantha – it's people what matter, an' you saved them, remember? You did what was right.'

She smiled. 'Thanks, Red.' She paused to take a mouthful of wine. 'But now you really must tell me your story. How did you get here? What happened to you?'

'It's a long story,' said Red. 'And most of it ain't so nice to hear.'

'Start by telling me how you got that scar,' said Liantha. 'And why you look so…' She trailed off, clearly unable to find the right words.

Red glanced around. 'I don't think we should talk about that here.'

'Why?' Liantha persisted. Everyone in earshot was listening now. 'Are you sick?'

Red laughed harshly. 'I ain't contagious, if that's what you're thinkin'. No, I'm not sick.'

'Then why have your eyes changed?' asked Liantha. 'You're so pale, but I heard someone say you'd been in Amoran. Please, Red – don't play with me. I'm your friend. You can tell me whatever it is.'

Red hesitated for a long moment. He didn't want to tell her, not because he didn't trust her, but because he didn't want to see the look that he knew would appear on her face. He didn't want to see her friendly concern turn to fear, or even anger.

But if he didn't tell her she would be upset anyway, and as he hesitated Teressa's words came back to him. He was going to have to tell people eventually, wasn't he? It couldn't stay secret forever. The truth was the only way.

'I died,' he said baldly. He pointed at the scar on his throat. 'This killed me.'

Liantha looked blank.

'An' then Kraego brought me back,' Red went on. 'I'm… I'm the Shadow That Walks now.'

Liantha drew back slightly. 'Don't say that, Red.'

Red growled and downed his cup of wine. 'Didn't want to, but you asked for the truth. There it is. I ain't gonna lie to you, Liantha. Never have, never will.'

She only stared. 'But…'

'Here.' Red gently took her small hand in his rough one, and pressed it against his throat. He kept it there until she pulled away.

Horror turned her face almost as pale as his. 'No,' she said softly.

'Yes,' Red corrected.

She stared into his eyes, brown looking into empty black, and he could see her fear growing.

'I ain't your enemy,' he told her. 'I swear. I'm still your friend, Liantha.'

She didn't reply, and he realised that utter silence had fallen. He looked up, and saw everyone staring at him.

Then the whispering started.

'The Shadow That Walks!'

'He's the heartless man…?'

'He's like the Dark Lord now?'

Even the griffins began to hiss among themselves.

'*Kraeai kran ae!* The cursed one!'

Red stood up. 'The power's on your side now. Our side. I swear by Gryphus' holy flames.'

One of Liantha's friends stood up too, so quickly his chair fell over. He pointed at Red. 'You're the Night God's servant! You're a monster!'

'Maybe.' Red glared at Liantha. 'See, sometimes the truth hurts.'

He turned and strode for the door.

His boots made no sound at all.

'Stop!' Kraego reared up from among the other griffins. 'Red, do not leave!'

Red stopped and looked back at him.

Kraego rounded on the others there. 'How dare you speak that way to my human?' he hissed. 'You know what he has done for you.'

'He is Kraeai kran ae!' another griffin hissed back. 'A human like him destroyed my home!'

'He cannot be trusted!' a second chimed in. Red knew her — Liantha's partner Seerae, Kraego's own half-sister. 'The last *Kraeai kran ae* ravaged the South,' she growled. 'This one will be no different.'

'No—,' Kraego began, but Red had already heard enough.

He said nothing, but turned for the door.

Kraego came after him. 'Red, do not leave. You cannot—,'

Red said nothing. The shadows by the door seemed to open up in front of him, inviting and comforting in their blackness. Without a thought, acting on some instinct he barely understood, he stepped into it and let darkness embrace him.

Chapter Twenty-One

Red's Choice

Red didn't stay in the shadows for long. He left them and returned to the real world once he sensed that he was far enough away, but as he emerged he felt as if the coldness inside him had deepened and grown. The fact that it made him feel good only made it worse.

He shivered, and walked silently down the inside of the tower until he came across a servant.

'Here, you,' he said.

The servant stopped and bowed. 'Yes?'

'Is there a Temple in the city?' Red asked.

The man nodded. 'Not far from here. Leave here by the ground floor and ya can't miss the dome, like.'

'Thanks.'

Red went on his way, down and down until he reached the bottom of the tower. By now it was almost dark outside, but he could see the last of the sun dipping below the horizon.

Sure enough, he could also see the dome of Monag's Sun Temple. It was small, but the gold sunwheel on the dome gleamed in the failing light.

Red hurried towards the front door. If he was going to pray, he should do it while there was some light left. Prayers to Gryphus were always heard most loudly during the day.

He paused in the doorway and looked inside. The Temple's single round room was deserted, and looked just as shabby as the Eyrie. But there were lamps burning on the walls, and an altar at the centre. It would do. Red stepped over the threshold.

The moment his foot touched the floor, the pain started.

It began as a kind of sickness – an uneasy feeling in the pit of his stomach. He kept going, and with every step the feeling grew. Spit gathered in his mouth, and he retched.

A sudden urge to run away gripped him and steadily mounted as he walked on.

Then, as he neared the altar, the sick feeling twisted and became pain.

Red groaned. The pain was in his heart, not his stomach. It stabbed at him, growing worse and worse, until it began to radiate into his arms and then up into his head.

He could feel himself sweating. Heat had come into his body, but now it felt sickly rather than comforting.

But he could see the altar ahead of him, and he forged on towards it, fighting the pain with every step. Surely, Gryphus would hear him. Surely, the sun god would recognise him as one of his children.

By the time he reached it, he was in agony. He tried to kneel, but collapsed instead, and pulling himself into a kneeling position felt like the greatest struggle of his life.

A gold sunwheel effigy had been placed on the altar. With another mighty effort, Red reached up towards it.

The moment he touched it he pulled back, swearing. The metal felt red-hot under his fingers – he looked at them and couldn't believe they weren't burned.

He clasped his hands together instead, and started his prayer; stumbling over the words. His voice sounded weak and even hoarser than before. It sounded like the voice of a man on his deathbed.

'Gryphus,' he rasped. 'Please, listen to me. It's me, Red. Kearney Redguard. I just… I just want you to know that I'm still yours. I know what I am now, but I didn't ask for it. I ain't gonna serve the Night God. I'd rather die. I'd rather be cut to pieces. I just want t'be a loyal Southerner. I want to serve you, not her. Please, just help me.' He looked up at the sunwheel, and put all his effort into raising his voice. 'Please. Just say somethin'. Just speak to me. Send a sign. Show me I ain't alone in this. Please.'

Nothing happened.

'Please,' Red said again. 'You're a god. I ain't askin' for much. Make the pain stop. Speak to me. Do somethin'! The South's gonna fall apart. We need you! I need you. Please!'

There was no reply.

'Just make the pain stop, to show me you're there,' Red pleaded. 'Show me I ain't damned.'

Utter silence was the only reply.

Red dragged himself to his feet. 'Fine,' he said. 'Do nothin'. Be useless just like you always have been. I don't need you. I'm gonna do this myself, even if I'm damned.'

With a last violent effort, he hit the sunwheel with the back of his hand and sent it flying before he turned and shuffled out of the Temple, wincing with the effort.

Outside, Kraego was waiting for him.

'You should not have gone in there,' the black griffin rumbled.

Red stepped back out into the night, and in an instant the pain left him. 'No,' he said. 'Yer right. Gryphus won't help me. He won't help anyone.'

'You do not need him, or any god,' said Kraego. 'You have me.'

'Yeah, an' looks like that's it,' said Red. 'They're never gonna trust me, Kraego. You saw them. They're scared of me. Some of 'em hate me too.'

'With your human cunning, you can persuade them to trust us,' said Kraego.

'I ain't no politician,' said Red. 'What'm I gonna tell them? All they've got now is my word to go on, an' everyone knows the Shadow That Walks is a liar.'

'Then we shall persuade them with deeds,' said Kraego. 'If we strike the first blow against Shar ourselves, it will show them that we mean what we have said.'

Red ran his finger down the scar on his throat. 'Hm. Yeah. That sounds like it'd work.'

'Speak, then,' said Kraego. 'Use your human gift and decide where we must go and what we must do there.'

Red spread his hands. 'I dunno, but I know where I want to go. Liranwee. My friends might still be there, an' it's my home. Was, anyhow.'

'Then Liranwee is where we shall go,' said Kraego. 'Together.'

*

Red wanted to leave immediately, but he knew he should at least tell the others he was going. By now Isleen, Neth and the others would have reached the Eyrie, so he went back there with Kraego to find them.

Isleen and Alaric had been given a shared room lower down in the tower – below the griffiners, in other words. Red found them both there, sharing a meal.

Isleen looked up when he entered, and smiled. 'There you are.

We heard…'

'Heard what?' Red asked tersely.

The smile disappeared. 'That'd you'd… had some difficulties,' said Isleen.

Red grimaced. 'News spreads fast 'round here. Yeah. Seems even old friends don't like what I've become. Can't say I blame them. But we just came here to tell you we're leavin'.'

'Leaving?' Isleen stood up. 'Captain, what are you thinking? Listen, I know this must be difficult for you, but you can't run away from it. You're still one of us, aren't you?'

'That's right!' Alaric stood up too. 'Alaric the Dashing wouldn't run away from his problems, and neither should you!'

Red rubbed his eyes. 'Alaric the Dashing ain't real, mate. This is real life – for the love of gods, get that through your skull! You can't just hide away in fantasies for the rest of your life. You'll wind up dead, or alone.'

Alaric stared at him with an expression of pathetic betrayal. 'But…'

'Anyway, we ain't running away,' Red went on quickly. 'We're goin' to do some scouting. If we can show people whose side we're on, that'll solve this faster than bandyin' words like some Eyrie Master in council.'

'Captain, no.' Isleen came towards him. 'You can't go alone. What if——?'

Red laughed harshly. 'What if what? I'm already dead. You stay here an' look after the others. We won't be gone long.'

'Where will you go?' Alaric asked timidly.

Red finally smiled. 'Home,' he said.

'They won't be glad to see you,' Isleen warned. 'After what happened…'

'Maybe not, but I gotta face it sooner or later,' said Red. 'Now listen – there's somethin' else I want you to do while I'm gone.'

'Yes?'

'If Teressa comes back before I do, I want you to protect her,' said Red. 'Vouch for her. The others here might try an' kill her on sight – don't let that happen. If anything happens to her, I'll hold you responsible, Isleen.'

Isleen looked shocked.

Alaric took her by the arm. 'That's unfair!' he protested. 'She's not a griffiner any more, and—,'

'and she's the best ally I've got right now,' said Red.

'I'll do what I can,' said Isleen. 'But she's only a—,'

'She's the best chance we've got!' Red interrupted. 'With her to spread the word about me, it'll make divisions in their ranks. Confuse 'em. Scare 'em, too. An' frankly, Isleen, I trust her more'n I trust you.'

Isleen stiffened. 'She's a traitor!' she snapped.

'Yeah,' said Red. 'An' you stabbed Queen Laela in the back an' helped Caedmon take her throne, so don't talk to me about betrayal. An' you had my father killed. Don't deny it.'

Isleen went pale. 'Captain, I—,'

Red softened. 'Don't worry about it. I ain't gonna chase you off. We've all done things we ain't proud of. But you owe me a debt, Isleen. You want my full trust, you gotta earn it. I reckon if you talked to Teressa, you'd find you had more in common with her than y'think. Now I'm off. I'll be back in a few days, probably.'

Isleen nodded formally. 'I understand.'

'An' you,' Red added, pointing at Alaric.

'Yes?' Alaric looked terrified.

'Look after her,' said Red. 'Try spendin' some time in the real world – you might even like it. After all, in the real world you've got Isleen.'

Alaric smiled and stood a little taller. 'I do. Thank you, Captain. I'll…' he took Isleen's hand and clutched it tightly. 'I'll defend her to the death!'

Red grinned. 'That's the spirit. See you two later.'

Kraego had been waiting in the corridor for him, and he led the way back up the tower.

'You are right not to trust her,' the black griffin rumbled. 'She killed my father as well.'

'Helped Shar do it, you mean,' said Red. 'Yeah, I know. An'I helped that Ahamay kill the Emperor, so maybe I'm no better. Let's get on an' get some sleep before we go. We'll tell Merca we're leavin' in the morning; she'll be busy right now. Mind you, she might not even notice.'

'The humans here are all mad,' said Kraego.

'Mad, I can manage,' said Red.

He reached the door to his quarters, and absent-mindedly went through it.

Inside, he found someone waiting for him.

Red's hand stayed on the doorknob. 'Liantha?'

The former Eyrie Mistress of New Eagleholm had been sitting on his bed, but now she stood up and came towards him.

'Red,' she said. 'Please come in.'

Red entered, leaving Kraego to come in after him. 'What's all this about?'

'I wanted to apologise,' said Liantha. 'I shouldn't have… I should have said something back there.'

'It's all right,' Red said gruffly. 'I knew you wouldn't take it well. How could you? The first man like me destroyed Old Eagleholm.'

'Yes…' Liantha sighed. 'And none of my people are going to forget that. Try and forgive them, Red. Almost everyone in that hall lost someone in the Eagleholm fire. That's not something anyone can forget.'

'Yeah…' Red walked past her and out onto the balcony. By now night had come, and the sky glittered with stars. There was no moon out tonight.

Liantha followed him, and came to stand beside him. Behind them both, Kraego lay down in his nest.

'I can't help but wonder,' said Red. 'If I'm like him now. I mean…'

'What is it?' asked Liantha.

'I dunno what I'll do,' said Red. 'I know the stories. The Shadow That Walks has a bloodlust inside him. I mean, all those things he did – how much of it did he want to do? What if he did some of it because he just… lost control? Or because the Night God forced him? An' if that's true, what'll happen to me? I've done nothin', but… I feel like I have. Or will. I feel guilty just existing.'

Liantha touched him. 'It's all right, Red. It's going to be fine.'

'But I feel like I don't belong to myself no more,' said Red. 'An' it's worse than it was when I was a slave. What if Teressa's right? What if I do the Night God's will without meanin' to? What if she can control me?'

'I think if she could, she would have done it by now,' said Liantha. 'You were right Red – you might be the Shadow That Walks now, but you're on our side. You can use these powers however you choose.'

'It is true!' Kraego interrupted. He came up behind them, looming over them both. 'The power was in me as well,' he said. 'But I was not controlled. I used it how I chose. The Night God tempted me, but I refused her. You too can refuse.'

'There,' said Liantha. 'You see? Listen to him; he knows what he's saying. I mean, he gave you the power, didn't he?'

'He did,' said Red. He had already started to feel better. 'You're right, Liantha, an' you too, Kraego. It's gonna be all right. We can do this.'

'And in the meantime, the others might not trust you, but I do,' said Liantha. 'I'm still your friend.'

Red put his arm around her. 'Thanks, Liantha. It means a lot to me, havin' you here. I mean it.'

Liantha put her own arm around him in return, a little hesitantly. 'I think you and I both need a friend just now. But I'm afraid it's true – you *are* cold. Be sure to hug me again if I catch a fever!'

Red chuckled. 'You got it.'

'I talked to your friend Lady Isleen,' Liantha added. 'She told me you're planning to fight back against the Northerners.'

'Yeah, I am,' said Red. 'Alone, if I have to.'

'You won't,' said Liantha. 'I'll come with you, and I'll order my council to do the same, and all my citizens who came here with me.'

'Really?' said Red.

'Yes,' said Liantha. 'You're the closest thing to a general we have. You've got Kraego, and he's easily the biggest griffin here. And you've been trained in fighting and military leadership. You're the obvious choice.'

'We are,' said Kraego. 'I trust that my sister understands that.'

'She does,' said Liantha. 'She wouldn't be fool enough to try and challenge you anyway.'

'And besides that, it is the nature of Kraeai kran ae to lead,' said Kraego. 'Not to follow. We have decided that we will go to Liranwee and learn more of what is happening. We will strike a blow against Shar, and that will be our call for others to follow us.'

'That's right,' Red nodded.

Liantha let go of him. 'What, alone?'

'Yeah,' said Red. 'We'll move faster by ourselves. But don't worry; we'll come back here afterwards. An' also, while we're gone, there's somethin' I've asked Isleen to do. If you want, you can help her.'

'What is it?' asked Liantha.

Red explained about Teressa.

Liantha looked doubtful. 'Northern traitors? Well… I suppose they could be helpful. I won't lie, though – my friends won't like it at all.'

'Then they'll just have to get used to it,' said Red. 'Can I count on you?'

'You can,' said Liantha. 'Followers are followers. I'll tell them that if they complain.'

'You can tell 'em if they lay a hand on any of 'em, they'll have me to answer to,' Red growled. 'An' Kraego as well, but I'm a lot worse.'

'How are you worse?' Kraego demanded.

''Cause I'm human,' said Red. 'Griffins like you do what they have to t'get what they want, but humans are the ones who get nasty just 'cause we can.'

'Understood,' Liantha smiled. 'I'll go and talk to the others and leave you to get some rest.'

'Thanks,' Red smiled at her. 'An' I mean it. Thanks for bein' here for me, Liantha. I needed it.'

'No,' Liantha smiled back. 'It was you who came to us when we needed you, Red. All of us. And we haven't forgotten it.'

*

Red went to bed that night without having eaten anything – not an uncommon thing nowadays. He still got hunger pangs, but now they were easier to ignore. He didn't know if he even needed to eat any more.

Tiredness was something else he could still feel, but he never slept easily now.

He lay on his back and stared at the ceiling. It was pitch black, but he could still see it. Darkness was no handicap to him now.

It's mine, he thought calmly. I own it. It owns me.

Words rose up in his mind. Words Kullervo had recited to him many years ago. Words his father Arenadd, had once whispered out of the shadows to strike terror into his enemies.

Red murmured them to himself, chanting them softly in the darkness.

'I am the shadow that comes in the night. I am the fear that lurks in your heart. I am the man without a heart. I am darkness. I am death. I am the Shadow That Walks.'

I am the shadow…

He fell asleep with those words in his ears.

Darkness filled his mind… and then there was light. Morning had come. But the sunlight coming in through the windows felt harsh and painful. It made his eyes ache.

He got up and walked out through the tower alone, searching for the others.

The building was utterly silent.

He looked in the first bedroom he found. There was a woman in there. Merca, lying in her bed.

At first he thought she was asleep – but then he saw the blood on her throat. Her eyes were wide open, the face locked in a final expression of horror.

Red ran through into the griffin's nest next door, and found Tarak there. She lay on her side, her entrails draped over the straw and her trough full of blood.

Red couldn't bear to look. He ran out, back to the corridor and on through the tower, searching everywhere, calling the names of his friends.

Everywhere he went, he found death. Isleen, stabbed to death in her bed. Alaric, lying on the open pages of a book with his pen still in his hand. Someone had dipped their hands in his blood and scrawled the words "…and then Alaric died" on the wall above him.

He found Liantha and Seerae, the one lying draped over the other with her head half torn off. Seerae's eyes had been cut out and crushed in her killer's hands.

He found Neth, slit open like a slaughtered pig, his friends stabbed to death as they had tried to fight back beside him.

Red searched every room on every level, and found nothing. Everyone dead.

But how? How could he have slept through it, how…?

He looked down at his own hands, and saw the truth.

Blood ran down to his elbows and dripped onto the floor. His fingers were caked in gore.

'No!' he screamed the word. 'No!'

In front of him, three people stood in a semicircle. All Northerners.

The first was a man, all grubby and wild, wearing nothing but shaggy animal skins. He held a wooden spear and wore a lunatic smile, and his hands and arms were soaked in blood.

The second was a man, robed and bearded, his long, curly hair draped over his shoulders. He held a dripping sickle and his hands dripped along with it.

The third was an old woman. One of her eyes was an empty, scarred socket, but the other eye glittered with hate. She too had been splashed with blood.

All three were gaunt and pale as death, and they stared at him with lifeless eyes.

All three spoke as one, their voices low and cold.

'Traegan. Arenadd. Saeddryn.' They smiled the smiles of wolves. 'Kearney.'

And he saw himself, there, standing with them, the eyes lifeless, the smile full of cruelty. Blood dripping from his hands.

One of them.

'No!' Red shouted, but his voice was silent.

The four of them began to chant.

'You are the shadow that comes in the night, you are the fear that lurks in their hearts. You are the man without a heart. You are darkness. You are death. You are the Shadow That Walks.'

And when Red tried to say no, tried to run, he did neither.

He looked around at the dead, and laughed until he cried.

*

'Red. Red!'

Red came awake in an instant. 'What?' he heard himself say.

Kraego's voice replied. 'Were you awake?'

Red sat up. There was no confusion, no drowsiness. His mind snapped back to full awareness in an instant. 'No,' he said. 'I was sleepin'. I...'

The giant griffin was standing over him, his tail swishing from side to side. 'I thought you were awake,' he said. 'You were... laughing.'

Red realised that Kraego sounded genuinely disturbed. 'Yeah,' he mumbled. 'Yeah, I think I would've been.' He sat there for a moment while the dream replayed itself in his mind. 'Oh gods,' he said. 'Was I here all night?'

'I was asleep,' said Kraego. 'Why would you not know where you were?'

'I dreamt…' Red slipped off the bed. 'I gotta go.'

He ran out of the room.

Chapter Twenty-Two

Southerners

Isleen and Alaric hadn't been up long. They'd been given a room to share in the Eyrie, but neither of them had had the time to settle in properly yet.

Not long after dawn, Isleen woke up and to her surprise she found Alaric already up and dressed, sitting at the small desk over by the wall. The pudgy storyteller was usually a heavy sleeper; he'd never gotten up before her.

Isleen sat up in bed. 'Are you all right?' she asked.

Alaric looked over at her. 'Oh. Good morning. Yes, I'm fine.'

Isleen, though, noticed how pale he looked. 'Did you sleep at all?'

'Not much,' Alaric admitted. 'I'm not used to having a proper bed yet. Anyway… I had things on my mind.'

'I know the feeling,' Isleen smiled and got out of bed. 'Well, we'll both have some time to rest before—,' she froze, and her smile vanished.

'What is it?' said Alaric.

Isleen looked past him. 'Captain,' she said. 'What is it?'

Alaric turned to look, and started violently when he saw Red standing in the doorway.

Red stood very still – unnaturally still. Both of them had noticed how deliberately he moved nowadays, never twitching or glancing around like an ordinary person. But his voice was its usual rough, damaged self.

'Are you all right?' he asked.

Isleen frowned. 'Yes, we're fine. Why? You look…' she trailed off, unable to find a way to finish without offending him.

'Awful, I know,' said Red, who actually did look worse than usual. His eyes were red-rimmed and his hair tousled – he looked as if he hadn't slept all night. Maybe he hadn't. 'Nothin' happened last night?' he persisted.

'Not that we noticed,' said Isleen. 'Why do you ask?'

Red looked at her, then at Alaric, then shook his head and left without another word.

'What was that all about?' Isleen asked once he'd gone.

Alaric kept his gaze on the doorway where Red had stood. 'He looked so frightened. Did you notice?'

'No,' said Isleen. 'But I believe you. What's happened? I would ask him, but I don't think he would tell me.'

'He wouldn't.' Alaric looked back at her, his own expression troubled. 'He's suffering, you know. He never says anything, but I can tell. It's written all over his face.'

'I know,' said Isleen. She shivered. 'I wish there was something we could do for him.'

'So do I,' said Alaric. He rubbed his eyes. 'I can't imagine how horrible it must be to be him. But he saved my life, and by Gryphus I'll follow him to the ends of the earth if I have to.'

Isleen smiled, making him blush. 'That sounds like something Alaric the Dashing might say! What were you doing all night, anyway? Writing?'

Alaric sighed. 'I tried. But I couldn't do it.'

'Never mind,' said Isleen. 'Try again later. I'm sure—,'

'No,' said Alaric. 'You don't understand. I was up all night. I haven't slept since yesterday. I was here at this desk while you were asleep, trying and trying… it's never been like this. I can't do it any more, Isleen. It's just gone.'

'Oh.' Isleen came over to him and put her hand on his shoulder. 'Don't worry, Alaric. It'll be fine. Try again when you feel ready.'

Alaric shook his head. 'The Captain was right. None of it's real. I've been thinking about that too. Every time I tried to write something, I remembered… no. He was right. I can't keep trying to hide away in a fantasy world. It's time to face what's real.' He drew himself up to his full, unimpressive height. 'So I'm quitting. No more stories. No more pretending. No more Alaric the Dashing. I'm sorry,' he added.

Isleen stared at him in surprise. 'Do you really mean that?'

'Yes,' said Alaric. 'In fact…'

He twisted around in his chair to face the desk again. There was an open book on it, its pages blank. Alaric grabbed a reed pen, dipped it in the inkpot, and scrawled some words across the page. His handwriting was clumsy and careless, and he didn't bother to try and keep it straight on the page.

"…Alaric the Dashing could feel the cold spreading in his body. The dagger

stuck in his back was like a spear of agony. 'Morgan' he proclaimed, 'how could you betray me?'

'Because ye are a Southerner, Alaric,' Morgan announced. 'Now die like the scum ye are.'

And then Alaric died, and his soul went away into the void where the Night God waited."

Alaric scrawled out the last few words, hesitated, and then added THE END before throwing the pen aside.

'There,' he said. 'It's done. Alaric the Dashing is dead. Now it'll just have to be Alaric the fat coward.'

Isleen had never heard him sound so angry or bitter. In fact, she had never seen him angry at all, not even during the worst humiliations they had had to endure in Amoran. 'Alaric!' she exclaimed.

Alaric, though, grinned. 'Excuse me. I have to go and find the Captain. I've got something to ask him.'

*

Red searched the tower, checking every room he had seen in his dream. But he didn't find anything. Everyone was fine, and his fear started to recede.

Just a dream.

But the knowledge that it hadn't really happened didn't do much to make him feel better. He headed for the dining hall to find some food, not really noticing anything around him, and remembered something his father had once told him.

'If you can dream it, you can do it.'

Red shuddered.

Would it always be like this? Was this what it was like to be the Shadow That Walked? Utterly alone, always able to feel the icy coldness where a heartbeat should be, with dreams of murder to torment him every night?

And what if it wasn't just dreaming? What if he lost control and started to act on the fantasies that had visited him? Or what if he sleepwalked?

What if one day he woke up and found that he really had done the things he had dreamt of doing?

Red reached the dining hall, and found that food had been laid out on the table for people to help themselves. He sat down at the first chair he found, and grabbed a small loaf of bread and some fried fish. He ate them without really tasting them, all the while struggling with his fears.

He'd vowed to use his powers to do what was right, but he knew, in a way that went deeper than any normal knowledge, that they could make a monster of him as well – if they hadn't already.

All right, he thought. *So what'm I gonna do about it?*

There had to be an answer. But what?

He was so deep in thought that it took him quite a while to realise that someone was speaking.

'Eh?' he said, turning his head to look. 'Oh,' he said, seeing who it was. 'It's you.'

Alaric coughed. 'Yes, excuse me, but—,'

'But what?' Red asked brusquely. 'Out with it.'

'Er,' Alaric shuffled his feet. 'I wanted to ask you for something.'

'Which is?' said Red.

'I want you to teach me how to fight,' said Alaric.

Red gave him a blank look. 'You what?'

'Yes,' said Alaric, more firmly. 'If there's going to be a war, I want to help.'

'Why d'you need me to teach you, then?' asked Red.

'Because you know how to fight,' said Alaric. 'And Isleen told me you were a Sergeant in the guards back in Liranwee, and sergeants help train new recruits, so you know how to teach.'

'Neth was a Sergeant too,' said Red. 'An' one of the other lads as well.'

'Maybe,' said Alaric. 'But you're the only one I trust. You're the only one here apart from Isleen who gives me any respect at all.'

Red looked at him in surprise.

'I know everyone thinks I'm useless,' Alaric added. 'Even you probably think it. But I don't want to be useless. I need to learn how to do something other than write legal documents and stupid stories.'

'"Stupid"?' Red repeated.

'Yes,' said Alaric. 'You were right, Captain. It's all nonsense. So will you teach me? I would consider it an honour.'

Red couldn't help but smile at the little man's earnest tone. 'All right,' he said. 'I'll give it a try. When I get back.'

Alaric beamed. 'Thank you!'

'An' while I'm gone,' Red added, 'find a stick or somethin' and practise with it. Or just practise with your hands. Can you throw a punch?'

'I think so,' said Alaric.

'All right, show me,' said Red. He held out a hand, palm forward. 'Punch my hand.'

Alaric scowled determinedly, and punched Red's palm as hard as he could.

Red chuckled. 'You never got into a bar fight in yer life, did you?'

'Of course not!'

'Well, let an old pro show you how it's done,' said Red. 'First… keep your wrist straight, like this. And don't tuck your thumb under yer fingers – you'll break it. Don't curl your fingers in so hard – keep 'em loose. Yeah, like that. And swing from the shoulder. Don't just use the fist. Use your whole body. Pretend like you want to punch through whatever it is. Now go on, try again.'

Alaric did. With Red's encouragement, he tried several more times until he'd gotten the hang of it.

'All right,' said Red. 'Practise that while I'm gone. But remember…'

'Yes?' the pudgy storyteller was listening keenly.

'When you get right down to it, fighting's all about hurtin' the other bugger worse than he hurts you,' said Red. 'An' that's not a joke. Most people don't really want to hurt anyone, or get hurt. If you're the meaner one, you'll probably win.'

'I doubt that will ever happen,' Alaric said cheerfully. 'Thank you, Captain.'

'I ain't a Captain any more,' said Red. 'Just call me Red.'

'All right, then. Thank you, Red.'

'No problem.' Red stood up. 'Now I'd better get goin'. There's work to do.'

*

Red went back to his own room, and found Kraego idly dozing in his nest next door. Even though Red walked silently now, the giant griffin still looked up when he entered.

'There you are. Where did you go?'

'I just—,' Red began, and stopped. If he couldn't confide in his partner, who could he confide in? 'I had a nightmare,' he said.

'Yes?' said Kraego.

'I dreamt that everyone was dead,' said Red. 'An' I'd killed them. It was so real… I had to see if everyone was all right.'

Kraego's tail swished. 'I would say that it was only a dream,' he rasped. 'But after I spoke to the Night God in my own dreams, I learnt to know better.'

Red's stomach lurched. 'D'you think it could come true, Kraego?'

'Not if you have the strength to stop it,' said Kraego.

'But what if I don't?' asked Red.

'Then there will be nothing either of us can do,' said Kraego.

'No…' Red went over to the bed and retrieved the short sword he had taken from the armoury. He stuffed it into his belt. 'If it turns out I can't control it, then I'm leaving. I'll get out of the country, go somewhere far away where there's nobody else. No-one I can hurt.'

'It will not happen,' Kraego insisted. 'Enough of this. We have things we must do.'

'Yeah,' said Red. 'We do, don't we?'

'Come, then,' said Kraego. 'We will use the shadows. Have you thought of a plan of what to do when we reach Liranwee?'

Red opened his mouth to say no, but then closed it again. The dream came back to him, and for a moment he just stood there, seeing it all in his mind. The circle of figures, all bloodstained and dead eyed, and himself standing among them. Odd to think that someone like Liantha would have been terrified to see them, but someone like Teressa would probably have knelt and called herself unworthy. But, of course, Northerners saw it differently, didn't they?

'Yeah…' Red said slowly. 'Yeah… I think I have.'

Chapter Twenty-Three

Recruitment

Ranulf Ranulfson, former sergeant in Liranwee's city guard, sat in the White Serpent and downed another mug of his favourite beer. There was already another one standing by, and he pulled it towards himself and sipped it more slowly. He'd had too much already, but he didn't give a damn. There wasn't anything left to do nowadays but drink.

Ranulf hadn't taken that much pride in his work, not like some. Guarding had just been a job, and mostly it was boring. But right now, he would have given anything to be out on patrol, walking unhurriedly through the streets of Liranwee with his old partner. Nowadays, he would give anything to be bored again.

But all of that was over now.

Liranwee had been taken. Overrun. The Northerners had come, thousands of them, with the army of griffins called the Unpartnered. The griffins had dropped firebombs and broken the gates down to let the Northerners in. Liranwee never stood a chance.

Not that they'd destroyed the city. A good part of it had burned down, and afterwards the Northerners had run wild through the streets, looting and killing.

But they hadn't destroyed everything. They'd installed a new council and Eyrie Master, and now the King of the North, Caedmon Taranisäii, had come to live in the Liranwee Eyrie. They'd rebuilt what they'd destroyed, or most of it, and they kept law and order in the city just as Lady Isleen had done. The members of the guard had been allowed to keep their jobs, if they agreed to answer to their new, Northerner, commander.

Ranulf, though, had quit his job along with many others, and now… nothing left to do but sit in the White Serpent and think about how things could have been. And miss people.

Funny to think of, really. Nobody really thought he cared that much about his job, not even him. His old patrolling partner, Red, used to leave him in the dust, always rushing off to volunteer for extra work, always taking it all so seriously…

Ranulf grimaced to himself at the thought of his old friend. Nowadays, of course, Red was just another person who was gone forever. He'd been the first to go, really.

Nobody ever would've expected someone like Red to be a traitor. Never. Not even when you knew that he had traitors in his family, what with his uncle being Branton Redguard, who'd betrayed his home city to a Northerner, and his father Danthirk having been killed for treason.

Red just wasn't the sort to go that way, never.

Ranulf downed another drink, and waved at the barman to bring him another one.

He didn't know what he believed any more. Traitor or not, Red had tried to warn him and he should have listened. Everyone should have listened. But they hadn't, and now they were paying the price.

Anyway, it wasn't like they didn't have plenty of other traitors in the city now. Even in the guard.

Ranulf growled to himself and snatched his next drink as it arrived. The guard as he'd known it didn't exist any more, and never would again. Not while it was being commanded by those Northern usurpers. And with the King himself living in Liranwee, there was no chance for anyone to fight back.

Anyone who attacked a Northerner went to prison. If they were judged to be a rebel, they'd be collared and sent to Amoran, never to be seen again. Bad enough that the Northerners were doing it, but with the guard under their control, now they were making Liranwee's citizens do it to each other.

People had been given rewards for ratting out their friends and neighbours, and plenty of them were willing to do it, too. Even Commander Talmon had been locked up for refusing to co-operate with the takeover of the guard.

Ranulf's head was spinning. He'd drunk too much.

He started on his next drink anyway. One for the road and then he'd go home and sleep it off. He'd have to be this drunk to get any sleep there; his old home had been his bunk in the guard barracks, but since he'd quit the only home he had was a stall in an abandoned stable. Or, when that was taken, a handy doorway.

'Hey, Ranulf.'

Ranulf looked up unsteadily. 'What?' he began, and scowled when he saw the guard uniform. 'Oh, it's you. Sod off, you.'

Young Elthan, though, sat down opposite him. 'Thought I'd find you here,' he said.

'An' I thought you'd be busy off kissin' the new Commander's arse,' said Ranulf.

'You ain't still bitter, are yer?' said Elthan. 'I just made the best of a bad situation. What about you? Still sleepin' in the gutter, then?'

Ranulf only muttered something and swallowed the last of his drink. 'I ain't drunk enough for this. Get me another one or sod off.'

'Y'look like you already had plenty,' said Elthan. 'But I'm here to celebrate, so all right.'

Ranulf thumped the empty mug down on the bench. 'Why, what's happened now? You throw another one of our old lads in prison for sayin' our city's been stolen out from under us?'

'No, I just got promoted,' said Elthan. 'An' you'd better keep that mouth shut, Ranulf, or you really will get arrested.'

'At least prison's got a roof over yer head,' said Ranulf.

'Nothing t'drink, though,' said Elthan. 'Oi, you! Bring us two pints!' he waved at the nearest barmaid. When the drinks arrived, he shoved one over to Ranulf. 'This one's on me,' he said. 'D'you even have any money to pay for the ones you've already drunk?'

Ranulf grunted and fished in his pocket for something which he dumped on the table between them.

It was a gold medal, still shiny. A broken, grubby griffin's feather hung next to it on the string.

Elthan touched it. 'Is this Red's medal?'

'Yeah,' said Ranulf.

'What, you ain't gonna trade this for beer are you?'

'Why not?' said Ranulf. 'That's real gold. It's gotta be worth a few pints.'

Elthan frowned and picked up the medal, rubbing his fingertips over the writing engraved on it. 'You got one too, right? Have y'still got it, or did you already drink it?'

Ranulf grunted again and picked up his mug.

'You sure you really wanna sell this?' Elthan persisted. 'I mean, we all know what Red did, but it's still a piece of the old days.'

'Who cares?' said Ranulf. 'I don't want it no more. Keep it if yer want an' sell it yerself.'

Elthan put it down on the bench. 'All right, but I dunno who'd buy it.'

'I'll take it,' said someone sitting to his left.

Both of them looked up.

'Were you listenin' in on us?' Elthan said sharply.

'Yeah.' The speaker was wearing a hood, and he didn't look up at either of them. 'I got good hearin'. But I'll take that medal if you don't want it.'

'Oh yeah? What'll you give us?'

'Information,' said the stranger.

Ranulf squinted at him. 'Who are yer, anyway? An' what information?'

The stranger shushed him. 'I've been watchin'. You don't look so happy about the situation here. Can't blame you, either. So if you want a chance t'do somethin' about it, I can help.'

'That's dangerous talk nowadays, stranger,' said Elthan. 'An' I'm gonna ask you to show us your face before we listen to you any more.'

'Why, so you can arrest me again?' said the stranger.

'Again?' Elthan gave him a suspicious look.

Ranulf started to get irritated. 'Look, take the damn hood off or sod off.'

'Fine, but keep quiet,' said the stranger. His voice was low and raspy. 'Or I'll disappear an' there won't be any more chances for either of you. I'm gonna try and help the pair of you just one last time, an' if you don't take it this time that's the last time, understood?'

'Fine, whatever,' said Elthan. 'Now stop the nonsense an' get on with it.'

The stranger took his hood off. Underneath he looked like someone who might have been tanned once, but now his skin was sickly pale. His thick red hair and beard had grown out and looked all raggedy and wild. The nose had been broken at some point, and in the bad light of the tavern his eyes were shadows.

Both of them stared at him.

'Wait,' said Ranulf. 'That ain't…?'

'It's me, Red,' Red growled. 'Now gimme back my medal, you drunk.'

Ranulf gaped at him as if he'd just fallen out of the sky. 'Red? Holy gods, but you're meant t'be…'

'Dead, I know,' said Red.

'We thought you'd died when the city fell,' said Elthan. 'Great Gryphus, what're you doing here? Where've you been all this time?'

'It's a long story,' said Red. 'But I came back here for you. Wasn't gonna leave my mates stuck here. I thought most of you might be dead already, but looks like you've been doin' all right, Elth.'

'Yeah, he just got promoted,' said Ranulf.

'So I heard,' said Red. 'I reckon you won't be draggin' me back to prison now, right?'

'No,' said Elthan. 'It was Isleen's Master of Law what put out that warrant on you, an' both of them are long gone. For gods' sakes, Red, what happened to you? You look half dead.'

'Hah.' It wasn't so much a laugh as a cough. 'Only half? Look, don't worry about me, I ain't got time to explain. D'you want to get out of here or not?'

'Where'd we be going?' Ranulf asked suspiciously. 'All the other cities're taken as well.'

'Not all of 'em,' said Red. 'There's a place I can take you where the Northerners ain't been. It's still free. I've got friends there, an' when the time comes we're gonna fight back. But first I'm gettin' people out to join us. Point is, we need you. An' you need us. Unless you'd rather live like this. Eh, Ranulf? You'd rather sleep in a gutter? An' you, Elthan? Would you rather be second-class in yer own home? Spend the rest of yer life bein' spat on by some Northerner what only got put in charge of you 'cause he's not a Southerner? An' don't lie about it. I told you – I've been watchin'. I know how it is.'

Elthan frowned. 'How can we trust you, Red? After what you did? You betrayed all of us.'

Red gave him a look of quiet outrage. 'You really think I did that? For Gryphus' sake, Elthan, I was yer friend. I was friends with both of you. An' then the moment there's an accusation you just believe it? Did you ever think that badly of me?'

'Didn't want to,' said Ranulf. 'But if you didn't do it, who did?'

'Morgan.' Red spat the name. 'Morgan did it. He was the spy. He killed Bear. He framed me. He tricked me an' took me to his King as a prisoner, an' then had me beaten around the head to make me talk. D'you know why I showed up here tryin' to warn everyone about the invasion? It's because I escaped.'

'Who's this Morgan—?' Ranulf began, but Elthan interrupted. 'You mean Morgan Taranisäii? That Morgan? The King's adopted son?'

'Yeah,' said Red. 'You know him?'

'I saw him,' said Elthan. 'He was here. They brought him back here, badly hurt. He almost died.'

'That's him,' said Red. 'I caught him an' took him to New Eagleholm, an' he got out of prison. He almost got hanged by a mob.'

'That's what I heard,' said Elthan. 'An' after he got better, he took an army an' went back there. Destroyed the whole city, they say. But...' he looked reflectively into his drink. 'If you say he's the real spy, I believe you.'

'C'mon,' said Ranulf. 'Why'd the King's son be out spyin'? Ain't he a griffiner?'

'Yeah, he is,' said Elthan. 'But... well, we ain't supposed to know, but I've heard the rumours. He's the King's chief spy. A master of disguise. It's said he infiltrated just about every city in the South before the invasion, or trained people to do it for him. I'll bet you any money you could name that he did it in Liranwee too.

'An' then when he realised we were on to him, he pinned the blame on me,' Red finished. 'You saw him, Ranulf. That blind beggar man, No-Eyes. That was him. He took off his eye-cloth, an' underneath... eyes. Black eyes.' Red gritted his teeth. 'I'm gonna kill that son of a bitch. I swore I would. I'm gonna kill his King as well, an' I'm gonna get the Northerners out of our land. Only question left is, are you with me?'

'Damn right,' Ranulf said immediately. 'An'...' he put his drink down. 'Red, I'm so sorry. I should've... but when I saw that stuff in your chest...'

'It's all right,' said Red. 'Forget it, mate. It's in the past now. What about you, Elthan?'

Elthan frowned. 'I'm sorry too, Red. An' don't blame yourself about what happened here. We should've listened, but even if we had it would've been too late.'

'All right, but are you comin'?' asked Red.

'Where're we goin'?'

'I'll tell you once we're out of the city. Well?'

'I'll... think about it.'

'Oh come on,' said Ranulf. 'What's wrong with you? You in love with your new job or somethin'? You'd rather stay here an' work for a bunch of Northerners? What kinda Southerner are you anyway?'

'Yeah, that's what I'm wonderin' too,' said Red. 'We're Southerners, remember? An' we're guards. We ain't scholars an' we ain't warriors. We're just guards. An' what does a guard do? Remember the oath? It's our job to see justice done. To protect our people. To lay our lives down for our home city, if we have to. But what's this I'm seein' here? Some bastard comes in here an' murders our people an' steals our city, an' you're all right with that? Forget about him bein' a king – he's a thief an' a murderer, an' so's his army. He's a criminal, an' we're guards, so who'd be better to bring him to justice? You tell me!'

'Keep yer voice down!' Elthan hissed. 'You want the whole tavern to hear?'

'I don't care, so long as *you* hear,' said Red. 'So did you?'

'Yeah…' Elthan calmed down and took a throatful of beer.

'Forget him,' said Ranulf. 'He ain't got the balls. Let's go, mate. I'm ready. An'… here.' He offered up the medal.

Red took it, and stuffed it into his pocket with a smile. 'Thanks, Ranulf.'

Ranulf shrugged. 'Like you said, it's yours. So's this.' He unbuckled the sword from around his waist and put it on the table.

Red grabbed it. 'My dad's sword!'

'Yeah, they took mine away when I quit,' said Ranulf. 'My armour too. But I'd kept yours after you dropped it. It's a bit rusty, but it's a decent blade.'

Red grinned and put the sword belt around his waist. 'Thanks. I was real sad about losin' it.'

'Thought so.' Ranulf drained his beer. 'Are we goin' or what?'

'Yeah.' Red put his hood back on and stood up.

Elthan stayed where he was, and avoided both their gazes.

Ranulf snorted. 'Oh, burn him. C'mon, Red.'

Red gave Elthan a last look. 'You oughta be ashamed.'

With that he slunk out of the tavern with Ranulf close behind, completely ignoring the protests of the unpaid bartender.

Outside, Red and Ranulf fell into step beside each other, as if they were still patrolling together and all the months in-between had never happened.

'Right,' said Red. 'Are you ready now, or d'you need to pick up your stuff before we go?'

Ranulf staggered slightly. 'Nah, I'm carryin' all I got left.'

'How long've you been out of a job, anyway?' asked Red.

'Ever since the takeover,' said Ranulf. 'I quit the moment they said we could stay if we worked under the new Commander. I dunno if Talmon's even still alive.'

'He is,' said Red. 'Bit knocked about, but he's alive.'

'How d'you know all this?' asked Ranulf.

'I told you – I've been watchin',' said Red. 'Gotten good at it, too.'

'All right, but how are we gonna get out of the city?'

'Same way I got in an' out last time,' said Red. 'C'mon an' I'll show you.'

Ranulf glanced at his old friend. He'd never been so glad to see anyone, but he couldn't shake the feeling that there was something odd about Red now. Something different. And it wasn't just how scruffy he'd gotten – Ranulf wasn't so neat nowadays either. No, it was something else, something he couldn't quite put a finger on. The voice had changed, definitely; Ranulf didn't recognise it at all. But it wasn't just the voice, no, it was something else. Something that frightened him.

The back of Ranulf's neck prickled. 'Red, I think someone's followin' us.'

'I know,' Red said calmly. 'It's just Elthan.' He hadn't even looked back.

Ranulf glanced over his shoulder, and sure enough…'What're you doin'?' he snapped. 'Sod off, traitor.'

Elthan hurried to catch up with them. 'Red, wait!'

Red stopped and turned to face him. He said nothing, and only stood and stared at him.

Elthan fidgeted. 'Look, I'm sorry. I should've… look, I know signin' up with the Northerners was cowardly. I just didn't know what else to do. D'you have any idea how crappy I feel? I've betrayed my own race, an' my own city, an' my friends as well.'

Red stayed silent, and Ranulf found himself doing the same.

'Look,' Elthan went on. 'I want to help. I've got a key to the armoury now. I can get you in there to pick up some weapons an' so forth. Might be able to recruit some more of the lads as well. Just let me do somethin'.'

Red finally spoke. 'What took you so long?'

Elthan glared at Ranulf. 'I had to pay off this great lump's bar tab. Well? Can I come?'

'Sure you can,' said Red. 'I knew you were gonna change your mind. That's why I didn't hide. So you could follow us.'

Elthan grinned in relief. 'All right. Are we goin' tonight?'

'Not if there's more guards who could join us,' said Red. 'Listen – I'll get Ranulf out, an' you'll go back to the barracks an' act like nothin' happened. You're gonna try an' talk some others into coming with us, an' when you're ready, leave me a message an' I'll show you the way out. You ain't gonna know it until you use it, in case you're caught. In the meantime, I've got work to do here.'

Elthan nodded. 'I got it. Where'll you leave the message?'

'Here at the White Serpent,' said Red. 'When it's time to meet up again, I'll tie somethin' onto the sign outside. You'll know it when you see it, an' when you do, go to the new guard tower – the one where we caught the Hangman. There's an empty house just down the street from it. That's where I'll be.'

'Yes Captain,' Elthan grinned. 'I'll see you there.'

'An' if you get into trouble,' Red added. 'Get the word out. I'll hear it, an' I'll come. That's a promise.'

'I'll remember.' Elthan nodded again and hurried away.

'Right then,' said Red. 'Now to get you out of Liranwee. There'll be others waiting, don't worry.'

'Who?' asked Ranulf.

'Lots of people,' said Red as they set off again. 'Everyone I could get. Some of the others from the old guard who quit like you. Most of 'em were so desperate, they'd have said yes if I just offered them food, an' forget the loyalty business.'

Ranulf chuckled. 'It's good t'be walkin' the city with you again, Red. It really is. I've missed it. Missed you, too.'

'An' me,' said Red. 'I thought I'd never see you again. Sometimes I'd think of you, an' the others as well, an' wonder if any of you were still alive. But I thought I'd never see Liranwee's walls again, or anyone behind 'em. Thought I'd never see Cymria again, come to that.'

'Eh?' said Ranulf. 'Why? Where'd you go.'

'Hrm,' Red grunted. 'I guess while we're walkin' I can fill you in a bit.'

So, while they headed through the streets to the south end of the city, Red gave Ranulf his story, or some of it, telling him about slavery in Amoran, and the massacre in the Imperial Palace, and about Kraego as well.

Ranulf listened in amazement. 'You're a griffiner now?'

'Yeah,' said Red. 'Kraego's waitin' for us with the others. Right, here we are.'

They'd reached the southern wall of the city where the shacks that made up the poorest part of it crowded right up to the edge. Red led the way to a particularly tumbledown old thing, whose roof had mostly caved in, and whose third wall was also the city wall.

'Not even rats'd live here,' he said. 'But…'

Inside, he lifted a slimy wooden board away to reveal a tunnel.

'Goes right under the wall,' he said. 'An' comes out in some trees way out from the city. I should warn you it's a bit of a crawl, an' a squeeze as well. Just as well you've lost weight.'

Ranulf gave the tunnel a dubious look. 'You sure about this?'

'I've used it dozens of times by now,' said Red. 'That's why I'm so filthy. That an' I ain't had time for a bath. Morgan used it to get in, too. They'd filled it in when I got back, but I dug it out again. Took days. Now c'mon, let's go.'

The tunnel did indeed turn out to be a tight squeeze. Ranulf had to crawl through it, sometimes wriggling along on his stomach when it got too narrow. It was pitch black as well, suffocatingly so, and full of the smell of dirt.

He could hear Red scrabbling along up ahead of him, sometimes muttering to himself. It was about the only comfort he had, but it was better than nothing as the journey went on and on and never seemed close to ending.

But it did end, eventually, when the tunnel suddenly ended in a vertical hole. Red pulled him up out of it, and into fresh air.

Ranulf collapsed, gasping. 'Argh. Son of a…'

'Yeah, not much fun, is it?' said Red. 'But we're out. See?'

Ranulf rolled onto his back, and saw trees above him, lit up by the faint light of dawn. They were out of the city.

Red sat down beside him. 'Rest up a bit, an' we'll go on when yer ready. Not far now.'

Ranulf heaved himself to his feet. 'I'll rest when we get there.'

Red stood up. 'You sure?'

'Yeah,' said Ranulf. 'One last push, right?'

'Right,' said Red. 'It's this way.'

They walked the last part together, southward through the trees until they reached Red's camp. A dozen small tents had been put up, disguised with branches so they would be just about invisible from the sky. People were already coming to meet them, but before any of them got close, something massive burst out of the undergrowth and loped towards them.

Ranulf threw himself flat. 'Holy shit!'

The giant griffin ignored him completely. He went straight to Red, and Red went to him without hesitating, and affectionately rubbed the huge creature's chest feathers. Ranulf backed off cautiously – he'd never been this close to a griffin before.

'It's all right,' Red said over his shoulder. 'This is Kraego. My partner. An' Kraego, this is Ranulf – my other partner.' He grinned. Ranulf made himself stand up straight, while Kraego glared at him. Then again, he was a griffin, and griffins always looked as if they were glaring. His eyes were bright blue, but they were set into a face covered in black feathers.

'He's a black griffin?' Ranulf exclaimed.

'Yeah,' said Red. 'Son of the Mighty Skandar himself. But he's on our side, of course.'

Kraego snorted and swished his tail.

'Right then,' Red went on. 'Time to meet the others.'

The others were gathering now, some of them stopping to salute Red and rap out a "sir!" or "Captain!".

Red saluted back. 'Morning, everyone. This is Ranulf, my old partner. Some of you already know him, some don't. He's with us now. An' I've recruited Elthan too. He's promised to find some others, an' steal some weapons an' armour for us. Now you take care of Ranulf. I'm goin' back.'

'Again?' one man asked. 'When are we gonna leave, sir? We can't have much more people, or we'll never get away without bein' spotted.'

'I ain't goin' back for more people this time,' said Red. 'I came back here to do one other thing too, an' once I've gotten Elthan out, I'm gonna do it. One last thing.'

'Which is?' Ranulf prompted.

Red cracked his knuckles. 'I'm gonna go an' have a word with the King.'

Chapter Twenty-Four

The Ghost of Liranwee

Strange things had begun happening in Liranwee. Some months after moving his government into the city, King Caedmon started to hear the reports come in.

Animals panicking for no obvious reason, sometimes even trying to flee the city altogether. Mysterious thefts, where doors and locks would be found broken without anyone having heard a sound. People disappearing without a trace.

And there were other reports. Stories of a ghostly figure that would vanish if anyone tried to approach it – a figure who would sometimes whisper in shadowy places, speaking of betrayal and murder, and revenge.

Caedmon had put it down to superstition and trickery, but it indicated something much more real and important: that there was rebellion in the air, and if things weren't handled carefully, the situation could get ugly.

He'd done his best, of course, to treat the Southerners sternly without being so harsh that they would fight back – nobody could rule for long by fear alone. But it was hard, and it would take generations before they got used to the new way of life and just accepted it as normal, as his own ancestors had once accepted Southern rule and even slavery.

And then, one day, after weeks of ghostly sightings and mysterious disappearances, a whole rank of the city guard vanished. Shortly afterward, the armoury was found left open, with a good chunk of its contents stolen, and Caedmon's new Commander of the Guard was found dead – his neck broken by a single brutal blow.

That night, Caedmon paced back and forth in his room, frowning to himself in thought.

Caradoc sat nearby, looking nervous. 'What are we going to do?' he asked.

Caedmon glanced up. Shar and Ereska were out flying over the Eyrie, as city-dwelling griffins liked to do, and father and son were alone.

'I'm not sure yet,' he said briefly. 'But it'll have to be decisive. This is the start of a rebellion, that's certain. What's not certain yet is who's behind it, but in any case we have to put it down, and fast. We strike hard, and fast, and in the right place.'

Caradoc listened seriously. He had turned nine not long after they came to the city, and Caedmon noticed how much more mature he seemed now.

'But where do we strike?' the boy asked.

'Well…' Caedmon stopped pacing. 'Considering that it's mostly guards and former guards who have been disappearing, I suspect it's one of them behind this. One of the ones who quit after the takeover. It may well be the former Commander Talmon – he escaped from prison about a month ago and hasn't been seen since.'

'Then should we look for him?' Caradoc suggested.

'We already are,' said Caedmon. 'But if he or somebody else is trying to gather support among the guard, then if anyone knows who it is and where they are, it will be one of them. There are bound to be at least a few of them who were offered the chance to join the perpetrators but turned them down. We should offer a reward for any information… but we should also show them the consequences of betrayal by dealing harshly with anyone we catch. We should also arrest some of them on principle – the more reluctant ones, or the ones found in dereliction of duty. That should be an effective way of showing them that we are not to be played with.'

'Won't they just hate us more?' asked Caradoc.

'They already do,' said Caedmon. 'The key to winning the obedience of people who hate you is to teach them fear. But long-term loyalty will mean more in the end, so we will reward the ones who do stay in line. Do you understand?'

'I think so,' Caradoc nodded. Caedmon had been discussing decisions like these with him for some time now, to teach him by example how to rule when his own time came. By now, he was more than used to it.

But, of course, he was still a child.

'What about the ghost?'

'There is no ghost,' Caedmon said irritably. 'When people are afraid, they invent things like this. And perhaps the rebels are hoping to scare us as well with these stories.'

Caradoc looked nervous. 'I think I'm a bit scared. Just a bit,' he added hastily.

Caedmon softened, and smiled. 'Don't worry, son. I'm here. I won't let anyone hurt you, and certainly not a ghost! There's no such thing, besides.'

'But you said sometimes people can come back from the dead,' said Caradoc.

'That's different,' said Caedmon. 'The Shadow That Walks isn't a ghost. Anyway, he would be on our side!'

'No he would not,' a voice interrupted.

Caedmon turned sharply. 'Who said that?'

There was nobody there.

'Not your side,' the voice continued. 'The Shadow That Walks serves the Night God, not you, Caedmon.'

A cold shiver raced down Caedmon's spine. 'Where are you? Let me see you, right now.'

A laugh was the only reply; a cold, harsh laugh.

Caedmon took a step back, towards Caradoc. 'Stay close to me,' he said. 'I don't like this… You! Wherever you are, show yourself. That's an order!'

'Don't you know me?' the voice asked. It was deep and rough, and now it grew low and spoke on, a soft chant from the shadows. 'I am the shadow that comes in the night…'

Caedmon's stomach twisted, and he pulled the sickle from his belt. 'Stop that!'

'…I am the fear that lurks in your heart…'

Caedmon turned this way and that, trying to find the source of the voice, but there was nothing and no-one there. Every door was closed, and there was nowhere to hide. There were only the shadows, and the voice, and a terrible coldness in the air.

'I am the Shadow That Walks,' the voice hissed.

Caedmon stood very still. 'This isn't possible,' he said, as calmly as he could.

'It is,' said the voice. 'I am Arenadd Taranisäii reborn. I serve the Night God, and you have offended her.'

The fear grew in Caedmon, sickening and smothering. 'Show yourself,' he said again. 'Now.'

But the voice only spoke on, relentlessly. 'Caedmon, son of Torc, you are a traitor and a murderer, and a usurper. You betrayed me. And for that, you are cursed.'

Caedmon pointed the sickle at where he thought the voice was coming from. 'Show yourself!'

'You were my apprentice,' said the voice. 'My heir. I trusted you. But you turned on me. You tried to kill me. You murdered my daughter, who was the rightful Queen. You stole her throne for yourself. And now you have gone against the will of the Night God by leaving your land, and making yourself no better than the Southerners who once made us their slaves! You are no rightful King, and no true Taranisäii either!'

Caradoc started to sob. 'Who is that? Father, who is that?'

'I don't know…' Caedmon held onto him with his free hand, but he couldn't find anything else to say. For the first time in years, all his confidence left him. For the first time in years, he had no answer to give. 'I'm doing the Night God's will,' he said at last, as strongly as he could. 'She sent my mother back to me, to help me take the throne. She wanted me to be King, and she wanted me to invade the South. It was my life's work.'

'Liar,' the voice hissed. 'You lie to me, you lie to your people, and you lie to yourself! You are the King of the North, not the South, and not Cymria. You have offended the Night God. Go back to Malvern. Take your armies out of the South and never return, and you will be forgiven for your crimes. If not, you will be punished.'

Caedmon turned around, still trying to see the man. *'Show yourself!'* he roared, trying desperately not to let his fear show.

A man stepped out of the shadows and into the lamplight. His clothes were ragged and dirty, but underneath them he was big and burly. A gold medal hung around his neck.

'Son of a bitch!' Caedmon swore. 'How on earth did you get in here?'

'Through the door, stupid,' the man snapped back. 'An' don't bother calling for the guards. I've already killed them all. Now listen up, you bastard, 'cause I got an ultimatum for you, an' I ain't gonna give it twice.'

'Who are you?' Caedmon demanded.

The man reached up and ripped off his hood, so both of them could see his red hair, and the lifeless black eyes beneath it. 'My name,' he said harshly, 'Is Captain Kearney Redguard. The last Redguard. Your spy Morgan stabbed me in the back, you had me tortured, an' the both of you destroyed my city an' took over my homeland. So let's just say, I ain't so fond of you.'

Caradoc whimpered. 'Oh Night God…'

Caedmon looked steadily back at the big Southerner. 'So are you here to kill me?'

'No,' said Red. 'Just to talk. But only this once. Listen now, or the next time you see me it'll be when my hands are around your neck.'

'Speak, then,' said Caedmon. 'And it had better be good, because they're going to be your last words.'

'Nah,' said Red. 'I don't really remember, but I think my last words were somethin' like "Let go of me you son of a filthy bastard's bastard!". Not so inspiring, really. Now listen up.'

He pointed at Caedmon's face. 'The Shadow That Walks has come, an' it's me. An' I am not on your side, or the Night God's side, or anyone's side except mine. So here's what you're gonna do. You're gonna take your armies, all of 'em, an' you're gonna leave. You're gonna go back to the North, an' you're never comin' back. An' if you don't do it, an' fast, I'm gonna make you suffer.'

Caedmon did not try and argue. He had seen Red's eyes, and that was all the proof he needed. They were Arenadd's eyes now, and Saeddyn's. The eyes of a dead man.

'I'm willing to die for my people,' he said quietly.

'So was I,' said Red. 'But that ain't what I'll do. I never took you for a coward, see. No, if you don't do as I've said, I'll come back. An' not for you. I'll come for him.' He pointed at Caradoc.

Caedmon stiffened. 'No. Don't you dare!'

'Oh, I will,' said Red. 'I mean it, blackrobe. You leave my country, or I'll come back, an' I'll take him. Your only son. I'll drag him away into the shadows, an' there won't be a damn thing anyone can do to stop me. An' then, I'll send him back to you in pieces. Legs first, so he stays alive long enough for you to know he's suffering before I take off his head.'

Caedmon held his son tightly. 'You wouldn't do that!'

'Oh yeah?' said Red. 'You wanna try me an' find out? Don't you know nothin' about the Shadows That Walk? We don't feel guilt. I ain't gonna lie – I enjoyed killin' those guards of yours. How much pleasure d'you reckon I'll get out of cutting your son to bits? If you're lucky, once I'm done with him, I might come back an' do the same to Morgan, an' if you're real lucky I might do it to you too an' put you out of your misery.'

'No!' Caradoc clutched his father's hand. 'You leave him alone!'

Red chuckled. 'Brave boy. He'll make a fine King one day. If he's still alive, an' I sure as sunrise don't mean to let that Morgan live. An' if you leave, that's how it'll be. You'll live to see him grow up, an' see him have kids of his own, an' become king just like his daddy. Me, I'm not gonna have any kids. There'll never be another Redguard. Might not be any more Taranisäiis either. But Caradoc might still have a chance. The choice is yours.' He nodded. 'Sleep well.'

With that, he turned and slid away into the shadows, vanishing like a bad dream.

Afterwards, neither Caedmon nor Caradoc dared move for a long moment. Caradoc didn't let go of his father's hand.

After a little while, the boy relaxed and started to cry.

Caedmon dropped his sickle and sat down, lifting his son onto his knee. 'It's all right, Caradoc. It's all right. Don't cry.'

But Caradoc only sobbed and clung to his father like the child he still was.

Caedmon held him back, fiercely. 'It's all right. I won't let him hurt you. I swear by the Night God, I won't let him touch you. I'll die to protect you if I have to, do you understand? I'll die before I let anything happen to you.'

'No!' Caradoc sobbed. 'No, don't. I don't want you to die.'

'And neither do I,' said Caedmon. 'But for you, I would. I swear it.'

'We've got to go,' said Caradoc. He took a few deep breaths and fiercely wiped his tears away with the back of his hand. 'We've got to go home, quick, before he comes back, we've got to do what he said!'

Caedmon's eyes narrowed. 'No,' he said. 'We're going to find him. We're going to catch him. And then we're going to find a way to kill him. I'll have him burned at the stake if I have to. I swear by the Night God's holy name.'

'But if we don't go, he'll kill us!' said Caradoc.

'That's why we have to find him first,' said Caedmon. He stood up, still holding his son's hand. 'Come on, Caradoc. We have work to do.'

*

Red left the city immediately after his talk with the King, but not through the secret passage. That was only necessary when he was with someone else. Now, on his own, he used the shadows and left by the open front gates, completely unnoticed. From there, he went back to the forest where the others camped, moving silently and effortlessly through a world of darkness that would have sucked the life out of him if he had any left to take.

It was terrifying, but exhilarating as well, and the more he used it the easier it became. But that easiness only scared him more. He didn't want it to become easier, any more than he had wanted the killing of the guard commander to thrill him as much as it had.

But it had, and he couldn't make himself forget the savage joy that had rushed through him when the life had left the Northerner's eyes, or when the blood of the guards outside the King's room had spurted over his hands and trickled down his arms.

And then afterwards, when he had spoken from the shadows and issued his threats… he had heard the ice in his own voice, and the fear in their eyes had given him pleasure as well – pleasure of a kind he did not remember feeling when he was alive.

But he had lied as well, in more ways than one. He had lied when he said that he didn't feel guilt.

He felt no guilt for the killings, or the threats, no. It wasn't like that. He felt guilt because he had enjoyed them so much, and that was different.

Was this what it was like? he asked himself as he stalked through the shadows. *Is this what it felt like to be him? Or her?*

The thought made him want to be sick. He told himself, as he had many times already, that he was doing this for a cause that was right. But that only made him wonder if the Dark Lord Arenadd had once told himself the same thing.

And Saeddryn, her too. Maybe every one of history's greatest monsters had done the same.

The smell of warm blood burned in his nostrils. All living things smelled like that to him now, but humans in particular.

He emerged from the shadows, and walked the last short distance to the camp.

The others were waiting – they had been ordered to pack up and be ready to leave the moment he came back, and he could see they had done just that. The tents had been folded, and the supplies he'd stolen put into packs. Everyone had been waiting, either in groups, or perched in trees to keep a lookout.

Talmon was one of the first to reach him. 'There you are, Captain.'

Red saluted his old Commander without thinking. 'Yes, sir!'

Talmon smiled. 'Old habits die hard, eh?'

Red relaxed and smiled back. 'They do, sir. Is everyone ready?'

Back when Red had known him in the old days, Talmon had worn his grey hair short. Now, it had grown out somewhat, but he'd shaved off the beard he had grown in prison. There was a scar on his forehead now, and more elsewhere. The Northerners didn't take kindly to defiance, it seemed.

'They are, Captain. And you?'

'Yeah, how'd it go?' asked Ranulf, coming to join them. He was wearing his old guard armour, which Elthan had stolen back for him along with his spear and sword. The armour fit him a little more loosely now.

Red hesitated. Everyone was listening with interest.

'Where's Kraego?' he asked.

'Hunting, I think,' said Elthan. 'He flew off.'

Red nodded. 'He'll find us again when he's ready. It's not easy to give a griffin the slip, especially when there's — how many are we now, Talmon?'

'Fifty-one,' said Talmon. 'Fifty-two counting you. Now how did it go? Did you get to the King?'

'Yeah,' Red nodded. He noticed that most of his listeners were keeping a slight distance. All of them had been told what he was by now. They listened as he described everything that had happened. Several of them cringed.

'You said that?' Elthan exclaimed.

'Yeah,' said Red. 'An' trust me, it worked. Man went as pale as a fish's belly.'

A good number of the group looked uncomfortable.

'I dunno,' Ranulf mumbled. 'Cuttin' up a kid... you ain't really gonna do that, are you?'

Red pulled a face. 'No way, but he's not gonna risk it, is he?'

'And if he does?' asked Talmon.

'Then I'll kidnap the kid,' said Red. 'Hold him hostage. That'll give us the upper hand when we're ready for open war.'

'I don't get why you didn't just kill the bastard,' said Ranulf.

'I wanted to,' said Red. 'But he's the best way to end this fast. With one man in charge, we've got him to negotiate with, an' he can take all of them out of here. But I thought it over, an' if he dies… well, Morgan'd be put in charge, but that'd just put us back where we started. If both of them died, there'd be a kid in charge. The council would take over, or there'd be a power struggle, an' we'd be contendin' with a bunch of different leaders, not just one. It'd get complicated is what I'm sayin'.'

Ranulf looked a little lost. 'Oh,' he said.

Talmon nodded sagely. 'You're smarter than you look, Captain. And clearly, you know what you're doing.'

'Yeah, but so do you,' said Red. 'That's why you're my second. Now, if everything's ready, let's head off.'

'Now can you tell us where we're goin'?' asked one of the few women in the crowd.

'Yeah.' Red rolled his shoulders to loosen them. 'We're goin' to Monag Island.'

Chapter Twenty-Five

Sacrifice

The journey back to Monag took months.

Red led his group south, away from Liranwee, with Talmon as his second in command and Ranulf and Elthan as assistants to both of them, one to handle the supplies and the other to keep everyone in line. Almost all of the new recruits were guards, and therefore knew how to march in formation, but most of the time they couldn't afford to do that, or even stay together. Therefore, at Talmon's suggestion, they split into several smaller groups and travelled between landmarks, meeting up again at each one. Kraego joined them not far out from Liranwee, and flew overhead to keep a lookout, sometimes stealing cattle for food. The giant griffin was disinclined to share his kills, but Red could help. He used his power to hunt or steal supplies along the way, and as the fastest and stealthiest of them, he moved from group to group, keeping everyone in touch.

The hardest part came when they reached New Eagleholm. None of them dared go too close except for Red and Kraego, who scouted it out and returned to confirm that the city was in Northern hands and the travellers would have to go around it.

They did, skirting around it as widely as possible, and pressed on through the wild country beyond it. There, they were able to join up again, but it was far harsher terrain than they had had to negotiate before, and it took all Red's new skills to keep them fed. With his newly heightened sense of smell, he was able to work out which plants were edible and how to track animals, which were easy enough for him to catch. The biggest threat aside from starvation came from the handful of wild griffins in the area, but few of them were bold enough to go near Kraego and when one did, he saw it off in a flurry of screeches and talon-blows.

Finally, when they reached the Southern-most shore of Cymria, it was time to stop.

'Make camp here,' Red told the others. 'Kraego an' me will fly over to Monag and bring a ship.'

Talmon, by now just as ragged and wild looking as everyone else, nodded. 'We'll wait here and see to it that there's plenty of smoke for you to see.'

Red nodded back, and hoisted himself onto Kraego's back. 'See you later. We'll be back by nightfall, most likely.'

Kraego took off, and flew out over the sea at a leisurely pace. Red sat easily on his back, used to flying by now. Kraego still refused to wear a harness like other partnered griffins, but Red had gotten used to that as well. It didn't matter so much if he fell off now, and anyway, he never felt as if he would. Kraego's power was in him now, and the two of them were bound together in a way that went beyond partnership, beyond friendship, beyond even brotherhood.

Now Kraego's wings carried both of them over the narrow channel between Monag and the mainland, and beyond the island's shores to the Eyrie tower where they had stayed before. Red was relieved to see that nothing looked too different, but he thought there were a couple more griffins flying overhead than before.

On the Eyrie roof, Merca and Tarak quickly arrived to meet them.

'There ya are,' Merca said brusquely. 'And not before time! This lot are eatin' us out of house and home so they are!'

'It's all right,' said Red. 'We'll be leavin' soon, but I'll need a ship to bring the others over from the mainland first. We have to regroup an' have a planning meeting before we're ready to start. How is everyone? Still alive?'

'They are, and growing more numerous by the day,' said Merca. 'We were happy enough to see most of them, but now with these Northerners…'

Red started. 'Northerners? You mean Teressa…?'

'Yes, Teressa, that's the one,' said Merca. 'She's sent a gang of her friends down here to bother us, and by Gryphus there was nearly a fight when they came, so there was! Some of us t'ort it was an invasion, so we did, but that Isleen put a stop to it. They're not liking it too well, they aren't. It's all a bit tense it is. They keep asking us when you're going to show.'

'Well I have now,' said Red. 'I'd better see 'em. Can you get someone t'fetch Teressa? I can have a quick word with her before I go get the others.'

'I would, but she's not here,' said Merca. 'I'll find one of her friends. Wait here, laddie.' She hurried off.

'She's as much of a weirdo as I remember,' Red murmured, mostly to himself.

Merca returned after a while, followed by two people. Red tensed instinctively when he saw them, and almost reached for his sword before he stopped himself.

They were Northerners, both of them, a man and a woman. Both of them looked aristocratic, finely clad and very upright, and sure enough a pair of griffins flew down to join them shortly after they arrived.

Red stood there for a moment, eyeing them, while they eyed him back just as cautiously.

But then the woman came forward, and knelt at his feet. 'Master,' she said.

The man came closer, peering at Red's face. He reached out. 'May I…?'

Red nodded briefly, and the man touched him on the neck and kept his hand there a moment, feeling for a pulse.

After a few moments, his face slacked in astonishment. 'By the Night God…'

He took a step back, and knelt as well, murmuring, 'Master.'

'Get up,' Red said shortly. 'I ain't a King an' I don't like bein' knelt to. Now, who are you?'

The man stood, and bowed. 'Lord Anfri, son of Lady Hafwen. And this is my wife, Lady Lowri.'

The woman also stood. 'You are the Shadow That Walks,' she said, in disbelief.

'I am,' Red nodded. 'You're shadow worshippers, like Teressa?'

'We are,' said Anfri. 'We were both junior griffiners in Malvern. We met Teressa in the Temple, and she converted us herself. When she told us about you… we knew we had to go and find you, no matter what it took.'

Lowri nodded. 'The first Shadow That Walks led our people to freedom. Now his successor has come, and we know our duty is to follow him, no matter where that might lead.'

'So you'll do as I say?' asked Red.

'To the death,' said Anfri, with complete sincerity.

'Good. How many of you are there, anyway?'

'Thirty of us,' said Lowri.

Red stared. 'Thirty?'

'Aye,' said Anfri. 'Most of us are griffiners. And more of us will come once they know about you. Word will spread.'

Red rubbed his forehead. 'Good gods. Where's Teressa? I gotta thank her.'

Both of them looked uncomfortable.

'Master, I don't want to make demands,' said Anfri. 'Especially when I've had no chance to prove my loyalty to you. But we also need your help.'

'With what?' said Red. 'Look, don't muck about – where's Teressa?'

'That's just it, you see,' said Lowri. 'She's not here. She's in Malvern. They've arrested her.'

'Shit!' Red looked at Anfri. 'When?'

'About a month ago,' said Anfri. 'She stayed as long as she could… she was arrested just before we got out of the city.'

'What'll they do with her, then?' asked Red. 'No, don't tell me… gods, I know what they do to traitors. They almost did it to me. They're gonna kill her, aren't they?'

'Yes,' said Anfri. 'But not for treachery. Only we believed her, you see. The unbelievers wouldn't listen to her. They don't think you exist, and they certainly don't believe that the Shadow That Walks could be a Southerner. She's been arrested for blasphemy. But the penalty—,'

'Death,' Red finished for him.

'Yes,' said Anfri. 'But I don't think they will have killed her yet. One of us is an apprentice priestess like her, and she says… well…'

'Says what?' Red snapped.

Anfri looked frightened. 'The Blood Moon is coming.'

*

Orak was not with Teressa when the arrest happened.

She had asked him to stay outside the city and wait for her while she talked to her followers. He wouldn't be able to protect her that way, but if he were with her he'd make her too conspicuous. Questions would be asked about why she wasn't in the Eyrie, and then it might come out that she had become a griffiner but not sworn her loyalty to the Eyrie and taken an apprenticeship as the law demanded.

Instead, she had decided to go in stealthily, and hope nobody noticed her.

And, at first, it had worked. She had gone to the houses of people she knew were members of her circle of secret worshippers, and given them the word that the Shadow That Walked had come again. She had asked them to spread the word to every other worshipper they knew, and had held several meetings in secret where she told them what had happened.

Most of them were sceptical, but they all listened, and some of them agreed to go to Monag immediately. Others left without making a decision, but either way she saw to it that the news got out.

She never found out who decided to betray her, but after several days, she embarked on the riskiest part of her mission: infiltrating the Eyrie itself. Luckily one of her followers was a servant there, and he helped her to get into the building. There she tracked down griffiners like Anfri and gave them the news about Red and Kraego.

The next day, she was arrested. She had decided to leave the city and meet up with Orak – he would want to see that she was all right, and it was time to start planning how they would get the others to Monag. But before she had gone very far at all, a pair of guards accosted her.

'Are you Teressa, the apprentice priestess?' one asked abruptly.

Teressa hesitated before saying yes.

'Then you're under arrest,' said the guard. 'For treason and blasphemy.'

She had tried to run away, but by then it was already too late. They took her away between them, and then to Malvern's main prison complex. If they'd known she was a griffiner, she would have been thrown into one of the cells under the Eyrie, but as far as they knew she was a commoner, and commoners went in a common prison.

It didn't matter one way or the other. A cell was a cell.

She lay in it now, curled up on her side, and felt her injuries throb relentlessly. There were a few of them by now: bruises on her face, and a deep cut on her chin.

There had been no trial. Commoners didn't get trials, and she hadn't told them she was a griffiner. There hadn't been any torture, either, and there should have been.

When she first came to the prison, they had given her a rough interrogation, demanding to know about this supposed Shadow That Walked, about Southerners, and who she had tried to talk into betraying their country.

She'd answered them with the truth. It was wrong to lie about something you truly believed in. They should know about what had happened; every Northerner should know what their duty was now. Though she had promised herself that, no matter what, she wouldn't tell them where to find Red she knew, deep down, that they could get it out of her if they wanted to.

They didn't believe her.

They hit her around the face and asked their questions, but they didn't believe the answers. But not because they thought she was lying.

'She's insane,' the guard commander finally said. 'Stop. Stop!'

They stopped hitting her.

'Enough of this,' the commander had ordered. 'We're not going to get anything out of her. She's raving. Put her back in her cell.'

So they had, and after that she had no way of knowing what was going to happen to her. Nobody bothered to inform her.

For the first few days in the cell, she waited – expecting them to come for her at any moment and take her to the scaffold or the chopping block.

But nobody came.

Time dragged out, day after day, week after week, and still nothing happened. No more interrogations, but no execution either. Nobody spoke to her, and she didn't see anyone at all except the guards patrolling past her cell, and the man who brought her food and emptied the toilet jar in the corner.

All she could do was sit or lie in the dark, and try and imagine what might happen to her. Would she be disembowelled as a traitor, or would she die for blasphemy instead? She didn't know what they did to blasphemers, but it must be death.

But when a month had passed, and then another began its relentless march, and still nothing happened, she started to wonder if they were just going to leave her here until she really did become as insane as they thought she was.

By now, she had already thought of suicide more than once. Anything, *anything* would be better than sitting here in the dark all alone, not knowing if she was going to live or die, not knowing what was happening to Orak or Red or anyone she had left behind.

I was a fool, she thought, day after day, more and more bitterly. Why hadn't she had the sense to protect herself? Why hadn't she lied to the guards? Why hadn't it ever occurred to her that someone might betray her? Had she really been stupid enough to think that she would be protected just because she was a follower of the Shadow That Walked, or of the Night God?

Everyone knew the Night God could not or did not protect her followers from death; her mercy was to bring death and peace to the suffering, not to save their lives. And the Shadow That Walked? What about him?

Teressa could see the sky through her cell window, and at night she would look out at the stars – and the moon, when it was visible – and pray. Prayer was all she had here.

She prayed to the Night God many times, uselessly asking for her help, or at least her forgiveness.

She knew it would never work. Either the Night God couldn't help her, or she just didn't care.

She prayed to Arenadd as well, and over time she found herself praying to him more and more often, and leaving the Night God behind. The Night God had never helped her, so far as she knew, but Arenadd had. He'd sent her to find his successor, and if she was going to die then it would be in his name, and in his service.

But no, she thought one night. No, not Arenadd's service. Red's service. He was her master now.

She remembered what he had said to her back then, when he gave her his permission to leave, and sometimes, when the loneliness got too much, she even imagined she could hear his voice.

"If you get into trouble, send a message. I'll come."

That was when she decided, and that night she prayed again – but not to the Night God, or Arenadd.

'Red,' she murmured, hands clasped. 'Captain Redguard. Help me. Ye said ye would come when I needed ye, and I need ye. Help me, Red.'

It was the only prayer that had made her feel any better in weeks.

'But if ye can't help me,' she added, 'If ye don't, then I'll die for ye. My life for ye, just as I promised. Aye…'

And then, the next day, they came for her at last.

A pair of guards opened the door, and one of them made an

impatient gesture at her.

'Get up.'

Teressa stumbled to her feet. 'Is it time?' she asked urgently. 'Are they going to—?'

The guard's reply was to grab her by the shoulder and pull her towards him. He took her by the wrist while his friend took the other, and snapped on a set of manacles.

'Now move.'

Teressa shuffled obediently out of the cell while they took up station on either side of her, holding her by the shoulders.

Her heart pounded so badly that she felt sick and dizzy with it. But she breathed deeply and forced herself not to panic, not now. She was a priestess, and the most loyal follower of the Shadow That Walked. She would go to her death bravely.

Arenadd, she prayed silently. *Help me be brave and die honourably, like ye.*

But when her guards took her out of the prison they didn't take her to the scaffold, but out into the street.

'Where are we going?' she asked, puzzled.

One of them slapped her across the head by way of an answer.

It was daylight outside, and her eyes ached. They hadn't been touched by light this bright in weeks, and she instinctively squeezed them shut and let the guards guide her along.

Her eyes took a long time to adjust – she opened them slowly and cautiously, and peered down at herself. Her silver robe was filthy and torn, and stained with blood from the congealing wound on her chin. She groaned to herself, and looked up blearily at her surroundings.

Ahead, she saw the dome of the Temple and realised what was going on. But she didn't try and say anything.

Inside the Temple was just as she remembered, dimly lit by the blue-glass lanterns she had always loved. An apprentice priestess like herself was sweeping the floor. She looked up when Teressa came near her, and the look of shock on her face quickly darkened into anger.

'Betrys,' Teressa said in surprise. 'It's me—,'

Betrys stepped forward and spat in her face.

The guard on Teressa's left pushed her away. 'Keep back!'

Betrys moved back. 'Traitor!' she yelled at Teressa. 'Blasphemer!'

Teressa had no hand free to wipe the spit off her face. She couldn't find anything to say at all; and only stared at her former friend in stunned silence.

The guards made her walk on, past the altar to the back of the Temple's main space, where the doors led to its private rooms. There, they took her to what had once been her own room, and took the manacles off before shoving her inside and locking the door on her.

Teressa slumped down on the bed, and wiped her face with the sleeve of her robe. So they'd given her to the Temple to deal with as a blasphemer. But what would that mean? The Temple didn't execute people.

The door opened again, and she looked up to see the High Priestess herself, with one of the thirteen lesser priestesses beside her.

'Holiness,' Teressa said blankly.

The High Priestess did not smile. 'Teressa. If you had any sense in you at all you'd be throwing yourself down at my feet and begging for forgiveness.'

'Well I won't,' Teressa said boldly. 'Because I won't betray myself, and anyway, it won't save me. I'll die with dignity or not at all.'

The High Priestess gave her a disgusted look. 'I won't waste my breath arguing with you,' she said. 'There's no point. We all know what you've done, and may you find forgiveness in the afterlife. For now—,' she nodded to the other priestess, who came in, carrying a bucket of water. 'Clean yourself up and say the death-prayers until nightfall.'

Teressa cringed. 'What—?'

'Be grateful,' the High Priestess added. 'You've been chosen for the highest honour, which you hardly deserve. The Blood Moon is tonight, and at midnight your blood will be given to the Night God. Until then, make your peace with her. We will send for you when the time comes.'

Teressa stared in horror – but only for a moment. 'Fool!' she yelled. 'Ye are blind! I tell ye, the Shadow That Walks has come, and I was doing his will by being here.'

'That's enough,' the other priestess snapped. 'We've heard the lunacy you've been spouting.'

'It's the truth,' said Teressa, calming down. 'He's come. The new Shadow That Walks has come, and it's our duty to——,'

The High Priestess started forward, and actually slapped her across the face. 'Silence! I won't have you saying this blasphemy in my Temple.'

But Teressa was immune to pain by now. She laughed in the High Priestess' face. 'Ye'll see,' she said. 'Ye'll all see. He'll come here, I swear. I called him. He'll come, and if ye don't bow to him, he'll kill ye for yer own blasphemy!'

The High Priestess shook her head in disgust and left, with her underling following. The door locked behind them.

Teressa knew she should be afraid, but she wasn't. Not any more. A kind of madness had filled her – a mad courage, maybe. She was ready to die. And when she did, she knew what would happen. She knew who would come for her. Tonight she would be sacrificed on the altar, and then she would go to be with Arenadd.

'Forever,' she said aloud, and knelt by the bucket of water to splash her face.

She washed herself vigorously, scrubbing her face, arms and legs and trying to clean her robe as well – though they wouldn't let her keep it when the time came.

When she was finished, she lay down on her old bed and stared at the ceiling with the stars she had painted on it so long ago. She knew she should pray now – she was expected to, at least.

But she didn't. She had prayed enough, and it hadn't done her the slightest bit of good.

Instead, she rolled onto her side and went to sleep. Maybe, she thought, she would dream of Arenadd.

Chapter Twenty-Six

A Vision of Evil

When Teressa woke up again it was night, and she could already hear the chanting of the priestesses outside.

The bucket of water was where she'd left it, and she got up and splashed her face again to wake herself up. Everything felt hazy and unreal.

Now, finally, feeling a little calmer, she wondered if she should pray after all. But to who? To what?

'Red,' she murmured to herself. 'Kearney…'

The door opened at that moment, and two junior priestesses entered.

Teressa stood up and eyed them resignedly. 'Is it time?' she asked.

'Yes,' said one of them. 'Take yer robe off.'

Teressa knew that they'd only tear it off by force if she didn't, so she stripped and stood there, shivering a little, while they came forward. One of them was holding a small pot of blue paste, and she silently dipped her fingers in it and began to draw designs on Teressa's body, forming spirals and moon symbols over her stomach, breasts and arms, with the shape of the full moon between her hips, over her womb.

'Now,' the first priestess said once the painting was finished. 'Come.'

They took her by the elbows and led her out of the room. She was barefoot – her shoes had been taken away from her in prison.

Completely naked, she stepped out into the main Temple. The thirteen senior priestesses were there, standing in a ring around the altar, one in front of each of the thirteen standing stones. The High Priestess was there too, by the altar and in front of the statue of the Night God herself, and she stood aside to let Teressa and her attendants come forward.

The altar had been fitted with manacles which were normally hidden, tucked away in little alcoves cut for just that purpose. Normally the altar had nothing on it except the silver divining bowl and the ceremonial dagger that worshippers used to offer their own blood to the Night God.

Now the bowl was gone, and the knife was tucked into the High Priestess' fur loincloth. Every one of the priestesses was dressed in their ceremonial outfits, each one bare-breasted with her face covered by a wooden animal mask. The High Priestess herself wore the mask of a griffin.

She nodded silently to the two junior priestesses holding Teressa, and they dragged her towards the altar. 'Lie down,' one said.

When Teressa saw the altar, with the faint stains of old sacrifices still visible on it, terror suddenly stabbed into her heart. She tried to pull away, so suddenly and violently that she broke their grip.

She didn't get far. Two of the senior priestesses stepped in her way, and pushed her back into the grasp of her captors, who grabbed her by the arms and twisted them behind her back.

Teressa wrenched at them, not even noticing the pain in her shoulders. 'No! Stop!'

Then she fought, really fought, with every scrap of strength she had, as they dragged her back to the altar by force and shoved her down on it. The manacles snapped closed around her wrists and ankles, and when the priestesses let go of her she could barely move.

'Let me go!' she screamed at them. 'Arenadd! Arenadd, help me! Red, help me!'

One of the junior priestesses stuffed a gag into her mouth. She tried to spit it out, but nearly choked on it instead. She could hardly breathe.

After that, there was nothing more she could do but lie there, while the chant went on. Above, through the hole in the roof, she could see the moon reaching its zenith. Soon it would be directly above her, and then it would begin to darken.

Below it, the statue of the Night God stared down on her, cold and pitiless. For now the moonlight lit up the statue from behind, but tonight the shadow would darken it as it darkened the moon. The moment the shadow covered the moon completely, they would kill her so that her blood would feed the Night God and bring the Blood Moon.

Worshippers had started to file into the Temple; she could hear them. Above and around her the chants went on, and the songs, the sacred songs. The moon finished its rising, and the shadow began to slide over it, bit by bit.

The High Priestess started to speak, while the other priestesses chanted more softly, providing a counterpoint to her loud, passionate voice.

'Tonight, the most sacred time has come!' she said. 'Tonight, the Night God's shining eye will be covered by a shadow, and she will be blind to us. Without the strength of her worshippers, she cannot survive.'

The people in the Temple gave a collective moan.

'But,' the High Priestess went on, 'with the offering of true Northern blood, the Night God will live!' she waved a hand over Teressa's naked body. 'This Northerner here will die in the name of the Night God, and her soul and her blood will feed her, and save her!'

The worshippers cheered.

Above, the moon darkened. The shadow was spreading, and fast. Soon the moonlight would be gone completely.

Frantically, Teressa pushed at the gag with her tongue. She had to get rid of it; she couldn't breathe, and she didn't want to die mute. After a couple of attempts it came loose, and she spat it out.

And then, without warning, the screaming began.

The High Priestess broke off mid-sentence and looked up sharply. Outside the circle, the gathered worshippers scattered, some of them shouting in fright.

Teressa turned her head with difficulty, and saw it. Saw… him.

Two griffins burst into the Temple, one grey, one black, and between them was a shadowy man. She saw him look straight at her, and heard him shout.

'No!'

The griffins charged, and an instant later, so did the man. She could see his face as he rushed straight at the altar, his expression full of horror and rage, mouth still open to bellow a war cry.

'*Redguard!*'

Teressa tried to reach toward him. 'Red!' she shouted back.

*

Red saw her, and heard her, even in the midst of his revulsion and the panic around him. He saw the circle of priestesses, some pulling their masks off to stare at him in shock. But more important than them, he saw the sacrifice. Teressa, naked and painted with blue patterns, chained on the altar like an animal for slaughter.

When he saw that, whatever plans he might have made beforehand flew out of his head. He drew his father's sword and charged, roaring his war cry with all his might.

One of the priestesses tried to stop him. He hurled her out of the way with his free hand, and sent her staggering to the ground. The others ran, shrieking in fright, and left his way to the altar clear.

Teressa struggled against the chains. 'Red!'

Red came on towards her. 'It's all right,' he said. 'I got you.'

Someone stepped in his way.

Red pointed his sword at her. 'Sod off out of the way, you.'

The High Priestess raised the sacrificial knife. 'No! Get out of here Southerner – you don't know what you're doing!'

'I ain't gonna warn you again,' Red growled.

'I can't,' said the High Priestess. 'Without the sacrifice, the Night God will—'

'I'm countin' on it.' Red shoved her out of the way and went to the altar, reaching out to undo the manacles. 'It's all right, Teressa, I'm gonna – argh!'

He reeled back, clutching at himself.

Above, the moon had darkened completely.

The High Priestess didn't wait to stab Red again. She pushed past him and rushed at Teressa, raising the sacrificial knife.

But Red was too fast for her. He whirled around silently, and brought his sword down on the High Priestess' back.

She screamed and staggered forward, and Red came up behind her and stabbed her to death. She groaned and toppled over, landing on top of Teressa. Blood streamed down over her shoulder and onto the altar… and then Red fell forward into absolute blackness.

*

Red opened his eyes and turned around, bewildered.

He was still in the Temple… or something that looked vaguely like it. The altar was still in front of him, but now there was nothing on it except a pool of blood. Around him the miniature stone circle had grown huge, expanding to fill the Temple.

But there was no Temple around him now. The mosaic on the floor had become grass, the stars painted on the ceiling had become a real, starry sky – a sky with no moon in it.

Around him, standing in front of the stones, were the priestesses, or a twisted version of them. Bare-breasted women, standing silently and staring at him through their masks – but, he realised, these weren't masks, but real. Women with the heads of animals. Thirteen of them.

'What the blazes?' he mumbled aloud. 'Where am I? What's goin' on?' he peered at the beast-women. 'An' what in the gods' names are they?'

'Oh, don't worry about them,' a voice said behind him. 'They won't hurt you.'

Red turned sharply, and saw him.

A tall, robed man with a pointed beard and curly hair. A Northerner, with a scar under his eye like a tear-track. There was a sardonic look on his face.

'Caedmon——?' Red began, and stopped. This wasn't Caedmon; it couldn't be.

The man only rolled his eyes. 'That's the Dark Lord Arenadd to you, Southerner.'

Red's own eyes narrowed. 'You. Why're you here? What is this place?'

'No idea,' said Arenadd. 'But what I'm more interested in is why *you're* here, Kearney Redguard.' He walked silently around the altar, trailing the tip of one finger through the pool of blood. 'I must say,' he added, 'We were expecting a sacrifice tonight, but we certainly didn't think it would come from you of all people. Even if you are the Shadow That Walks, I didn't think you were into that sort of thing.'

'What?' said Red. 'What sacrifice? I stopped the sacrifice.'

'Ahem,' Arenadd coughed and held up his bloodied finger. 'I believe I can see true Northern blood on this altar. Blood which you spilled.'

Red frowned. 'You mean the priestess——? Dammit!'

'Yes, I'm afraid it counts,' said Arenadd. 'But if it's any consolation, I seriously doubt that not having the sacrifice would have killed the Night God, or done anything very much. Most of what people believe about her is nonsense, you know. You did save Teressa's life, though, and I'd like to thank you for that.'

'Yeah, she worships you,' said Red. 'It's creepy. Where are we, anyway?'

Arenadd shrugged. 'It gives her life meaning, so she's welcome to it. And as I said, I don't really know what this place is. But I came here myself once or twice.' He shrugged again. 'Being a Southerner you wouldn't know about it, of course. But he who sacrifices on the night of the Blood Moon is granted a meeting with the Night God. Something like that anyway. But I suspect it only works if the man in question is the Shadow That Walks. The living don't generally get to see her.'

Red turned around quickly, scanning the black landscape. 'Where is she, then?'

'She won't come,' said Arenadd. 'She sent me instead.'

'Why?' asked Red.

'Well, she *said* it's because you're a Southerner,' said Arenadd. 'But...' he frowned.

'But?' Red prompted.

Arenadd lowered his voice. 'Just between you and me, I think she's staying away because she's afraid of you.'

'Afraid?' Red repeated. 'Why? What could I do to her?'

'I don't know,' said Arenadd. 'But you are very powerful. I shall have to think about that. There's not much else to do in the void, you know. Just thinking and watching the affairs of the living.'

Red eyed him. 'I've seen you before,' he said. 'Haven't I? When the Hangman got me, that was you I saw. I felt your hands draggin' me away into the void. An' then when I died in Amoran...'

'Yes, that was me,' said Arenadd. 'I came for your soul. I come for everyone's soul.'

'But I'm a Southerner,' said Red. 'My soul should go with Gryphus.'

'Gryphus?' Arenadd snorted. 'He doesn't have anything to do with the dead – that's my master's business. And mine too now.' He smiled humourlessly. 'All men, you see, are equal, Kearney Redguard. We're born equal and we die equal. The gods favour no-one.'

'Seems neither of 'em want anything to do with me nowadays,' Red muttered. 'I can't go in Gryphus' temples any more, an' the Night God won't come see me either.'

'Good!' said Arenadd. 'Consider yourself lucky. Your lot's going to be complicated enough without them interfering. Trust me, boy, you want nothing to do with the gods.'

Red eyed him. 'An' what about you? Whose side are you on?'

'Me?' Arenadd looked up at the starry sky. 'Nobody's side except my own. Do you have anything you really need to know before you go? We can't stand here and chatter forever. If you're lucky, I might even tell you something useful. I do know a lot.' His mouth tightened. 'More than I really want to, come to that.'

Red thought quickly. 'Can I die?' he asked.

'You already did, you blockhead,' Arenadd said impatiently.

'I mean can I die properly,' Red snapped back. 'Can I be killed?'

'Yes, you can,' said Arenadd. 'My children put paid to Saeddryn, didn't they? You'll just have to hope Caedmon doesn't know how they did it. If not, then as far as I know you'll live forever. You won't age, you can't get sick, injuries can put you down for a while if they're bad enough but they'll heal fast. Try not to get too attached to anyone – if you're sensible you'll outlive them all. Oh… and don't fall in love.'

Red frowned. 'What?'

'Well, all right, if you really must, go ahead and fall into some woman's arms,' said Arenadd. 'Or some man's if that's your thing. But you'd better not let it go any further than that. If you bed any woman, she'll die. I don't know about men. But unless you're celibate, you'll kill people. You're deadly, all right – even your cock can kill.'

Red winced. 'Really?'

'And you thought the pox was bad,' said Arenadd. He nodded. 'Goodbye.'

'Wait!' Red took a step towards him. 'What should I do?'

Arenadd shrugged again. 'Whatever you think is right. Whatever your heart tells you to do. You still have one, you know. Just not a very good one. But you have one. Now, go back.' He inclined his head. 'Maybe you'll see me again some day – pray that you do, Kearney Redguard.'

He vanished.

*

Red blinked again, and the Temple returned. He looked around, confused – he was still standing by the altar, and nothing had changed.

In front of him, the High Priestess' corpse slid off Teressa and thumped onto the floor. Behind him, screams split the air as Orak and Kraego charged back and forth, scattering and killing the assembled worshippers.

Red quickly shook off his confusion, and stepped forward to where Teressa waited. He sheathed his sword, and wrenched the chains off her with his bare hands. The moment she was free she rolled straight off the altar and threw herself against him.

Red put a protective arm around her, and turned to look at the chaos in the Temple. Not many people were left.

'Stop!' Red roared.

Kraego and Orak hesitated, and loped towards him. Of the people left in the Temple, some of those who were still alive had pressed themselves against the walls or dived behind pillars for some semblance of shelter. Others lay on the floor, injured or dying.

Red stood tall and glared at them, while Kraego came to stand beside him and Orak went to check on his human.

'I'm the Shadow That Walks!' he shouted, the words echoing in the great stone space.

Silence fell.

'My name is Kearney Redguard,' Red added. 'I'm a Southerner, an' proud of it! I'm also the Shadow That Walks, an' this is Kraego, son of Skandar, who brought me back!'

'I am Kraego!' Kraego screeched. 'I am the dark griffin, and my human is Kraeai kran ae!'

'It's true!' Teressa said suddenly. 'This is the Shadow That Walks! I follow him, and he come to save me, just as I said he would. If ye are true Northerners, then ye must follow him too! It's our sacred duty.'

'Liar!' one man bravely shouted back. 'A Southerner can't be the Shadow That Walks!'

'Believe it, you blackrobe son of a bitch,' Red growled, and twisted sideways into the shadows.

He thought he heard a new wave of screams as he vanished.

*

Red didn't like using the shadows, and he didn't go far with them. Just out into the city and away, far enough to reach a quiet spot where he and the two griffins might not be noticed. Besides, he didn't want to drag Teressa too far with him – it had been bad for him when he was alive, and it would be bad for her too.

Once they were out again, he took his tunic off and quietly offered it to the shivering Northerner.

'Here,' he said. 'I don't feel the cold much any more.'

Teressa clutched it, but didn't put it on. For a moment she just stood there staring at it, and then she suddenly grabbed him by the shoulder and kissed him full on the mouth.

Red let her do it, but then he gently pushed her away. 'Don't,' he said.

Teressa started to sob. 'Ye saved me,' she said. 'I, I swear, master… Red, I—'

Red wrapped the tunic around her, and held her, though he doubted his cold body would give her much comfort. 'It's all right,' he said. 'Teressa, it's all right. Breathe deep an' be brave.'

She shuddered against him. 'I swear,' she said. 'I swear I'll never worship the Night God again.'

'I ain't surprised!' said Red, trying to sound irreverent to cheer her up. 'After they nearly… but it's all right now. You're safe.'

'Ye came for me,' said Teressa.

''Course I did,' said Red. 'I told you, didn't I? I said if you're in trouble, send me a message an' I'll come. Well you did, an' I did. Them friends of yours, Anfri an' whats-her-name, they came to Monag an' they told me about you gettin' arrested. So me an' Kraego went right away to get you out.'

'I prayed to ye,' said Teressa. 'I prayed to the Night God, and Arenadd, and to ye. But it was ye who answered my prayers. It's ye I follow now, Red. It's ye I worship.'

'Well don't,' Red said shortly. 'I ain't a god an' I didn't hear no prayers. Now let's get out of here.'

Teressa looked troubled. 'If ye ask me not to worship ye, then… then I'll worship nothing.'

'It'd be a good idea,' said Red. He looked up. 'Kraego!'

Kraego and Orak came hurrying up, and Orak went straight to Teressa. 'My human,' the grey griffin said urgently. 'Are you hurt?'

Teressa let go of Red and went to him. 'No. I'm fine, Orak. Thank ye for coming for me.'

'Of course I came for you,' said Orak, a little irritably. 'You are my human. I waited outside the city, searching for an opportunity to get you back. Kraego found me, and I went with him. Together, we were strong enough. Now come – we must leave the city at once.'

Teressa took several deep breaths, and finally put Red's tunic on. 'Yes… we should go.'

Red hauled himself onto Kraego's back. 'Follow us,' he said. 'We won't use the shadows. We're goin' the old-fashioned way.'

Teressa got onto Orak's back, and clung on, shivering, as the grey griffin took to the air. She wouldn't last long in flight without proper clothes. But for now it was more important to escape, and fast, before other griffins came in pursuit.

And besides… for now the cold didn't matter. It was a sensation, and for a while she had thought she would never feel anything again. Now she savoured it, and as the two griffins flew out of Malvern together, one just behind the other, she looked ahead and let her gaze settle on Red.

I shouldn't have kissed him, she thought.

It had been stupidity of the first order. He wasn't some mortal man to be embraced; he was the Shadow That Walked. He was above her, beyond her; he was an immortal, and alone in that respect – unreachable by any ordinary human, and no mortal would be worthy of him.

She supposed she had done what she had done on a mad impulse more than anything else. He'd saved her life, and the sight of him had filled her with so much joy that she couldn't contain herself. He wasn't just her master; he was her saviour. A saviour who didn't want the awe and worship he deserved.

She thought about it obsessively during the long, cold flight that followed, maybe partly as a way to distract herself from the shock starting to close in on her mind. Her heart pattered frantically, and terror tinged around the edges of her mind. Part of her wanted to panic. But if she did that now, she might fall to her death.

She forced herself to think of other things instead, hoping to push the fear away by considering ways of repaying Red for what he had done for her. Her attempts to honour him like the holy man he was only seemed to confuse and annoy him, so therefore she would honour him in a way that didn't bother him so much.

But how? He seemed to value honesty, not worship. Honesty, courage, loyalty and strength. But were these things that she had, or could have? Hadn't she already lied to him, by not telling him everything she was going to do in the North? And hadn't she shown that she was weak, by being captured and needing to be rescued?

No… she had lied, and so proven that she did not have honesty or true loyalty. And by forcing him to rescue her, she had shown that she did not have courage or strength either.

But I will! she told herself fiercely. She was a Northerner, a true full-blooded Northerner, and every Northerner was a warrior somewhere deep inside. She would show him that Northerners weren't cowards or liars, or traitors, the way some in the South said they were. She would prove that she could be as brave as him.

That's what I'll do, then, she thought.

In that moment, she made her decision.

In the Temple they had taken away her silver robe, and she would take that as a sign. From now on, she would no longer be a priestess of the Night God. From now on she would worship the Shadow That Walked alone, and be what he needed her to be.

There was a war coming, and he didn't need a priestess for that; he needed fighters. Warriors.

So that was what she would be. She would learn how to fight like a true Northern warrior, and she would fight loyally by his side until she was dead, or until victory was his. She would ask him to teach her, or, if not him, Anfri or some other Northerner who knew fighting would teach her.

She would not disappoint Red again. She would earn his respect, and repay her debt to him.

Teressa's black eyes narrowed, and she set her jaw as ferociously as she could.

'Never,' she whispered aloud, the words lost in the wind. 'Never again.'

*

Red had made a camp in a clearing just outside the walls of Malvern, in a patch of forest left there by royal decree. There was a small stream not far away, and an empty fireplace set up. Teressa sat down beside it, shivering. 'We shouldn't stay here for too long. They'll come searching.'

'Yeah, I know,' said Red. He retrieved the bag he'd left hanging from a tree branch, and fished out a flint and tinder. After a few tries he managed to get the fire lit, and he passed the bag to Teressa.

'There's some food and stuff in there. I'm gonna nip back into the city and get you something to wear, okay?'

Teressa held her hands out over the fire to warm them. 'Be careful, Red.'

Red patted her awkwardly. 'I don't need to be careful – I got the shadows now. You just rest. C'mon, Kraego.'

The black griffin stretched. 'We will not be gone for long. Orak, wait for us.'

Orak shuffled closer to his human. 'I shall.'

Red climbed onto Kraego's back, and the black griffin took flight – off into the sky, and the shadows as well. Both of them knew where they were going, and this time neither one of them needed to leave the shadows.

Red left Kraego waiting in the main square by the statue of Arenadd and Skandar, and slipped off into the temple, which was still in a state of chaos. From there it was easy enough to follow Teressa's scent, and that led him to a back room. There were stars painted on the ceiling here, and a wardrobe, and inside it he found what he was after.

Red slung it on his back and returned to Kraego's side, still invisible, his mind still full of the vision he had had. Arenadd… the Dark Lord Arenadd. He'd spoken to him. And after everything Red had been told about him, he'd been nothing like what he would have expected. He hadn't seemed bloodthirsty or cruel to him, or evil. All Red had seen was haughty rudeness and sarcasm – and something else.

Red frowned as he got back onto Kraego. Had there been something else hidden in Arenadd's face and voice? He concentrated on the memory, knowing it was important. He'd interrogated witnesses and accused criminals, and he knew how it worked. You had to know when someone was hiding something, when they were lying – what they were holding back. And Arenadd had been hiding something, he was certain of it.

But what?

Kraego returned to the light, landing neatly and silently in the clearing where the fire was still burning. Red jumped down, and looked around for Teressa. She wasn't there, and neither was Orak.

'Damn – where'd they go?' Red put the bag down. 'Hang on Kraego. I'll be back.'

Kraego huffed and lay down by the fire, and Red sniffed the air. He could smell both Teressa and Orak, and he relaxed a bit when he realised they weren't far away. He headed off in their direction.

The moon was still bright, and its light shone on the waters of the stream, on the other side of a birch thicket. Orak was there, silently keeping watch, and there was Teressa.

She was in the water, though it must have been freezing, and Red's lucky tunic hung on a branch nearby. Teressa had her back to him, and she was busy washing herself, scrubbing furiously at her skin with handfuls of sand.

Red paused, embarrassed, and started to turn away — but he couldn't help but linger for a moment longer, just watching her. She was pale and slender, curiously graceful in her nakedness, her true form revealed now the flowing priestess' robe was gone. The painted spirals were coming away from her skin, blue-tinted water dripping from her hands, but to Red's surprise he saw that there were other marks on her; thin spiralling patterns, also in blue, traced down her back. And these spirals did not wash away.

Feeling very guilty now, Red silently turned away and returned to the campfire. He didn't bother to try and warm his hands over it — he already knew that wouldn't work. Forbidden thoughts crossed his mind, and he found himself remembering Lady Ahamay, and how she had moved against him, so warm and alive.

'Gods,' Red muttered. He remembered Arenadd's warning and knew, right then and there, that the traitorous Erebian would now be the last woman he'd ever touch. And maybe Teressa would be the last ever to kiss or embrace him.

A slow, quiet acceptance came over him. He would be alone, he knew. Alone forever. Nobody would ever touch him again, not really. That was what it meant to be the Shadow That Walked.

Teressa came back into the clearing, the tunic wrapped around her. Her hair was dripping. 'Red,' she said. 'What is it?'

He looked up. 'Hrm?'

Teressa sat down beside him, and touched his forearm. 'Ye look so sad.'

Red rubbed his eyes, and picked up the bag. 'It's nothing. Here, I got this back.'

She opened it, and examined the contents with obvious surprise. 'My things – where were they?'

'In yer old room. Don't ask me why.'

Teressa dragged out the spare robe. 'Thank ye, Red.'

Red accepted his tunic back from her. 'It's nothing,' he said gruffly. He looked away politely, but couldn't stop himself from asking, 'What are those marks on your back? The spirals?'

There was a rustle of cloth from behind him. 'Ye mean the tattoos?'

'Yeah. They remind me of Caedmon's a bit.'

'Every Northerner takes the tattoos when they're old enough,' said Teressa. 'It's part of the adulthood ceremony. Mine were put on me in the Temple.' She sighed. 'I'm finished.'

Red turned around. 'Reminds me of when I got my guard tattoo,' he said. 'I reckon that was the day I became a man.'

Teressa looked up at him. 'How old were ye?'

'Sixteen. You?'

She smiled. 'Sixteen.' The smile disappeared. 'I can never go back now. That place was my home. The priestesses were my family. And now...'

Red wanted to put an arm around her shoulders, but a sudden pang at his heart held him back. 'I know,' he said. 'I know. The guards were my family, and they tried to kill me too. But at least yer safe now, right?'

'Aye,' said Teressa. 'Ye saved me, Red. And... and I suppose ye and I will find a place to live when this is over.'

Again, Red stopped himself from touching her. 'Liranwee,' he said, throat tight. 'When this is over I'll give you a home there. I promise. You'll like it there. I built that city, and it's where I'll always belong.'

Teressa moved closer to him – he could feel her warmth, hear her heart. 'Tell me about it,' she said. 'I want to know everything.'

Red smiled sadly. 'Liranwee,' he murmured. 'It's the greatest city in the South. It's where we'll all go in the end – I know it.'

'Aye,' said Teressa. 'We will.'

Chapter Twenty-Seven

Strike Again

Several tense weeks passed in Liranwee, while Caedmon waited.

Caradoc stayed by his father's side all that time, though some had suggested he should be sent away to some secret location, or maybe even all the way to Amoran. But the King had been definite about that.

'He's my son, and I won't have anyone else protect him,' he said. 'Even from the Shadow That Walks.'

There was no point in lying about that any longer. Caedmon could have kept the encounter with Red a secret, but he had spread the word instead, warning his followers that they had a dangerous new enemy. And when word came from Malvern about the massacre in the Temple, the rumours of a new Shadow That Walked changed from suspicion to solid fact.

People came to see Caedmon then. Other griffiners, mostly. They came demanding explanations, looking for guidance. They were afraid; Caradoc could see it as easily as his father did.

'Stay alert,' Caedmon told them. 'Watch for signs. Feelings of coldness and unease. Animals panicking.'

'But then what?' the Master of War asked when he heard this. 'If we know he's there, what do we do about it?'

Caedmon tried to answer that, but his answers weren't what he wished they could be. Don't panic. Try and find a sunwheel; it might scare him. Light every candle you've got so there aren't as many shadows for him to hide in. Stay close to your partner.

It wouldn't do much, and he knew it. So did they, most likely. But what else could he possibly tell them?

'My mother was the Shadow That Walks, remember?' he told Caradoc one day. 'You know that.'

Caradoc nodded. 'She was meant to kill Laela Half-Breed so you could be King.'

'Yes,' said Caedmon. 'But not many of us like to admit that she failed. Nobody wants to admit that someone like her could fail, but

"

she did. The half-breed tricked her, and killed her. In the end, it was up to me to win the throne myself, when even the Shadow That Walked had failed.'

Caradoc looked even more scared then, but Caedmon shook his head. 'No, son, it's a good thing, don't you see? What happened to my mother was terrible, but it's proof that the Shadow That Walks can fail, and can be killed. If she could fail, then this Southern pretender can fail as well. And I think he's more likely to. My mother was a great warrior even when she was alive, but this man, this Kearney Redguard – you and I know him already, don't we? We met him before we first came here, when Morgan took him prisoner. And we know he's stupid. Remember, Caradoc? Just a stupid Southerner. He might have the power now, but he won't know what to do with it.'

Caradoc looked a little happier. 'But how do we stop him?'

'Simple,' said Caedmon. 'We trick him. Trap him. He can't go into the shadows once we have him chained. And then once we have him we can work out a way to kill him. Remember, son: we're smarter than him. And he can't stop a whole army by himself. We've got our people, and the Unpartnered, and we have the Amoranis as well, don't we?'

Caradoc nodded. 'You said they helped the half-breed kill Grandma Saeddryn. They can help us too, can't they?'

'I'm sure they can,' said Caedmon.

And then, days later, the Amoranis were gone.

A man came to see the King – a griffiner, who had flown all the way from Withypool. He was an Amorani, an offsider of the Prince who had gone back to Amoran for his father's birthday some time ago, and in very little time after his arrival in Liranwee he was allowed in to see the King.

Once the two griffins had greeted each other, the Amorani man bowed politely to Caedmon.

'Sire,' he said. 'There is news.'

'Yes?' Caedmon prompted.

The man looked uncomfortable. 'We are leaving. My people and I must return to Amoran at once.'

'Why?' Caedmon asked sharply. 'The Emperor and I had an agreement, and that agreement stays in effect until the war is finished.'

'That is understood,' said the man. 'But something has changed. The order to return does not come from the Emperor, but from his successor.'

'Successor?' said Caedmon. 'You mean the Emperor—?'

'Dead,' said the man. 'Assassinated by an Erebian spy, along with all his closest relatives. But one grandchild remains and has been made Empress-elect. She has commanded us to leave Cymria at once and to have no more dealings with you and your people.'

Caedmon muttered a Northern swearword. *'Twllt din!* The agreement with the Emperor should still apply to this successor. I demand an explanation.'

'I am sorry,' said the Amorani. 'But no explanation has been given. I can only repeat what the Empress-elect has commanded, and I am forbidden to disobey her on pain of death. But if you have a message for her in return, I have been asked to deliver it to her.'

'Can your people stay here until the matter is resolved?' asked Caedmon.

'No, Sire. We must withdraw immediately and return to Amoran, or I and my fellow commanders will be sentenced to death.'

'Understood,' Caedmon said curtly. 'Stay here in Liranwee until my message is ready for you to take. I should have it for you by tomorrow.'

'Yes, Sire.' The Amorani bowed and left.

Caedmon swore again after he had gone. *'Coc y gath!'*

'This is not good,' Shar said unnecessarily.

'Oh really?' Caedmon snapped back. 'Do you have any idea how perilous things are going to be here with the Amoranis gone?'

'It does not matter,' said Shar. 'We have the Southerners beaten.'

'And without the Amoranis, they outnumber us ten to one,' said Caedmon. 'Do you know what would happen if they banded together? We wouldn't stand a chance.'

'But they cannot,' said Shar. 'Surely… you and I both know that the Southern humans have never been together as one people – they have always been in separate territories. When you and I were youngsters they fought against each other.'

'But they won't now,' said Caedmon. 'Not now. Not when we've given them a common enemy. All they need now is a leader, and we both know who that could well be.'

'Kraeai kran ae,' Shar hissed. 'But you do not think that

Southerners would follow the cursed one? He may be one of them, but his powers belong to the North, and they have always hated and feared the one who carries them.'

'I wouldn't be surprised if he could make them change their minds soon enough,' said Caedmon. 'With this thing in Malvern, rescuing that traitor priestess – all it would take is a few more exploits like that to bring them around.'

'Then what do you suggest?' said Shar. 'If you kill him then, that may only inspire them.'

'Yes… we can't afford to create a martyr,' said Caedmon. 'We have to kill him before they start seeing him as a hero – if they don't already. We don't know enough about him yet to be certain. And if not… then we'll have to find a way to change the way they see him, won't we? If they love him, then we'll find a way to make them hate him. Yes…' he frowned to himself, as the idea matured in his mind.

'Yes, we'll find a way. One way or another. This Red thinks he can be a hero after what he's become, but I'll make another Dark Lord of him. I'll turn his own people on him, and if I do it well enough they might even give him to me themselves.'

'He will still be powerful,' Shar pointed out.

'But he can't fight this battle alone,' said Caedmon. 'Without followers, he'll fail. And he will. I'll see to it personally.' He glanced over at Caradoc, who had sat there by Ereska's side and listened to it all in silence. 'For our future.'

'If you wish to do this, you must find him first,' Shar observed.

'And I will,' said Caedmon. 'That part will be simple enough.'

And it would be. All of them already knew that.

Two days later, the visitors all four of them had been waiting for finally arrived.

Caedmon came hurrying to the Eyrie rooftop as the spotted griffin landed, with Shar, Caradoc and Ereska close by.

Echo landed as nimbly as always, and crouched low to let his partner dismount.

Morgan, though, did not have much grace left. He climbed down clumsily, and his bow to his King was a little stiff.

Caedmon helped him up, and greeted him with a hug. 'Morgan.'

Morgan gave him a quick hug back. 'Sire. Sorry it took me so long.'

'It's fine, Morgan,' Caedmon said gruffly. 'How are you?'

Morgan didn't answer that question, but all of them could see how different he looked now. He had healed from what had happened to him, more or less, but even Caradoc knew that he would never be the same again.

His face was scarred now, and one arm had a twist. He walked with a limp, and the rope had left a permanent mark on his throat. But scars on the body were one thing. They could be ugly, but they were only what could be seen on the outside.

Morgan had scars on his soul now, and they showed in his eyes, and his voice, and the bitter lines around his mouth.

'What do you need me to do, Sire?' he asked.

'Come on,' said Caedmon, with surprising gentleness. 'Come inside and have something to eat. You too, Echo. Caradoc!' he added more sharply. 'Come here and say something to your brother.'

Caradoc came over, a little timid. 'Hello, Morgan. Does your arm hurt badly today?'

Morgan finally smiled, and ruffled the boy's hair. 'Not so badly, Caradoc. It's good to see you again.'

'I'm glad you didn't die,' Caradoc said, very solemn.

'So am I,' said Morgan. He sighed. 'So am I.'

Inside, the three humans sat down together and shared some food. The griffins stayed close by and conversed amongst themselves in rapid griffish.

'Morgan,' Caedmon said. 'I'm so sorry. What happened to you — if I could have done something…'

'It's all right,' said Morgan. 'I know whose fault it was, and it wasn't yours.'

'Yes, well, those people from New Eagleholm — but now they've paid the price, haven't they?' said Caedmon.

Morgan's mouth thinned. 'They have. I left Arwydd in charge. She can handle it.'

'Oh yes.' Caedmon smiled. 'How is she? It was touching to see how well she looked after you.'

'I want to marry her,' Morgan said baldly. 'She asked me before I left, and I said yes.'

'Excellent!' said Caedmon. 'I'm happy for you, Morgan — you take good care of her. I'm sure you will.'

'I will,' said Morgan. 'But now will you tell me what you want me to do?'

'Yes, of course,' said Caedmon. 'But it won't be easy, and you may not want to do it. I hate asking you after what you've already gone through on my behalf, and if you don't want to do this then you have my permission to say no.'

'That depends,' said Morgan. 'What is it?'

'We have a rat that needs catching,' said Caedmon. 'A red one.'

Morgan listened in silence while his master explained. His expression barely flickered.

'I know the Shadows That Walk,' Caedmon said afterwards. 'I know how they think. The Night God is supposed to give each one a mission, but with this one, I doubt she spoke to him at all. So that only leaves his own desires. No doubt he wants to chase us out of the South, but he'll want one other thing, won't he? Every Shadow That Walks does.'

'Revenge,' Morgan said softly.

'Yes. Revenge on the ones he blames for his death. I don't know how he died, but I'm sure he blames me. But more than me, he'll blame you. We both know what happened between you two, and we know what he said to you while we had him locked up.'

Morgan sighed. 'He looked me in the eye and said he was going to kill me one day. He promised it.'

'Exactly,' said Caedmon. 'And that's why you're the one who's going to catch him. He hates me, but he hates you more, and he'll go anywhere he has to if he thinks he might find you there.' He glanced at Caradoc. 'And you know what he's threatened to do. The longer we can keep him away from my son, the better. So if you're afraid of taking this on, think of that.'

'I understand,' said Morgan.

'And I do as well,' said Echo. 'Shar has explained it to me. It would be our glory to bring this red rat down.'

'And the griffin as well,' said Caedmon. 'This Kraego.'

'It will be your task to finish him, Eck-hoo,' said Shar. 'The human may be immortal, but Kraego is not. Remember my promise, spotted griffin.'

'I do,' said Echo. 'I have never forgotten it, Shar.' He flicked his tail. 'I will fight the dark griffin, and I will kill him for you.'

'He might be too strong for you, Echo,' said Morgan.

'But I will defeat him by cunning,' said Echo. 'It has always been my greatest weapon. This Kraego will be a mindless brute like his father. But I am as sly as a human, yes?'

'You are,' Morgan smiled.

'So that is how it will be,' Echo finished. 'I shall kill Kraego, and you will capture the red human, or see to it that he is disgraced in the eyes of his kind. Either way, he will be unpartnered and unfit to lead others.'

'Exactly,' said Caedmon. He inclined his head towards Morgan with respect. 'You've sacrificed a lot for your country, Morgan, and no matter what happens, you'll be honoured for it. I'll see to it that a statue of you goes next to the one of your brother in Malvern. That's a promise.'

'No,' Morgan said coldly. 'Put it in Liranwee. Soon enough it'll be our new capital, won't it?'

'Yes,' said Caedmon. 'Yes, it will be. The greatest city in the South.'

Chapter Twenty-Eight

Drinks with Friends

After a long and sometimes fraught journey back through the South, Red, Kraego, Orak and Teressa arrived back in Monag.

Not much had changed while they were gone, but Anfri and his fellow Northerners had been joined by several more that had arrived during Red's absence. All of them gathered to meet Teressa, and Red watched with some surprise while they bowed respectfully to her and greeted her in their own language.

'We thought ye must have died,' one said.

'I came close,' said Teressa, speaking Cymrian for Red's benefit. 'But the Shadow That Walks saved me. Just as I knew he would,' she added with a smile.

All of them looked at Red, some with puzzlement, but all with awe.

'I had some doubts, I admit it,' said Anfri. 'But you saved Teressa's life. That's all the proof I needed that you're on our side.'

Red sensed that something needed to be said here, not just to Anfri but for everyone listening.

'I'm on the side of anyone who tries to do what's right,' he said. 'Northerner, Southerner, griffin, Amorani – there's no difference to me when all's said an' done. I dunno much about being the Shadow That Walks, or not yet, but I do know that what the King's doing is wrong. He's got no right to come an' take our land from us, or sell us like meat in the marketplace. I know us Southerners did the same to you once, but that was a long time ago.'

His tone turned sombre, and he continued. 'I knew a man once, or a kind of man. His name was Kullervo. He's dead now, but I won't forget what he told me. He said "the past is dead an' gone. What matters is makin' the future better."'

'That's what I'm gonna try an' do. I ain't gonna conquer the North, or kill the King unless I have to.'

The Northerners looked relieved.

'All I want to do is save the South,' said Red. 'An' put a stop to this war. Anyone who wants to help me do that is welcome.'

'And we will,' said Teressa. 'We'll help ye.'

'We will!' Anfri said hastily, while his friends murmured agreement.

'Right then,' said Red. 'Now that's been sorted out, let's go relax. I dunno about you, but I could use a drink.'

'We'll go to the main dining hall straight away, sir,' said Anfri.

'Nah,' said Red. He smiled at Kraego. 'I might be a griffiner now, an' the Shadow That Walks an' all that other stuff, but at heart I'm still just a city guard. I'm goin' to the pub. Come join me if you want.'

They looked puzzled, but Teressa laughed.

'I'll come!' she said. 'I'll tell the others, too.'

Kraego snorted his irritation, but said nothing.

There was a pub in Monag, as it turned out – just one, with the unlikely name of The Surly Griffin. It featured a scowling griffin on the sign, who for some reason had green feathers.

'Never mind, as long as it's got halfway decent beer,' Red said cheerfully.

Quite a few people from the Eyrie chose to join him – humans, of course; very few normal buildings had room for even one griffin.

Red took up a handy table, and others came to sit around him; Teressa and Anfri, Liantha, Neth, even Isleen and Alaric, the latter looking a little bruised but proud.

Red had managed to scrounge some money on the journey back, and he used it to buy a round of drinks.

'Doesn't matter what you asked for, they've only got beer an' the other beer,' he said over the chatter of the other drinkers.

They made an odd group: Northerners, Southerners, guards, griffiners, nobles and commoners. But they sat together around Red and toasted each other – hesitantly, but with growing sincerity.

'To the South! To victory! To the Shadow That Walks and the dark griffin!'

'Damn right!' Red roared, and drank deeply.

They took turns buying rounds, and Red saw to it that everyone finished what they took.

'This is how you do it, see?' he said after the first few. 'This is how you make friends the easy way. A nice pub, a few beers, an' no pretentions or trappings in the way.'

He told stories, too, and so did the others, taking turns to talk about their lives.

Red talked about Kullervo, and Amoran, and Teressa talked about life as a priestess. Liantha talked about her childhood growing up in the ruins of Old Eagleholm, and her foster-father, Roland the hatchery keeper.

'He was the wisest, kindest man I ever met,' she said.

'Me too,' said Red. 'Almost. There was only one other I knew.'

'Aye, so there was,' said Teressa.

Red raised his mug. 'To Kullervo Taranisäii,' he said. 'The best man I ever met. You ain't gonna be forgotten, Kullervo. No matter what.'

'Never!' Isleen agreed. 'Not in Amoran, and not here.'

'To Kullervo!' the others echoed. 'Kullervo the man-griffin!'

After things had quietened down, Red turned to Teressa. 'I wish you could've met him properly,' he said.

'So do I,' said Teressa. 'But at least I saw him once.'

'Yeah…' Red said slowly. 'That reminds me.'

'Yes?' said Teressa.

'I nearly forgot. But what did he tell you before he died? Will you tell me now?'

Teressa hesitated.

'Well?' said Red.

So she told him. She told him what Kullervo had said, and how she had acted on his words by finding first the heart, and then Arenadd's body. Red listened in astonishment.

'I'm so sorry,' she said afterward. 'I should never have done it without asking ye. I never stopped blaming myself.'

'But you say he wouldn't wake up?' said Red.

Teressa shook her head. 'I tried everything. His body was there, and it was breathing, but…'

'…nobody at home,' said Red. 'I know it.'

'How?' asked Teressa.

'I saw him,' said Red. 'In the Temple. See, you ain't the only one who kept things back. I tried to stop the sacrifice, but I ended up bein' the one to do it. The High Priestess died instead of you, but it still counted. An' then I saw him. I had a vision.'

Teressa tensed. 'What was it like? What was he like?'

Red described it to her, as well as he could remember. 'See?' he finished. 'You've fixed his body up, but he ain't in it. He's in the void still, with his master.'

'Then why?' said Teressa. 'Why send me to do that?'

'Maybe he's hopin' to escape,' said Red. 'An' he wanted to make sure there was a body for him when he did. Eh? Why else?'

'If he comes back, he'll be on our side,' said Teressa. 'I'm sure of it. He wanted me to join ye, didn't he?'

'I asked him whose side he was on,' said Red. 'He said he was on his own side. He also said I might see him again one day, an' I should hope so. Dunno what he meant by that. I don't reckon he'd help us, Teressa. I dunno what he wants to do. But he wants to come back, I'm sure of it.'

'I'm so sorry,' Teressa said again. 'I should have said something, I should have realised...'

'Yeah, well.' Red stared into his beer. 'Ain't you heard the stories, Teressa? Us Dark Lords always rise again.'

Other Books By K.J. Taylor

The Price of Magic

Broken Prophecy

The Land of Bad Fantasy

Tales of Cymria

The Fallen Moon
The Dark Griffin
The Griffin's Flight
The Griffin's War

The Risen Sun
The Shadow's Heir
The Shadowed Throne
The Shadow's Heart

The Southern Star
The Last Guard
The Silent Guard
The Cursed Guard

The Drachengott
Wind
Earth
Fire
Water